M000222927

THE SIN OF SAINTS

The Sin of Saints: Book 1 of The Benevolence & Blood Series by Lauren M. Leasure

Published by Kindle Direct Publishing

Copyright © 2022 Lauren M. Leasure

All rights reserved. No portion of this book may be reproduced in any form without permission from the publisher, except as permitted by U.S. copyright law. For permissions contact info@laurenmleasure.com

Cover by Ivy at Beautiful Book Covers

Paperback ISBN: 978-0-578-26812-5

THE BENEVOLENCE & BLOOD SERIES

THE

Sin

OF

Saints

LAUREN M. LEASURE

Dedicated to you — may you find the hope, healing, and happiness you deserve.

Stay in Touch

www.instagram.com/laurenmleasure
www.facebook.com/laurenmleasure

Receive special offers, giveaways, discounts, bonus content, and updates from the author by signing up for the newsletter at www.laurenmleasure.com

Content Warning
This book includes content that may be sensitive for some readers, including
- Profanity
- Violence and death
- Blood and gore
- Loss of family members
- Explicit sexual content
- Mental health and suicide
- Sexual violence
- Mention of pregnancy loss
- Drugs and addiction

ROUGHWATER ISLAND

SILENT BAY

CABILLIA

PORT OF XOMM

PORT OF CABILLIA

AERA

RHEDROSIAN MTS

XOM

TAITHA

LAKE
DEADKEEP

DEEPWATER
LAKES

THE PLAINS   DRY GULCH

MAPLENOOK   BLINDBARROW

ONYX PASS

JULIA

ONYXIAN MTS

WIDORA

ESERENE

ANICOLE

CONTINENT OF
ASTRAN

EDDENA

NESAN

ARAQINA

WIDOW'S
SEA

EDWATER

OVEDEL

KRURIA

CONTINENT OF
LOSINA

GALYRA

IA

The Benevolent Saints

Katia, Keeper of the Benevolent Saints
Tolar, Saint of Wealth
Onera, Saint of Miracles
Aanh, Saint of the Home
Soren, Saint of Heaven

The Blood Saints

Rhedros, Keeper of the Blood Saints
Faldyr, Saint of War
Liara, Saint of Hell
Idros, Saint of Storms
Noros, Saint of Pain
Cyen, Saint of Death

Pronunciation Guide

People

Petra Gaignory – PET-ruh GAYN-er-ee
Larka – LARK-uh
Evarius Castemont – ev-AIR-ee-us CAST-uh-mont
Calomyr – CAL-uh-mere
Solise – SOH-lees
Irabel – EE-ruh-bel
Sarek – SARE-ek
Marita – muh-REE-tuh
Wrena – REN-uh
Tyrak – TEE-rik
Kauvras – KOVE-ris
Ludovicus – lu-DOH-vuh-kiss
Raolin – ROW-lin
Balthazar – BAL-thuh-zar
Arturius – ar-TUR-ee-us
Anton – ANT-awn
Higgins – HIG-ins
Garit – GARE-it
Elin – EE-lin
Umfray – UM-fray
Belin – BAY-lin
Ythan – EE-thin

Places

Eserene – ES-er-een
Widoras – wid-DOOR-is
Sidus – SIGH-dis
Prisma – PRIZ-muh
Ockhull – OCK-ul
Taitha – TAY-tha
Cabillia – cuh-BILL-ee-uh
Xomma – ZO-muh
Nesan – nuh-SAN
Eddena – eh-DEEN-uh
Malarrey – muh-LAR-ee
Astran – AST-ran

Chapter 1
Now

"Fucking shit," I muttered before immediately clapping my hand over my mouth and glancing up to my tutor. Marita's eyes narrowed as she stared down her nose at me. "Apologies," I offered, raising my eyebrows. I could have sworn that the guard who stood alert by the door let slip an almost imperceptible laugh. *Almost.*

I watched Marita's embroidery needle continue its journey through the fabric, rounding out the butter-yellow petal of a foreign flower I didn't recognize. "You do know that kind of language will not be tolerated by the Board, Petra."

My head dropped back to my task while I rolled my eyes. "I know, Marita, I just–"

"Ah," Marita cut in. "*Lady* Marita. You must be conscious of titles. You know what will happen if you're not. You have only two weeks left."

"I know, *Lady* Marita," I sneered. She returned the eye roll and added a sigh. "I'm trying to kick the habit." Certain parts of my

19

upbringing were harder to let go of than others. The language was one of them.

She placed her embroidery hoop in her lap and leaned forward in her chair, hooking a finger under my chin and tilting my face to hers. "I've watched many young women walk into that throne room and say goodbye to their families for the last time. You are already older than the other girls in your Initiation class and even though you are now a Castemont, it does not mean you are safe." Marita's tone was sharp, though the edges were softened by good intentions.

I watched her gray eyes turn to solid ice, the worry emanating from her gaze enough to pin me where I sat on the pristine floor. I felt as if I were seeing Marita for the first time, the planes of her cheekbones, the pleasant angle of her eyes. Marita was actually...beautiful. I didn't think she had seen more than forty-five years by the absence of deep lines in her face. Since she had been assigned as my tutor three months ago, she was always clad in a veil. I had assumed the hair beneath was as gray as her eyes. Today, a single coarse hair had escaped her bonnet, resting almost invisibly across her forehead. Blonde. I was almost taken aback by the normalcy of it.

"I'll be *fine*."

Though I wasn't sure who I was trying to convince more, Marita or myself.

On paper, my family name was Castemont, but that wouldn't do me any favors with the Board of Blood. The blood in my veins was far from royal. The Board of Blood declined the invitation to the wedding of my mother and Lord Castemont just three months ago. "The Board will be indisposed," the messenger said. They weren't indisposed, though. The reason they didn't come was that they vehemently disapproved of a marriage between a Royal and a commoner.

Which meant their opinion of me was set in stone.

The disapproval of the Board did nothing to quell the love between my mother and Lord Castemont though, and I sat behind them in the Grand Cathedral as the Benevolent Saints watched over their union. My mother took her vows with her love for her Lord evident in every word. Lord Castemont returned the

20

sentiment, quietly promising to love and protect my mother, and in turn, me, at all costs.

That protection, however, did not extend to my dealings with the Board of Blood.

I slipped the final pin through my dress pattern, assessing the blank canvas that would soon exhibit the disgustingly gaudy traditional features of a pure white Eserenian Initiation gown. I relished the grounding feeling of the cool marble floor beneath my thighs, the same marble that covered the walls in the drawing room attached to my bedroom. It was too bright and rigid for a room that was supposed to evoke quiet comfort. Everything in this room was too...formal. An uncomfortable set of chairs and a matching settee in powder blue, baroque art in heavy gold frames, a crystal chandelier the size of my old bedroom.

Things had changed rapidly over the past four years. I often had to find reminders in the little things that this was real. That *I* was real. That I was okay.

"If I didn't know any better, I'd say that making my own dress for this Saints damned Initiation was its own punishment," I remarked as I rose from the floor.

"Petra!" Marita barked.

"It was either 'Saints damned' or 'fucking.' I chose the lesser of two evils," I answered, palms raised in the air. Marita rolled her eyes. It had only taken about a week of her constant company to see the spirited spitfire that lurked just beneath the hard exterior of a royal tutor. I was able to coax more of her personality out the longer we spent together, and I enjoyed the little glimpses I got of the real Marita. She coaxed my personality from me too, my distrustful exterior falling away quickly.

"I'm not going to be there to defend you, you know," she replied, turning her eyes back down to her embroidery. Every time my squalid upbringing was evident in the company of the Royals, Marita had defended me, explaining away my slip in language, in behavior, in appearance. She had been firm with me, stressing the importance of the task ahead, yet always acted as a soft place to land. She was my...friend? Yes, I'd call her my friend. As close to a friend as I'd had since Larka was taken from me. "No one but the Initiates and the Board of Blood are allowed in the throne room that day. Not even your mother and father."

"My *step*-father," I corrected her quickly, the same way she had corrected me. "Besides, I can defend myself."

Her eyes were rimmed with concern. The same concern pooled in the pit of my stomach, cold and sour. I felt the slight tang of acid in the back of my throat. I hadn't yet come to terms with what lay ahead of me. "I have no doubt in my mind that you are *able* to defend yourself, girl. However, you will not be allowed to. You understand that, right?"

I took a deep breath, walking toward the cupboard that held the needles and thread. I wasn't entirely sure whether or not my goal was to survive Initiation, because the Royal Court did not sound like anything I wanted to be a part of. Death did not scare me the way it should have. "Sure fuckin' do."

◆ ◆ ◆

I covered half my plate with creamy potatoes. Lord Castemont let us do away with the servants when it was just the three of us at dinner. My mother had expressed the awkwardness she felt being served a meal she didn't cook and sitting idly by while the table was cleared and the dishes cleaned by hands that weren't hers.

It hadn't seemed to bother her in the past.

"Two weeks to go, Petra," my mother remarked while refilling her wine glass. My mother only indulged in more than one glass when she was nervous. She had two glasses the night before her wedding and two the night before she was sworn in as a Lady of the Court.

This was her third.

I nodded absentmindedly, my mind preoccupied by the height of my heels that I tapped under the table. Marita ordered me to wear these heels every waking moment of every day. I was to learn to walk on these ridiculous fucking sticks before my Initiation. As if the gargantuan ruffles and jewels were not enough. My feet *ached.*

22

Covering my potatoes with a heaping scoop of sweet corn, I noticed my mother had already funneled half of her newest glass of wine down her throat.

"The fuck is wrong with you, Ma?" I asked without thinking, once again clapping my hand over my mouth. Old habits die hard.

Castemont did his best to hide his snicker, but his mouth full of lamb burst open at my comment. He quickly turned it into a cough and covered his mouth with his napkin. "Excuse me," he tried to say.

"Evarius, please," my mother said sharply as she turned to him. "Two weeks. She has *two weeks* to learn how to behave well enough to stand in front of the Board of Blood."

I grabbed a roll from the basket to my left and the tray of butter to my right. I considered grabbing my knife to spread the butter, but decided against it, instead dipping my roll directly into the butter tray, scooping a melting glob directly into my mouth.

"Petra!" my mother scolded me. I threw my hands up and widened my eyes at her as I chewed.

Castemont was doing his best — but failing — to conceal a laugh. "Why waste a clean knife?" I said, mouth full. I didn't care if I lived in a royal house — well, a Low Royal house. And not so much a house but a mansion-sized section of the Low Royal Castle. But still mine. I watched my mother give an exasperated look to Castemont, silently urging him to aid her in this battle.

"She's put in tremendous effort, Irabel," he said in a tone that was only half comforting. "She'll be just fine." He inhaled deeply, stuffing another bite of lamb in his mouth. I watched as he chewed, his face contemplative, his square jaw working over more than just the meat. He was a handsome man, thick black hair smattered with silver, the clean style highlighting the sharp cut of his cheeks and the deep brown of his eyes. It was a face I had only recently begun to appreciate.

People had begun to whisper about the Lord's love life in the years before he met us. He was the only one of twelve Eserenian Lords not to take a wife. He had been betrothed a few years before, to a foreign noblewoman's daughter who lived in Eserene. She was taken by a fever not long after she accepted his proposal, around the same time our lives fell apart for the second time. Then he met my mother, all because I was desperate and delinquent. And it's because of his generosity, his faith, that we survived. Even when I railed against every kindness.

Had it been any other Lord, we would not be in this position. The Lords, Ladies, Barons, and Baronesses of the Low Royal Court were terribly aloof. They had drawn a clear line in the sand between themselves and *others*. Not only had we been *others*, we were filth under their boots, the mud puddles they stepped around.

"Lady Marita tells me you're still working on your gown for Initiation. Tell me, do you have much left to do?" Castemont asked, my mother clearly egging him on.

I couldn't tell the truth. I should have finished that Saints damned monstrosity a week ago. "If I tell you, it would give away the surprise," I chided. My mother saw right through it, inhaling to undoubtedly push me on the subject.

Suddenly, Tyrak barged through the door, the action so loud and fast that I was surprised the door remained on its hinges. "My Lord, a word?" The look on his face was grave.

Tyrak's olive-skinned hand was on the gilded hilt of the sword that swung on his hip. I could sense the frenzy of urgency radiating from his body. Even though Tyrak's dark eyes were filled with wild worry, Castemont's face stayed neutral, nodding to us as he excused himself from the table and entered the hallway, Tyrak close behind.

Tyrak was Castemont's head guard and had been since they both entered the court at the age of twenty-one. Not sixteen or seventeen. No Initiation was held for the men of royal standing. Just a small ceremony and a romp through the city to celebrate coming of age, adding lovers to their list and drinking a lion's share of mead and ale. Nothing like what the women had to endure.

My mother and I looked at each other silently as the door closed, the air thick between us. I knew almost nothing about any other countries and their relations to Eserene and Widoras until becoming a Castemont. And still, what I had learned was basic. It was, however, enough to piece together the fact that there had

24

long been unrest stirring across the continent of Astran. The borders between the three countries of Astran shared tenuous relations since the dawn of recorded history, but the grumblings were growing into shouts.

"I sometimes forget that we live in a capital city," my mother muttered.

"Well, it wasn't necessarily important knowledge until you became a part of its royalty." I took a sip of wine. "I forget that there's a life outside the city walls."

Castemont told us that we, as royals, generally didn't worry about what happened beyond city walls, across country lines, or on the dirt of other continents. Tyrak's intrusion, however, produced a small kernel of fear that had been buried away deep in my gut.

Sensing the shift, my mother reached across the table and laid her hand flat in the middle, the emerald in her betrothal ring catching the candlelight of the silver chandelier hanging overhead. I laid my hand across hers, something we'd do on the dark days in the ragged kitchen of my childhood home, when we pined for our life before loss and devastation, when her face was blank and vacant. Her hand was as maddeningly delicate as it was then, and I fought the bitterness that began to rise in the back of my throat. "I'm sure it's just a small military movement that Tyrak feels is worth reporting. Or maybe a skirmish along one of the borders. Saints know *that's* not news," she offered, lifting one side of her mouth.

"Maybe," I replied. "Probably." Still, my heartbeat had increased the moment Tyrak had stormed in and refused to settle. I removed my hand from my mother's before she could feel the sweat forming on my palms. I wiped both hands on the heavy crimson velvet of my skirts, watching as the fabric darkened to the color of blood under my touch. I knew it was only because of the fibers being pushed in the other direction, but the sight was unsettling nonetheless. I knew the pressure of my new life was building, but I did my absolute best to lock it away, to ignore it completely.

Castemont pushed through the door, leaving Tyrak in the hall. "Not to worry, my loves," he offered as he reclaimed his seat at the table. My mother raised an eyebrow, expectantly waiting for more information from her husband. "A small band of rebels infiltrated the Cabillian border carrying leechthorn. They've been dealt with."

"Leechthorn?" I asked, the volume of my voice surprising everyone at the table, including myself.

Castemont resumed cutting into the lamb on his plate, looking uninterested. "A plant that only grows in Cabillia." He placed a piece in his mouth, chewing thoughtfully, and took a deep dreg of his wine. "It's dried in the sun, ground into a powder, and smoked from a pipe. Horribly addictive, but I'm told the high feels like walking among the Benevolent Saints themselves. One drag and you're enslaved for life. The longer you go without it, the stronger you get. And if you can't get your fix in time," he said, his voice grim, "you'll rip yourself to shreds."

"Well, remind me never to try that out," I said jokingly, trying to lighten the dark mood that had swept over the dining room. "How dismal."

"And it's made its way into Widoras?" my mother asked, her gaze boring into his cheek, her face painted with worry.

"It's been in Widoras for some time now," he said quietly, not raising his eyes from his plate. "All is well. It's under control. Nothing new. Nothing of note."

A sinking feeling hit my chest out of nowhere, my mind swirling with bits of my past I had worked so hard to bury. Clouds of smoke, flaming debris falling, the screams, *her* screams–

"The corn is delicious. It must be fresh," he said, quickly placing a forkful of sweet corn in his mouth. My mother's gaze did not leave his face. He loudly cleared his throat.

The subject was dismissed.

Chapter 2

Four Years Ago

A harsh whisper cleaved through the frigid night. "Petra."

"Yes?" I answered.

"I can't sleep." The other side of the bed moved as Larka turned to face me. The contours of her face were illuminated by the silvery moonlight pouring in from the sole window in our bedroom. I could see her long lashes dancing. She always blinked too much when she was excited. Even at twenty three, her eyes were the thing to give away her excitement.

"What do you think it'll be like?" she asked.

"I have no idea," I replied, whispering into the night. "Nothing to compare it to." I could practically hear Larka's eyes roll at my bland answer. Our bed was comfortable enough — small, if anything, but enough for the two of us. My sister and I had shared this same bed our entire lives. She was three years my senior, though some said we didn't look anything like sisters. While her hair was silken, fine, and golden blonde like our mother's, mine was coarse, wild, and caramel brown, supposedly matching some distant cousin I'd never met. Her eyes were the color of ice, while mine resembled tree bark. And though we were both taller than average, she was all fluid grace while I was awkward and clumsy.

"The harbor is going to be crowded. What if the ships crash into each other? No, they wouldn't. They're captains for a reason, right? Saints, it's going to be amazing," she continued, whimsy entering her voice as she droned on, answering her own questions as she went.

I laughed. "I hope there's one from Eddena," I replied. Eddena's lapis lazuli mines were known across the world. The stone was crushed into a fine powder to dye textiles, and the color was my absolute favorite. Larka and I swore that one day we'd go to Eddena and mine some for ourselves. We'd laid out a plan to see the whole world, actually, as soon as we could save enough money to make sure our parents would be all right while we were gone.

"You *always* talk about Eddena. What about Zidderune? I bet their sails are lovely," she crooned. I noticed the sound of light footsteps on the road outside, not at all an odd occurrence considering Copper Street was used heavily by Inkwell residents, but strange considering the hour and...had they paused?

I rolled my eyes, shifting my attention back to the conversation, ignoring my paranoia. "You want to see the Zidderunian ship because you know the Zidderunian Prince will be the one captaining it," I sneered.

She snorted. "That doesn't hurt either. You've heard what they say about him."

I sighed. Tomorrow marked Eserene's first time hosting Cindregala. The celebration marked the end of the War of Kings, when Faldyr, Blood Saint of War, sent a tide so high that it destroyed many coastal cities, Eserene included. Katia, Keeper of Benevolent Saints called upon her kelpies to keep the wave from washing too far inland and destroying the whole world. The festivities were held in one of 120 cities around the world each year, each a coastal city that had been swamped by Faldyr's tidal wrath. Eserene was the very last city on the list, and after tomorrow the list would return to the first city.

Tomorrow was also my twentieth birthday.

The entire city had been preparing for the event for months. Dilapidated buildings had been restored, streets had been recobbled and swept and swept again, shrubbery had been planted, tassels and banners hung from every corner. The city gleamed like a jewel on the Invisible King's crown. That is, except for our district, Inkwell.

The noblemen and women that would be arriving for Cindregala had no business in the slums of Inkwell among the poor and the wretched and the rats, save for a few of the most depraved who sought anonymity in the Painted Empress Brothel. The city saw no reason to clean up the district, so Inkwell remained caked with the same soot and dirt it always had.

"I'm nervous," I whispered to Larka.

"Why?"

"I'm not sure. I'm just...nervous. Big crowd. Lots of strangers."

Larka scoffed. "You worry too much."

"Someone's gotta," I countered. But she was right. Larka had a tendency to say the wrong things at the wrong time, and the thought of being around so many people tomorrow who could unknowingly antagonize her set me on edge. Larka let out a giggle and turned onto her back, sighing deeply. The heavy moonlight did nothing to warm the night breeze that slipped through the planks of our bare walls. Our father had tried to nail the gaps shut more than once, but it seemed that for every gap he sealed, two more replaced it. His hands shook all the while, the tremors having worsened over the last few years.

"Fresh air does us good, Da!" Larka cheerfully chimed a few months ago as our father stood exasperated in our room, his frustration visible in the creases of his face.

"Maybe in the summer, girl, but come winter ye won't be saying the same thing," he rasped, trying to keep his tone even. He held a rock in his hand in place of a mallet, not able to afford a replacement after a tremor sent the old one crashing to the ground while he patched up the roof one rainy spring day.

Larka just moved in to embrace him, assuring him that we would be fine. She and my Da had always had a special bond, some sort of deeper understanding of one another, like their souls were molded from the same clay, by the same hands.

Those gaps whistled and hummed as an autumn gust assaulted the house. Larka said nothing, so neither did I. I hoped that Ma and Da couldn't hear the creaking of the planks from their room downstairs. Guilt already wracked them. I didn't need to add more.

"How's it feel?" Larka asked.

"How's what feel?"

"To be almost twenty!"

"Feels like being nineteen." I shrugged. Larka snorted, throwing her hands in the air in a dramatic display of exasperation.

She pulled the thin blanket up to rest under both of our chins. "Enjoy our last night together, Petra."

"What? Why is it our last night together?" I said, a sour feeling settling in my chest.

"Because the second the Prince of Zidderune spots me, he's going to whisk me away on his beautiful ship with the red sails and I'll live in luxury for the rest of my days."

I rolled my eyes. "Larka, Zidderune's royal color is green."

"I'll be sure to write you," she said before rolling over.

◆ ◆ ◆

I awoke to an empty bed, but Larka's heat lingered on her side. The stale smell of plain porridge wafted from the lower level into our bedroom. Larka often complained about porridge being one of our only dishes in Inkwell, but to be honest, I didn't mind it. Porridge was food, and food was sustenance.

I padded down the stairs into our miniscule kitchen, my mother and father chatting across from each other at the stacked crates we called a table, a mug of warm water in my mother's hands. A pot of porridge sat on the stove, and I peered in to see that we wouldn't have much to eat this morning. "G'morning Ma, g'morning Da," I chimed as I planted a kiss on each of their heads.

Both of my parents had lived their entire lives in Inkwell, their parents and grandparents before them as well. They were simply used to the fact that there was never much money to go around. Residents in Inkwell took care of each other, though, even if the district was large enough that it really could have been its own city. My Ma and Da met when they were both seventeen and were married the following year, garnering raised eyebrows when Larka was born just a few months later.

My father's hands had been shaky for as long as I could remember. He often said the Benevolent Saints made him too strong, so the Blood Saints had to knock him down a peg. His subsequent laughs were always edged with the smallest bit of empty melancholy. The tremors had worsened to the point of almost complete dependence on his family for the smallest of tasks, and working was out of the question. Unable to feed himself what little food we had without his movements sending it flying across the room, we had all grown used to feeding him. He took the humiliation with grace and smothered it in humor. "Those damned Blood Saints," he'd say.

"Happiest of birthdays, my love," my father said, offering a warm smile, his hazel eyes bright. I mirrored his excitement.

"Happy birthday, Petra," my mother said, rising from her wobbly chair to give me a hug. While life in Inkwell usually made women hardy and stalwart, my mother had retained the fragility of her youth. She was sensitive, overly perceptive, and too soft-spoken for her own good.

"Big day," Da said, the smile still plastered to his face. While my mother was quiet and mild, his accent was thoroughly Inkwellian, harsh and intentional. He raised his shoulders to emphasize his excitement. My mother matched his smile. "Yer Ma and I are planning on walking down to the docks in about an hour. Might stop along the way to see Selina and Kolvar." I grabbed a bowl and spooned in my small helping of porridge. "What're yer plans?"

"I thought Larka and I would do the same and see where the day takes us. We'd like to see the carnival, too." I leaned against the creaky counter, savoring the warmth of the porridge and the hot stove next to me. Three more spoonfuls and my bowl was empty, but I was too excited to pay attention to my hunger. "Larka is convinced the Prince of Zidderune is going to pick her out of the crowd and take her away to be his wife."

My father almost spat out his water as he laughed. Ma giggled too, the airiness of it a warm spot in the cold autumn air that seeped through our walls. "She's got a better chance of shooting gold coins out her arse," he huffed.

"Sarek!" my mother scolded, laughing along with him. For all of my mother's softness, Larka and I had inherited our father's mouth.

Larka breezed in the front door, hearing her name in our conversation. I quickly caught sight of a thin, visibly dirty man peering into our front door from the other side of the street. I didn't recognize him, and I peeked out the gap in the shutters over the window to find the spot where he'd been now empty. Fucking creep. Probably staring after Larka. Most men did. "You think I couldn't captivate a prince?" Larka said playfully, spooning her own bowl of porridge.

"I think the prince would find ye beautiful, just as everyone else does," my father continued, scratching the scruff that had appeared on his cheeks over the last few days, his hands shaking all the while. "But the second ye open that mouth, he's bound to throw ye overboard."

"That's enough, Sarek!" Ma's voice cracked into a laugh.

"Hey, if the prince can't handle what I have to say," Larka said, "then he's no fuckin' prince for me." Ma slapped her hands over her face as the rest of us chuckled.

I had always admired Larka's confidence. She had the beauty to match it, her hair shining like spun gold in the sunlight that streamed through the window my mother had unshuttered. Her nose was more petite than mine, too, a perfect slope ending in a point that made her appear much more innocent than she was. My nose was stronger, straighter. Her lips sat in a perfect pout atop her dainty chin where mine were thinner, and though we both had high cheekbones, hers were sharp enough to slice the heart from a man's chest. While she was outspoken and blunt all the time, I was more mild and timid when it came to public settings. Her certainty was a stark contrast to my constant anxiety. My tongue was just as sharp as hers though, even if I didn't use it as often.

32

Had she not been tainted by an Inkwell birth, her beauty would have been a prize to the Royal Court.

"I need to get ready," I said, beginning to head to the front door.

"Your throne awaits," she said flippantly, referring to the hovel we called an outhouse. I rolled my eyes and excused myself.

◆ ◆ ◆

Inkwell was an afterthought of the city. The district reserved for Eserene's poorest residents was shoved into the only remaining space that was left as the city was established, just making it inside the eastern wall when it was erected after the War of Kings. Gormill Road was the main street in Inkwell and one of our favorite places to wander. The eastern wall of Eserene served as an ever-changing mural of paint and flyers and chaos that the road ran against. Starving artists found space where they could add to the chaos, layering over the work of other artists, advertisements for brothels and pubs, and general filth.

On the west side of the street sat small shops filled with what we could get in Inkwell — mostly stale oats, root vegetables, mussels, burlap, and firewood. There was a seamstress, Caroline, who was far too talented for Inkwell, always sure to wave to me and Larka when we passed. There was a reeking bait shop for the fishermen who made their measly salaries fishing in the harbor, unable to afford larger boats to venture into deeper, more lucrative waters. Shops selling odds and ends, most of them stolen no doubt, dotted the lane, trying to pull in any currency they could to feed their families. Cottages patched with whatever materials were available punctuated the lane as well, and the chimneys of the ones who could afford firewood pumped thick black smoke into the sky.

Today, though, most chimneys sat idle as the residents of Inkwell woke up to Cindregala.

The gem of Gormill Road was at the end of it. The street spilled out onto the Eserenian waterfront. With the filth of Inkwell to one's back, one wouldn't know they were in the slums of the city by looking across the harbor.

Sapphire and teal and the deepest navy swirled together like clouds in the night sky to create Pellucid Harbor. It was a sight that took the breath straight from one's lungs whether they scrounged for survival in Inkwell or dined on imported meats and fruits in the highest reaches of the High Royal Castle.

Arm in arm, Larka and I strolled toward the waterfront, eagerly awaiting the sight of the colorful patchwork quilt of sails. The street was humming with activity as Inkwell residents funneled toward the waterfront. It was the first and only Cindregala that Eserenian citizens would see in their lifetime, and the Benevolent Saints had granted the city the perfect day.

We could just begin to see our breath fog the air in front of us as autumn's chill began to give way to another harsh Eserenian winter. Past the shops and the shanties that made up Gormill Road, we climbed the slight hill that blocked the district's view of Pellucid Harbor. We made it to the top just as the sun crested the northeast wall behind us, illuminating what laid in front of us.

Words failed me. My jaw hung on its hinges. Larka and I both stopped in our tracks, enraptured by the hundreds of ships that had sailed into the harbor under the cover of night. Colors I had never even seen lay before me. Reds and oranges that appeared to be on fire; yellow that looked like it was cut directly from the sun. Black that swallowed all the light around it, somehow capturing the essence of the dead of night in the bright morning light. Every shade of every color I could ever imagine — multiplied by a thousand — greeted us.

My eyes searched the painter's palette before me as we silently walked forward with the crowd, all just as dumbstruck as we were. As we descended the hill, I turned to my right and saw the throngs of people spilling out of the other districts. There were thousands, like grains of sand through an hourglass. Music played from somewhere — everywhere. The chill that had inhabited my bones melted away as Larka and I looked at each other and laughed, words still escaping us.

I watched as the waterfront of Sidus filled with people that were almost as poor as us, the district just barely passing the threshold of being worthy enough to be cleaned and shined for today's festivities. The district of Prisma's waterfront was bursting with people who never had to worry about their chances of eating on any given day. They had the money for homes and clothes and good horses. On a day like today, their houses would be full of loved ones celebrating with tables of food, much of which would go to waste, a feast for the rats. I tried not to think of it.

The other districts were not as fortunate to have such easy access to the waterfront, but the waterfront was open to all Eserene residents. The Cliffs of Malarrey rose proudly toward the west end of the city, the jagged edges and sheer cliff face a natural deterrent for any attackers.

"Pardon me. Excuse me. Thank you." I muttered niceties as I all but shouldered my way through layers of people crowding the barrier at the waterfront. I felt a palm graze my backside and whipped around to find a man in his thirties with missing teeth and a drunken grin. I froze.

"I think the fuck not," Larka spat, her hand connecting with his cheek. The man stepped back, stunned. "Hands to yourself, prick," she muttered, pulling me along.

My face had reddened, my cheeks hot. "*Saints,* Larka," I whispered to her.

"Do you want a man to just *take* what he wants from you?" She opened her mouth in a dramatic gag, ever the purveyor of theatrics. "All men are lousy pigs, Petra. Can't trust any of them. Take no shit from men who try to take from you. Take no shit from anyone, really." I knew she was right, but it had always been hard for me to speak up. Besides, she seemed to like being my voice.

Rising high above the harbor and the lower districts of Eserene, the castle was a series of daggers in the blue sky, the entire castle built on a pedestal, only accessible by a road that wound around and around the base. The lower levels that surrounded the High Royal Castle were reserved for Low Royalty — the lords and barons held private residences among the turrets, conducting their daily duties under the eyes of the High Royal Court. Dukes and counts held residences just above in the High Royal Castle. And jutting from the lower levels...

The King's Keep. The spires and reaches seemed to skim the clouds some days, leaving scars in the mist as the sky floated by. It provided the perfect vantage point to view the sprawling harbor — and the peasants that now surrounded it. I wondered if the King was watching now.

They called him the Invisible King. King Belin had never once stood on a terrace waving to his people. Never paraded through the city streets to the cheers of the lowborn, flowers thrown at the feet of his steed. His age, his appearance, his mannerisms — all a mystery. He had come to power after King Umfray had died of the red delirium, drowning in his own blood as delusions called him to meet the Benevolent Saints. King Umfray's sole heir had been a terrible drunk, meeting his demise at the bottom of the harbor one winter night ten years prior. It was a mess trying to find an eligible family member to continue Umfray's legacy. No brothers, no nephews, no obvious choices. King Belin was an obscure cousin, somehow falling next in line for a throne he had never shown his face for. He took the throne just over four years ago, more than enough time to greet his people.

And still the people loved the faceless king, scrambling to catch a glimpse of his windowless carriage any time he had to leave the city for business.

Today, the Royal Guard had cordoned off a swath of the waterfront where plush sofas and velvet chairs and food-laden tables were arranged with a perfect view of the harbor. Eserene's elite were bundled in the furs of rare beasts, excessively wrapped in luxurious fabrics from far off places. Guards stood every few feet around the stanchion, ready to protect the royals from us common folk. I thought my eyes would roll straight out of their sockets.

"Petra! Larka!" I heard, spinning to the left to meet Elin's brown eyes and full cheeks, my arm unhooking from Larka's. Elin was Larka's best friend and had been since we were young. I never thought she liked me much, simply tolerating me for the sake of her friendship with Larka. They'd always been close, but in recent years they'd become inseparable. Larka squealed as she gave Elin a squeeze, the girls giggling. "Can you believe how beautiful it is?" Elin remarked excitedly, one arm still around Larka.

Larka nodded emphatically, the girls falling into the chatter I was so used to hearing, arms linked together. I couldn't focus on their conversation as I scanned the harbor for my Eddenian lapis lazuli. "Let's try to get closer," I leaned in and told Larka and Elin, who barely nodded in acknowledgement as I followed them through the crowd. The smudges of color that were the sails became clearer, sigils and crests taking shape as we neared the water.

Suddenly, I was on the ground.

I hadn't even recognized the feeling of being pushed before my tailbone hit the gravel, an instant ache traveling through my spine. *Shit.* My cheeks burned with embarrassment. I began to collect myself, hoping no one had seen the fall, when an outstretched hand entered my vision. Calloused, rugged, honest.

I glanced up to meet the gaze of the kind stranger, finding his eyes–

His right eye was a startling blue, the color so intense it reminded me of the waters lapping in the harbor. But his left eye... The inner half of his left eye was the same blue as his right. The other half, though, was the color of a broken bottle of ale — gleaming emerald.

Like nothing I'd ever seen before.

"Are you okay?" he asked.

Chapter 3

Now

My mother joined Lady Marita and me in the drawing room as I sat sprawled on the floor, sewing together the panels of my soon-to-be-Eserenian nightmare. After receiving a quiet yet hysterical earful from my mother for lying about the status of said gown, she decided she'd sit in while I sewed, making easy conversation with a prim and proper Marita.

Marita was forbidden to divulge the forms of punishment inflicted upon Initiates if they stepped out of line or didn't meet the Board's standards. She told me she knew very little about the entire process. She was simply allowed to tell me that there was to be pain, that it was cruel in nature, that I would not be allowed to defend myself. As much as I knew the notion should rattle me, it simply didn't. I did not fear physical punishment nor death; I had thrown my fair share of fists on the streets of Inkwell as a child and dodged death just as many times. I feared what came after Initiation, if I made it, when I was an official member of the Low Royal Court. I would be immediately placed on the marriage market and married off to the "most suitable match," which was most likely going to be based on which family had a son and advantage to offer.

I couldn't decide whether I'd rather ask for a blade to the throat now.

"Lord Castemont is well respected," my mother said to me from her chair as if reading the thoughts in my mind. "The men who will pursue you are well aware of his status and will not risk losing their hides nor reputations by his hand. We will not approve your marriage unless the man is kind, Petra." Her hands were folded delicately in her lap, her right pointer finger idly drawing circles against the back of her left hand — another nervous habit of hers.

"Why do I have to be married, Ma?"

"Because that's the way it is in the Royal Court."

Marita's gaze darted swiftly from my mother to me, treading carefully as a spectator to what could easily erupt into an explosive argument.

I took a deep breath. "This *wasn't* the way it was. What would Solise have thought of this?"

She flinched at the mention of that name. "Petra, you're twenty-four years old. It's high time you were married. Is this about–"

"No, Ma. This isn't about *him.*" My heart ached at the words. "You didn't care when, or even *if*, I married before we came to this fucking court."

"Things were different, Petra," she said, the idle circles she drew against her hand gaining speed, Marita's eyes widening at my language.

"You never would have married Larka off, and she was almost my age when she–"

"Enough, Petra. Things. Were. *Different.*" I saw quiet rage enter her expression and I knew my next words needed to be chosen carefully. Royal life had hardened her slightly, gilding her voice with a power she had not possessed as an Inkwellian. But underneath the golden exterior was the same frail woman.

Neither of us averted our gazes from each other. I put all my focus into keeping my face a blank mask, not wanting to give into the tears that threatened to appear, clutching the needle between my fingers so tightly my knuckles turned white.

My mother tightened her lips into a thin line. "Larka was not a part of this court." The words stung, the crushing reality of my new life hitting me once again. She watched the wave wash over me as I processed her words, a flicker of apology in the same ice-blue eyes that Larka had, the split-second look replaced by the same quiet rage as before.

My only response was a curt nod before turning my attention back to my work. I would finish sewing my panels together today, leaving tomorrow to begin adding the ostentatious displays of wealth that were supposed to prove my worth to the Board of Blood.

Suddenly my spine began to tingle, my shoulders rising in response, my face wrinkling with discomfort. And I saw it again — the explosion, the lead in my gut when I realized it was gunpowder, the sound of breaking bones and the smell of burning skin and–

"Best hurry up, girl," Marita barked, looking at my gown and snapping me from my trance. The goosebumps remained on my skin as reality flooded my brain.

I am here, I thought. *I am here. And I am okay.*

I silently continued my stitching, not looking up until the last stitch was sewn.

◆ ◆ ◆

"Good morning, my Lady," chimed a handmaiden, pulling me from the depths of a nightmare, the deck of a ship with a sail made of fire. I blinked the image from my eyes, focusing on her face as she started toward the curtains. There were a dozen handmaidens that rotated through duties in the Castemont residence, and I had a hard time remembering her name. Shit, I couldn't remember a single one of my handmaidens' names. Not for lack of trying, but because there wasn't room in my head for much more. I recognized the soft pout of her lips, though, and the roundness of her deep brown cheeks. Her face was as kind as she was.

40

"Good morning," I replied, purposely avoiding addressing her by name as she moved from one massive window to the next, letting the sunlight cast the room in a golden sheen. I sat up and stretched, still unused to the presence of *handmaidens* in my quarters when a few short years ago our entire house could fit into my new bedroom three times over.

"Your mother has requested you join her for breakfast in the courtyard," she said softly, tying back the curtains.

"Fuck," I muttered under my breath. The young woman flinched slightly, an almost imperceptible movement but one I caught nonetheless. "Apologies," I quickly said, standing and stepping into the plush slippers that awaited my feet. "Grew up in a very different place than this."

"Yes, my Lady. As did I," she said before drawing her gaze down. "Apologies," she said, a guilty tone in her quiet voice.

"For?"

"Speaking out of turn."

I grimaced. "You're allowed to talk."

She looked up at me, skin flushed. "Thank you, my Lady, but I won't be bothering you further. Is there anything else you need?"

I studied her face. The way she stood. Feet together. Hands folded in front, slightly wringing her fingers in embarrassment or shame or...fear?

"I'm serious. You're allowed to speak. Say whatever you want. I don't care. Saints know I could use a friend around here." I said, immediately regretting the slip in my façade of royalty. I turned to make my bed.

The young woman rushed over, all but shooing me away. "Please, my Lady, allow me."

I hated this. I *hated* this. This was awkward. I could make my own bed. "I'm so sorry, but what is your name again?"

"Wrena, my Lady," she said as she continued to straighten my sheets.

"Wrena, I'm Petra. You can call me Petra. You don't have to refer to me as a lady."

"Yes, Miss Petra."

"*Miss Petra?*" I snorted, stifling a laugh. "How old are you Wrena?" She looked close to my age.

"I'm twenty-five."

"And I'm twenty-four. Therefore, you don't need to be calling me by any Saints forsaken title. We are peers." She averted her gaze as she finished making the bed and returned to her rigid standing position. "Okay?"

"Okay, Petra," she said with a soft smile.

"See? Not so bad, is it?" It was that moment that I realized... I was lonely. Mind-numbingly, atrociously, really *fucking* lonely. Marita's company was pleasant, but I wasn't sure the last time I'd seen another person my age, aside from the occasional younger guard, and they didn't dare look too long in my direction.

I surveyed Wrena again. We had both taken paths in life that led us to the Low Royal Castle. The only difference was the positions we held. "Well, Wrena, I've been here for about four months now and I think this is the longest conversation I've had with anyone remotely close to my age."

Another soft laugh rose from Wrena. The sound was surprisingly refreshing. *Normal.* It stirred memories of Larka's laugh. A pang hit my chest, lightning quick and searing, but I quickly swallowed the hurt. "There are actually quite a few handmaidens around your age, my La—" she caught herself. "Petra," she said, bobbing her head slightly to emphasize the titleless-ness of it. "Kleia, Ayin, Charlot, all of us are close in age."

"Well feel free to pass along the message that I don't bite," I said as cheerfully as I could, but the loneliness coated my words.

"I will. We're told to keep conversations to a minimum, and you've always seemed so sad, so no one thought it was appropriate to speak with you."

Sad. I was *visibly* sad. "I'm not sad," I said with a smile. "I'm just...adjusting. And like I said, I could use some friends here. You and your handmaidens are always permitted to speak in my presence." *In my presence.* What an uncomfortable phrase. I almost wrinkled my nose. "Hell, do more than speak. Scream, sing, I don't care. So long as you don't call me a lady."

"Thank you, Petra." We exchanged smiles. I began to turn to my bathing chamber to prepare for what was bound to be an uncomfortable breakfast with my mother. "Is there anything else I can get you?"

I paused before saying half-jokingly, "A way out of here."

◆ ◆ ◆

"G'morning, Ma," I droned as I pulled out a chair at a small table in the courtyard. The wrought iron chair was intricately delicate, but it groaned as I scraped it across the stone patio. An unpleasantness in a pleasant place. Just like me.

"Good morning, Petra," my mother said, her lilting voice heavy with impending conversation. I took a moment to ground myself, taking in my surroundings to remind myself that this was real life. A deep breath filled my nostrils with the scent of the jasmine snaking along the trellises that lined the gazebo overhead. A fat bumblebee buzzed lazily along the flowers. A fountain babbled peacefully behind me. Guards stood a healthy distance away near the two exits — one back to the Low Royal portion of the castle, and the other an informal entrance into the King's Keep which currently loomed threateningly overhead.

I turned to the table and surveyed the array of food. This was food we could have never dreamed of a few years ago. The food on the table in front of me would have fed our family for a *week*. I reached for the steaming teapot to my right, gingerly filling my teacup, spilling a few drops onto the navy tablecloth. "Shit," I whispered. I heard my mother's exasperated sigh. I looked up at her and returned her sigh. "Yes?"

"I'm worried, Petra," she said, and I could hear it in her voice. Some of the fragility she had worked so diligently to harden peeked through. "If you don't pass Initiation, you know what will happen."

For many, it was death. The other option was exile. The young women who didn't pass Initiation into the court to enter the marriage market were either killed on the spot or cast out of the city walls to the Onyx Pass, forbidden to enter Eserene for the rest of their lives. Their families, their friends, their possessions, their *lives*, all left behind. Outside the walls between Eserene and the nearest village, Blindbarrow, all manner of beasts both human and animal prowled through the Onyx Pass. Not one exiled Initiate had ever made it to Blindbarrow. The choice between death or exile was made in the moment by the Board of Blood, based on how sadistic they were feeling.

The practice was barbaric.

The practice was something I never had to consider under our Inkwell roof.

And the practice was now my future.

I stabbed a chunk of melon with my fork, absentmindedly piling fruit on my plate. "I'm very aware of what could happen, Ma. I'm very aware of the *probability* of it happening." I said quietly. Somberly. I didn't meet her gaze. I couldn't.

It was true. I wasn't so detached from reality that I believed I had a fair shot of passing Initiation. I knew the chances of me passing were low. But I knew there *was* a chance. I wasn't sure if I had been clinging to that small chance as a way to cope with what was almost certain death, or to make my mother feel better.

And I didn't know how to feel about that.

"Do you realize that if you do not pass, if you are not Initiated, you will never see your family again? You will never see *me* again?" I saw tears threaten to spill over her lids as her voice cracked. "Less than two weeks now, Petra! That could be all the time we have together."

I pursed my lips, an acidic, burning feeling pooling in my stomach. "I can't think about it, Ma."

"You *must!*" She was almost shouting now, tears spilling over her eyes, her linen napkin balled in one tiny, delicate hand. The hysterics were echoes of the shrieks and screams that had preceded complete despondency in years past. I hadn't seen this side of her in a long time. "You must think about this. You must, Petra. I need you to pass. I cannot lose my baby. My *other* baby."

The words were a cannonball in my chest. I nodded slowly. "You won't, Ma. You won't lose me."

She was distraught now. I could see the guards side-eyeing our table, the awkwardness of being a bystander to an argument rippling off of them. Her jerky movements were so at odds with the peaceful surroundings of the courtyard that I winced.

"Ma!" I said with force in my voice. "I will do everything in my power to pass Initiation, okay?" I calmed my voice. "I may have been raised in Inkwell, but that doesn't mean I'm a fuckin' animal. An animal." I caught myself.

"I can't lose you. I can't lose you. *I can't lose you.*" She said, rocking back and forth in her chair now, fists flailing, tears leaving dark stains on her sky blue dress.

I once again took on the role of the parent, reaching my hand across the table, laying it flat in front of her. An attempt to calm her down. The simple gesture silenced her breathing for a split second. Another sob, a deep breath, and she was as composed as she could be. She laid her hand across mine, a knowing glance in her swollen, reddened eyes.

"You will not lose me." But somewhere not so deep in my soul, I knew that wasn't true.

Chapter 4

Then

"I'm fine," I said, grabbing the stranger's outstretched hand, my eyes never leaving his. The softness of my voice sounded too feminine, too refined to be mine. "Thank you," I breathed. His golden-brown skin was at home in the autumn sun that was still shining on the harbor, his short, shaggy dark hair, the kind my hands would love to be tangled in. His eyes were...beautiful. The colors seemed alive, a far cry from the deep brown of my eyes.

"Try to be more careful." His voice was smoky and edged with the richness of the earth beneath my feet, but there was a distinct playfulness to it.

"Mhm," was all I could manage. Fucking Saints, I felt like Larka meeting the Zidderunian Prince. I shook my head to clear the smoke that his voice had blown across my senses. "Enjoy Cindregala," I said, and turned away into the crowd, following Larka and Elin who hadn't even seen my tumble.

"Wait," he called, once again reaching out a hand, this time gently placing it on my shoulder. I turned back to him, looking into those eyes that for some reason had me in a Saints damned chokehold. I wanted out. I raised an eyebrow, expectantly waiting, unable to keep from studying the line between blue and green in his left eye.

He said nothing, those eyes roving my face as if committing it to memory. I knew I should shrink under his gaze, but something deep inside of me kept me propped up. His jaw was square, darkened with stubble. I could tell by the way his cheekbones sat that his eyes would crinkle when he smiled. I stared up at him, looming almost a foot taller than me, his heady scent of smoke and cedar—

"What's your name?" he asked, a coaxing smile curving his lips.

"I have to go. My sister is leaving. Thanks again," I muttered, swiftly turning and finding the back of Larka's head in the crowd. I took a deep breath and walked as quickly as I could without looking like an absolute idiot.

What the hell was that?

Shaking the lingering fog from my head, I fell into stride beside Larka and Elin who were chatting about the meaning of the symbol on the green sail closest to shore. Clouds still swirled through my mind, replaying what had just happened.

"That arrow is *definitely* a symbol for...something else," Larka said, wiggling her eyebrows and snickering. I was immediately pulled back into the present, knowing exactly where Larka was headed with this.

Elin scoffed, rolling her eyes. "Why do you say that?"

"You can't look at that and tell me it isn't phallic," she laughed. A man walking in front of us turned around at the word, which only made Larka's laugh deepen.

"Larka!" I growled. But her laugh continued, the sound blending with the music and the people and the waves.

I knew that she and I would likely never see the world like we planned, needing to help provide for our parents. But in that moment, laughing with Larka as the sun danced through her hair, the melodious laughs echoing from her mouth, I was swept with a wave of gratitude. It came from nowhere, an unfamiliar fullness that bloomed in my chest, but it hummed with a welcome warmth.

"Girls!" We heard voices from ahead and spotted our parents with Selina and Kolvar, Elin's parents.

"Isn't it incredible?" my mother quietly gushed as we approached their group. Their cheeks were still red from the bite that was now leaving the air thanks to the sun. My father's eyes were brighter than I'd ever seen them. In that moment he was a picture of his younger self, tremors minor enough to conceal.

"It's so much better than I imagined," said Larka, scanning the harbor once again.

"There he is, Larka! There's yer Zidderunian Prince! What's his name again?" my father taunted.

"Who cares? Look at the size of that ship!" she laughed.

"Ever think maybe he's compensating?" my father quipped, and Larka gave him a light elbow in the ribs.

"We're going to head to my mother's house in Sidus," said Kolvar, his arm around Elin's shoulder. "We're going to try to convince her to make the journey down here, but the old goat is a crotchety one, let me tell ya."

"Good luck with that one," my father chuckled. We said our farewells, Elin and her family taking off toward Sidus.

My father clasped his shaking hands together. "My ladies," he said in his best High Royal accent, his chest puffing out. "A gift for ye." He reached into his pocket, pulling out two silver pieces and handing them to us, using all of his concentration to shakily deposit one in each of our hands. My mother beamed beside him. "I hear the carnival is up and running in Bellenau Square. Go have some fun. Happy birthday, Petra."

Our eyes widened. Larka spoke first. "Dad, you don't have to-"

"Ah!" he cut in. "I won't hear it."

I spoke next. "This could be used for-"

"I said I won't hear it. Ye girls work so hard to keep our home together. Now *go have fun.*" He waved his hands, shooing us away.

Larka and I looked at each other, faint smiles on both of our faces. A silver piece wouldn't get us much, but the atmosphere and the music and the crowd were magic, and we were swept away in it.

The walk from the waterfront to Ockull's Bellenau Square was only about ten minutes, but I could have sworn we passed half of Eserene's residents on the streets mingling with sailors from other cities. I had never seen anything like it — the merriment, the alcohol, the chaos.

◆ ◆ ◆

Turning the corner of Ivy Avenue into Bellenau Square, more sights and sounds and smells descended on my senses than had ever before. A grand arch had been erected over the entrance to the square, covered in flowers the likes I had never seen before. Violet and yellow petals glowed in the sunlight, welcoming Eserenian residents to wonders they'd only ever experience once.

The square was lined with stalls serving food from across the world — food I had never even heard of. Spun sugar from Azmar. Fried dandelion roots from Anicole. A jumble of noodles and what looked like some sort of shellfish from Myrefall. I knew that Larka's stomach was just as empty as mine was, but we seemed to have an unspoken agreement that we would not be spending our precious silver pieces on food.

Vendors peddling wares were interspersed between the food stalls. Larka and I leisurely smelled exotic spices and teas until the stall owners chased us away for loitering. We ran our hands over the only silk we'd ever touched. We picked through buckets of glass beads in hues that matched the sails in the harbor. Handwoven bags, braided shawls, ceramic bowls, and windchimes made of shells along with intricate jewelry were a vibrant spectacle that lulled me into a trance.

"I wish Ma and Da hadn't raised us so honest," Larka scoffed, inspecting a blown glass vase the same color as her eyes. "It would be so easy for me to pocket stuff here."

"How would you pocket a *vase?*"

"Well, not the vase. But I could tuck ten scarves under my cloak and no one would notice." She said it far too loudly, and I lowered my eyes in embarrassment, in case anyone had heard. "I'm not saying I *would,* just that I *could.*"

Our parents had instilled in us that everything we had must be earned. So many people made their money in Inkwell by selling stolen goods, but no matter how empty our bellies were, no matter how cold our hearth was, they made it clear that we were never to resort to thievery.

"Come on," Larka said, growing bored of the blown glass. "This coin is burning a hole in my pocket. Ignore the hole that's already there."

I laughed as she pulled me away from the stall, down another row of tents.

This was the best day of my life.

◆ ◆ ◆

"How about the ring toss?" I suggested.

"The *ring toss?* We are not wasting our money on something so pathetic," Larka declared in her usual snarky tone. "Come *on*." She grabbed my arm, leading us deeper and deeper into the carnival crowd.

The crowd swirled busily around us in the midmorning sun as Larka and I surveyed the stalls. "Oh!" shouted Larka. "A soothsayer!"

She pointed to a small tent toward the end of the row. A sign hung from the awning, the words scrawled in shaky script. *Lady Ingra of Skystead: Soothsayer and Prophet of the Saints, Benevolent and Blood.*

"You're fucking joking, Larka," I said with a scowl.

"I'm fucking not, *Petra.*" she retorted. "Come on! I've always wanted to see a soothsayer."

"It's *my* birthday."

"Well it's also *my* Cindregala."

I pulled the silver piece from my pocket, flipping it over in my hand. Genuine excitement lined Larka's face. "Really? This is what you want?" I asked.

"Really," she said firmly. Determined. "You can't tell me you don't want it too."

I sighed, then gave a slight nod of my head. Larka squealed, grabbing my arm and dragging me toward the tent.

Parting the heavy aubergine curtains, the thick smell of incense wafted outside. The feel of the smoke around my head was suffocating.

"Enter," a small, raspy voice uttered. Larka walked through first, dramatically waving her hand in front of her face, stirring tendrils of smoke. I followed behind her, now completely overcome with the aroma of incense. It coated my throat. It was dark except for a taper in each corner of the tent and the tiny glow of the burning incense. We could just make out the outline of a woman's face sitting in the corner, a low table with two cushions before her. "Sit, please," she rasped.

Larka plopped down on a flat cushion without hesitation, quiet excitement rippling off of her. I took my time lowering myself to the floor, a distant sense of discomfort settling over my chest. Anxious, as always.

"You wish to know what the Saints have planned for your future?" the old woman said, her face coming into focus now that I was closer. Her face matched her voice — withered and wrinkled, deep brown, the hood of her cloak resting atop a head of wispy gray hair.

"We do," Larka said excitedly, quickly turning her face to me. She placed her silver piece on the table. My silver piece had grown warm in my hand, the weight of it burning through my skin. "Come on, Petra," Larka urged.

"The girl is unsure," the soothsayer said, barely above a whisper.

I swallowed hard, still feeling Larka's excitement. I placed my silver piece on the table. "I'm not unsure. Here you go."

The old woman nodded. "I am Ingra," She slid the silver pieces toward herself with dark spindly fingers wrinkled with age. "I am able to see certain aspects of your future, the aspects that my Saints allow me to see."

"Benevolent Saints only, please. I just want to know if I marry the Prince of Zidderune," Larka giggled. "Nothing from the Blood Saints."

Ingra did not laugh. "I will tell you what I see. I cannot look for specific scenarios nor plead favor from a specific side."

I almost heard the smile leave Larka's face as she nodded. "Yes, okay. Me first."

"My Saints are telling me your future will not be what you imagine it to be," Ingra said, turning to me, her dark eyes pinning me in place. "My Saints ask that I start with you." I gave a nervous laugh, nodding my head.

"Okay."

"Tell me your name, sweet one," she purred.

"Petra. Petra Gaignory."

"Ahh, Petra. Beautiful name," she droned. "The Blood Saints..." she started. My face wrinkled at the mention of the dark ones. "The Blood Saints are showing me...blood."

"Blood?" I scoffed, fighting back the laugh in my voice. How convenient that the damned Blood Saints showed her blood. Larka giggled beside me. I just about rolled my eyes when Ingra started speaking again.

"Your blood will spill, girl, from your eyes like they're hoping." Who is hoping my eyes will bleed? I stilled, cocking my head, my gaze narrowing. "The beasts of the Onyx Pass prowl the mountains with your blood on their jowls." Larka went rigid then.

"I'm from Inkwell. Why would I ever leave the Eserenian walls?" I asked incredulously. We had only ever heard legends of the Onyx Pass; warriors cutting down monsters as they rode to their next assignment, beggars and vagrants trying to find their way somewhere else, few making it through the horrors of the pass. And the unlucky Royal Initiates who did not pass whatever tests they were put through, cast out to die in the forest between the jaws of monsters.

"My Saints will not say why you will leave," she rasped. "My Saints are showing me fearsome beasts laying slain in your wake. Wolfhounds opened from shoulder to gut. Oxbears sliced across the neck. Veridian raptors without wings, left with bleeding stumps, and Rivodian crows combusting in midair. Bones cracking, fracturing in places that won't heal." Her words quickened. Cold sweat began trickling from my temple. The incense smoke was suddenly choking me, the walls closing in. I needed to get out, I needed–

"You were born of sin, were you not?

"Our parents were married when Petra was conceived," Larka said matter-of-factly. "If you're looking for a child born of sin, that's me."

"Mmm..." Ingra hummed, digesting her words. "Cabillia. The country to our north. My Benevolent Saints are showing me Cabillia. Fields of violet wildflowers, and...oh." She stopped.

"What?" I breathed. The incense suddenly smelled like burnt lavender. Sharp. Sour. An affront to the fragile scent of a lavender field.

"Firestorm. My Blood Saints are showing me a firestorm. Many firestorms, actually." I was silent. "And my Saints have closed the curtains."

"What? Cabillia? I don't understand. Why is there a firestorm?" I pleaded.

"My Saints will not say. My Saints have shown me all they can show me. You must be patient."

Larka turned to me, a twinkle of mischief in her eyes. The humanity of the look softened my posture, my muscles relaxing. I could tell she stifled a laugh. She didn't believe a word the soothsayer spoke. It further slowed my heartbeat. I reminded myself that a *real* soothsayer would not be at the carnival. A *real* soothsayer would be serving a king or a lord of some far off land, advising them on military strategies and the movements of their enemies.

Ingra gave me a grim nod before turning her attention to Larka. I felt the sweat begin to evaporate from my palms.

She is not a real soothsayer.

I am okay. I am okay. I am okay.

Larka leaned expectantly toward the soothsayer across from her. Ingra took a deep breath, holding it for a few seconds before releasing it in a heavy sigh. "And your name, pretty girl?"

"Larka Gaignory." Larka smiled.

"Larka. Hmm. 'Means birdsong." Larka nodded.

Ingra leaned back slightly, her black eyes searching the ceiling of her tent. She was silent for a few beats, her steady breathing the only sound, her breath creating whirls of smoke above us.

"Darkness. My Saints are showing me darkness," the soothsayer said quietly, somberly.

My heart rate increased again. "Darkness?" Larka scoffed. Sweat began to dampen my palms once again. "Your Blood Saints or your Benevolent Saints?"

"All of my Saints are showing me nothing."

"Maybe you should ask them nicely," Larka taunted, not at all thrown by the words leaving the soothsayer's mouth.

Ingra was once again silent. My throat began to feel acidic, uncomfortable.

"That is all my Saints are showing me, Miss Larka," Ingra breathed.

Larka clicked her tongue. "That's no fun. What a ripoff." She scrambled to her feet, muttering. "You get blood and fire and sin and I get *darkness?* What a load of shit."

I nodded to the soothsayer as I turned to leave, but the look in her eyes stopped me for a moment. Desperation. Fear. Warning. Her black eyes glowed. "Thank you," I said quietly as I exited. Ingra was silent.

I squinted as I reentered the sunlight. Larka was still muttering about her lost coin. "I can't believe we spent our silver pieces on *that.*" She combed her fingers through her hair and turned to me, instantly noticing the paleness of my face. "What's the matter with you?"

"I... I just...that was..." I stammered.

"Like I said, *a load of shit.* If I'm spending a silver piece, I expect to hear *something.* Fuck!" she exclaimed, kicking at the ground, attracting the attention of a passing family. I was silent, sorting through the words we had just heard. "You don't actually believe that, do you?" I looked at her. "*Shit,* you do. Petra, this was a soothsayer at a carnival. She isn't real. She's just here to make money, probably to spend on liquor by the look of her."

"Yeah," I said quietly, nodding. "You're right. She isn't real." I tried to calm myself down. "She isn't real," I repeated.

Larka searched my face, a puzzled look on hers. "Why are you so shaken up?"

"I'm not," I said, shaking my head to clear my thoughts again. The smell of the incense clung to my clothes and hair, smothering me. It was better than burning lavender, but still suffocating. "I'm shaken up that we got scammed out of the only spare silver pieces we'll see all year." I managed to let loose a laugh which Larka echoed.

"We can't tell Ma and Da that this is what we spent it on," Larka said, looping her arm through mine and leading us back into the rows of tents and booths.

"You're the older sister," I chided. "You can be the one to explain."

As we walked away from the tent discussing what we'd tell our parents, I felt the weight of eyes burning into my back. I turned my head slightly, just enough to see Ingra standing outside of her tent, watching us walk away, a hand clutching her Saints' beads to her heart.

Chapter 5

Now

I stood in front of the gilded mirror, running my palms across the shimmering bodice of my Initiation gown. I had stayed up until dawn sewing each crystal into place, wrapping my body in the shattered ice of the famed Eserenian stones. The light from the silver chandelier in my wardrobe danced across each and every facet, the glint of the crystals shimmering on every surface, gracing my cheeks with radiant sparks. The sight of the dancing lights across my skin was familiar, each streak of shine leaving a trail of emptiness in its wake, echoes of a past life. I pushed the thought away. The corset held me in a death grip and I almost blushed at the sight of my figure, the way the soft straps laid across my upper arms. My gaze traveled to my skirts — massive, flowing rosettes and ruffles covered every inch, a small train resting behind me, patiently waiting to whisper over the marble floors.

Four days. I had four days until I stood for Initiation in front of the Board of Blood. Four days until my fate was sealed. The Board of Blood would arrive tomorrow to begin the process, a feast marking the official start of the ceremonies. All Initiates and their family were invited to a grand dining hall – one of many in the castle. The purpose, however, was for the Board to begin assessing each Initiate, side-eyeing her manners and grammar and *breedability*, as Marita called it. I fought the shudder that scraped against my insides.

I could hear Marita pacing outside the door of my wardrobe, whispering a prayer to every Benevolent Saint she could think of, hand on her chin. "Lady Marita," I called, the soft femininity of my voice so foreign to me that I almost flinched. Marita appeared in the doorway, her expression troubled, her light brown eyebrows knit together. "I'm ready to practice."

I stepped from the pedestal, the fabric of my gown swooshing and swaying with the movement. My high heels clicked gracefully, and I repeated *heel-toe, heel-toe, heel-toe* just as she had taught me, as I floated through the wardrobe to meet Marita. She gave a curt nod and led me out to the marble floor of my drawing room.

Back and forth. Back and forth. Back and forth I walked. Curtsy. Lower eyes. Present wrist. Curtsy. Lower eyes. Present wrist. Marita wasn't permitted to tell me *why* this action must take place, and my stomach turned at the uncertainty of it. I had missed out on the traditional education that all the other Initiates received, so I had no idea why the actual *fuck* the ceremony even existed. Or why they needed my wrist.

After what felt like an hour of the same movements, Marita finally approached me, my eyes gazing down at her due to the height of my heels. The look on her face was forlorn, desperate. "Do you think I'm ready?"

A sorrowful smile turned her lips up, the desperation remaining in her eyes. "You've worked harder than I've seen anyone work." Not a real answer. Before I could say anything, she began to speak the words I would hear from the Board of Blood in four days. "Repeat after me. For the crown you will bleed," she breathed, the look of urgency intensifying.

"For the crown I will bleed," I repeated.

"For the Court you will bear."

"For the Court I will bear."

"For the King you will live."

"For the King I will live."

"And for the realm you will die."

"For the realm," I said, my breath catching in my throat. "I will die."

Marita nodded slightly, stepping back. "You are ready, girl." Her smile turned hollow. Thick, opaque sorrow still flooded her eyes, as if she were already seeing me laying dead and naked in a heap outside the city walls.

"I am ready," I said softly. I had put in the hours. I had made a conscious effort to watch my language, my tone, my facial expressions. I would do everything I possibly could do so I could stay with my mother. I would not disappoint Lord Castemont. And if I made it through, I would deal with how to be the perfect wife.

I would prove my worth and marry a nobleman. I would do that for my mother. For my *family*.

Looking out at the wall towering above the city below, I quelled the urge to run straight for the cliffs.

◆ ◆ ◆

"Isn't that what you want though?" Wrena asked, perched rigidly on the edge of my bed, hands neatly folded in her lap. I had coaxed her into relaxing for a moment and insisted she sit with me. She had been visibly uncomfortable, but her words began to relax as we spoke.

"You have to understand that a few years ago my life was very different," I said tightly. My hands rested on my abdomen as I stared up at the painted roses on my ceiling. "I never considered marriage because I never thought I'd be able to leave my parents. My sister and I had planned on traveling, but we knew it might not happen. And when I finally met someone...it just didn't work out that way."

Wrena cocked her head. "A life married to a nobleman doesn't sound so awful." She blinked wistfully.

I propped myself up on an elbow. "Give me a fuckin' break," I scoffed. Wrena recoiled, eyes widening. Shit. "I'm sorry. I'm working on that." I laid back down. "I'm just saying, I'm not

58

opposed to the idea of marriage, I just never thought it would happen. Now I'm set up to enter the marriage court, Benevolent Saints willing I make it through Initiation."

"I would love to be married one day," Wrena said quietly, longing in her voice.

"Oh yeah? Any suitors thus far?" I prodded. I hadn't noticed at first, probably due to the veil my general misery cast over the world, but Wrena was beautiful. Wrena was *very* beautiful. Her olive skin was plump and dewy, and though her chocolate hair was fastened in a low bun, I could tell it was long and wild like the sea. Her nose had a slight bump in the middle, the imperfection of it somehow perfectly complementing her deep brown eyes. A small freckle sat below her left eye. Something about her face was daylight and summer wind and soft grass.

She cast those brown eyes away from me. "Maidens take a vow of celibacy."

If I had been drinking, I would have sprayed a mouthful through the air. "Excuse me?" She nodded. "What the actual fu–" I caught myself. "What?"

"Our lives are dedicated to the service of the court, which is a service of the realm."

"I never knew that." Why would I? I had only been in the castle for just over three months, the rest of my existence spent scraping by in Inkwell. "I don't think I could have survived this long without sex." Her face blanched. This poor girl must have thought me mad. "Okay. Say you *could* get married. To anyone you want. Who would you choose?" She straightened more, which I hadn't thought possible. She cast her eyes down, a nervous smile cracking her lips.

"Miss Petra, I–"

"Just Petra!" I snapped. "Come on! Anyone in the world." I poked. She nervously tucked a strand of hair that wasn't there behind her ear.

"Anyone?" she asked quietly. I nodded mischievously. She pondered for a moment, her eyes dancing around the room. I watched shadows dance across her face before a smile mirrored the mischief of my own. "Prince Rayner of Zidderune."

I paled. My ears began to ring. The edges of my vision went cloudy. I saw the blurry image of bloody water like the roses that stared down from my ceiling. Wrena felt the change immediately, reaching a small hand out and placing it on my arm. A Saints damned mention of a name and I was spiraling.

"Are you well, Petra? Did I say something?" She was so sweet. *So* sweet. She had no idea what she had just unlocked, what had tumbled out of a box within a box within a box in my brain that I had kept vaulted and hidden since moving to the castle.

"Yes, Wrena, I'm sorry. I–" A sob broke, thick and suffocating. Wrena rose, quickly shuffling to my side, lowering to her knees so we were face to face.

"Petra, what is it? What happened? What do you need?" I was frozen. Her eyes searched my face which was contorting to hold back tears. "Petra!"

I took a deep breath. Counted one. Two. Three. I closed my eyes. Counted again. Opened them. *I am okay.* Wrena's desperate eyes bored into mine. "I'm fine. Thank you. I think I'd like to go to sleep now." I had to grind the words out.

Wrena nodded quickly. "Yes, my Lady." I didn't have the energy to correct her as she began pulling the blanket out for me, urging me under. "I'm so sorry, my Lady, I didn't mean to–"

"You did nothing wrong," I said absently. "Goodnight."

She quickly walked to the door. "Goodnight, Petra," she breathed.

Chapter 6
Then

We had weaseled our way through the throngs of people and were leaning on the railing overlooking the harbor. Front row seats to the explosion of color and culture. Ships of every size and make crowded the harbor. Row boats floated in between the ships, taking crewmembers to shore to participate in the drinking, dancing, and debauchery that Eserene provided.

"Holy Saints! Look at that one!" Larka said, pointing dramatically in the direction of a group of ships.

"You'll have to be more specific," I countered.

"The black ship with the silver sail. Have you ever seen anything like it?" Her eyes were wide, blinking rapidly, the sunlight reflecting from the water bouncing in her eyes.

The ship *was* spectacular. The wood was the deepest black I had ever seen, at war with the brightly colored sails that flew from the ships around it. The sail gleamed in the sunlight, somehow capturing the essence of molten silver in the form of fabric.

"Taitha, capital of Cabillia," a smoky voice offered from our left.

I turned to meet the same mismatched eyes I had earlier today. *Benevolent Saints.*

Larka's gaze didn't move from the ship. "Taitha?" she said. "I didn't even know they had ships. Much less ships like *that*. Aren't they landlocked?" He didn't have time to answer before she started again. "Must have some money if they're paying for ships from the middle of the country."

A wave of discomfort washed over me, my stomach souring at the feel of the stranger next to me. He looked out to the harbor. "Cabillia has hundreds of miles of waterfront. The capital would be mad to pass up the opportunity to have ships," he said with the same playfulness that had struck me earlier.

"Huh," Larka murmured. She didn't even register the stranger beside us who had interjected himself into our conversation. I glanced sideways at the man. His clothes told me he sure as hell was not from Inkwell. Actually, his clothes looked like they didn't come from Eserene at all. But the way the sunlight caught in his black hair was easily distracting me from surveying his clothing.

"Where do you live?" I blurted without thinking, my tone sharper than intended. Neither Larka nor the man seemed to notice.

"Oh," he said with a nervous laugh, his hand gripping the back of his neck. "Ockhull." Larka didn't bat an eye at the mention of the middle-class district, but something in his tone made me grimace. It was hard not to look at him, not to study his profile as he watched the ships bob in the harbor, and at the same time my body tensed at the sight of him. "Remember what I said earlier," he added in quickly, turning to the crowd to leave. "Be careful."

"Who the fuck was that?" Larka finally exclaimed, tearing her eyes from the opulent ship.

"'Don't know," I answered, trying to shake the prickly feeling the conversation left me with. "I ran into–"

The air cleaved with hammering bells and screams. "FIRE!"

Five hundred feet to our left in the harbor, the bow of a warship was engulfed in angry flames. The sails — lapis lazuli. Eddena. I froze in panic, the crowd around us scattering as the ship moved in our direction at a fever pitch and the flames spread to the masts. The crew began to jump overboard as the sail caught fire, their shocked screams echoing off the seawall as the frigid water stole their breath away. Nearby rowboats took on water as crew members pulled themselves aboard, frantically rowing out of the way of the inferno. At the rate it was moving, there were maybe forty-five seconds before it reached the seawall.

"COME ON!" Larka yelled beside me, and I realized she was yelling to the rowboats of men. Garbled screams erupted as the ship collided with swimming sailors that couldn't move out of the way in time, the blunt force knocking them unconscious before the flames could reach them. Heads slipped underwater in the chaos, and I lost track of who resurfaced and who didn't. Bodies began to float. Blood pouring from head wounds painted a rose garden across the water.

Thirty seconds.

The flaming ship was still heading directly toward us, a rowboat teeming with crewmen directly in its path feverishly paddling for shore. I could tell that if they cut to the side, it'd be too late. It was then that I realized what their only option was, what they were going to attempt. One man stood at the bow holding a bundle of rope, swinging it over his head.

"THROW IT!" Larka screamed, looking around her for someone, *anyone*, to help, and I knew what she was doing. She was going to try to pull the boat to the shore. It would be quicker than paddling if there was enough strength to drag it in.

Like a lasso bound for a calf, the sailor heaved the rope to where we stood atop the seawall. Three men had seen the plan set in motion and quickly crowded around Larka, ready to pull. The Eddenian ship blazed toward the rowboat, toward the shore, blue sails turning orange–

Larka caught the end of the rope, quickly pulling as much of it onto land as she could, the men falling into formation behind her. I stood dumbfounded, frozen in place, my mind running a million miles a second but my legs bound in invisible shackles.

Twenty seconds.

The rowboat began to pick up speed as their makeshift rescue team pulled and pulled. It was working. Holy *shit*, it was working. The craft glided over the water. The blazing ship was still speeding toward them, but they were closing the distance to shore.

Larka let out a war cry, her face blood red with the effort, veins popping from her neck. The men behind her heaved and heaved. All I could do was watch.

The ship was closing in on the rowboat and the men aboard screamed, some of them paddling furiously with their hands, *anything* to propel them forward. They suddenly began to lose momentum.

"We need leverage!" Larka shouted, and all at once, the team of brute force shifted to the left, catching the rope on a railing post and pulling it taut. The rowboat gained speed again, heading for the seawall at breakneck speed. All they'd have to do is hop up and they'd make it. They were *right there.*

The railing post snapped in half with a loud crack, Larka and the three men falling to the ground, the rope slackening.

Ten seconds.

The team rose, but the slackened rope had looped around Larka's calf in the chaos of the fall, somehow wrapping around her leg in a knot. She flailed her arms out, screaming in pain as she clawed at the rope, but her cries were drowned out by the screams of people fleeing, scrambling, watching.

Her lower leg snapped in two, the crack audible even over the turmoil that whirled around us. She collapsed back to the ground, her face colliding with the earth, the three men behind her pulling with all their strength, not realizing she'd been caught.

My world slowed down as the flaming ship closed in on the rowboat, the men screaming and diving overboard as a last ditch attempt at survival. Explosions rang out from the ship as the sides disintegrated in a boom of power.

Gunpowder.

The ship crashed into the rowboat, detonating the remaining sailors. Screams were cut short.

"Petra!" Larka screamed, her eyes full of undiluted, raw terror. The rope had caught on the ship's debris as it began to sink. Larka was being dragged toward the harbor, her mangled leg still wrapped in the rope. The three men had abandoned Larka and disappeared into the crowd, fleeing the impending collision.

Five seconds.

64

Finally, *finally* my legs gained feeling and I was running toward my sister as she slid closer and closer to the water. Her scream pierced the air and I realized that blood was pouring from her leg now, the bone protruding at a nauseating angle. "Larka!" I bellowed. My feet were moving too slowly, *too slowly.*

Four seconds.

Another blast. I saw white. My ears *screeched.* Chunks of flaming wood rained down over the remaining crowd, most frozen with shock as they watched the horror unfold. The explosion had thrown me back, erasing the progress I had made toward her.

Three seconds.

I saw it before I knew what was happening. A wooden plank fell from the sky, a blazing tail of fire behind it. It speared Larka through her throat. Blood spattered and spilled from her mouth. Her eyes stayed locked on mine as I sat helplessly in the grass.

Two seconds.

The rope made its final pull as chunks of debris sank, and she went over the edge. The harbor claimed its prize. Her contorted body slid into the water at the exact second the flaming remnants of the ship finally collided with the seawall, her scream cut short by the explosion filling my vision and blowing me back once again.

Nothing. I saw nothing. But the darkness was warm, comforting, so enticing that I wanted to let it take me right there. I think Larka was calling me to it, but her voice was obscured by crackling fires and the screams of strangers.

My mind imploded on itself.

I opened my eyes, my ears still ringing furiously and my vision doubled. The ringing in my ears was deafening, *roaring.* My vision was blurry as I realized that the ringing in my ears was the sound of my own screams. I couldn't see. I couldn't hear. I couldn't breathe.

I tasted blood and realized I was covered in it as I dragged my hand across my face. I had to get up. I had to find Larka. I stood, blinking the blood from my eyes, and started toward the blaze that had swallowed my sister.

Someone grabbed my arm, forcefully pulling me back. I fought, knowing Larka was just below the seawall waiting for me to come save her. Back, back, back and away I was pulled. I flailed my arms and punched at the air, *needing* to get to my sister.

Arms closed around me and a face appeared in front of me. Those eyes. His mouth was screaming. I didn't hear him. His hands held my face as I writhed and fought. I felt blood run from my forehead to my cheek. I was dizzy and tired. I was so tired.

I needed to get to Larka.

My vision went dark. My body went loose. And I let the emptiness swallow me whole.

◆ ◆ ◆

Darkness. Nothing. Black.

A sliver of light. Blue sky and...smoke.

Bells ringing. *So many bells ringing.* Screaming. I knew that voice. *Ma.*

My eyes were swollen and coated in grit. I pried them open to see the silhouette of my mother against the flames, falling to her knees and ripping at her hair.

"Petra!" I heard from far away. So, so far away. Movement. Frantic, furious movement. *Da.* My face was in his hands as he became clear then blurry, clear then blurry. My vision shook. "Petra!" he screamed, his eyes moving from my face to the inferno that raged at the seawall. My mother wailed. Why was she crying? Where was Larka?

My throat was full of gravel as I tried to speak. "Da, we should go home," I rasped. "Where's Larka?" My dad searched my face, wiping the sweat from his brow and leaving a trail of blood in the wake of his hand. "Da, where's Larka? Oh, Da, you're bleeding," I coughed.

"Petra, you need to stay here," he said, his shaking hands pinning my shoulders down.

"Da, you're bleeding," I repeated. I didn't see any cuts. Why was there so much blood on his face?

"Petra, *stay here,*" he shouted.

"We have to find Larka, Da," I said back, searching the crowd and the flames for her. Why was my mother crying?

I tasted blood and pain split through my skull. "We have to find Larka," I cried.

I fell back under the spell of darkness.

Chapter 7

Now

It felt like a funeral. We stood in the entrance hall of the Low Royal Castle, the other Initiates standing as rigidly as I did in our simple gowns, a far cry from the frothy monstrosities we would be wearing in three days' time. My turquoise satin gown pooled on the floor beneath me, the color of Pellucid Harbor, the color of a past life.

It was the first time I had seen any of the other Initiates, and to say I was the obvious outlier was an understatement. Though my thick caramel hair was curled and coiffed in the same fashion as the others, I still looked noticeably different. My face was simply more womanly, more angled, my body more well-defined. I was taller than the others, too, and I was certainly the only one who did not still hold her virginity.

I met Cora when I arrived for the greeting ceremony, the two of us exchanging an awkward nod as our parents introduced us. She was *young*, maybe seventeen at most, the roundness of youth still visible in her cheeks. Her hair and brows were a rich dark brown, close to black, and her skin was just as rich. Her father was Baron Evenmark, a plump fellow with the same hair and brows as his daughter. Her mother was slight and aloof, seemingly removed from the entire gathering.

Estelle was the daughter of Lord and Lady Ascelin, the former of whom had been taken by a fever just a year ago. Estelle's older brother stood in his place, chin raised proudly but clearly shaken by the responsibility that lay before him. Estelle's gown was a pale yellow, the color offset by her sandy brown skin and jet black hair.

Next came Alira and Willow, twin daughters of Baron and Baroness Dumond, the softness of their blue eyes indicative of eighteen years or thereabouts. Both girls were dressed in shades of purple, Alira in lilac and Willow in aubergine, the silk pooling identically at their feet. Even their blonde curls were identical, pinned tastefully at the napes of their necks.

Iridia lowered herself into an almost awkward curtsy as she was introduced to Lord Castemont by her father, Lord Pouissard. She tucked a tightly coiled curl behind her ear as she stood up again, her dark eyes searching for her mother. Lady Pouissard had been flitting about the room for a few minutes, making conversation as if she weren't sending her daughter off to what could be her death. Clearly it wasn't a concern for her.

Rounding out the Initiates was Augusta, a girl of no more than eighteen with wild red hair that was barely contained by the ribbon tied around it, a youthful flush to her cheeks that matched that of her mother, Lady Seavale. Lord Seavale stood a few inches taller than his wife, his handsome face still as a stone.

I was *ancient* among this crowd of mere children. At twenty-four years old, I should have been married for at least six years by now and a mother three or four times over. Though the other girls were polite and cordial, I could feel the antipathy and dejection radiating from where they stood. I was an *other*.

In a room full of people, I was utterly and completely alone.

We stood in a half-moon across the entrance hall, the wide, curved staircase looming over us, each Initiate pushed forward with her parents behind her. Each nobleman's head guard stood in the back, hand on the hilt of the sword at their side. "Do I look okay?" I whispered to my mother. There had been no rule against speaking, but the occupants of the hall had fallen into an unarticulated, agreed upon silence. I didn't want to be the one to break it.

Her hand rested on my upper arm. "You look beautiful, dear," she whispered back, her tone hopeful on the surface but tainted with a distant emotion I could not place. Lord Castemont leaned in, placing his hand on my other arm and giving it a reassuring squeeze.

"Just do as you practiced," he breathed. I nodded.

The beasts of the Onyx Pass prowl the mountains with your blood on their jowls.

No. I wouldn't think about the soothsayer.

I could do this. I would do this. I *had* to do this.

The two guards standing on either side of the towering set of doors straightened as the noise of hooves stirred outside, skidding to a halt. The room went eerily still. The left guard opened his mouth, the sound of the intake of breath piercing the quiet. "Presenting the esteemed seven, the designated sons of the Benevolent Saints, the honorable members of the Board of Blood, Eserene's authority of Royal Initiation." My stomach dropped. The guards stepped toward the door, pulling open each side in perfect unison, the clank of the heavy wood echoing deafeningly throughout the hall. My mind quickly flashed to an explosion, the sound, the shock–

Sunlight poured in, a stark contrast to the somber, padded darkness of the entrance hall. Only six silhouettes stood in the doorway.

"Sir Anton," the guard called, and the figure on the right stepped through the doorway into the gloom of the hall. Away from the too-strong sunlight, his face came into focus as he bowed slightly and surveyed each Initiate with burning amber eyes. He was deathly pale, skin milky white, almost translucent. His shoulder length hair was black, pinned back at the sides to reveal angular cheekbones. Something about his face, the way his chin met his lips under a sharp nose made me even more uneasy than I had been before. I felt like I was going to vomit.

"Sir Balthazar." The second figure stepped forward, joining Anton in eyeing each Initiate. They looked similar, the severe cheekbones stretching taut pale skin. The biggest difference was his eyes, a faceted shine of crystalline blue. "Sir Higgins." Higgins stepped forward, his eyes the same green as my mother's engagement ring. But he was shorter than the others, more solid, his skin a few shades darker, but with the same jet black hair. "Sir Raolin." His eyes were shockingly red, the most unnatural ruby tone I'd ever seen. His face was rounder, reminiscent of a man who may not have always been so wicked. "Sir Arturius." Even still, the trend of unnerving eyes continued as jade irises struck against his dark hair, his imposing figure a few inches taller than his counterparts. "Sir Garit." Amethyst eyes traveled the room like it was a feast to be devoured, his neck long and disconcertingly graceful. The shade of his eyes stirred something in me, something that I wasn't yet ready to rouse.

Stillness fell again.

"Sir Ludovicus the Wicked." *The what?* A seventh silhouette materialized in the doorway, breezing in at a more leisurely pace than those before him. His hands were behind his back, the only noise in the hall was the fall of his boots on the ground. He had similar features to the other members, yet somehow sharper, more harsh. And his eyes — his eyes were pitch black, swallowing all the light that other eyes would have reflected. He quickly glanced around the room before his gaze fixed on me. I tensed, fighting the urge to step back.

Ludovicus came to a stop in front of me. He towered almost a foot above me, causing me to look almost straight up to meet his stare. *Always look them in the eye,* Marita told me. The instructions played again and again in my head as his onyx eyes bored into mine. My throat felt like it was closing, like I couldn't get enough air. "Well," he hissed, raising a hand to my face and placing a long, pointed fingernail beneath my chin. "How delightful to meet you, love. Aren't you exquisite?" His voice was a knife on glass, gritty and rough across the fibers of my soul.

I felt Castemont stir behind me. "It's a pleasure to see you, Sir Ludovicus," he declared, the waver in his voice almost imperceptible. He stepped forward, extending a hand to the man

— no, the creature — in front of me. Ludovicus' eyes remained on me for a moment before breaking to meet Lord Castemont's gaze, extending a hand to meet his. "Are you doing well, old friend?" Lord Castemont asked.

"Ah, Lord Evarius Castemont," Ludovicus answered, the abrasiveness of his voice prickling the back of my neck. "I am doing well. Our sincere apologies for missing your nuptials, Lady Castemont," he hissed toward my mother. She stayed silent. "As you heard, we were...indisposed." The brothers shifted uncomfortably behind him. He turned back to Castemont. "Well Evarius, you've got a pig to send to market after all. My brothers in blood and I were getting worried. Such a shame she isn't *really* yours." I cringed. I felt Castemont's energy shift at the jeer and could tell he was planning his next words delicately.

"Petra may not be my daughter by blood, but I have come to love her as my own. The Benevolent Saints smiled upon me the day I met her. I am proud to present her to the Board for Initiation." The pride was audible in his voice. If this all went to shit, if I were to die in three days, at least I had that.

Ludovicus' piercing eyes shot back to me. Once again, I did not back down from his stare. "Tell me, child, how old are you?"

I swallowed, considering the implications of my answer. "I am twenty-four years old, Sir." I ground out the last word.

His eyebrows raised. His chin dipped. "Twenty-four? And you're just now standing for Initiation?" Was he kidding? Was this a test? He knew this, he knew that I just came into this position.

"As you know, my wife Irabel and I only met a few years ago. They were...lowborn," he said, and I could hear his wince at the formal word for what we were.

"Ah, yes. A charity case, I remember now. How heartwarming."

"No, good Sir. I love Irabel with every beat of my heart, meaning I love Petra just the same. You'll see that she will be a valuable addition to the Royal Court."

The other six brothers stirred slightly in their boots. "Yes, I'm sure she will be," Ludovicus hissed, finally tearing his gaze from me and rejoining the others in the middle of the hall. "I'm sure you will all be valuable additions to the Royal Court." He resumed a slow walk around the room, assessing each Initiate with his bottomless gaze. "We are honored to be the authority that oversees all Initiations. Thank you for hosting us." He smoothed the lapel of his jacket. I watched as the guards at the front doors followed him with their eyes, discomfort evident on their faces. He clicked his long, pointed fingernails together, the rhythmic tapping echoing throughout the silent hall.

He sighed loudly. "Shall we feast?"

Chapter 8

Then

There was no body to bury.

Among the jagged edges of wood and debris, what remained of my sister was unrecognizable. Unsalvageable. Taken by the tide.

Selina and Kolvar organized a small vigil on the front steps of our home. I don't think my mother would have been able to walk further than the front door. She wailed and howled to the sky as an Inkwell priest said a prayer to the Benevolent Saints that Larka be welcomed by all five of them, kept safe from the six Blood Saints until she could be reunited with her family one day.

A cigar. A cigar had set the Eddenian ship ablaze when it had been knocked from the hands of a sailor by his drunken crewmate. They had been in a friendly race with another ship and gained too much speed for the harbor.

I sat in the grass on the edge of the water, staring at the scorched mortar and blackened grass and gravel. The only reminder that it had happened. The only reminder that the nightmare I was having was not a nightmare at all, but real life.

That Larka was dead.

It had been two weeks. Two weeks since the explosion. Two weeks since the harbor was stained red with the lifeblood of my sister. Two weeks since Cindregala took only a brief pause and continued on with music and dancing and exotic food and wine once the bulk of the disaster was cleared.

I heard the explosion over and over again in my mind, watching as chunks of wood and metal flew through the air like sea birds, swooping down only to crash in the dirt and the water. I could smell the burning ship, taste the blood in my mouth. Feel the paralysis that had struck my legs as I watched everything unfold.

I could have saved her. If I had just pushed a little harder, thought a little quicker, I could have run to her. I could have pushed her out of the way. I could have been the one to sprint into the danger, fearless and without a second thought. I could have been the one who died. I *should* have been the one who died.

And with every explosion that sounded in my mind, so came Ingra's words.

Three days after Larka died, I stumbled from Inkwell to Bellenau Square, eyes swollen, clothes dirty. I had to find Ingra, demand answers, ask her why the hell she didn't warn us, how the hell she knew what was going to happen. People cleared out of my way as I wandered through the streets to the town square, not giving much thought to what was presumably another drunk.

But when I turned the corner to the row where the soothsayer told us of our fates, her tent was gone.

I walked up and down the rows of tents and booths to make sure I hadn't been mistaken, hadn't confused one row for another, but she was nowhere to be found. I stood in front of the empty spot, the faint smell of incense lingering in the air like a taunt. I sank to the ground, gripping my knees to my chin, rocking back and forth on the balls of my feet. Fuck the passersby. Fuck their whispers. Fuck this.

I leaned forward, falling to my knees, and sobbed.

Chapter 9

Now

Which fork was for salad? Shit. Marita had made me point out the utensils in a traditional place setting at least a dozen times, but under the gaze of the Board of Blood, my mind was blank. There were so many fucking forks. I don't think my family had even owned as many forks as there were in front of me right now. *This one.* But before I grabbed it, I panicked.

I delicately unfolded my napkin, raising it to dab a nonexistent drop of dressing from my mouth, hoping no one would notice considering I hadn't even touched my salad yet. I glanced around the table and took note of the fork the other Initiates chose. Had I picked up the fork I was thinking of, it would have been very wrong.

The large dining table had room for three dozen, decorated tastefully with twisted gold candelabras and white tapers. They matched the chandelier that hung above, casting the room in a honeyed light. The only sound in the room was Ludovicus' faint humming and the clicking of his fingernails.

"We are delighted to be a part of your annual Initiation process once again," he cooed, his deep black eyes working their way around the table. "I trust that each and every one of you fine young ladies have properly prepared?" His eyes locked with mine as he uttered the word "young." There were a few slight nods around the table as salads were picked at and wine was sipped. He straightened, gently tugging on the lapels of his jacket. "As is tradition, we will hold formal interviews on the morrow to assess your readiness. We want to make sure you are of sound mind to take part in this honorable occasion." His voice was spindly, thin, yet elicited a feral response in me. "A day of rest will follow, allowing you to be at your very best come Initiation Day." He folded his hands on the table. "Let us discuss the rules. Don't fret, as they're very simple. Sir Anton?"

Anton started in a voice that plucked at my nerves. "You shall only speak when spoken to." His gaze was severe, his amber eyes boring into each Initiate with unmatched intensity.

"All acts shall be done in the name of the King, the country, and the Benevolent Saints," rasped Raolin, his voice low and oddly sultry. His red eyes glowed in the amber light of the dining hall.

Garit took a sip of his wine before speaking, his lips stained crimson. "You shall not raise a weapon, be it a hand, a fist, a knife or sword, at any time, in any way, to anyone during your Initiation." There it was. Marita had warned me that I was not to defend myself. She never elaborated as to why, but it had been hammered into my head that I was to remain quiet and steadfast throughout the entire ritual. Hearing the words slither from Garit's lips felt surreal. I felt the nervous energy of the room intensify.

"You shall not inhibit, infringe upon, encourage, or in any way influence another Initiate," began Arturius, the long, sharpened nail of his pointer finger scraping quietly across the deep red tablecloth. So I'd be going through this truly alone.

"And remember," began Ludovicus, his voice echoing off the marble floors, a chill crawling down my spine. "Should you fail Initiation, you will be immediately cast out of the city walls and barred from returning." A faint smile danced upon his lips.

My stomach churned, and I assumed the other Initiates felt the same because all forks were idle. "Or be greeted swiftly by death."

"But why?" My mouth had let the words loose before I even realized I was speaking. Every pair of eyes in the room turned to me. I opened my mouth to apologize then closed it, sweat threatening to bead on my brow. *Shit shit shit shit shit.* I felt my mother and Castemont tense on either side of me, my mother's breaths quickening.

Ludovicus cocked his head, a predator assessing his prey. With one thin eyebrow raised, he pushed his chair back from the head of the table and stood. "Why, you ask?" Hands behind his back, he began slowly stalking toward me. No one dared look at him, but I remembered to keep his gaze, fighting back the instinct telling me to look away, to run and hide. He inched closer and closer until he was behind me and my stare was forced to break. "Please stand, Petra Castemont," he said almost tauntingly, the emphasis on my last name dripping in sarcasm.

I removed my napkin from my lap, folded it neatly on the table and smoothed over my silky skirts as I rose, my chin high. *For my family,* I thought to myself, chanting Marita's words in my mind like a war cry. *For my family. For my family.* I turned to face him, immediately finding his burning gaze.

"It seems the common girl has not learned how to behave. Do you agree, brothers?" he said, beginning his strut around the table again, his hands still leisurely behind his back.

"Aye," the other members said in a monotone chorus.

"The reason we do this, sweet Petra, is to ensure the strength of the Royal Court. Do we want whiny girls birthing whiny babies? No. We want women who will better the Royal Court with every babe she births. Women who are strong. Resilient. Well-mannered, well-groomed, well-behaved."

Each word made a heat bubble behind my rib cage that I didn't know how to quell. Why did I have to open my mouth? "And what do we do with a girl who doesn't know how to behave?" He stopped walking, facing me again. "Who doesn't follow the rules?" Ludovicus looked expectantly around the room. My pulse quickened, blasting in my ears. The edges of my vision started closing in.

78

Silence. Stinging, hissing silence that closed in on my brain. I stayed firm, holding his stare. "Death, Petra." His tongue curled around my name like a snake. My mouth went dry. "Girls who don't behave face death, either at the hands of the fine brothers you see here or the teeth of the beasts that lurk in the Onyx Pass." I wanted my mother to jump in, wished for Castemont to say something, *anything* to make this man stop. "Is that what you want, Petra? Do you wish to die?"

I clenched my jaw, knowing my life hinged on the next words from my mouth. He stood across the table from me, yet the heat from his look was like burning coals to my skin. "No, Sir Ludovicus. I do not wish to die."

He cocked his head again, a wide mouthed smile on his lips. "Ah, good. You had me worried for a moment, what with your recklessness." I wasn't going to die tonight, but I hadn't relaxed yet. He began his pacing back to his seat, perching elegantly in the high backed crimson velvet chair. I remained standing, afraid to move, afraid to blink, eyes still on him. "You may sit, dear."

I slowly lowered myself back to my seat. My mother's hand flew to my knee under the table, clenching so hard that even through the layers of skirts, even with her delicate hands, it was painful. Breathe. *I am okay.* "I just despise when we must ruin such an enjoyable evening with the humdrum of real life." He clicked his tongue, shaking his head. "Now, where were we?"

The kitchen door swung open, servers pouring in with the main dish. "Ah, yes. We are just delighted to be here."

◆ ◆ ◆

I shouldn't have been awake. I had returned to my room after a tense tea with my mother and Castemont. For a while, no one had spoken, the silence so fragile I could almost feel its brittle edges. Castemont had presented me with a box wrapped in navy ribbon before I left for bed, telling me I didn't have to open it then. I took that offer, just wanting to get to the privacy of my rooms so I could crumble.

The tears began the moment I closed my bedroom door and steadily increased into deep sobs that erupted from my chest. I flung the box onto a dresser in my wardrobe then collapsed onto the bed, every part of me tired. I began to feel numbness sink in after an hour and my eyes glazed over after two. I stared at the wall, clinging to a pillow that was soaked beneath my cheek.

The slightest knock on the door broke the sound of my ragged breathing. "Yes?" I choked out, needing to clear my throat to be able to raise my voice enough for the visitor to hear.

Wrena cracked the door open, poking her head through, holding a tray of milk and small biscuits. "Is there anything I can get you Petra? I noticed the candlelight under your door and thought you may still be awake." I sat up, my lip beginning to quiver again. I opened my mouth to speak but knew if I started, the sobs would come again. I saw her note the puffiness of my eyes, the redness of my nose. "Would you like me to come in?" I nodded, dropping my head, clutching my pillow to my chest.

She took a tentative seat on the mattress next to me. "I may be overstepping, but if you'd like a friend, I am here to listen." The softness, the sincerity of her voice made the urge to weep stronger. *A friend.* I hadn't really had friends in Inkwell. I had Larka, until I didn't.

I raised my head, assessing the stranger in front of me. I knew nothing about her aside from the fact that she grew up poor like I had. I didn't know if she was trustworthy, if she would taunt me behind my back with the other handmaidens, if she would laugh in my face. I didn't trust easily, not anymore. But in that moment, in that moment when I felt like the world was cracking in half under me and the sky was going to shatter into a million tiny pieces, in what could be one of the last few moments of my life, I broke.

And Wrena listened. To everything. Growing up in Inkwell without a pot to piss in. The warmth the memories of that childhood brought me even when our hearth was cold. Running against the wind on the waterfront next to Larka as my father watched us, his hands shaking as he sat smiling in the grass watching his daughters without a care in the world. I left out the soothsayer, still feeling the guilt of my sister's death, the prickly edges working their way into my mind regardless. I told her about watching the flame go out in Larka's eyes. Seeing my father deteriorate, unable to function on his own. Feeling the relationship I had with my mother beginning to crack and leaning on Solise. The kind healer's words as she explained what had happened to my father. The questions that had never been answered.

I told her of the other half of my heart and the day he was buried. I told her about how stupid and brash I had been, but how it led Lord Castemont to us. How I rejected the idea of my mother marrying him. I told her about rescinding that rejection when I realized that I was depriving my mother of happiness simply because my own happiness had died. I told her how Castemont truly loved me, and though he would never be my father, he tried his hardest to fill the role.

Wrena listened to every detail, from the times I had the eerie feeling I was being watched to the worry I felt the night before Cindregala. I told her about the disaster that was tonight and how I had genuinely feared for my life. That I still did. That my lack of a royal upbringing and a proper education were going to damn me. That it was one of my last nights alive.

By the time my mouth was dry and my words ran out, she and I had both reclined back on the bed, staring at the painted ceiling. "Wow," she whispered.

And...I laughed. A deep, cackling laugh. Wrena was startled beside me, propping herself up on an elbow as I rolled on the other side of the bed, tears streaming from my eyes. "You know what?" I said, finally catching my breath. "'Wow' is right." I burst into laughter again, and Wrena joined in. And for a moment, we were just two girls side by side, laughing at absolutely nothing and everything, and I was back in Inkwell with Larka.

◆ ◆ ◆

Midnight came and went but still Wrena stayed. "I haven't visited Inkwell," Wrena said. "But I assume it's very similar to the place where I grew up." We had moved to sit across from each other on the bed, our legs folded beneath us. Crumbs fell to the sheets like stars on a white sky as we picked at the biscuits.

"Tell me," I urged. "I can be a friend, too."

She sighed, her eyes going a bit cloudy, contemplative. "I think it's about as far from Eserene as you can get in Widoras. Across the Onyxian Mountains, the northwestern part of the country. There's a forest so vast that you could walk for three days and still not find the end of it, so thick that the sun is blotted out in parts. Falsend Forest. There are clearings that make it appear you've made it through only to be thrust back into the wood again, lost and disoriented. But if you know where to turn, if you follow the right trails, you'll find Maplenook." She smiled the most heartbreakingly beautiful smile I had ever seen. "It was small and poor, and..." The smile slowly faded. I stayed quiet, watching her face as memories danced through her mind. "We had nothing. Nobody really had anything, and traders and merchants visited only once or twice a year. Almost everything we had we made or found or hunted. But the men knew how to brew, so there was always ale, always wine, and always people who were kinder than they were rich. We had what we needed — one little pub, a butcher, and a brothel, of course." We both laughed.

"That does sound like Inkwell," I said as our laughter died down. She stayed silent, still staring into the distance, remembering. "What happened?"

She knew the question was coming. I could tell by the way she nodded, slowly, considerately. She took another biscuit, breaking it in two and popping one piece in her mouth, chewing thoughtfully and swallowing hard. "Kauvras."

"Kauvras?"

"He destroyed everything, and what he didn't destroy, he took. Well, technically it wasn't him, but his henchmen. The people marched single file out of Maplenook. I watched my parents leave." Her voice was disconcertingly even.

Confusion washed over my face. "I don't understand. Why?" Confusion now washed over Wrena's face.

"You don't know who Kauvras is?" she asked. Her surprise made me cower a bit. Should I know who Kauvras is? I shook my head. She giggled — *giggled* slightly as she shook her head. "People always say Eserene is cut off from the rest of the world, but this is a bit mad." It was true — the walls contained us and kept us safe, but the walls also kept the world out. I knew nothing about the world beyond Eserene aside from the Onyx Pass and the names of a few cities, usually the ones with the rumored handsome princes thanks to Larka. I had my Inkwellian upbringing and lack of education to thank for my minimal knowledge of the outside world.

"Kauvras is the estranged younger brother of former King Umfray. Kauvras was always...strange." I never even knew Umfray had a brother. "Kauvras started a cult of rebels in Cabillia about twenty-five years ago. Supposedly, it had nothing to do with his brother. It was under the guise that he was upset about the increased trade the Cabillian King had arranged with countries across the sea, most notably Nesan, which they had been at war with over territory a hundred years ago. Some people just couldn't seem to bury the hatchet. The trade raised prices and raised taxes, which benefitted Nesan. He began preaching in the alleys and on the corners of Taitha, the capital of Cabillia, that the king was bedding the Nesanian Queen; that the man was weak for letting a woman pull the strings. No one knows if that was true, and to this day Nesanian citizens deny it.

"I've heard rumors that Kauvras' real issue with Nesan started because the love of his life was taken from him by a Nesanian Prince. I don't know much about that. But the seeds of discontent had been sown long before Kauvras began his conquest. Some say it never quite settled after the War of Kings. Cabillia had been on the brink of collapse for a long, long time. It just needed a push."

"And that was Kauvras," I said, my eyes widening at the fact I had never heard of this, at the fact that this was happening.

"That was Kauvras. His following grew quickly. Like wildfire. And before anyone knew it, he had overthrown the Cabillian King and took the throne for himself, setting King Divos ablaze and hanging his body from the gates of the castle." She placed the second half of her biscuit in her mouth, pausing to chew as if she hadn't just described a horrific scene. I cringed a little at the mention of flames, but quickly righted my mind. "You really don't know any of this?"

I shook my head. "None of it."

"Blood Saints. Well, under the rule of Kauvras, relations with Nesan fell apart. They pulled their trade agreement, and since the countries of Losina are allied against Astran, they all pulled their trade agreements too. The people then grew frustrated at the increased demand upon their own shoulders, having grown used to the imported luxuries from the countries across the sea." Losina. I had never heard of Losina. I made a mental note to remember the names she was throwing out, trying to keep track of them all. "The people turned on Kauvras, and the grumblings turned to riots in the streets. They were demanding his abdication."

"But he didn't abdicate, did he?"

"You're catching on." A small smile. "A group of Kauvras' rivals met one night in a field of dead wildflowers near just outside of Taitha to discuss their next move in pushing Kauvras out." *A field of flowers*...my heart thudded so hard against my ribs I thought they might crack, Ingra's words whispering in my mind. "Kauvras had guards on constant patrol of the city, so when one came upon this secretive meeting, the Blood Saints unleashed hell. The rival group charged at the guard, prepared to kill with their rusty daggers and swords. But the guard knew that even with his training, his chances of coming out victorious against a group of fifteen men were slim, so at the last moment, he threw his torch down. The dried wildflowers caught fire, and the smoke was as purple as the flowers."

A field of violet wildflowers. I was frozen as I listened to her words. I didn't want to believe what I was hearing. "The fire didn't spread the way he had intended, but the men stopped dead in their tracks as the guard stepped further away. As the dried wildflowers caught flame and smoke hit the men's' nostrils, their eyes went dim. He watched as the men dropped their weapons, swaying slightly, their pupils dilating. And within ten seconds, they were on their knees, screaming and tearing the hair from their heads. Then they turned to each other, screaming like wild animals, clawing and ripping at each others' skin until blood stained the ground. Throats torn from necks, hearts from chests, arms and legs from sockets. The guard stared in disbelief as the fifteen men completely destroyed each other; left nothing but a heap of steaming gore." I felt nauseous, but Wrena's voice didn't waver even once. "The guard rushed back to Kauvras to tell him what happened, to tell him the horror he had witnessed. Kauvras didn't think it was horrific, though. Kauvras saw an opportunity." She paused, looking toward the window. "It's late now, Petra, and you have quite a day tomorrow."

"Absolutely fucking not," I said, straight-faced. "I am hearing this for the first time, and I'd like to hear all of it, please and thank you." She let out a laugh, but my stare was intent on her. I pushed the soothsayer's words from my head, needing to hear the full story before letting my mind panic.

"Whatever you say, my Lady," she said, bowing her head. "Kauvras instructed his guards to round up the poor, the homeless, the inept and bring them to the castle. Bundles of the dried wildflowers from the field were gathered, and the subjects were locked in rooms with flaming flowers." Every muscle in my body went taut. "Kauvras just watched. He wanted to see what would happen, what this smoke would make them do. He observed that a single inhalation of the smoke created the most euphoric high followed by rage. He was smart and knew to always take measures to protect himself and his guards from inhaling it. It was highly addictive, but the high was short. When they were denied their fix, their eyes would bleed, their skin would peel, and they would eventually tear at their flesh and bones until they died by their own hand."

Bleeding eyes. I was going to be sick. "Leechthorn?" I whispered, remembering Tyrak's sudden interruption at dinner almost two weeks ago. My mind whirled in circles, connecting the dots between the words of Wrena and the soothsayer.

Wrena nodded her head in approval. If she noticed the distress on my face, she didn't show it. "Leechthorn, yes. So you know *some* things. After watching dozens of mothers rip their own children to shreds and young men claw the throats from their fathers, Kauvras realized that unlike other drugs, people were getting stronger the longer they went without leechthorn. The initial high only lasts for a few seconds, but then they explode with rage. Once they calm down, they're relatively docile until the craving starts to build again. But...he found that the mere promise of another fix was enough to control the poor souls who relied on it, that they would follow his every order for the guarantee of a single hit.

"He visited the sage in Taitha to explore his new discovery further. The old man only knew leechthorn had been ground up and used as a salve. He didn't know of any other uses, no matter how much Kauvras questioned him. Kauvras didn't like that answer, so he bashed his head in."

My mind was spiraling. Ingra's words pounded against the inside of my skull. My breathing was ragged as I tried to digest her words, but Wrena was lost in the story, her own memories haunting her face.

"It started. He rounded up the residents of Taitha and forced a pipe to their lips. Even the children, even the sick and the elderly. He owned them all. Total control." Her face was downcast now. "His original goal was to sack Nesan, but he began to hear...voices, as they say." My brows raised. "He claimed the Benevolent Saints came to him and told him of a prophecy, of a bastard born to Katia, Keeper of the Benevolent Saints. Personally, I think he was dealing in blood magic which is why he started to go mad," she said quietly. "He claimed the Benevolent Saints told him that when the chosen one was found, he would feel the confirmation in his soul. He was to wed the chosen one, use their powers to destroy this world, start anew, and ascend."

My stomach roiled. "Ascend?"

"Ascend to what, no one knows. My theory is that he thinks he'll ascend to sainthood. Others say it will make him the rightful emperor of the realm." She swallowed hard. "So he sent his guards and his growing army to conquer city after city, village after village, expanding his battalion of ravenous fiends, erasing their entire lives with leechthorn. Those who protest he kills on the spot, or hands them to his sadistic guards to do what they please. Says that his opposers were sent by the Blood Saints as obstacles to his mission. He denies his subjects until they're at their strongest, on the brink of destroying themselves. They'll do anything for that fix. Steal, maim, kill."

"And they came to Maplenook?" I whispered. My fingernails were digging into my palms.

"They came to Maplenook. And they destroyed Maplenook." Her eyes watered and I watched as she swallowed hard, the tears retreating.

"How did you—"

"Luck. Pure luck, Petra." She looked me in the eyes, her normally soft gaze intense. "Maplenook was a lot closer to Taitha than Eserene is. The meager traders that came through the town brought some news of Kauvras, but not much. I really didn't know much when...when it happened.

"My mother, my older brother Josef, and I had finished breakfast when we heard the screams. Blood curdling. When we got outside, we saw them. Every one of Kauvras' men had masks over their faces to protect them from the smoke and bundles of leechthorn in their fists. My father had been collecting water from the well. He was caught in the mess of fleeing villagers. And I watched as a soldier the size of a mountain in a bear mask grabbed my father by the back of his head and held his lips to a burning pipe." Wrena took a deep breath. "My mother dropped to her knees. I'm not sure if there would ever have been a chance she'd recover from that alone.

"Josef turned to me, simply saying *woodpile* and grabbed my mother, hauling her back inside, the best protection he could think of. The woodpile had been where we played as children, an alcove that could fit a small child situated between two stacks of wood. I was sixteen at that point, far too large to fit in the spot, but I shimmied my way in and waited, praying to the Saints that the masked men didn't find me, find my mother and brother. From a small gap between logs, I could see into the street." Wrena stopped, and I could tell by the look on her face that she was preparing herself to speak the words that would come next. "They dragged my mother out by her hair. She was *wailing*, screaming for the Benevolent Saints as two guards held her down and put the pipe to her lips. I swear I saw her skin go gray. And Josef..." she swallowed. "Josef screamed as he watched my mother all but die, flailing and punching and kicking at the guards around him. Until the man in the bear mask grabbed him from behind and put a blade to his throat, and that was it." Her voice threatened to break. Her next words came quickly, as if she were afraid that they'd get stuck. "He fell to the ground and his body was twitching, and there was blood spilling from his mouth and he was *dying*." A tear slid down her cheek. I knew the feeling of seeing a sibling die, seeing a sibling spit blood and the deep *knowing* of what it meant.

"At the last second, he turned his head to face me, and we locked eyes through the gap in the logs. And I watched him take his last breath." She straightened. "They lined up all the prisoners, their new soldiers, and counted off as they marched into the woods, away from the village, back to Taitha with almost a hundred new recruits, my mother included. And that was it. I buried Josef beside the house, in the vegetable garden."

We were silent for a long while, the sound of an occasional sniff punctuating the quiet. We had both watched as the life was extinguished from our siblings, a pain that was hard to put into words, only understood by those who had experienced it. We had both watched everything be ripped away. She inhaled. "I made it through the forest somehow. I don't remember much of the days I wandered, but I ended up in a small town called Julia on the Hudna River. My feet were bloodied and my clothes were torn. There was a convoy of refugees from other villages leaving for Eserene escorted by two men. I don't remember asking, I just remember suddenly being a part of this group of bundled women with screaming children and bloody feet.

"One of the two men leading the convoy took a liking to me, and I to him." She paused, her eyes softening at the memory. "He was a soldier in the Eserenian army, deployed on missions to retrieve refugees from any number of horrors across the continent, not just Kauvras. His brother had ascended to the Royal Guard and he was able to secure me this position. I would sneak down to the pubs on my nights off to see him, steal a few moments with him." She looked off wistfully, a sad smile pulling at her lips. "He told me that as soon as the situation in Taitha calmed down, as soon as he didn't need to lead convoys of refugees, he would leave the Eserenian army, find steady work and save up enough money so I wouldn't need to hold this position. King Umfray was still alive, but the red delirium had been setting in. And Kauvras wasn't fit to rule of course. He could never tell me, but I think that King Belin was already in the castle at that point, preparing to take the throne upon Umfray's death. King Umfray declared that any refugees who were let in were forbidden to discuss what was going on outside of Eserene's walls. I had to blindly trust that he would make good on his promise, that he could one day tell me what was happening and why it was so secretive. And I did trust him."

I willed my mind to give her my full attention, to stop sorting through my own past and listen to her. "You think Belin was already here?"

She sighed. "I think so. I've drawn it out a million times, considered every possibility. Did King Umfray sound like the kind of man who would let refugees into Eserene?" No. He hadn't been. He was a good king to his people but not to those outside the walls. "I didn't know much about the King, only what I could get from the little that was revealed to me and what I heard in passing in the halls of the Low Royal Castle."

"And your soldier continued to be sent out for refugees?"

"Yes. He was gone for weeks at a time and our time together was precious. No vow of celibacy or life of service was worth a single day without him. I loved him more than I could fathom and I would spend every waking moment of eternity with him if I could. I would have died for him."

A familiar pain erupted in my chest, joining the other wounds that had opened tonight. "And then...?"

She went quiet again. "He was slaughtered by Kauvras' men the next year on his way back to Julia to escort another convoy." I knew it had been coming but I had held out hope. "The day his brother delivered the news was also the day I looked at the calendar and realized my cycle was late. I didn't even have time to grieve until..." Her hand rested on her belly, a slow nod to her head. "Until I was grieving again. Came and went before I knew it. My last piece of him..." Silence. A blank stare. "Gone."

My Saints. "Wrena, I—"

"No," she cut me off, her face softening again. She looked at me. She really looked at me. I saw in her eyes something one could only see if they had shared the deepest parts of their soul, laid bare their darkest days. "Thank you," she said.

"Thank *you,*" I replied. We didn't have to explain further.

"It is growing close to dawn, " she remarked, looking out the crack in the curtains. I nodded, and she noted the apprehension on my face. "You're going to do absolutely fine, Petra." The words were almost convincing.

The interview swirled in my head with the information I just learned. Wrena's pain had permeated my soul. My entire body ached with the weight of her heartbreak, crashing against my own with jagged edges. My brain burned, the thoughts overlapping at every corner. How the hell was I supposed to sort through this?

"Do you think he'll come here?" I asked suddenly. "Kauvras, or his men?"

Wrena pursed her lips. "We're so far removed from the rest of the continent," she explained. "I'd be surprised if they made it here any time soon. I'm not sure any city has the resources to lay siege to a city with walls as fortified as Eserene's." I nodded, thinking of the wall that had been the backdrop of my entire life — a comforting, constant presence. The thought of anything beyond the wall made me uncomfortable. I didn't like to consider the possibilities of life anywhere else, of the beasts that prowled between.

Wrena began to stir and I realized my eyes burned with exhaustion. "Goodnight, Wrena," I said, smiling as she gathered the tray from the bed, rising to her feet.

She smiled. "Goodnight, Petra."

I rolled over as dawn broke. I saw Larka's face and a man with Wrena's eyes and men in masks.

90

Chapter 10
Then

Ma, Da, and I ate every measly meal in silence, my mother dutifully spooning porridge or potatoes or beets into my father's mouth as his hands trembled under the table. Ma and I found work when we could at the washbasin on Gormill Road, but she was often so sick with grief that I carried most of the weight. I couldn't be in our house very long, so it worked out as well as it could have. Memories of Larka were painted on the walls, plastered to the ceiling, blowing on the breeze through the gaps in the planks.

I often sat on the waterfront on the grass and gravel that had been scorched, now laced with frost. The black char on the mortar and stones of the seawall had faded more and more each time Idros sent a storm. The wind churned the water in the harbor, the waves crashing into the wall, washing away one of the last pieces I had of Larka. A small section of scarred bricks was all that remained.

It was the dead of winter. My cloak was hardly enough to keep the cold from my bones, but still I sat on the thin layer of ice. My fingers and toes had gone numb an hour ago, my gaze intent on the sea. Every time the wind blew, I prayed that I'd hear a whisper of her, catch the smell of her, feel her ghost. But all I ever got was the frigid, salty air and the calls of gulls.

"I've seen you out here a few times," I heard a voice call from behind me, footsteps approaching. I turned and saw Elin. I hadn't seen her since the vigil on our doorsteps, when she stood still, red faced, numb. She sat down beside me, her cloak looking worse for wear. "I always want to come talk. I just...didn't know how." I said nothing, still staring into the harbor, the lighthouse's bulb ever turning.

"Well, here you are," I said blankly.

"H-how are you doing?" she asked sincerely, and I could hear the tension, the questioning in her voice. I didn't answer right away and I saw her turn back toward the harbor out of my peripherals.

I took a deep breath. "Everyday, every Saints damned day, I hear that explosion." There was no emotion in my voice, in my head. Just icy, raging numbness. "I see the blood spilling from her lips and her throat. I feel the jolt of that ship hitting the seawall." I was spitting each word through gritted teeth now, my jaw already aching. Something pushed against the inside of my ribcage, white hot pressure burning within me. I wanted to scream, to claw at my chest, to just make it stop. "If the man who had lit the Saints damned cigar had not gone up in flames that day, I would have hunted him down and set him ablaze myself." Elin was silent next to me. "Every plan we had, everything we wanted to do, it's all gone. Everything is gone." She turned to me and I to her, taking in her brown eyes, as large as saucers and worn, gaunt with grief.

"Why didn't you help her?"

Her tiny words were ice and boiling water. Frozen stone and fire. The storm in my chest crept its way up the back of my throat, pooling in my eyes as tears. "What?"

"Why didn't you help her?" she asked again, every ounce of sympathy that had been in her voice gone.

I realized I had never once been alone with Elin. Larka had always been around. Pain flashed through my gut at the proximity of this person, my mind crumbling, the smell of smoke, and–

"She was perfect," she whispered. "It should have been you."

My eyes stayed on the ocean, the view growing blurry behind the tears still gathering in my eyes. And as much as I wanted to turn to Elin and beat her face in, smash her head on the ground, I couldn't. I couldn't blame her for the words that broke my ribs and pierced my heart.

Because it should have been me.

Elin was right. Larka was perfect. She had been full of the things that made such a dreary life beautiful — laughter and humor and enough snark to shock anyone. If she were the sun, I was the rain, gray and stormy and full of uneasiness. People only endured the rain for the sake of the sun.

"I need you to go," I said flatly.

"It's because I'm right." Her words were just as flat.

"I. Need. You. To. Go," I spat through a clenched jaw. Without another word, she gathered her cloak and rose. I kept my eyes on the harbor, the familiar feeling of being watched bouncing right off my back. Let them stare. Let them whisper. There was nothing that could be said that I didn't already believe.

Because it should have been me.

♦ ♦ ♦

"How much can you give me?" I plopped the tarnished bracelet on the counter, keeping the hood of my cloak over my head. I wasn't sure what kind of metal it was. I just wanted it out of my possession.

"'Gonna take more work than it's worth. Nothin' I can do for ye," the shopkeeper said, his thick, burly Inkwell accent a perfect match for his haggard face.

"Please," I said.

"This piece 'a shit won't be worth three silvers at market. Waste 'a my time." His hands were on either side of the counter, his dark eyes staring lazily down at me.

"I'll take one silver," I pleaded. *Something.*

"Out!" he barked, pointing to the door.

I gathered the chain in my hand, the cold bite of the metal burning a hole in my palm. I didn't want to steal. Make an honest living or go hungry. That's how we'd been raised. But priorities change when the hunger runs so deep that death is no longer a far off someday but rather a countdown of weeks, maybe days. My father was deteriorating quickly and needed his strength, my mother unable to work between her grief and caring for my father. My odd shifts at the washbasin were not enough to keep our family afloat.

I felt the crooked weight of what I'd done heavy on me. I hadn't set out to be a thief that day, but the opportunity presented itself and I took it. An old woman had been purchasing tea at a market stand, digging through her cloth bag in search of coins when she dropped it, the contents splaying across the street. I had been walking to Larka's spot on the waterfront when I saw it happen, bending down to help the old woman gather her belongings.

And there it was.

Among the coins and the bits of parchment was the coiled silver chain. I didn't think. I just pocketed it, handing everything back to the woman, scrambling to be on my way and out of her line of sight, like she could see the shame on my face clear as day.

I walked around with it in my pocket for half the day, the debate in my mind raging, screaming at me. *Find her, and give it back. Sell it. It's tarnished anyway. It's not worth much. Go find the woman. You need to sell it. Get it out of your possession. Now.*

I'd been on my way to the waterfront in search of Larka's ghost again but pivoted back to town, headed to the pathetic shanty we called a jewelry shop.

But apparently they weren't pathetic enough to purchase a piece of trash.

And it started then, taking opportunities when they were presented to steal jewelry, eyeglasses, anything I could get my hands on. Each time I brought something in, the shopkeeper would eye me, then the item. He had to know they were stolen, but his need for money outweighed any conscience he had.

94

I was surviving. *We* were surviving. The white hot rage would boil in my chest at times, slamming against my skin, fighting to get out. All I could do was take the rage, ball it into my fist like dough, and mold it into motivation to survive.

As winter melted into spring and the sun began to warm the city, our house remained cold. I couldn't stand it. The streets, however, weren't cold. When I managed to escape for a few hours, when I was a huntress and the measly wealth of Inkwell was my prey, I wasn't Petra Gaignory. I wasn't the surviving sister. I wasn't cold or poor or pathetic. I simply was.

I had surpassed the feeling of guilt I would experience when I'd nick something from a pocket or a purse or a saddlebag. The shimmer of a thrill bloomed into something else. Now I was proud. There were days I swore that the Benevolent Saints smiled on me as it seemed my finds were laid out just for me. Maybe it was the Blood Saints tempting me. But then I reminded myself that none of the Saints were doing *shit* for me. This fortune, this small slice of survival...this was my own doing.

No one was ever the wiser. No one suspected a thing, least of all my parents. It was never enough to make them question what I was bringing home. "Good day at the washbasin," I'd say, or "Sidus woman paid me to clean her house," plopping down a fresh bag of oatmeal on the countertop, my mother's eyes glowing momentarily at the bounty that lay before her. I always kept my eyes low and my hood lower as I stood before the man at the shop. He simply paid me for whatever I brought that day and nodded as I turned to leave.

◆ ◆ ◆

Da's tremors had begun to snake their way up his arms, the spasms of his shoulders jolting his entire body. He often sat with his eyes closed, too exhausted to fight them anymore, letting them throw his body around like he was a buoy in rough water. I had bought him a mallet to replace the one that had busted, even though I knew he couldn't use it. He spent so much time staring at it, eyes vacant and distant, that it didn't take long for me to regret buying it for him.

The idea of a healer had never been mentioned. It was as if a silent agreement existed that if we brought it up, it would only make things worse, since we didn't have the coin to afford it. But now... I had become stealthy, learning how to crouch in the shadows and disappear into nothing. I had become too brave for my own good, and I knew that. But I had built up a small stash of coins, just enough for a visit from a healer.

I walked through the front door one evening to find my mother spooning potato stew into my father's mouth at our makeshift table, broth dribbling down his chin as he struggled to close his mouth around the spoon. His eyes were distressingly empty, the weight of the last six months dragging the corners down. He had grown all but despondent, answering questions with one word, if that. He had once been lighter than the wind, even with his affliction, and now he was a husk of his former self.

The one bright spot, the one thing that was somewhat of a comfort, was that he had begun taking walks in the evening. He always demanded to go on his walks alone. He relished the tiny slice of independence. Though the tremors made him a bit slower, he was still relatively steady on his feet.

After my mother dabbed the broth from his chin, he cleared his throat and rose, wobbling with the effort. "I'll be walking now," he said curtly. My mother rose to get his cloak, fastening the buttons and tie.

"Let me join you, Da," I offered, stepping toward him.

"Nae, Petra. Let me do this one thing on my own." His tone was short, agitated. He shouldered past me and out the door as the last light of day was swallowed by the blackness of the sky.

My mother and I stood in the kitchen for a moment, simply looking at each other, so many unspoken words between us. Her arms were crossed in front of her. "Petra, I need to know, how are—"

"I have money for a healer," I cut her off, unable to bear the question I knew would come eventually. Her eyes widened, brows raised. She said nothing. I looked at the woman in front of me. Her face was lined with grief, the deep crevices in direct opposition to her thick, chestnut hair, still somehow resisting the graying of age. So small, so fragile. This woman was a stranger, no longer the mother I knew. She needed this as much as he did. "I think we should use it."

She raised her hands to her mouth slowly, looking toward the floor. "I will not ask how you've been getting this coin," she said quietly. "But do not get caught, Petra." Her voice was grave, layered with the anxiety of a mother but the desperation of a beggar.

I nodded, silent understanding radiating from my face. I turned toward the small pot of stew on the stove and filled a bowl. My mother and I sat down at the table. "It's gotten worse," I whispered. Her eyes closed. My voice was cold, emotionless, as if I were making a simple observation about the weather. She nodded slowly.

"I know." A single tear fell from her eye, rolling over her sharp cheekbone and falling to the raw wood of our makeshift table. "I don't know what to do."

"The healer is the first step," I said. "She can tell us what to do." I laid my spoon in my bowl, no longer hungry. "I will go see her tomorrow, have her come to the house."

"Don't tell your father."

"I won't." If he knew, he'd call it off, send the healer away.

"He's been forgetting things." Her voice was so small, so defeated that I felt my heart crack, each piece sinking lower and lower. "Yesterday he forgot Larka's name." Her voice broke, a sob erupting from deep in her chest. A pit opened in my stomach, and I clawed at the bit of hope I had as it was sucked toward the hole. "I don't like that he's walking alone."

I nodded. "I'll make arrangements for the healer." I rose abruptly from my chair and padded up the stairs to the room Larka and I had shared.

Chapter 11
Now

Marita had laid out the gown I was to wear to my interview while I choked down a single piece of buttered toast. Dusky violet satin skirts floated across the marble, and I had to contain the rolling of my eyes when I saw Marita pull out the petticoat. The bodice was simple black velvet with sleeves that hung off the shoulder. She had pinned my hair up in spirals of caramel to show my neck and collarbone, somehow taming the coarse, unruly waves.

I stood in the mirror of my wardrobe, Marita tightening my corset as my mother and Lord Castemont waited in the drawing room. Marita tied the bow on my corset and moved to one of the bureaus. "You still haven't opened the gift from Lord Castemont," she said, picking up the box I had completely forgotten about and handing it to me. I didn't want a gift. I wanted *out*. Reluctantly, I took the box from her, gently tugging on the deep blue ribbon and pulling the lid from the box.

On a black velvet pillow sat a dainty gold diadem. Strong columns of gold made it appear as if the sun's rays were gifted to anyone who bore it. It was accented with diamonds on the tip of each spire, somehow delicate yet imposing, understated yet captivating all at the same time. And uncomfortably familiar. Marita gasped quietly. "Petra, do you know what this is?"

"A nauseatingly expensive gift?" I muttered, staring into the crystalline points.

"This diadem is modeled after the Crown of Katia, Keeper of the Benevolent Saints."

I examined it closer. I had seen paintings of Katia in her crown, the very source of the sun's rays. I knew little about her, though, or any of the Saints. I nodded slightly, bending forward to allow Marita to place it on my head, careful not to look in the mirror for fear of vomiting. "Will I be okay, Marita?" I needed to hear the words.

"You, girl," Marita started, "will be absolutely perfect. And would you like to know how I know that?" I nodded. "Because the Benevolent Saints smile upon you. You rose from the dirt and ashes like a phoenix, did you not? You have done everything you could, and you are going to be just fine." The tone of her voice was almost convincing.

I took a deep breath, steeling myself for what was to come next, and looked ahead into the mirror. My posture was straight, my neck elongated, my hands folded elegantly in front of me. Regular meals had filled out my shape. And the diadem — it shone so brightly, so triumphantly that my breath caught in my throat. For the first time, I looked royal. I *felt* royal.

All of the features I'd felt made me plain now glowed in the low light. My brown eyes were lit with conviction, the colors set dancing as they beheld the diadem.

Holy shit.

Make it through the interview, through Initiation, and I'd officially be a member of the Royal Court.

"Are you ready, Lady Petra?" she asked firmly.

"I'm ready."

◆ ◆ ◆

My mother and Castemont walked on either side of me, escorting me to a room in an obscure wing of the castle where the interview would take place. I had no idea where we were, every corridor foreign to me. Neither my mother nor Castemont could advise me on what to expect. Only Initiates were permitted to know what happens in an interview.

We arrived at the large double doors at exactly 2 o' clock, just as instructed. Every heartbeat was an eternity as I waited for the first part of this nightmare to begin.

Beat.

Things could have been different. So, so different.

Beat.

I could have lived a very different life.

Beat.

Had *he* patrolled these halls? Guarded these doors?

If I thought about it any longer, I was going to vomit. *I am okay,* I told myself. *I am okay,*

The doors clicked open and a guard stepped forward, extending his hand into a formal drawing room. I didn't dare look my mother in the eyes at this moment, so I dipped my head toward her slightly and felt her kiss my cheek, and a gentle hand pushed my back urging me forward.

"Lady Petra Castemont," the guard declared as I walked past him. The room was decorated similarly to the dining hall we ate in last night — heavy velvet curtains and tapestries in rich reds and navies, plush carpet that threatened to swallow the high heels I wore. In the center of the room was a long table, seven chairs filled on one side by the Board and one empty chair facing them.

Seven sets of perverted gemstone eyes stripped me naked as I approached them, and I fought every urge to turn and walk back out. Their gazes were thirsty, greedy. How old were they? I had a hard time discerning as they somehow looked both young and ancient. Garit rose, gesturing to the chair in front of the table. "Please, Lady Petra, have a seat."

I curtsied to them and lowered myself into the velvet chair, the excessive cushions seemingly moving to suffocate me. The Board's chairs were higher than mine by mere inches, the sight of them looking down on me making me feel like an ant staring up at seven lions.

I am okay. I am okay. I am okay.

"I trust you slept well, my Lady?" Anton hissed. Ludovicus' stare was almost painful, the heat once again like coals on my skin.

"Yes, good Sir," I said, dutifully bowing my head.

Eerie silence pushed in on me, the velvet suffocating. "Pray tell, what do you know about today's interview?" rasped Arturius.

"Nothing, Sir. Nothing has been disclosed to me."

"Ah, good answer," he purred back.

"When is your birthday, Petra?" Raolin asked.

"One month after the first full moon of autumn." My voice stayed surprisingly level.

"And how old are you?" he continued.

"Twenty-four, Sir."

Each mouth curled into a wicked smile. "So you were born on the Night of the Holy Stone of Blood Saints?" Balthazar said, his voice disconcertingly low and smooth as he referenced the day that came only once every three hundred years. I nodded to the men. Sideways glances darted between the men. The only stare that stayed constant, that stayed on me, belonged to Ludovicus. "And in Inkwell, nonetheless."

"Now tell me, how does a grimy peasant from Inkwell find herself living in the castle?" Higgins all but growled. His chin was propped up on a fist, his voice more gravelly than the others but still underlined with the same otherworldly hiss. I didn't let the words sting. I wouldn't. They knew this story well, had detested the idea of a peasant in the castle since the beginning.

"Well, my good Sirs of the Board, my mother remarried after my father passed. Lord Castemont has been very kind and allowed me to move into their castle residence with them."

"My condolences," Raolin cut in, lowering his head momentarily. "And may I ask, how did your father pass?"

Fucking bastard. They already knew. "A tragic fall, Sir," I said quietly but firmly, looking each of them in the eyes. I wouldn't let them see the uncertainty in my eyes.

"Suicide? How awful," Balthazar said, long-nailed fingers covering his mouth.

"Not suicide, Sir," I cut in. It wasn't suicide. But it hadn't been a fall either.

"It's a shame he won't rest with the Benevolent Saints. Suicide is a sin, after all," Raolin added, disregarding what I had said. "A shame he will be separated from your sister for eternity. I'm sure he's being pulled apart limb by limb by the Blood Saints now." The others murmured in agreement.

My jaw clenched so hard I thought my molars would shatter. The seven sets of eyes bore into my soul, once again stripping me bare, looking for any weakness, any foothold they could gain on me. Should I just take it? Should I correct them? "Yes," I said, just barely loosening my jaw enough so the words didn't sound strained. "A shame."

So *this* was what the interview was for. They wanted to see me break. They wanted me to crack, see if I'd crumble under the ghosts of everyone I've loved.

I wouldn't.

"And your sister," started Ludovicus. I knew he had been waiting to plunge that dagger into my heart, to be the one to make me bleed. "How did she perish?"

My eyes stayed locked on his, and I swore that in his eyes I saw the smoke billowing from the Eddenian ship, flaming bits of lapis canvas floating to the ground like feathers on the wind. "My sister..." I started, swallowing hard, straightening in the chair as it threatened to swallow me. "My sister passed away in an accident at the Cindregala celebration in Eserene four years ago." I quickly built walls in my mind, hiding the most painful parts of that day, reinforcing my level facade. "She died trying to save a rowboat full of sailors after their ship went up in flames."

"Oh! A horrible tragedy," Ludovicus said, the sarcasm dripping from his voice. "How valiant of her. And did you try to save her?"

The burning fury bubbled violently behind my ribs at the question that I knew he had been working toward. For a moment, I let the steam climb up the back of my throat like smoke from a volcano threatening to erupt. I remembered a cold day on the waterfront with Elin, when she told me the truth everyone already knew. My face remained neutral as I had practiced with Marita, though I had no idea I would be faced with this. *They will* not *win.*

"I was too far away. By the time I got to her, the ship hit the seawall and the explosion blew me back." I knew it wasn't the whole truth, but I knew that if I told the whole truth I would implode in a tornado of vitriol and guilt. They'd probably toss me into the Onyx Pass before Initiation even started.

Ludovicus tapped a long fingernail against his chin. "That is a lie." The words hit like a hot brand on my chest. I didn't try to keep my face calm and neutral. My mouth opened, then closed as I realized the firestorm I was about to unleash. Maybe *this* was the firestorm the soothsayer warned me of.

No. The guilt was a blade, mine to bear, but it would not be a weapon used to end my life. If what Ingra said was true, I would end up in the Onyx Pass at some point. I may as well try to exercise *some* control over when. Ludovicus watched as the emotions washed over my face, his eyebrows raised, observing. I stayed silent. "We have been told that you *were* in fact close enough to assist your sweet sister in her heroic act."

They'd been *told*? "That is interesting," I worked out, breathing no life into the guilt that coated every one of my bones, carrying on like this was a normal conversation. "You seem to have been told wrong." Someone had been watching me?

"Do you doubt the word of the Board of Blood?" snapped Garit, a thin brow cocking.

"Of course not, good Sirs," I quickly answered. "If I could have saved my sister that day, I would have. Unfortunately, I was too far away at the time." I would deal with the guilt later.

A bland smile broke on Ludovicus' face. The fucking bastard was *smiling.* An unnerving silence swept the room. I smoothed my skirts, keeping my eyes focused on Ludovicus. "Why, my sweet one, do you think that we were told otherwise?"

He was going to push this. I leaned forward ever so slightly, praying that this would be over soon before I detonated. "Only the Benevolent Saints may know."

"I will admit that you may be the first...*impure* Initiate we've ever had," Ludovicus hissed, his brothers murmuring in agreement. "Another shame *he* too is with the Saints now."

No. *No.* Anything but this. *Breathe in. Breathe out. I am okay.* Every muscle in my body tensed as Garit leaned to Ludovicus. "We've met him, brother. Don't you remember?"

"How could I forget? So kind! So...unassuming."

Bile rose in my throat as they looked at me expectantly. "Yes," I started, doing everything to keep my voice from wavering. "He was very kind."

"If only he'd been there to help your sister the day she died."

"If only. But he wasn't around that day." I didn't want to put that on him, didn't want to disturb his ghost.

"A lie."

I could do this. "He wasn't."

Ludovicus nodded. "And are you also planning on lying about the thievery you've committed?" Good fucking Saints.

"I have told nothing but the truth today, good Sir." The lie burned my mouth as I told it, the bitterness coating my tongue. "I will tell you I am not proud of stealing, however I had to provide for my family during a desperate time." I kept my tone even.

"We have an honest thief!" Higgins laughed, clapping his hands in amusement. "What a curious thing." The other brothers joined in with chuckles and snickers, but Ludovicus stayed solemn, his hands steepled under his chin.

Eerie silence once again smothered the room in a thick blanket. I wanted to gasp for air. "You do not belong here. I trust you are aware of that, my darling?" He placed his hands on the table, clicking his fingernails leisurely. "You are far older than any Initiate we've ever welcomed into the Royal Court. Not to mention, my love, the absence of a proper upbringing and fine lineage." Ludovicus leaned back in his chair. "But I believe we see something promising in you, don't we gentlemen?" More murmurs of agreement. "Something that will be worth the shit stain you'll leave on this Royal Court."

I tried not to flinch at the insult. I once again smoothed my skirts, taking the time to tuck a loose strand of hair behind my ear. Looking in the mirror this morning, I felt regal for the first time. I let that image carry me forward, let Katia's crown on my head gild my bones.

"I may not have been born to a Lord and Lady. I may have moved from the slums of the city just months ago. I may not have received a proper education nor training in etiquette or grammar or the arts like the other Initiates have, but I have accepted this role without question. I have pushed my beliefs aside, uprooted my entire life, and stepped up the way that I was expected to, for the good of my family. For the good of my *new* family." I took a deep breath, looking down the line of spindly men. "So, my good Sirs, forgive me if I lack certain elements of a perfect Initiate, but please know I grew up tripping over rats, not the hems of ballgowns."

The members of the Board of Blood had gone preternaturally still. Ludovicus finally tapped a finger nail, breaking the lethal placidity that had fallen over the room, and raised one hand to prop up his chin. "That is all, Lady Petra. You are excused." I couldn't read the emotion in his voice, on his face. I stood, curtsied as I was supposed to, and walked out of the room where my mother and Castemont waited anxiously.

Without a word, they escorted me down the hall, back the way we came. As soon as we turned the corner and we were out of sight of the drawing room doors, I fell to my knees and relinquished control of my body to the sobs that erupted. I felt hands on my shoulders – one of my mother's and one of Lord Castemont's, though the pair remained silent as I shattered.

◆ ◆ ◆

I shut the door behind me, leaning against it as I took in a deep breath. My mind quickly descended into the deepest parts of despair. *This will be one of the last times you see your mother. Don't just sit here in your room.* But how could I look at her when I knew what was going to happen? How could I look at her knowing she was about to lose all that remained of her old life?

My bodice was too tight, my skirts too heavy, the sleeves on my arms too restricting. I wanted them *off*. In a frenzy, I tore at the corset on my back, my fingers struggling to find the loose ends as I began to sweat, my breath coming in ragged gasps. The loose end was buried in my gown, my fingers fumbling across the stitches and seams. I was suffocating. I kicked my high heels off, the feeling of my bare heels sinking into the floor overwhelming. I rushed to the wardrobe, eager to do something, *anything* to be free of the chokehold this gown had on my body. I felt my face heat, the flush traveling down my neck to my chest. The boning of the bodice was digging into my waist, the fabric growing heavier by the second until I was sure the weight would drag me to the pits of Hell. My heart was going to explode.

A pair of scissors left by a seamstress sat on the bureau and I lunged for them, immediately cutting through the bodice until it fell to the floor. I tore through the skirts like a blade through butter, letting the dusky satin pool at my feet. I tossed the scissors to the floor and clawed at the hair at the nape of my neck, grabbing at pins and clips as I sobbed, my head about to burst from pressure and the burning heat smashing into my ribcage. I wanted to scream, to let out the fury that blazed inside of me. My rage could incinerate this entire room, my dread and horror could level this castle.

I was going to die.

When the pins and velvet and satin lay in a heap on the floor, I stared at my naked body in the mirror, only the delicate golden diadem remaining on my head. It glinted in the honeyed light of my wardrobe. Having access to more food, *better* food had defined my shape, emphasizing how much of a woman I was compared to the younger Initiates. The despair deepened.

But the diadem was a beacon atop my head. They were the sun's rays, and they shone just for me. I held onto the strange wisp of comfort it brought me.

Why the fuck did the young women of Eserene need to go through Initiaton? The tradition was barbaric, beyond cruel. If the Board of Blood was responsible for the Initiation processes across all the cities of Astran, were they equally as brutal in other cities? Were Taithan Initiates interrogated as I had been? Did the young women of the Royal Court of Anicole face the same scrutiny?

I plucked the diadem from my head and placed it back on the velvet pillow, reaching for a needlessly expensive sky blue silk robe. Energy bubbled inside of me and before I could think twice

I was ringing the small bell given to me to call a handmaiden. I hadn't rung it once since moving in here, but I was hoping Wrena's offer to be a friend still stood.

"Yes, my Lady?" a petite handmaiden asked, immediately appearing from the hallway.

"Um, I'm sorry to disturb you," I mumbled, embarrassed. "Is Wrena around?"

"I'll fetch her right away, my Lady." I didn't think to ask her to call me Petra. I should have. I should have asked her name, I should have invited her in. I paced back and forth, my bare feet still aching from the heels that still lay discarded on the marble floor. *Breathe*, I told myself.

A small knock sounded at the door, and I rushed to open it, finding Wrena in a muslin dress the color of butter that made her tan skin look radiant, her long chocolate hair loose. I realized her eyes were the same deep brown as mine, concern creasing the corners. "Can you talk?"

"Of course. I apologize for my appearance. I had been dismissed from duties and I—"

I grabbed her hand, cutting her off and dragging her to my bed. I didn't care what she was wearing. "I'm going to die."

"Why would you say such a thing?" But she knew. She knew exactly why I would say it.

"I need you to tell me everything you know about Initiation," I urged her. "I know so little. I haven't been told much of anything."

She pulled back a bit, a puzzled look on her face. "I don't believe you're supposed to know. I don't believe anyone is." I shook my head, my brows furrowed, urging her on. She straightened, smoothing her dress across her lap. "What *do* you know?"

"All I knew about Initiation was that it existed and that those who failed were killed or cast out. Until my mother wed Castemont, that was it. I know now that at some point I will be walking across the room, curtsying, and raising my wrist. Marita was forbidden to tell me the reasons. And that I am not allowed to defend myself from whatever pain they choose to inflict." The look that flashed across Wrena's face made nausea set in. "It's what the daughters of all the Low Royals must do to enter the Royal Court and the marriage market. And if I fail..." I gave her a grave look.

Wrena nodded slowly, her face frozen with concern. "That's all?"

"That's all."

She nodded, swallowing hard. "I don't know much, only what rumors circulated in Maplenook and what the other handmaidens say, so I'm not sure how accurate it is..."

"Tell me." How did rumors make it to Maplenook when I hadn't even heard them in Inkwell?

"I don't know if this is the truth. I don't want to give you the wrong information and send you unprepared."

"I'm already wildly unprepared. *Tell me.*"

Her eyes pinned me in place and I could tell she was searching for words. "If rumors are to be believed, this is the twenty-fourth year the tradition has taken place. No one is sure exactly why it started, but the seven brothers of the Board of Blood were established to conduct the ceremony."

"How?"

"I was told that they just...appeared one day. King Umfray announced that they were to begin an Initiation process for young ladies entering the Royal Court. And that was it. No one is sure why Eserene does it, but–"

"Why Eserene does it? Isn't it for the same reason all the other cities do it?"

Wrena furrowed her brow in question. "The other cities?" She stared at me another second, assessing. "Initiation is an Eserenian tradition. It isn't practiced anywhere else." Another emotion washed over her face, but I couldn't place it. Fear? Paranoia? "Forgive me, Petra, but I'm not sure if you're supposed to have this knowledge. I know I'm not."

I hadn't been able to spend any time with the other Initiates, hadn't been able to ask them of their expectations, their experiences, and their anxieties. "I need you to tell me, Wrena."

Tense contemplation contorted her face, the torturous battle between right and wrong visible in her eyes. She took a deep breath. "I don't know if it's because you're so new here, because

108

you grew up in the slums, or because you're not supposed to know — Saints know *the help* isn't supposed to know this — but I will tell you."

"I won't tell a soul what I know. And I won't tell them it came from you."

Another look of uneasiness across her face, then a slow nod. "Around the time that Kauvras started gaining traction in the north, King Umfray became worried at the weak state of his Royal Court. He was worried his brother would try to claim the throne. It had been ninety-five years since the War of Kings. The soldiers who fought were long dead, and the war was a distant memory that lived outside the walls of Eserene. The Royal Court grew soft — marriages lost significance as the daughters of Low Royals married laborers and sailors, albeit for love. Some of the men bounced from brothel to brothel, siring mountains of bastards and never taking wives at all. Noblemen and women divorced and remarried and muddied the Royal bloodline. The Royal Court was more a formality than an authority.

"When news of Kauvras' latest campaign reached King Umfray, the old man immediately took action. He cut the rot out at the root, having every lovestruck daughter, every debauched son, every disgraced Lord and Lady and Baron and Baroness cut down by his guards." My eyes were wide. Never, *ever* had I heard of this. Was I not told for a reason? Did Inkwell prefer to move on from the insult of its royal connections being slaughtered just for associating with the slums? This was but a year before my birth. Lord Castemont lived through it — survived it. "You never knew?"

I shook my head. "Never."

Wrena nodded, continuing. "I heard that the city reeled for a bit. They were scarred from the carnage that had occurred in the streets. A year later, on the Night of the Holy Stone of Blood Saints, it is said that a group of brothers appeared at the city gates, requesting an audience with King Umfray. The Board of Blood."

The Night of the Holy Stone of Blood Saints happened only once every three hundred years, when the moon passed in front of the sun, making the moon look like it's made of obsidian and casting the land in a darkness heavier than the night.

The night I was born.

I said nothing, keeping my face still. "No one had ever heard of these men. I've been told that Umfray had been praying to Onera, Saint of Miracles, and the moment his head guard told him of the mysterious visitors, he sprinted toward the gates, sure that Onera had granted him his miracle. The Board of Blood made a show of telling him that the Benevolent Saints had sent them to cure the city of its decay, to build a Royal Court so strong that no rebel cult stood a chance of penetrating it. He accepted their offer immediately without question.

"So they established an order, a structure. The sons and daughters of Lords and Barons would marry, produce as many offspring as possible, and restore the former glory of the court. The boys would start training as warriors from an early age, the weak and unworthy..." she paused. "...weeding themselves out." My stomach turned, and I had to remind myself to breathe. I wasn't sure when I had begun holding my breath in the first place. "And the girls would be raised as proper ladies, gaining an education and the skills to take care of a family, and strong enough to produce offspring that would uphold the Royal lineage."

"And Initiation would stamp out the weak and unworthy." I said, a sick understanding sweeping through my bones.

Wrena nodded. "That's what I've been told, but I don't know if it's true."

In the deepest part of my soul, in the pits that lay covered with the steel reserve I'd been forced to forge, I knew it was true. "They want to ensure only the strongest survive. And then what? What's the point? No one gets past the walls."

"The men become generals and captains in the Royal Army, the best of them ascending to the Royal Guard."

"I forget we even have an army," I muttered. Eserene's walls were two hundred feet high and the harbor was so vast that not even cannonballs would make it to shore from behind the breakwall. The Cliffs of Malarrey were vertical with few footholds. Why the hell would we need an army?

"They are more symbolic than functional, I can tell you that, even with the finest warriors bearing arms," she said, scoffing. A nostalgic smile pulled on the corners of her lips. "I assume they became even more pointless as the years went on with what I'd heard from..." She trailed off, catching herself from talking about her late lover. I made a mental note to ask his name after she finished. She shook her head quickly. "They've never seen battle, and likely never will. Saints willing, of course. But Umfray always kept them organized and ready in case Kauvras' forces came calling."

I leaned back, picking out my favorite painted rose on the ceiling. Wrena stayed sitting, the nervous energy fluttering off of her in palpable waves. "So we're breeding mares." Wrena said nothing. I lifted my head, looking at her. "What? We're basically breeding mares, are we not?"

"Yes..." she trailed off, her mouth forming around words she wanted to say but couldn't spit out.

I sat up again, searching her face. "Tell me."

She was visibly distressed. "I don't even know if it's true."

"*Tell me.* Please."

"It's just...there are rumors, as there always are." She went quiet. I raised my eyebrows toward her, tipping my head forward. "The Board of Blood is supposedly searching for something. A child of the Saints."

"The one that Kauvras is looking for? That he claimed the Saints told him to find? The chosen one?"

"The very same." She wrung her hands in her lap, her fingers going white in the spots she squeezed. "They believe that immortality flows through the veins of the individual. And if they find this person..." She exhaled as if banishing the thoughts from her lungs. "They're just meaningless whispers, Petra." But I could tell by the sound of her voice that she believed it.

"And the Board of Blood claims the Saints spoke to them as well?"

"I don't know what they claim. All I know is what I've heard, and that's it. I assumed you already knew this."

Growing up in Inkwell, the damned Benevolent Saints rarely showed face. The Blood Saints, yes. But the Benevolent Saints seemed to be a farce. A severe illness overcome here, a bountiful harvest of mussels there. I felt shimmers of their presence only when I swiped someone else's valuables, knowing I'd be able to feed my family. I quickly reminded myself that it wasn't Tolar, Saint of Wealth who granted me the little I could get. That was *me*.

I could only assume that the Saints the Board of Blood had heard from were the Saints who carried the same name.

"And..." Her voice went quiet, pained. "Again, I don't know if it's true, but..." Barely above a whisper. "The reason they have you raise your wrist is because the Initiation requires a blood sacrifice."

"A blood sacrifice? What the fuck?"

"They'll...*taste* your blood. To honor the Saints."

"What fucking Saint requires a *blood sacrifice?*" Realization hit me. "None of them. Not even the damned Blood Saints. They want the blood of each Initiate to test their theory of immortality." My volume increased, the panic setting in. "They believe that the child of the Saints is a girl in the Low Royal Court? And all of this was put into place because Umfray didn't want his brother to take over?" There were no other ceremonies in Eserene that required any sacrifice of the sort, much less blood. I was being fucked by my minimal knowledge of Eserene and the world beyond.

"I don't know, Petra. This is just what I've heard." Her voice took on a soothing tone, like she had just told me the most horrendous news and was trying to comfort me. Like she had just told me the history behind my cause of death and now tried to shush me into peace of mind.

The idea of a blade to my wrist didn't bother me. The idea of the sight of my blood dripping down my wrist didn't bother me, either. What bothered me was that no one mentioned the fact that there would be men *drinking my blood.* That no one, not Marita, not Lord Castemont, not even my own mother had told me, though the latter may not have known. That the Board of Blood was called that for a reason, that my blood would be sipped and I would be cast aside like an empty cup. I ran my fingers through my hair, ripping through the knots and tangles left behind from the pins I had removed.

"The Benevolent Saints will smile upon you, Petra."

"The Benevolent Saints aren't real," I muttered evenly.

Wrena gasped. "Petra! How could you say–"

"The Benevolent Saints aren't real," I repeated, emphasizing each word with painful clarity. "I will be dead between the peaks of the Onyx Pass in two days' time, Wrena, because a group of fucking men want to slit my wrists and throw me to the beasts for being unworthy. If the Benevolent Saints are real, then they sure as hell don't smile upon me."

◆ ◆ ◆

I put all my effort into maintaining a sense of normalcy at breakfast. This was to be our rest day, used to make any final preparations before a life in the Royal Court. I had a sick feeling, however, that it was intended to allow families to spend time with their daughters for what could be the last time. A small, sick mercy granted by the Board of Blood.

My mother and Castemont were silent, the unmistakable tension pulsing through the air like a live being. Ma's face had been drawn, forlorn, slightly reddened all morning. She was trying to keep me from seeing her fear. No, not her fear. Fear needed uncertainty to grow. She was certain that she would be losing another daughter come tomorrow.

Another daughter gone without a body to bury.

The few bites of porridge I managed to choke down threatened to make their way back up, the irony of what was one of my last meals not lost on me. I placed a spoonful in my mouth, holding it there, savoring the warmth, the texture bringing me back to our pitiful kitchen. The oats may have been of a finer quality now, but it was still porridge.

I opened my mouth to say something but then closed it as the absence of words made itself apparent. "You are afraid," Castemont said evenly, calmly. His voice was warm, even under the layer of uncertainty that covered the room. It hadn't been a question, but I answered anyway.

"I am." My tone matched his, my stare equally as steady. I hadn't looked directly at him all morning, afraid that if I did, the anger I felt at him for withholding everything that Wrena told me would burst forward like a tidal wave. I didn't want to sour one of my last mornings with my mother.

113

A sob broke from her lips suddenly, and she quickly covered her mouth with her napkin, taking a deep breath. "You face a considerable challenge tomorrow, Petra," he stated. Each word plucked at my anger, the strings buzzing as the pitch got higher and higher. He folded his napkin and placed it on the table. "One that you had no knowledge of until very recently."

Something snapped inside of me. A tiny, inconsequential twig on a forest floor. Something so small that almost I didn't even notice it until heat bloomed in my chest. A flash of anger ricocheted through my body just then. "Why didn't you tell me?"

He cleared his throat. "It is forbidden to speak of the secrets of Initiation."

"I've been here less than four months." My tone began to sharpen, escaping my mouth in such a way that I almost didn't recognize it as my own. I had never spoken to him in this way, even when I disapproved of the relationship he had with my mother. I placed my fist on the table, knuckles white. "Why didn't you tell me that my *blood* was to be *sacrificed* to a bunch of fucking Saints that haven't done shit for me?"

His face went pale. "How do you know that?"

"*Why* didn't you tell me?" My voice echoed through the room. I heard the sound of Tyrak's boots stirring in the hallway.

"Evarius?" my mother asked, confusion on her face. "What is she talking about?"

So she didn't know. The kind man who had taken my mother in, taken *me* in, sat dumbfounded across from me; his mouth slightly agape as I saw his eyes widen, working over the words I had spoken.

"I am under oath. The sacred rites of the Initiation are a secret only shared by those who have entered into the Royal Court," he said carefully.

"Evarius?" my mother repeated.

"Tell her. Tell her what is going to happen to me tomorrow," My teeth were gritted so hard that my head began to pound.

"The sacred rites of the Initiation are a secret−"

I threw myself from my seat, my chair clattering to the floor as I leaned over the table.

"Fucking TELL HER!" I screamed. The rage that was becoming familiar boiled in my chest. I welcomed it, *relished* it. It was new and shiny and churning in a way that demanded to be released. "I wasn't raised preparing for this day! I have processed all of this in the last four months! Now turn to your Saints damned wife and *tell* her what is going to happen to her daughter, her *only remaining daughter*, tomorrow." The voice was mine but I didn't feel like I was speaking. The words flew from my mouth sharper than daggers, gilded in Royal gold but forged in the depths of Inkwell.

My mother was sobbing at this point, her body convulsing. I saw her try to form a *please,* but a sob stole it from her lips. Castemont said nothing, his silence deafening as his jaw clenched and unclenched.

"You lying piece of *shit.* You absolute fucking piece of–"

His chair flew back like mine had as he shot to his feet. "I am your Lord and you will respect me as such, girl!" His voice boomed through the hall, the tone so foreign it almost made me recoil. His face was etched with a rage I hadn't even seen a hint of before, his features turning animalistic.

"*Fuck* your oath, Castemont," I sneered. "You've watched me *drown* as I navigated this blindly. You couldn't have thrown me a line? Anything to better prepare me? You *lied* over and over." I jabbed my finger at him from across the table. "Why did you tell me Initiation is held in every city on Astran when it's only here? Why is it only Eserenian girls?" Tears threatened my eyes but they turned to steam as the heat rose up the back of my throat. "You've known me for almost four years, Castemont. *Four years.* You claim you love me yet you send me to the slaughterhouse, bound and gagged!"

"Petra!" my mother screamed.

"I trusted you! My mother trusted you!"

"The Initiation is held for a reason, Petra! Like it or not, only the strong enter the court. This is the way and has been since–"

"Since the Board of Blood showed up at the city gates? Since the Night of the Holy Stone of Blood Saints signaled to Umfray that these fuckers *must* be divine? Sent by the Saints? And King Belin is happy to continue the tradition?" I was almost hysterical now as my skin burned.

"Who told you?" he gritted out. A controlled heat bloomed in his eyes, thinly hiding a feral animal of rage behind it.

"Not you, that's for damn sure!"

He circled the table, the sound of his boots on the marble echoing deafeningly as he approached me. "Who. Told. You?" I began to back away, but my eyes never left his.

We stopped moving as I hit the wall, refusing to cower even as he stood half a foot over me, looking down his nose at me.

"Not. *You.*" I repeated the words through gritted teeth. His palm connected with my cheek, the breath knocked from my lungs at the sheer shock of the blow, saliva flying from my mouth. My mother screamed his name, sprinting from her seat between us, pushing him back from me. I met his gaze again even as tears welled in my eyes, the sting of his palm like a hot iron on my face. I knew that the redness would fade, but I was forever branded by his hand. "This is your fault," I said in a low tone, refusing to let him see me break. "You will live the rest of your life knowing that *you* killed me." He said nothing as he stared down at me, nostrils flaring.

The jovial man I had once known him as was dead to me; the patience he'd shown me since we met snuffed out as quickly as a candle on an open windowsill. I had entered this dining room holding onto a sliver of hope that Wrena's words weren't true, and I would be leaving with the confirmation that they were. I would die and my mother would be left to sort through this morning's events.

I walked out of the room, each click of my high heels a twist of the knife as I stepped around the toppled chairs. My mother's ragged breathing was the only sound that followed me out of the dining hall.

Tyrak turned to me, hand on the hilt of his sword, taking in my reddened face. His face was emotionless, but his dark eyes were rimmed with the slightest hint of concern. He stepped out of my way without a word as I hurried to my quarters.

Fuck Castemont. *Fuck* the Board. *Fuck* my lack of education, my cluelessness, and the secrecy. He saw how I struggled and still kept quiet. Oath or no oath, I was his family. Apparently I was expected to sacrifice everything for my family, yet he was not expected to do the same due to some fucking *oath?*

I slammed my door behind me, the rage roiling through me like a tempest. Before I knew what I was doing, I was storming to the window and ripping at the curtains until they fell from the rod, crumpling on the floor. A war cry exploded from my throat as I swept my arms across my vanity, mirrors, perfume bottles, and trays shattering on the cold marble floor. I tore the sheets from my bed, the vase of flowers from my nightstand, the sconces on the wall, all of them hitting the floor, echoing throughout my bedroom. I threw my wardrobe door open, pulling gowns from racks, emptying the drawers of the bureau in my rage as I ripped and tore my way closer and closer to my Initiation gown.

But the diadem.

I stopped. It sat on the black velvet pillow, perfectly illuminated by candlelight, as if it were watching my rampage. Tears streaming down my face, Lord Castemont's handprint still on my cheek, I picked it up, placed it on my uncombed head, calming my sobs to whimpers.

Standing in front of the mirror, I surveyed the mess I'd become. The stranger who stared back at me had been broken again and again, brown eyes dulled by enough anguish for ten lifetimes. I closed my eyes, letting the familiar smoke weave through the spires of the diadem and settle around my head. Clarity.

My chances were grim, but I would not accept the fact that seven men had the authority to grant life or impose death. I would not accept the fact that they were killing young women — Saints damned *children* — looking for some fabled chosen one. No. Maybe others had come to the same conclusion but had too much to lose. I, on the other hand, had nothing left.

For that reason, I would chew up the Board and spit them out, drawing their blood as they planned to draw mine. And if I died, if the Board deemed me unworthy or uncouth or whatever the fuck they killed for, I would go down in an explosion that rivaled the one brewing in my chest.

I knew the Benevolent Saints wouldn't smile upon me come tomorrow. The Blood Saints, maybe.

But I didn't need the Saints. I hadn't ever needed them, in fact. I had always been my own hero for no other reason than necessity. Tomorrow wouldn't be any different.

Marita was right. I was a phoenix, and I would rise in a burst of fire or die setting everything ablaze.

Chapter 12
Then

"Da, you have a visitor," I said softly, peeking my head around the corner to where he laid on his bed. I hoped he couldn't detect the nervousness in my voice. He turned his head, brows furrowed, shoulders jerking violently. "Can you come to the kitchen?" He didn't answer, but I heard him stir as I walked to the front door.

"Thank you for coming, Solise," I said to the healer that stood on our front steps, ushering her inside. She was a squat, a sturdy woman with silver hair pulled into a low bun, her deep brown face lined with years of mending the poor of Inkwell. She looked far too kind for this part of town. She nodded as she stepped inside.

My father rounded the corner, shakily stopping in his tracks, his eyes assessing who had arrived. The small woman in a black robe. The case she carried at her side. His daughter, his *only* daughter, staring nervously back at him.

My mother, who had been sitting at the table, rose and rushed to his side, placing a calming hand on his arm. "My darling, Petra has arranged for a healer to see you."

He was silent, his eyes flicking from me to the healer who began pulling vials from her bag and setting them in rows on the table. Solise paid no mind to the noticeably shaking man in the corner, humming quietly to herself despite the thick tension radiating off of my father. "W-Why?"

"We'd like to see if she can help you," I said, my eyebrows raised, silently pleading that he would accept. "With your tremors." I offered a small, innocent smile. Solise had already taken the silver for the visit. I couldn't ask for it back if my father declined.

The silence continued save for Solise's humming. He looked back and forth between me and my mother, then nodded slowly, stepping toward the table and lowering himself into one of the rickety chairs. Solise finished setting up, turning to face my father and pressing her hands together.

"Hello, Sarek. My name is Solise," she said with a smile. Her presence was calming and warm, but there was something familiar about her face, something, when the candlelight hit just right, that set me the slightest bit on edge.

"I don't m-mean to be r-rude, Solise," was all he said. Was his voice shaking?

She waved a hand. "I understand your reluctance. Now, when did your tremors start?" she asked, her gaze traveling across his body.

My father looked to me, his face blank. I gave him an encouraging nod. "I always h-had shaky hands, even as a b-boy," he choked out. I hadn't heard him speak this much since Larka's death. His voice *was* shaking. I winced. "And when I w-was sixteen, they s-started getting w-worse."

"And you've watched it worsen?" she asked, looking toward my mother.

My mother nodded. "Yes. We met at seventeen, and the shaking was noticeable, but nothing like it is today. And then..." She raised her palms to the ceiling. "It has kept him from work since the girls were young." My father averted his eyes in shame. "He had been able to feed himself, clothe himself...until recently."

Solise's face turned pensive, sober. She moved toward him, picking up one of his arms from his lap, holding it in her

120

hands as it jerked and spasmed. We were all quiet as her gaze ran up his arm to his shoulder as it slammed into the chair. Every few seconds the chair would screech an inch across the floor with the force of his movements.

"Did you ever have a fall, Sarek? Any kind of violent accident?"

"No, ma'am."

"Any fights where you may have been knocked in the head?"

"No ma'am."

"And your legs?"

"Still f-fine. I can walk on m-my own. It sometimes t-takes me longer-er, but no f-falls." The way he ended the sentence made it sound like he was going to say "yet." My heart began to fracture. It had felt sick, heavy before, but the sound of his voice, the sorrow in his words fragmented the very core of me.

A small smile lit Solise's face. "Well, Sarek, I'm glad to hear that," she said, her voice soothing. My father's face softened ever so slightly. A little win. "Have you noticed that you've been forgetting things more often?"

My mother and I looked at each other, the same dread on our faces. "Nae," my father answered.

"Yes," my mother cut in. "He has been forgetting things." The pain in her voice was palpable, unmistakable. My father cocked his head to her, confused.

"Nae," my father repeated.

"It started small, maybe a year ago. Things like the names of old friends, street names across town and the like. I thought nothing of it. Then it got a bit more considerable. He forgot what the town was preparing for, why decorations were being placed and buildings fixed up. I had to remind him of Cindregala three or four times—"

"Nae!" my father spat.

"Aye, Sarek." She nodded at him, her eyes wide with concern. I had no idea this had been occurring at the time. Had Larka known? "Then..."

"Then Cindregala," Solise said so my mother didn't have to, nodding, reading the pain on her face as she remembered the horror, the screams. Eserene as a whole may not have taken much pause when Larka died, but Inkwell remembered. Larka had been one of their own, even if they hadn't known her. Though we didn't know Solise before today, there was a certain level of understanding, almost an inherent friendship the people of Inkwell shared.

"Yes. And so much had happened, there was so much grief, and I wasn't paying much attention to his mind or what he was saying." My mother's voice picked up, the tears rising in her eyes. "And then he forgot her name. He *forgot* Larka's name." The tears were spilling rapidly now, her voice rising with the hysterics.

His brown eyes fell somewhere distant, his face slackening as reality hit him like a mallet to the gut. Vacant. Defeated. The room was silent aside from the screeching of the chair every few seconds.

Solise stared at him intently, pursing her lips. A momentary flicker of pain crossed her face. "I'm going to give you a tonic," she said evenly, my father turning his gaze to meet hers. "I want you to drink it morning and evening. It's bitter, but it should help with the memory." He nodded.

He shot a shaky palm out, shaking his head. "We don't have the coin."

"Then it is a gift," she answered. "For a man who needs it."

He flinched, his head shaking even more vigorously. "Nae, I can't accept th-that−"

"I'm afraid I must insist, Sarek," she said with a playful smile, the mood in the room lightening slightly. "Please."

He stayed still for a moment, considering. Finally, he lowered his head in thanks. "The tremors will continue to plague you, I'm afraid, but so long as you continue to walk, to use the muscles in your legs, you should not lose your mobility." Part of me relaxed with relief and I could tell by the shift in his shoulders that he felt the same thing. Solise began packing bottles and vials back into her case. I walked her to the door, planning to thank her and send her on her way, but something about the way she carried herself told me to follow her outside and shut the door behind us.

She turned to me as the door clicked shut. Her lips were pressed into a thin line, her eyes creased with worry, and any relief I had felt was gone in an instant. "I wished to speak with your mother, too," she muttered quietly, looking at the closed door. "But you need to know that he will continue to worsen, Petra." Her voice was grave, her eyes dark. I clenched my jaw, searching her face. "It would be cruel of me to tell him of his fate as he has deteriorated so much, but his best years are behind him." My stomach fell to the floor. Words tried to form on my tongue but I swallowed them back. "The tonic *will* help his memory for some time, but it will not stop the inevitable. He will continue to deteriorate until his heart can't withstand the tremors. What I told him about walking was true — make sure he continues to move. That will slow it down, keep it from creeping to his legs, keep the muscles from wasting." I shook my head, her words in my brain but not sticking in any way that made sense. "Quassus mors is what it looks like to me," she said, her voice low and somber. "Rare. I've seen only one case in my days, while I was training at the academy."

No. *No.* This wasn't actually happening. I had hired a counterfeit healer, a poser. Just like Ingra hadn't been a real soothsayer.

"Make sure he is taking the tonic," she emphasized, her eyes boring into mine. Something about the look pulled my attention from the burning in my mind. "It will make the biggest difference for him. It is expensive to make, but when he runs out, come to me and I will mix you more."

"We aren't going to be able to pay–"

"My son Novis pulled the rope behind Larka at Cindregala," she breathed. My body went numb. "He told me everything had happened so suddenly that he hadn't the time to reach her before she went over the edge. Instinct took over and he backed into the crowd. He was...distraught." She covered her mouth for a moment, contemplative. "He couldn't keep food down. His sleep was interrupted by screaming nightmares in the days after. He had been struck in the head with a flaming chunk of wood, and though the wound wasn't severe, he wouldn't let me tend to it. He told me he deserved the pain for standing by as your sister died." My mouth went dry. "I stood in the back of the crowd at the vigil held on these very steps just days after and noticed the slight shaking of your father. Much less violent then," she added quietly. She looked at the door behind me once again. "He's deteriorated quickly, from what I can see. When you came to me to ask for aid, I recognized you, knew who I'd be seeing today."

I fought through the numbness. "Your son did what he could." It was all I could manage to choke out. I wanted to scream at him for letting her die but hold him and tell him I knew, I *understood* the guilt.

"He stepped off the Cliffs of Malarrey the night of the vigil."

Her words were a cannonball in my chest, tearing through my ribs to hit me directly in the heart, then dropping heavy into my stomach. I opened my mouth to speak, the words drowned by the shock as my head shook. "I know the grief your parents carry. The grief *you* carry. I will do what I can to make him as comfortable as possible, to shoulder some of the burden I know weighs heavy upon your family." My head was still shaking as I stared at her in disbelief, her words still ricocheting through my skull. I was going to vomit. I was going to scream. The emotion swelled so severely inside of me that it threatened to break the few ribs that the cannonball had left whole. She nodded in understanding, giving my arm a light squeeze as she turned to leave.

"Petra," Solise called from the top step. I stood in place, as frozen as I was that miserable day. "I'm sorry," I heard her say as she descended the stairs into the street of the poor, the wretched, and the rats.

◆ ◆ ◆

My mother fought to keep herself together as she padded down the narrow, creaky stairs from my bedroom to find my father still sitting in the kitchen chair, a vial of tonic sitting on the table. I knew better than to say anything to him then, allowing him the space to sort out what was sprung upon him.

Wanting things to feel as normal as possible, I had pulled her upstairs under the guise of needing help reattaching a fallen curtain, sitting her on my thin mattress and relaying what Solise had told me outside. I told her she needed to keep quiet so as not to alert Da of anything more amiss than what already was. I held her as she sobbed silently, her body convulsing violently in my arms.

I was so close to breaking, mere inches from it, but I had to hold everyone else together. I couldn't do that if I was in pieces.

My mother rushed to my father, quickly taking a seat beside him and raising the tonic to his lips. He choked it down, pausing twice to gag. "She wasn't kidding. Shit's r-rancid." A slight smile pulled at his lips and he let a small chuckle go despite himself. I saw my mother's face soften at the noise, the first time he'd laughed since the day of Cindregala, before it turned into a nightmare. "Th-thank you," he said, his voice small, weak, wavering. I closed the distance between us, leaning down behind him to wrap an arm across his quaking shoulders. His hand rested across my forearm.

"Anything for you, Da." My mother placed her hand on my father's knee, my own hand coming to rest atop hers. She and I exchanged a glance so thick with unspoken words it threatened to drown me.

We hadn't reached a conclusion as to whether we should tell him the truth. Whether we should tell him that the tremors would kill him. She and I both said nothing as the three of us sat together. "W-where did you g-get the money?" he finally asked, pulling me from my worried trance.

"Please, Da, don't worry about it."

I saw my mother purse her lips at him as he scanned her face. Her eyes were the size of saucers we couldn't afford, aglow in the low candle light of the kitchen.

"Petra," he croaked. "Don't get caught."

◆ ◆ ◆

We fell into a routine. I provided. Ma took care of Da. And Da did his best to function. He continued his nightly walks, showing the smallest signs of excitement when the shadows grew longer each day and the sun sank toward the Cliffs of Malarrey. The thought of the cliffs set my soul into a dizzying, sorrowful downfall, trying to think of the faces of the men behind Larka. This man, Novis, had died because he didn't save Larka.

I hadn't been alone in my guilt.

It was then that I felt the appeal of the cliffs, the sweet relief that waited for me at the bottom. Just one step and I would be with Larka again. I could explain to her what had happened. I could apologize. We would laugh at the absurdity of a cigar lighting an entire ship on fire.

It would be so, so easy.

Ma waited anxiously by the door while Da was gone and I tidied up. "He will be fine," she murmured, more to herself than to me. "He walks the same route every night. Solise said this was *good.*" But her fingernails were quickly chewed to nubs, the skin of her cuticles picked to shreds. He'd soon round the corner onto our street, clumsily climb the steps, and fall into my mother's arms.

It was enough. It had to be enough.

◆ ◆ ◆

It had been a shit day. A single skein of yarn was all I'd managed to lift. A hobbling old woman had a canvas bag filled to the brim with yarn. I told myself she wouldn't miss one when she had yards and yards of it, quickly silencing any whispers of guilt surrounding my source of income and replacing them with a creeping thrill.

The man at the shop lifted his brow, eyeing me from behind his counter. I hadn't bothered to learn his name, hadn't wanted to, because if this all went to shit, I refused to implicate anyone else. "Tough out there today?" he said, pulling the skein toward him across the counter and running his fingers over the yarn.

I didn't answer, instead taking the half coin he placed on the counter and stalking out of the shop.

I turned the corner to my street, paying little attention to anything but my thoughts of my next trip to Solise, when I was suddenly on the ground, my cloak splayed around me.

"Watch where the *fuck* you're going," I snapped, the bite in my voice so unlike me. I gathered myself before looking up to see who I'd collided with.

Those eyes. One blue, the other half blue, half green. I raised my eyebrows in disbelief. "You," I whispered.

His sharp honey-brown cheeks lifted up in a smile, the smell of smoke and cedar clinging to my clothes. "Didn't I tell you to be more careful?" There was that smoky voice, full of low burning fire and melted chocolate and early autumn leaves and earth.

My heart seemed to remember before my brain did, because it began to beat wildly before the memories flooded in. I remembered the day, the fact that he had been nearby just before everything happened. The blue and green collided in his eye the same way the burning ship collided with the seawall. I needed to go, I needed to *run*. His stare set me back on the gravel by the harbor. His stare sent me back to when Larka was alive.

I quickly stood, saying nothing and hurrying toward my house. He called from behind me, the same way he had that day. "Are you okay?"

I froze, my moth-eaten cloak fluttering at my sides. Turning, I spat back at him. "What?"

"Are you okay? Were you hurt that day? In the explosion? In the stampede?" Genuine worry flashed across his face as he clenched his jaw.

I searched his face. He looked to be a few years my senior, towering almost a foot over me. I remembered Larka's words as she told me men are pigs, that they aren't trustworthy. "What's your game?"

"What?"

"What's your fucking game?" I repeated, irritated.

"I don't... There is no game. I just want to know if you're okay. You had a pretty nasty gash on your forehead." What? I only had a few scrapes and bruises, no gash. But the sincerity of his words struck me. No one had asked if I was okay after that day, understandably so since I was still breathing.

And the truth was that no, I absolutely was not okay. I replayed Larka's final moments in my head every Saints damned day, her screams echoing through my skull. I heard the snap of her leg, saw her clawing at the rope. I heard the gunpowder ignite, saw the bodies of sailors floating face down in the harbor.

I had made it out with nothing but nicks and scrapes and an aching head. My torn cloak was the only lasting evidence that I had even been in attendance that day.

"I'm fine, thank you." I spun back toward my house and walked as quickly as my legs would carry me.

"Wait!" he shouted, the same way he had on the day of Cindregala. I clenched my jaw, just wanting to get home. To get away from any reminder of that day.

"What's your name?" he called.

I debated turning on my heel and ignoring him, afraid that if I told him, it would invite him in again. Some small part of me urged my mouth to speak. "Petra."

"Calomyr," he said, placing his hand on his chest. I nodded and turned once again.

"Do try to be more careful, Petra," he called after me, his voice taunting but tinged with the sorrow of someone who had witnessed a soul leave a body, a life coming to an end.

I threw a hand in the air, waving him away as I walked toward the house. "Watch where you're going, *Calomyr.*" He answered with a low chuckle, like church bells dripping honey.

Chapter 13

Now

From where I lay on my bed, I could hear the ruffle of skirts on the floor every so often. They'd draw near, pace, and retreat.

My mother. What I hadn't determined was whether she was more upset at what she learned or the explosive manner in which she learned it. I sat up to run to the door half a dozen times, each time falling back, knowing I wouldn't be able to look her in the eyes. I knew that the pain I saw there would break me as it had so many times before.

I had never considered how I'd spend my last full day alive. Fuming with rage while I laid on a mattress worth more than our Inkwell home was not what I would have pictured. For some reason, the thought of tomorrow was no longer turning my stomach. Was this what it was like to accept one's own mortality? Or had I simply resigned myself to the fact that I was going to fight to the death tomorrow, dragging as many Saints damned Board members to the purgatory with me? It had been awhile since I had seriously considered my own death.

The whisper of skirts on the floor in the hall returned. They paused, and then—

A knock.

I rose, hesitating as I walked to the door, knowing that the chances of me making it through this conversation without breaking were slim.

And there she was. Small, elegant. No trace of a past life of poverty, struggle, or grief. Her life had changed dramatically, and I realized that once the wedding happened, she and I rarely had time to spend together. She had filled out as much as I had, dining on the finest imported pastries and gourmet meats. Her sallow face had color like I'd never seen, her blue eyes bright once again. She was *beautiful*.

And I may have hated her for it.

I wordlessly ushered her through the door, leading her to the powder blue velvet chairs in the drawing room. We faced each other, neither taking the initiative to look the other in the eyes.

"He's sorry," she said, her voice low.

I raised an eyebrow, finally meeting her stare. "Excuse me?"

"He's sorry, Petra."

I took a deep breath, my knuckles going white on the arms of the chair. A wave of grief hit me then. Was I grieving the loss of the Castemont I thought I knew? "You came to my quarters the day before I am to die to tell me *he's sorry?*" She flinched at my harsh tone, and I almost did too.

"He's been under a lot of stress and—"

"And what?" I cut her off, leaning forward in my chair. "And that explains why he couldn't tell me, tell *you* what I'd be facing tomorrow? Why he is offering his step-daughter, the only remaining child of the woman he loves to a team of fucking butchers?"

"He is under sacred oath and—"

"No. You don't get to speak right now, Ma. You lost that privilege when you walked in here to *apologize for him.*" I had never spoken to my mother in this way, not even when I was the sole provider, or when her helplessness drove me so crazy I wanted to scream in her face. The imbalance of power was almost welcomed. "I don't know what's worse, the fact that he couldn't come apologize to me himself, or the fact that your first words to me were about *him.*" This man had gone from our savior to my destruction. "He watched me struggle, knew I had no knowledge of Initiation and the traditions and expectations, and he *still* chose to stay quiet, to let me suffer through this. He saw how Ludovicus spoke to me. He saw how I broke after the interview. And he *still* chose to stay quiet. Not so much as a 'keep an eye out for Ludovicus' or 'they're going to try to rile you up, don't let them.' Who would have known if he had helped me? How would anyone find out?" Tears streamed down my face now, the anger flooding my chest like a high tide rushing in. "This is not my story, this is not my choice, and this is not my happily ever after. I have gone through this *alone,* and I've gone through it for *you,* so that you can live *your* happily ever after. And the only reason I even know what to expect is because of the fucking rumors that a handmaiden has heard."

"Who was it, Petra?" she asked quietly.

"Why does it matter?" I shot back.

"The rites are sacred and to be known by only those who have completed Initiation."

I scoffed. "Give me a fucking break, Ma. Pull your head out of Castemont's ass." She flinched, her mouth dropping open. "It wasn't so long ago that we were fighting for our survival together. Oh, wait," I seethed, venom dripping from every word, "*I* fought for our survival. You let the grief destroy you. I didn't have that luxury. Not until I had secured our survival *by myself.*" She sat back, closing her jaw, her face plastered with infuriating innocence, as if she had no idea of the sacrifices I had made. I hated that she looked so well, her skin supple, her bodice fitted.

"Solise helped," she breathed.

My vision turned red. "Are you saying that her help invalidates all I did? She was more of a mother to me in those years than you were!"

I saw her jaw work as she contemplated her next words. "That mouth is going to get you killed."

My mouth fell agape. It was so insensitive, so unlike her. "What's going to get me killed, Ma, is your husband's decision to keep me in the dark."

"He has clothed you, fed you, made sure you had–"

"What about the years that I clothed you? That I fed you? That you were too despondent to care whether we lived or died or even had a roof to live or die under?" Her jaw stayed set as my pitch turned into a scream. "You're forgetting that the whole reason you met him is because of *me!* Because of the things I had to do to ensure our survival. And now he expects me to die for a Saints damned tradition and you're going to go along with it? What the fuck is wrong with you?!" She stood abruptly, my words still echoing off the marble floors. "I should have listened to Solise, should have trusted her word. What happened to 'I can't lose you?' What happened to your tears at breakfast, begging me to try, begging me to put in the effort? If I'd have known what it entailed, what would happen, I could have *tried.* I could have put effort into things that *mattered.*" She swiftly rose and began walking to the door. "That's your husband, Ma, but I'm your daughter. Remember that."

"He was under a sacred oath," she whispered, as if the justification was enough for her. She threw herself through the door, latching it behind her.

I expected the tears to come, but all I could do was lay my head back and stare at the ceiling.

◆ ◆ ◆

Neither my mother nor Castemont came to see me for the rest of the afternoon.

I paced my rooms debating whether I should call for them. Each of my heel-clad steps echoed across the marble floors and walls, a metronome to accompany my misery.

I wanted to run. I wanted to grab what I could and run home. I knew how to survive in Inkwell. I could do it again. But how was I supposed to leave? I had no idea where I even was in the castle. The little I'd seen of it was not enough to give me any clue how to get out. My windows looked over a courtyard always cast in shadow, so there was no telling which way the slums of the southeast of Eserene lay. And if I made it past the guards outside my door, then what?

I stopped in the middle of the floor, the echoes resounding until they fell into piercing, suffocating silence. It was the kind of silence that screamed in my ears, held my brain in its claws.

Breathe.

I am okay.

But before I knew it, my feet were carrying me to my wardrobe. Heels kicked off and to the side. A bag. The simplest dresses I owned. The ones best for running. Extra socks. A cloak. A few pieces of jewelry to sell.

Bag over my shoulder, I sprinted for the door, unsure of where I was going but intent on getting the hell away from this prison. I pushed the doors open and–

"You can't outrun fate, child." Marita stood in the doorway, a bottle of wine in one hand, two glasses clutched in the other.

I stared at her, my chest heaving as she stepped in and closed the door behind her. She looked me up and down, the red fury on my face, the crumpled gown I wore, my bare feet poking out from beneath the hem.

She silently walked through the drawing room and set the wine bottle and glasses on one of the small end tables, turned back to me, and opened her arms.

I don't remember running to her. I don't remember folding my arms around her as she pulled me in. But suddenly she was holding me up as I began to collapse, my entire world coming down with me.

"I can't do it," I sobbed into her shoulder. "I can't do it Marita." Her hand ran in smooth circles across my back. "No one told me. Castemont didn't tell me. You didn't tell me."

"I'm so sorry, Petra," she whispered. And I knew she was. I knew she was bound to the court with her life. I knew that the consequences she'd face if she had warned me would be cruel. But Castemont was *family.* Castemont would not have faced execution had he disclosed secrets. She pulled away, looking into my eyes with her own that were weeping too. She sniffled, running her thumb across my wet cheek. "Now, girl, you know what would happen if anyone found out I was bringing this to you, yes?" I nodded. One corner of her mouth lifted in a wicked smile. "But since we're keeping secrets..." She turned to the table and popped the cork from the wine, filling the two glasses and handing me one with a slight smile. "I think you could use this."

The smile that bloomed across my face was genuine, despite the cheeks I knew were red, despite the runny nose and watery eyes. We sat in the same chairs where my mother and I sat just hours ago. Where we had what could have been our last conversation.

"When I was seventeen," she started abruptly, "both of my parents were taken by the red delirium. Within three months they were here and then they were gone." I flinched at her words. And I realized I knew nothing about Marita, nothing of her past. "I had no family in the city, no one I felt I could rely upon. So I marched myself from Ockhull to Inkwell and up the steps of the Painted Empress." I inhaled sharply. Marita took a long sip of her wine, running her tongue across her teeth before looking up at me again. "I trust you know about the Painted Empress, girl?"

"Yes," I breathed, my jaw clenched and eyes wide.

"Then you know the kind of establishment that Mr. Evrod runs does not cater to the wants or needs or well-being of his employees. Only his patrons. His depraved patrons, his sadistic patrons, the ones that are vile and sick and twisted, who worship only the Blood Saints, or no Saints at all." I tried to respond, but the words caught in my throat. I managed a slight nod as I remembered the noises that would come from the windows of the Painted Empress, the men who stalked and stumbled in and out.

"The money I made from my customers...it wasn't much, and Evrod took most of it. We were permitted to live outside the brothel and keep shifts rather than be on call at all hours, a small mercy, I suppose. But I could never save up enough. So I spent four years under that roof." I wanted to vomit. Marita's eyes were distant, but I knew what she was seeing.

"There was a nobleman," she continued, her tone even. "Young. Maybe five or six years older than I. He would visit me

134

often." Her face began to melt into disgust. She lifted her glass and finished her wine. "He... He enjoyed pain. Inflicting it. He liked to see me hurt. He liked to watch me...watch me bleed. He never visited without his blade." Once again, vomit rose in my throat. I wanted to ask why and who and how and what the actual fuck happened to her. "But, like most stupid noblemen, he would bring his guard along. And when the hallways were too crowded or otherwise...occupied, he had to stand guard in the room. He was massive, a giant of a man. But always silent. And always watching. I had quickly learned to pay him no mind.

"And it was one of those days when all of the rooms overflowed and the hallways were crowded with mistresses and their customers, that the guard was forced to wait inside while his Lord..." She didn't finish her sentence. She didn't have to. "He had been feeling particularly sadistic, and I was bloody from chin to toe. I remember the feeling of the wounds stinging every inch of me. But my mind was numb. Gone." Marita swallowed hard. "And for the first time, I looked over his shoulder and saw the guard staring at me, the sorrow on his face etched into every feature. I will never forget that look, those dark eyes, not until the day I die. Saints, I can see it now, so clearly. And he just watched me as I bled, as his master held me down. Watched me with pure despair and heartbreak and hopelessness."

Marita leaned forward and refilled her wine glass, her face turning thoughtful. "I cleaned myself up as best I could after they left. I couldn't look at my body too long. Then Evrod woke me up in the dead of night and told me I had a customer. The cuts had clotted but were still sticky and raw, and every brush of my dressing gown on my skin was torture. I didn't think I could make it through another customer. Then the door opened and...the guard stood there.

"He rushed into the room, hardly looking at me, and he told me we didn't have much time. He pulled rolls of bandages from a small bag along with a large tin of salve. 'Please,' he urged me, and his voice was so sincere, Petra. So, so incredibly sincere. 'Let me help.' He gestured at my robe and I dropped it. He dutifully cleaned and dressed every single cut his master had left on me, apologizing all the while. Then he dug some clothes out of his bag and told me to dress. Just a simple brown tunic and black pants with boots that were a bit too big. I was silent the entire time. I didn't know what to say. I don't think I could have spoken even if I tried.

"He whisked me out of the brothel, easily hiding me from Evrod who was buzzing around making sure his late-night customers were 'satisfied.'" She shuddered lightly. "And he brought me to his sister, who worked in the Low Royal Castle as a tutor for the young women preparing for Initiation. A little training, and here I am. She passed a few years back, unfortunately. But she is the reason I'm here."

"What about the Lord? Who was he?"

A slight shake of her head. "There are more than a hundred Lords in this castle, girl. And you haven't been here long enough to name half."

"Does he know you're here?" My mind was whirling in circles.

"I'm not sure if he knows, girl. He may not recognize me when my most recognizable features are covered up." She pulled back the white cuff of her frock, the one that covered every inch of skin beside her face and hands.

I was almost ill at the sight of her forearm. Scars so deep, so knotted that I didn't know how she survived them in the first place. A few were spiked with the marks of crude stitches. They snaked across her skin like vines, creating a map of every night she spent with that man. She pushed her sleeve back down to her wrist, her fingers curling to hold it in place. "The veil helps, too."

The woman in front of me had trudged through the depths of Hell and had the scars to prove it. "The reason I'm telling you this, Petra, is because if I can make it through that, if I can survive that, you can survive this." I blinked at her, her words bouncing off of me. Though I didn't intend to, my head began shaking. "The truth is, I know little more about Initiation than you do. We're trained to instruct you on basic etiquette and self-control, and that's it. From the bottom of my heart, I am so sorry I have no real help to give you."

My head continued to shake. "Marita, I had no idea."

"Good," she laughed. "I like it that way." She took a deep breath and leaned back. "But even after all of it, I still wonder what happened to the Lord to make him that way."

"What do you mean?"

"People aren't born hateful. People aren't born with the desire to hurt, to draw blood." Her voice was small, thoughtful. "I want to know what happened to him to make him a monster." I nodded slowly. She was right.

Though I hadn't even sipped from my glass, she leaned forward and topped it off. "To you, Petra," she said, raising her glass to clink against mine. "May you burn the wicked to ash and rise again."

◆ ◆ ◆

The echoes of Marita's story rang through my head as Wrena and I laid on my bed in silence, staring at the rose painted ceiling.

The last time I ever would.

Though we had only known each other a short time, she had become dear to me quickly, much like Marita. She knew much more about me than anyone else in the castle, even my mother. And I felt I knew her well, too.

"So who do you hope to marry when you're placed on the marriage market like a prize cow?" she asked playfully.

The tone of her voice and the words she said brought a slight smile to my face. "A cow?" I laughed. "I guess that's better than Ludovicus calling me a pig. I never thought of it like that, but shit. I guess I will be a prize cow on the market. No, actually I'll be just a regular old cow. Emphasis on *old*."

Wrena's laugh was a bell in the dim light of the remnants of the sunset. I had taken my dinner in my room and requested Wrena join me. She once again sat and listened to me, dampening any emotions on her face in favor of letting me express mine.

"Will I still be your handmaiden when you're married off?" *When.* The positivity was a sorrowful reminder of what was to come, but I entertained the thought.

"Would you like to be?" I asked.

"Well, yes."

"You *want* to be a handmaiden?"

She pursed her lips, looking around the room.

"Then it's settled." I cut her off before she could reply. "When I'm royal I will release you of your duties and you can live with me in my residence. *I* will allow you to marry. I'll set up a meeting between you and the Prince of Zidderune myself." She let a soft giggle float through the room. We sat in companionable silence, ignoring the reality that snaked down my spine. "I'm assuming you'll be reassigned after tomorrow."

She propped herself up on an elbow. "None of that talk."

"I'm only being realistic."

"None of it!" she cut in.

"Thank you," I blurted. "For listening. For being a friend when you didn't have to be."

She turned her head toward me. "You needed one. But I think I did too." She smiled softly. "Plus, the Initiate I last served was dreadful. Everyday with her was a nightmare at best, a walk through the deepest pits of Hell at worst."

"Oh?"

"Daughter of Lord and Lady Saursky. Lady Cherina was her name." She sneered as she said it, contorting her face in disgust. "Wretched creature. She squeezed every drop she could out of that title. She'd send us on errands across the castle, asking for biscuits or wine or cherries, and when we'd return, she'd berate us, telling us we got the wrong ones or too many or not enough. She slapped Kleia clean across the face for looking her in the eye."

"Saints," I said, wincing.

"So, my Lady Petra, you are a dream," she sighed.

"And did she make it through Initiation?"

"Unfortunately." We both laughed. "That bitch."

"If I were allowed to wander the castle as I pleased, I'd fetch those biscuits myself."

Wrena laughed. "What do they think would happen if you roamed the castle?" My shoulders rose in a shrug. "Are they intentionally keeping you from meeting the other Initiates and from leaving your rooms?"

"I'm not sure. I met them all for the first time yesterday. I was told to request a handmaiden should I need anything, and that I was never to wander on my own."

"Strange, it hasn't been a requirement for past Initiates," she offered.

My head snapped to her. "Are you saying the other Initiates are not confined to their quarters?" She winced, offering an apologetic squeeze of my arm. *Unbelievable.* Shit was getting worse and worse. I wouldn't let that thought fester though. I couldn't. "It *is* my last night..." She shot me a look. "And I've seen only a small corner of this castle. My room, Castemont Hall, and the entry hall and one dining room. Nothing beyond that." Well, a little beyond that, but I was keeping that to myself.

"You're not suggesting—"

"No, I'm not suggesting. I'm *telling* you that tonight, my very last night alive, I am going to leave these quarters and fetch my own damn biscuits from the kitchens. Maybe take a stroll." I shrugged my shoulders.

"That doesn't sound like a good idea," Wrena said, genuine worry lacing her voice.

"Who cares? I'm going to *die* tomorrow."

"And how do you suppose you're going to get past the guards outside your door? Outside Castemont Hall? Do you even know how to get to the kitchens?"

"No, but you do."

"Petra, as your handmaiden, I can't condone—"

"Well then I'm releasing you of your handmaiden duties early. You're now my friend."

"Then as your friend, I can't condone this."

"Fine, then you're my handmaiden. And your lady *commands* you to accompany her on a grand adventure to the kitchens." I saw the knowing in her eyes. She knew I was going to do it whether she helped me or not.

Exasperated, she sat up. "You sure?" she asked.

"Absolutely."

◆ ◆ ◆

The idea that the main doors to my quarters were guarded but the service entrance was not seemed beyond foolish. Did they think that my Inkwellian upbringing made me too stupid to consider escaping through the service halls? Wrena had vanished for a moment, returning with a bundle under her arm. "Here," she said, motioning for me to put on the handmaiden's uniform.

"Brilliant," I smiled, stripping out of my nightgown and stepping into the same pale blue frock as she did the same. She opened the service door and ushered me through.

"This will take us straight to the kitchens. You go in, grab the biscuits, and you come out. Got it?" Her sternness was surprising, and I realized that I may not face the consequences of this night after tomorrow, but she would. I nodded, a sudden sick feeling pounding through my veins and pooling in my stomach. I took a deep breath and steadied myself, walking behind Wrena through the dark, narrow halls. It was eerily quiet, and I realized it must be far past midnight.

We descended a small flight of stairs and turned right, a long corridor ahead of us. Wrena was silent as she made one last left turn and stopped in front of a door. "Back wall with the windows, to the left, in a white ceramic jar. Get back here as quickly as you can," she whispered. The urgency in her voice made my skin crawl.

I had to do this. My last night on this earth would not be spent in the same place I had been for the last four months. This small, insignificant rebellion would make me feel whole, if just for one moment, before I was dumped at the Onyx Pass or left to bleed out on the floor of the throne room.

I cracked the heavy wooden door open, peering through. Large windows looked over the north side of Eserene, the torches on top of the walls glowing orbs in the distance. Moonlight poured in, illuminating the dull stone floors as if the Benevolent Saints shone directly through the windows. Rows of counters and tables and ovens filled the room, the faintest smell of garlic hanging in the air. I stepped through the door, closing it softly behind me, feeling the frantic energy from Wrena piercing through the wood.

Back wall with the windows. Behind a row of counters, I saw a table in the corner with a hodgepodge of items — stacked plates and spare silverware and a pile of napkins and–

A white ceramic jar. I padded silently across the kitchen, relishing the savory feeling of defiance, of rebellion, of–

Voices. I hit the floor, ducking behind the counter as a male voice grew closer, louder. I saw another door a dozen feet to the left of the door I had slipped through. *Please, Saints, no.* I waited on my hands and knees, ready to pivot the moment they entered the kitchens, ready to keep in the shadows like I had so many times on the streets of Inkwell.

The door burst open. "Twenty-four years. That's what, 120, 140 Initiates?" That voice was...

Castemont. What the fuck was he doing here? I made a conscious effort to keep my mouth shut, keep my legs from carrying me across the room and launching myself at him.

"One hundred and thirty-six, to be exact. Though I'm surprised the Saints gave us *that*. But we've set the stage and wish to reap our reward. We've had fun over the years, but the work has been done. Our reward is nigh." The voice was a knife on glass. Goosebumps rose from my skin and the back of my neck almost hurt with the sensation it stirred across my skin.

Ludovicus.

"And you will get your reward." My eyes widened. I heard liquid pouring into glasses.

"If you're wrong, I will snap the ribs of that pretty little wife of yours," he hissed. *No.* Their footsteps echoed across the room and the echo kept me from hearing which way they were moving.

"That won't be necessary, old friend," Castemont answered, the sound of ale hitting a glass punctuating his statement. "I have not a doubt in my mind." His voice wavered ever so slightly, and I heard Ludovicus inhale sharply.

"You love her." His statement was abrupt, cut with disgust.

Castemont chuckled. "Love is a strong word. I'll admit she's grown on me, but she's mostly useless outside the bedroom."

My head spun. My rage surpassed the familiar white hot boil. An all-consuming, scalding heat exploded in my chest, spreading throughout my body like lava. It took every ounce of power, every Saints damned piece of my bloody soul to keep quiet. I swore steam rose from my skin. My body felt like crackling embers, flames spitting and dying on the stone floor.

"May all of the Saints smile upon us both tomorrow," Ludovicus said, the sound of clinking glasses and retreating footsteps echoing through the kitchens. My fingernails bit into my palms. I couldn't get enough air.

The second the door closed behind them I sprinted for the service door, ripping it open and throwing myself through it. "I thought you were going to be seen. Who was that?" Wrena whispered urgently, her voice strained with worry.

"Castemont and Ludovicus," I panted through gritted teeth. She cocked her head, eyebrows raised. "You're right, I think they're looking for the chosen one."

"What did they say?"

The door flew open behind us.

Castemont.

Chapter 14

Then

Da started bringing back souvenirs from his walks. A flower he'd picked from the waterfront lawn, the stem crumpled and broken from gripping it so hard, refusing to lose it to the tremors. A smooth stone he'd found on the side of Gormill Road, damp with sweat from his palms, along with feathers, leaves, bits of parchment... He found beauty in the simple and ordinary. A pile of *things* began to grow on our table, getting bigger each day.

That was my father coming back.

The tonic had helped his memory. Even better, it had seemed to lift his spirits. He still had moments when the grief left him hurting, visibly broken. But the light was shining through the trees, breaking up the shadows one by one.

"This f-feather comes from a ciakoo. I haven't seen one s-since I was a b-boy, and I found this feather on the s-side of the s-street! Can y-you believe it? Very r-rare!" His voice bordered on excitement, the dampening effects of the last several months keeping it from cresting. I took the feather from his shaking hand, lightly running my finger down the vane. At first glance, it was black, but as I looked closer I saw the base was a deep, rich purple that faded into an even deeper blue, the color of the night sky in the dead of winter.

"Wow," I whispered.

"'Means good fortune is c-coming our way."

"Is that so?" I laughed, placing it on the table and turning to prepare his evening dose of tonic.

"Mhm, that's what the l-legends say," he said, tipping his head back as I lifted the vial to his mouth. He winced at the bitterness but choked it down. "Thanks, love."

"You look like you're feeling better." I leaned against the decrepit counter.

He sat back, his shoulders slamming against the chair. "I think I a-am," he mumbled. "And y-ye? How are ye f-feeling?"

The question hit me the same way it did when the stranger — Calomyr, I remembered — asked me a few weeks back. The pain rang like a bell in my chest, the vibrations buzzing against my ribs. Should I tell him? Should I burden him with my pain when he had so much of his own?

I longed to be a child again, running to him with every hurt. He'd scoop me up, his tremors only a ripple then. I wanted to run to him with this. "Actually, I'm not doing well, Da. I'm really not." I watched the dim happiness we had shared just moments earlier shatter in his eyes, his body thrashing.

"W-why?" he asked.

"Since everything happened, I can't escape it. The sound of it, the sight of it, the smell of burning wood and gunpowder. I watch her die every day of my life, Da."

"Watch who die?"

And there it was. The progression of time was never far from my mind, but I had hoped the tonic was working to slow it down. As my father spoke those words, the reality of it slammed into me. I watched as he searched my face for answers, finding only circles the color of the ciakoo feather under my eyes and the sheen of forming tears. "Larka?" he said abruptly, and my heart stopped momentarily.

144

"Yes, Da. I watched Larka—"

"Larka, w-where's Petra? Can you f-fetch her for m-me please?" he asked, concern in his voice. "I'd like t-to show her what I found." I closed my eyes, my lips a thin line. I would not break in front of him. *I would not break in front of him.*

"I'm going to get Ma for you, okay Da?" I said, planting a kiss on his head and walking to where my mother sat reading in their bedroom. She took one look at the tears spilling over my lids, the silver trail down my cheeks, and nodded.

She knew.

◆ ◆ ◆

The makeshift table in the kitchen was full of Da's finds, and even though the tonic wasn't preserving his memory as much as we'd hoped it would, the small pile of odds and ends made me smile. They were tangible evidence of my father's happiness, his soul — things he'd seen and thought were worthwhile to pick up, hold on to, and show his family.

My mother wrapped his cloak around his convulsing shoulders while he stood near the front door, pushing the two buttons through their loops and tying the straps over them. I had been able to purchase him the cloak a month ago, the double fasteners ensuring it wouldn't come loose on his walks like his old one sometimes did. Even so, he had managed to snag the hem on something already, so there was a tiny tear on its edge.

My latest unsavory endeavor landed me a small golden pendant in the shape of the sun that hung on a golden chain. The man at the shop gave me enough to feed my family for a week. With the money for minced beef, Ma and I decided we should make meat pies, Da's favorite.

"I can smell 'em a-already," he said excitedly, pointing his nose in the air.

"Gimme a break. We haven't even mixed the dough for the crust yet," my mother shot back.

"It matters nae. I c-can still smell 'em."

"They'll be ready when you get back. Be careful," my mother called.

He waved a hand and walked out the door, my mother's face laced with apprehensive worry as it always was when he left.

She began to measure out flour, adding heaping cups to the only bowl we owned. "Do you think the walks are still a good idea?" she asked quietly.

"You heard Solise, Ma," I said, sprinkling some flour on the countertop to roll out the crust. "He needs to keep moving."

"Maybe one of us should start to go with him," she said, not looking up from her work.

"*You* can be the one to suggest that to him." I blew air out of my mouth, imagining the cantankerous reaction a suggestion like that would surely elicit.

She cut chunks of butter into the bowl, the first butter we'd been able to purchase in as long as I could remember. "Maybe one of us should start to follow him, you know? Stay back, of course, but just keep an eye on him as he wanders."

I grimaced. "And what do we say when he turns around and sees us? Huh?"

I placed the meat in a pan on the stove, melted butter bubbling around it. The smell was mouthwatering and almost foreign. I had eaten a meat pie only once before when Larka and I were little and there was an extra silver in the budget. "But pies are supposed to be sweet!" Larka yelled when my mother placed it on the table in front of her. I remember that evening so vividly — her toothless grin, my father's laugh, and of course, the most amazing meal I'd ever eaten.

I pushed the meat around as my mother rolled out the dough, using the handle of the mallet as a makeshift rolling pin. "Maybe next time I land a big score, we can invest in a proper rolling pin, Ma."

She paused her rolling, not turning to look at me. "Petra..." she started and sighed. "You can't keep stealing." Continuing her rolling, she let out another big sigh. "I am worried sick of what will happen if you–"

"It won't happen, Ma," I assured her. Miniscule splashes of boiling butter kissed my hands as I stirred, the sensation so odd that I didn't know whether to pull my hand away or leave it. "I'm always careful. I stick to the shadows and only go for easy targets."

146

"It isn't right."

I raised my eyebrows, my stare boring into the back of her head. "You think that I don't know that?"

"I know you do, but–"

"But what? What would we do if I *didn't* steal? Starve? It was either this or a job at the Painted Empress." She cringed at the mention of it. "I do what I need to do, Ma. Never any more. Only enough to keep us alive. What state would Da be in now if I hadn't called upon Solise? What would you be rolling that dough with, huh? You wouldn't be rolling dough at all, because we couldn't afford it. You're not the one working, so you can't say *shit* about what I do." I hadn't felt the anger start to form until the last few words had shot from my mouth. She finally turned to face me.

"I don't work, Petra, because I have to take care of your father." Her tone was firm, even.

"And if you didn't, I would have to. We have our roles, we can each play them how we choose." My tone was equally as firm and even as hers. "Unless you'd like me to inquire with Mr. Evrod about a position at the Painted Empress?"

She went quiet. I won't lie and say I haven't thought of a job at the closest brothel to our home. The two men I'd lain with as a teenager were good enough lovers — nothing to be too excited about, though one of them did ask about Larka almost immediately after rolling off of me. But it wasn't necessarily unpleasant. Because of that, the Painted Empress didn't seem like such a bad place in theory. But every time I walked by the brothel, heard the screams rising from deep inside, I wasn't sure it was a pleasure house. Those screams didn't sound like ecstasy, and the men stumbling drunk to and from the doors made me feel ill. Even the slogan made my stomach turn. *We'll fulfill your every fantasy — even the most depraved.*

It had to be theft.

We continued our tasks in silence. I added salt and pepper to the minced meat as well as some chopped rosemary Solise had given me last time I went to her for more tonic. The smell enveloped me, made me feel a comfort I had known so few times in my life. I savored this moment, letting the tension between my mother and I melt away as I stirred the meat, taking in the sight and sound and smell of having satisfying food.

I helped my mother line the small tins with the dough for a flaky crust, spooning the meat in and covering it with more dough. My stomach was beginning to growl as my mother slipped each into the small oven, glancing out the gap in the shutters to the street. "I've noticed this man a few times recently," she said nonchalantly.

I furrowed my brows. "What man?"

"Come look."

Peering through the gap, I saw him. A man slight in stature with wispy blonde hair and a cloak just a bit too nice to have been purchased in Inkwell. Dusk had almost closed upon the city, shadows obscured into darkness. "You've noticed him *a few* times?"

"Yes, always just waiting there." Her tone revealed no worry, but I had long felt the gaze of strangers on me in a way that made me feel...*watched.*

His eyes were shifty, moving from the ground to the sky to the passing crowds. A heavy feeling collected in my chest. I couldn't help but grimace, squeezing my eyes shut. It was nothing. It had to be nothing. I was worrying too much, just like I always did. My mother continued cleaning up, wiping down the rickety counters. "Thank you," she said quietly, almost inaudibly.

I lowered myself to one of the kitchen chairs. "For?"

"Doing what you do. Providing. So I can stay with him." I fiddled with a small pebble that was a part of my father's collection. "I think the tonic has stopped working." Her words were heavy with sorrow and longing.

I inhaled deeply, knowing that once I acknowledged it, it was real. These were the final seconds before we entered the free fall of his affliction again. "I do too."

"Now what?" she asked, finally turning to face me. I watched my mother fight back tears, something a child shouldn't have to see their mother do as often as I had.

I sighed, throwing my head back to look at the unlevel ceiling. "I think we both know the answer, Ma. We just don't want to admit it." She raised her thumb to her mouth, chewing on the nail nervously. "Solise said there's nothing else she can do."

We sat in silence for a long while, the bubbling of the pies in the oven punctuating the silence every so often, the smell filling the house with a warmth we hadn't felt in months. Would he remember that meat pies were his favorite when he returned home? Eventually my mother rose and pulled the pies from the oven. He'd be back soon, and I was praying to the Saints that he would remember.

My mother jumped as a knock on the door sounded then, the beats so close together it sounded like a hummingbird's wings. It didn't stop until I threw the door open to find Elin standing breathless on the front steps.

"It's your Da."

Chapter 15
Now

I stared up at Castemont, the man who had become the closest thing I'd ever have to a father again. His face was sober as he glared down at me. I said nothing as he pinned me in place with that look.

"What, pray tell, are you doing, Petra?" he started, and a warm relief flooded into my fingertips at the notion of him caving first. The sweetness of his voice didn't match the disdain that was now fastened to his face. He sounded the part of loving, concerned step-father but the face he wore belonged to an executioner. My lips hardened into a line as I visualized my eyes like daggers to his shoulders, pinning him in place as he had done to me. *I am in control. I am okay.* "I assume *this* is who you've been receiving your information from?" I felt Wrena shrink even smaller beside me.

"Aye, but I threatened to harm her if she didn't tell me all she knew." The lie fell from my lips easily. He raised an eyebrow and I felt Wrena straighten slightly.

"Is that so?" he purred. The tone of his voice was maddening. I nodded, my eyes still locked on his. "And what were you doing in the kitchens?"

He probably thought I was up to something nefarious. I was too embarrassed to tell him I had risked my life, *Wrena's* life, for a handful of fucking biscuits. I stayed silent. He gave a slight nod. "Back to your quarters. Immediately. Take the servants' halls so no one sees you." Still I stood, still I stared, imagining myself towering above him. He was nothing. "You," he pointed to Wrena. "With me."

"No," I said.

He turned his attention back to me, a brow lifting. "No?"

"No. She had nothing to do with this." I stepped toward him, staring up at his face. "She is not to be punished."

"Petra, darling, you have no authority in this castle until you complete Initiation." His tone was patronizing. But he was right. I stared him down with every ounce of resolve I had.

I turned to Wrena. "Thank you for your kindness," I said flatly, trying to convey the panic and the apologies through my eyes. All I could see in hers was fear, and I was afraid that if I looked too long, my eyes would mirror hers. I turned away, blinking tears from my eyes, praying to the Saints I could keep them at bay until I was in my own bedroom. I heard the echo of the wooden door to the kitchens slam shut, the noise reverberating through the halls and straight to my bones.

Alone in my room, the night sky closed in. The stars burned holes in my head and the moonlight filled me with nausea. A light breeze blew through, moving the billowy curtains like ghosts. No one came knocking.

◆ ◆ ◆

The sunlight assaulted my eyes as they opened, and I had a half second until the dread pooled into my stomach.

Initiation Day.

I rose, hearing footsteps in the hall come and go. I sat on the edge of my bed wondering if Wrena had been reassigned early, if she was okay, if the head mistress would punish her. If

Castemont would punish her. I pushed the thought from my mind, the nausea from last night returning in an instant. The marble floor was cool beneath my feet, and I reminded myself that this was real, that I was real.

A soft knock on the door of my bedroom. "Yes?" My mother floated in, eyes downcast. My face immediately hardened, emotionally shielding myself from whatever she was going to say.

"Let's get you ready." It was barely above a whisper. I nodded, my jaw still clenched, and stood.

◆ ◆ ◆

She said nothing of the night before. If Castemont had told her, she at least had the sense to keep quiet.

I didn't have the stomach to look at myself in the mirror right now, the way the gown skimmed my curves, the way my mother had pinned up my brown hair. I did, however, stare at the delicate gold diadem on the bureau, the only thing that had felt...like comfort. Like strength. Like it was mine. Even if it had come from Castemont.

"It suits you," my mother murmured, following my gaze to the diadem as she fastened my corset. Each tug pushed more and more air out of my lungs. I better get used to it considering my lungs would most likely be airless by nightfall. Maybe punctured, too. "You know it was created in the image of the crown that sits on the head of Katia."

Katia, Keeper of the Benevolent Saints. From what I knew, the legends said that she was the one who led the Benevolent Saints in battles against the Blood Saints and their Keeper, Rhedros. She commanded an army of monsters; kelpies rose from the sea at her call, soulhags emerged from the dirt, scaled drivas descended from the heavens, breathing fire on all those in their path. She was the one who had the final say on blessings granted, mercies denied. They called her the Heart of the Eleven Saints.

"I didn't receive a formal education, if you remember." It was true. That had little to do with her and more to do with our family's lack of funds. Most of what I learned of the Saints had been since moving into the castle. I had known their names and what they presided over, maybe a story here and there. But Larka and I learned what we knew about the Saints from the little our parents told us, and they weren't the most devout followers. We took their names in vain simply because everyone else did. Like I told Wrena, if the Benevolent Saints were real, they didn't smile upon me. No word on the Blood Saints, yet.

My mother huffed. "I did my best." I wasn't sure if I believed her. She hadn't done her best in a long, long time, and definitely not since moving into the Low Royal Castle.

She finished tying the corset, giving it a final tug that almost pulled me off the pedestal. My hands fell to my sides and the texture of the ruffles caused bile to rise in my throat. This was it.

My mother picked up the diadem from the bureau, motioning for me to kneel. She nestled it among the braided coronet that framed my face, and something about the action struck a bolt of melancholy through my heart. I stood and stepped down from the pedestal, meeting her gaze. The silence was strained, and every word that came to mind dissolved like sugar in water. I could tell she was wrestling with her next words as well.

I simply lowered my head and bent into a low curtsy. She nodded back, ushering me out the door of my wardrobe and toward the hall. "Excuse me, Ma," I said curtly, motioning to the restroom. She nodded and headed for the drawing room.

I locked the door behind me and leaned against it, savoring the slightly cool wood beneath my bare shoulders. I just needed one last second, one final moment to breathe. Then I saw it.

On the countertop that held a bowl of clean water sat a small piece of black velvet. I could tell from where I stood that it was folded in half. It didn't look like it belonged in the neat pile of hand towels that sat to the right of the bowl. I approached, slowly lifting back the top piece of velvet.

A dagger with simple golden cross guards and a dark wooden grip stared back at me. A single diamond cut into an oval sat at the top of the handle. My eyes widened as I instinctively looked in the mirror, eyeing the closed door behind me. Beside the dagger on the bed of velvet was a sheath that was connected to a strap — a thigh strap, I realized. Whose was this? Who had been in my quarters?

I folded the velvet over the weapon, realizing this was not the time to be concerned with something so trivial compared to my life ending. As I reached the door, though, I paused. Had this been left *for* me? If someone had left this by mistake and came back to retrieve it, they could easily pin me as the thief, especially considering my past. But this wasn't a handkerchief someone left behind by mistake, taken with more pressing matters. This was a weapon arranged on a bed of velvet, the sheath and strap laid delicately behind it. Maybe it *had* been left for me. I knew I didn't have much time before my mother came to see what was taking me so long.

Before I could blink, I slung my leg on the counter, hiking up the layers of skirts and petticoats to my hip. I grabbed the dagger, holding it closely to my eyes. The inscription was so light that I had to turn the dagger to read it.

THE MERCY OF KATIA

I flipped it, seeing words inscribed on the other side as well.

THE FURY OF RHEDROS

More of the Saints' bullshit. I hadn't the slightest idea how to wield the thing, but I supposed that having a blade was better than being empty handed. Right?

Quickly, I slid the strap up my leg, fumbling with the ends to tighten it. Sheathing the dagger, I let my skirts drop to the ground. I took a few small jumps to ensure it was secure against my leg, my heart pounding so intensely I was sure my mother would hear it on the other side of the door.

One last look in the mirror, a deep breath, and I was ready as I would ever be.

◆ ◆ ◆

Castemont stared at me as I exited my quarters, my mother trailing behind me. This man who had become so dear to me, who

154

I had grown to trust...that trust now crumbled before me, ash and dust replacing the warmth that had once been. "You look absolutely lovely, darling," he said sweetly. I said nothing, locking my eyes with his and turning down the hall. The dagger burned against my leg as I fought back the urge to sink it into his chest. My mother and Castemont walked side by side behind me, Tyrak's steady presence bringing up the rear.

The tang of salt air floated from Pellucid Harbor to the breezeway outside Castemont Hall. The smell wrapped me in the comfort of Inkwell. Of *home.* A home I would never see again.

Before the pain of that realization could take over, I pushed it over the breezeway, letting it shatter on the city streets below. And as it splintered into thousands of tiny pieces, I heard a ruffle behind me. On the other railing of the breezeway perched a ciakoo.

It was a split second; just long enough for the bird to see me, cock its head, and take off again before my mother or Castemont noticed. Against the sky and sun, its feathers were molten night, the dark blue and deep violet and emerald like liquid on its wings. I let the sight of it drip into my veins. It was enough to keep me walking.

The doors to the throne room lay ahead and my heartbeat made its way to the back of my throat. My heartbeat stopped altogether as I looked to the left wall.

Wrena's arms were bound over her head, her shoulders unnaturally bent behind her, her throat slit from ear to ear. Slow trickles of blood still dripped down her naked body, pooling on the stones beneath her.

I stumbled back, my head shaking violently as bile rose in my throat. The sob came from so deep it was silent, my body folding in half. "The sacred rites of the Initiation are a secret only shared by those who have entered into the Royal Court," Castemont said in a low voice behind me, repeating the words he said to me in the dining hall two days prior. My mother was silent. Stars whirled in my vision as I began to wretch, nothing coming up as my body painfully convulsed. *I killed her. It's my fault she's dead. I killed her. I killed her. I killed her.* The guilt took over, the pounding at my chest like boulders down a mountain. And as those boulders crashed down one by one, I remembered.

I had never asked the name of her lover.

I felt a large hand on my bare shoulder, the callouses telling me it was Castemont's. He pushed me slightly to the right, and this time not only my heart stopped but my lungs, my brain, my very sense of being.

Hanging in the same position, only recognizable by the warm, familiar face, was Marita. She was naked as Wrena was, evidence of her four years at the Painted Empress like hash marks across her body, slashes of thickened skin covered in blood. The hair that had been under her bonnet was shorn to the root, her eyes bulging open. The blood...so much blood, her body plated in crimson. In the silence of the entry hall, the dripping echoed around me.

Drip. Drip. Drip.

I didn't have the strength to bend over and wretch. I didn't have the strength to hit the floor. I didn't have the strength to turn around and dig my thumbs into Castemont's eyes or slit his throat deeply enough to kill him. I wanted to push him over the breezeway, watch him flail and scream. I closed my eyes, letting the scorching fury build, set my skin ablaze, the blood in my veins as thick as the molten night I had seen in the sky just minutes ago.

If I broke now, if I erupted into the fire that was burning so bright within me, I'd have no chance of standing against any of the Board members. I wiped my lips on my wrist, my mouth acidic and eyes burning, and righted myself.

I slowly turned to the two people who stood behind me. I met my mother's gaze first. She quickly averted hers once again as I realized her eyes were swollen, reddened. She shook her head.

Turning my head to Castemont, I noted his stern face, but the left corner of his mouth rose ever so slightly.

"Why?" I whispered, keeping my tone as even as possible. My jaw was painfully clenched.

"We were unable to verify whether Marita gave you information as well," he said steadily, his arms behind his back.

"She didn't," I hissed.

"We couldn't take any risks." Lava boiled inside me and I tried my hardest to swallow it back. If I lunged on Castemont now, I'd be taken away before even seeing the Board of Blood. I held his stare as I took one big breath, two, then three. I looked at my mother once more. Nothing. Not even an apologetic glance. I wished more than anything to watch him bleed, watch him suffer as Wrena and Marita — my *friends* — had suffered. I swallowed my violence and turned around.

I lost everything four years ago. The people who meant the most to me, all of them, gone. I had coped with it as best I could, pushed through it, gritted my teeth through the pain. Now, once again, two of the most important people in my life were taken from me. I fought back images of them dying, begging for mercy. I heard their screams just as I still heard Larka's. Saw their dead eyes as I saw Da's. Felt the crevice in my heart crack open once again as I thought of the only man I'd ever loved rotting in the ground. My heart hardened in that moment, all because of this man who had promised to be a father to me.

Chapter 16

Then

The jagged gashes wrapped from the left side of his rib cage to his back, the wounds so deep I could see muscle and bones. Darkness had descended but I could see his wounds were still wet, though they no longer oozed. His brown eyes were open to the sky, watching for any signs of a ciakoo's silhouette against the stars.

And he was completely still.

"Pulled 'im in 'bout half mile off shore," a gruff fisherman said.

"I was walking from the market and saw the commotion," Elin said somberly.

"Looks like 'e lost a fight with the Cliffs of Malarrey," the fisherman said, his voice low. "Condolences, my ladies." He bowed his head and walked back toward the docks.

I wasn't looking at my father. It was impossible. I looked at the body on the ground, pale and foreign. The eyes, his familiar shape, but nothing else. No. This wasn't him. It couldn't be him. He never walked the cliffs.

My knees buckled not of my own accord and I hit the grass next to him, staring into those empty eyes, searching, seeking anything that didn't look right, anything that would prove that the body that laid before me did not belong to my father. But then I noticed his cheekbones, his full lips. The tunic he had left the house in earlier, torn to shreds by the rocks below the cliffs. His hands were clenched, muscles flexed, and I knew that if I pried his hands open, I'd have my answer, that this was not my father. This man's hands would be empty, meaning it *couldn't* be my father.

I pulled his fingers back, the ringing in my ears deafening. His grip finally gave, and out tumbled a tiny stone the size of my pinky nail, burning blue. Lapis lazuli.

It's strange — I heard nothing when the core of me died. I thought I'd hear my own screams echoing through my head, the pounding of my fists upon my father's motionless chest, the sobs erupting from my mother behind me. But there was nothing. It was just icy, infinite silence as I watched the life I knew disintegrate in front of me once again, the ashes falling like snow to the ground.

I put all my strength into beating my father's chest, begging him to wake up, to tell me about the stone he somehow found, to tell me why the *fuck* he was on the Cliffs of Malarrey. The blood from his wounds rained in showers upon me with every impact of my fist, my mother holding his cheeks and screaming into his face to *wake the fuck up*. Quassus mors was supposed to take his life, not a fall. Not now. *Not yet.*

Everything around me screeched to a halt, the only thing in this world was him. Getting him back. Getting him home. Shoveling steaming forkfuls of meat pies into his mouth and finishing with the tonic. Then we'd put him to sleep and tell him how we saw a lifeless man on the beach who looked unbelievably like him.

A crowd had begun to gather around us, the shadows of bystanders blocking the only moonlight we had. I roared at the crowd like an animal, feral in the pursuit of his life. A familiar voice sounded from behind me and a hand rested upon my shoulder, even as that very shoulder heaved my clenched fists into my father's chest. "Petra," the voice said, distant through the deafening ringing in my ears. "Petra." The hand began to guide me back and I whirled around, prepared to strike the one who dared to prevent me from saving my father.

Solise stared up at me, dragging me from my father and passing me to bystanders who blocked my path and pushed me away. I swung my fists in every direction I could, connecting with cheeks and backs and shoulders until finally my arms were pinned to my side.

My screams were savage and through the crowd I caught a glimpse of my mother being dragged away too, her body thrashing as my father's had, as mine had, fighting every hand that held her back. "Drink," Solise called through the raging fog in my mind. "Drink, Petra!" She poured something into my screaming mouth. I was choking on it, gagging, spitting it into the air until a warm darkness began to close around the sides of my vision.

I let it swallow me whole, plunging into a world where my father was alive, Larka was alive, and the meat pies were ready to eat.

◆ ◆ ◆

My tongue was dried to the roof of my mouth when I awoke, my eyes full of grit. I squinted in the muffled light filtering in through the window, breathing in the smell of dust and a lingering scent of cooked food and—

Da. I shot up, my head pounding in protest at the speed. I was in my parents' room, my skin soaked with sweat and freezing, vague echoes ringing through my head. My mother laid to my left facing the wall, her petite body curled in on itself as she slept. I leaned my head back against the wall and closed my eyes.

Solise stood at the stove stirring oatmeal in the only pot we owned. Hearing me enter the kitchen, she rested the spoon on the counter and strode to me, arms outstretched, silent. I accepted her hug and the moment my body hit hers, the gravity of last night hit me. This woman who had shown our family such kindness was doing so again.

160

My father was *dead*. My sweet, innocent, loving father had died. Tears began to flow silently, dripping onto Solise's robe. Her hand circled my back softly as I remembered everything in vivid detail. The bitter taste of the arri root that Solise had poured in my mouth rose thickly in the back of my throat, the sleep it had induced still heavy in my brain. I pulled away from Solise and collapsed into a chair at the makeshift table. I couldn't look at his pile of things that still lay there undisturbed. Every time I tried to open my mouth to speak, my head pounded harder, louder. Solise saw me struggle and pulled the pot from the stove, placing it on a rolled up dishrag before taking a seat across from me.

"How are you feeling?" she said softly, kindly. My mouth opened and closed like a fish out of water. I squeezed my eyes shut, sure that if I did so hard enough I would open them to a world where half of my family wasn't dead. The tiny piece of lapis lazuli my father had held sat near the corner of the table, separate from the pile of his other finds. I reached for the stone, turning it over in my palm.

I opened my mouth to speak, but once again the words caught in my throat. Solise reached a hand toward me. "You don't need to speak." I closed my mouth as she rose, preparing me a bowl of porridge. I stared at the lump of slop in the bowl, the steam rising from it. Had my Da's wound steamed in the cool air?

"Where is he?" I whispered. My throat was as raw as if I had swallowed a handful of gravel. The weight in my gut matched that feeling.

"I took him to my house." I lifted my eyes to her. "I examined him for an exact cause of death and stitched the wound the best I could. You will need to bury him within the day, Petra." My eyelids were heavy with exhaustion of every kind. "I brought you the clothes he wore — dressed him in some of the clothes Novis left behind."

I nodded. "And...and he fell?" I choked out.

"So it seems, child," she said woefully, her tone as stiff with mourning as mine. "Words cannot express how sorry I am." I said nothing. A wave of nausea overtook me and I leaned over and began vomiting on the dank wooden floor, intent on expelling last night from my body. Solise quickly arrived at my side, gathering

161

my tangled hair and resuming circles on my back as I heaved with every ounce of strength I had. I wretched until my body shook, my eyes were blurry, and my nose was running, then I leaned back and collapsed against the back of the chair. Solise wet a rag and placed it on my forehead as my mother stumbled into the kitchen.

Our eyes met, a million words passing between us as I watched her replay the scenes of last night, clutching her elbows across her chest. She looked so small. After a few moments, she fell to the floor and wailed.

Chapter 17

Now

Resolve was an iron fist around my heart, squeezing, pumping the blood through my veins. As I walked into the throne room alone, six other doors arranged around the hall opened too, the other Initiates stepping forward as I did, their traditional pure white gowns just as excessive as mine. "Please, ladies," crooned an indistinguishable voice belonging to a member of the Board of Blood. "Gather here."

The seven members sat on a raised dais draped with crimson velvet curtains. The men were arranged in a straight line in lavish chairs that matched the drapes, each sitting leisurely. *Fucking bastards.* A behemoth of a throne rose behind them, empty, the deep mahogany gilded in gold. The Invisible King's throne.

I wondered if he held court in his throne room. I wondered if he even held court at all. I realized I hadn't asked Castemont if he'd ever met the Invisible King. Where was King Belin now? What did he think of this?

The Initiates and I stood together in front of the dais. The doors to the throne room suddenly slammed shut, the clangs echoing through the cavernous hall. I felt their eyes penetrating my skin, one set burning the most of all. The onyx black eyes of Ludovicus roved over my body, one eyebrow slightly raised and a lazy smile on his milky face. I wasn't sure if he knew Castemont had caught me last night. Caught me and Wrena. I shivered, willing my body to stay still.

"My, my," crooned the same breathy voice that had called us to gather. Raolin. His ruby eyes reminded me of the rats that crawled through Inkwell. "You all look absolutely splendid."

"Truly," Garit added, his long fingernails tapping together. The brothers wore matching suits of black, silver stitching accenting the lapels as the dull sheen of leather glowed underneath.

I felt tension and uneasiness ripple off the other Initiates. I was standing closest to the east wall of the throne room, trying to keep my eyes from wandering around the hall. Alira stood next to me, her hands neatly folded in front of her. Did she know what was going to happen today? Were she and her sister Willow kept in the dark as I had been?

Marble columns the color of bone shot up from the matching floors, each carved with ancient scenes of the Saints' greatest legends. Twenty-two columns in total, eleven on each side of the hall, two for each Saint. I saw Aanh, Saint of the Home, building a house of pure gold, protecting it with her life. Idros, Saint of Storms, was depicted pushing thunder clouds together, lightning snaking out beneath. Cyen, Saint of Death, stood over the graves of the departed. I shivered at the sight of his lifeless eyes.

The pillars reserved for the Keepers were gilded in gold as the throne was. A battle scene was etched into each column that belonged to Katia and Rhedros, though it wasn't clear who had the upper hand. Katia's crown shot sun rays to the sky while Rhedros' crown cast a shadow downward.

The columns supported a mezzanine that shadowed the back half of the expansive room, no doubt for guards with bows ready to extinguish any attackers while court was held. It was empty. We were completely at the mercy of the Board.

Not me, though. The dagger pulsed at my thigh.

Ludovicus rose, placing his hands behind his back while descending the steps of the dais, weaving between us at a sickeningly slow pace. "Today you will learn the innermost secrets of the Royal Court. Those who succeed are sworn to secrecy to protect the sanctity of our court. Those who fail will be killed on site or cast into the Onyx Pass. Not a single Initiate has ever made it through the Pass to Blindbarrow." His eyebrows raised as he stopped in front of Augusta, the furthest to the left. "I'm in a good mood today, but I'm not sure whether I can say the same for my brothers. Pray that if you fall, you fall swiftly."

A spindly finger lifted Augusta's chin as he inspected her face then stepped back and inspected her body. "Now that we've gotten to know each and every one of you, it is time to see if you're worthy of royal standing. If you should be so fortunate as to pass Initiation and ascend to the Royal Court, you will be placed upon the marriage market and married off to the most suitable match." He moved down the line, inspecting each Initiate as he had Augusta. "Your duty as women is to produce strong Eserenian leaders and wives to wed them. Should you be unable to provide," he emphasized the word with a diseased tone, "you will meet the same fate as the failed Initiates. You have purposely been denied information throughout your life in order to protect the sanctity of this process, and if you are found to be disseminating any confidential information, you will meet the same fate as the failed Initiates. Am I clear?" We all nodded and I swallowed hard, my throat bobbing as he neared me.

"And should you break any rule, be found of any infraction," he stepped closer to me, finger hooking under my chin, his voice lowering, "we will find *great* joy in peeling the scalp from your head or watching the beasts of the Onyx Pass rip the eyes from your face." He spoke the last words so low that only I could hear them. I remembered what Ingra had said. *The beasts...with your blood on their jowls.* I pushed the soothsayer's words from my mind. I kept my eyes on his, my gaze a solid cover

for the fire that was burning in my head. He was so close, *so* close...
I could grab the dagger and plunge it into his chest.

He released my chin, returning to his seat upon the dais. The
room was eerily still, the lack of guards at each door making me
feel more exposed than I had expected. I suppose I had grown
used to the near constant company of guards. I thought of the
carnage that hung outside the door I walked through, wondered
if the blood still dripped from Wrena and Marita to the stone
floor. I shook the thought from my head.

"As you know, we are the Board of Blood. My brothers and I
were handpicked by the Saints to conduct Initiation across the
continent, ushering in a new generation of royalty each year." But
were they really? "The Saints spoke directly to us twenty-four
years ago, calling for the beginning of a new tradition."

"Augusta, darling, please step forward," Anton called. The girl
took an apprehensive step, the ruffles of her gown swishing
behind her. "Tell me of one sacrifice you have made in your life."
I had to keep my face straight, confusion sweeping down the row
of Initiates.

She paused. "Could you please elaborate, Sir Anton?"

"I asked you to tell me of one sacrifice you have made in your
life," he repeated, annoyance lacing his words. "It's a simple
query."

She shifted uncomfortably, the sudden attention making her
visibly shake. "Each year, I choose to abstain from frivolous
spending during the week of Saint Tolar's Day," she muttered
quietly. The innocence in her voice told me that she genuinely
thought of this as a sacrifice. As the daughter of a nobleman, I
suppose it was a sacrifice. She did not understand that this
"frivolous spending" was not normal for most Eserenian
residents.

Anton's face lit with amusement. "A whole week?" His words
dripped with sarcasm like the bodies in the hall dripped with
blood. "How conscientious of you."

"Thank you, Sir," she said, not catching the mockery in his
voice. The other brothers let out quiet chuckles.

"You may return to your place."

166

"Iridia, please step forward," Arturius crooned. His voice was raspier than Anton's, the grit sending a chill down my spine. "Tell me of one sacrifice you have made."

She stepped forward, planting her feet on the ground. After hearing the question asked of Augusta, Iridia had an answer ready. "When I was eleven, my father, who as you know is Lord Pouissard, took me to Inkwell where we spent a whole day passing out bread and ale. I sacrificed an entire day to help the less fortunate." I bristled at the mention of home. I wondered if I had accepted food from her, if I unknowingly ate the bread of a rich girl who I'd die beside in this very throne room a few years later.

"Goodness, me." Arturius' words were rife with the same sarcasm as Anton's had been. "How devastating."

The Board of Blood moved down the line, reacting to answers like giving away a piece of precious jewelry and settling for a brown mare instead of a black stallion.

"Petra," Ludovicus hissed. "Please step forward." A million ideas ran through my mind. Should I lie and say something that aligned with the other Initiates' answers? No. I needed to get through this as cleanly as possible. "Tell me of one sacrifice you've made."

I swallowed and stepped forward. My palms dampened and I plunged them in the ruffles of my skirts. Seven sets of perverted gemstone eyes were on my body. Before I could stop myself, I was speaking.

"I once gave up my pillow for my Da so he could tuck it behind his back to help ease the impact of his tremors while he slept. It was my only pillow, but he suffered from quassus mors, and he wasn't getting any sleep." The words tumbled from me as I felt the thin mattress against my head, the scratchy blanket pulled up to my chin.

Silence. I could sense the baffled look on Alira's face beside me. "Ah," Ludovicus sighed, cocking his head. "A true sacrifice. You may step back." I let out a breath I didn't know I was holding in.

"Sacrifice, ladies, is one of the crucial pillars of the Royal Court. You must be able to look sacrifice in the face and not shy away. It is a way to get the Saints' attention — we must commit sin in order to be forgiven." His words were low, thick.

Commit sin? Sacrifice? What the actual *fuck*?

"Each year on the Eve of Keeper Katia's Day, a lowly commoner is selected. They are brought to the castle, flayed, and dismembered on the Altar of Katia." His nonchalant tone did not match what he was saying. "Their screams alert the Benevolent Saints that one of their children is in danger. Each member of the Royal Court is required to take part in some way, whether they peel a bit of skin from the muscle, saw through bone, sever the heart from their chest. Each member commits a sin under the watch of the Benevolent Saints." I once again fought to keep my face straight, but I could tell someone down the line was beginning to sway, dangerously close to fainting.

Each year... That meant Castemont took part in this. My mother would one day take part in this. *No.*

"The Benevolent Saints gift us with their forgiveness as they always do," Balthazar murmured. "Benevolence always washes the Blood away."

Willow collapsed. Alira immediately dropped to her side, propping her up.

"Ah!" Ludovicus shouted. "Up, Alira." She immediately dropped her twin, returning to a standing position with a red face. "Collect her, Higgins," Ludovicus called, and the large man rose and prowled toward the fallen girl.

"No, please," Alira begged, her stance still rigid. "Please, Sirs, she probably fainted from nervousness, from being in awe of your presence. Please don't take her away." Oh my Saints, were we about to watch her die? "Please!" screamed Alira.

"You are not to speak out of turn!" Anton shouted. Her face contorted around her sobs as she fought the urge to run to Willow. "What do we think, brothers?" he asked, turning down the line of the vampiric men. "Onyx Pass? Or shall we kill her now?" Alira choked on her sobs.

"Death. Now," Arturius stated. Alira screamed. "We call upon Cyen, Saint of Death, to join us in this throne room."

"Oh, but she's unconscious, brother," Garit chided. "I'd rather watch her awaken to realize death will be meeting her soon." Murmurs of agreement.

168

Higgins slung her over his shoulder and placed her in a far corner of the room, shackling her hands together then running the chain around a column depicting Tolar's bounty. She was still slumped over. I prayed she would somehow be dead before she had the chance to wake up.

"I'm not sure we've ever had someone fall so early," Garit laughed, his voice slick like oil.

Ludovicus rasped out a low laugh. "The fun hasn't even started."

Chapter 18
Then

I wanted to faint, to slip into an unconsciousness that was nothing but darkness. "Are you sure?" Solise said. I looked to my mother and we both nodded. My mother's cheeks had not dried since she collapsed on the kitchen floor yesterday, the day a blur of screaming and rage and despair and tears.

Solise nodded and gingerly pulled back the sheet, revealing my father's familiar face. He looked peaceful, like he had simply fallen asleep, but his skin was too gray. My mother's face was plastered with longing, regret as the rise and fall of her chest quickened once again. A steady stream of tears still poured from her eyes, her nose rubbed raw and red.

I gave Solise a slight nod and she covered his face again. "You must arrange a burial today. His body will not keep much longer." I knew Solise was doing everything she could to help, but hearing my father be referred to as nothing more than a body was a dagger to my heart. My mother had slipped into despondency, which had happened multiple times over the past few hours. I wished I could join her in that detached state, floating aimlessly through my emotions, but I had to be the steady one here since she clearly couldn't be.

We had no money for the funeral he deserved, for a plot of land under a shady tree where the vines twisted into the sky. Even in death, the city shit on Inkwell. There was a designated section of the city's cemetery for those without the funds to secure their loved ones a peaceful resting place — the Backwoods, they called it. It was only established because in the years before I was born it had been common to see dead bodies rotting in the street. Families had no choice but to leave them outside the walls of their homes. The rats began to overrun Inkwell, and as soon as they made their way into other districts, the city sprung into action.

It was an unregulated area, and people often came upon unmarked graves as they dug a resting place for their loved ones. It was not manicured or sustained like the rest of the cemetery. It had garnered the name because of the unkempt trees that grew gnarled and wild, the grass and weeds knee high. Small stones marked the graves, some taken by the overgrowth of time. Mice skittered through the weeds. It was somehow both eerie and peaceful, ghostly yet exploding with life.

I left Ma with Solise and walked quietly through the city until I reached the cemetery, a portion of green grass with fences that bordered the northern side of Prisma and the southern side of Ockhull. We were close to Ockhull's well-known patisserie, the scent of fresh honey apple bread and iced biscuits wafting through the air. As I entered the gates of the cemetery and strode through the immaculately kept grounds, I kept my gaze forward, ignoring the welling emotion in my throat. Straight through to the back, to a place an outsider might assume wasn't a part of the cemetery at all. To the Backwoods.

Birds chirped overhead, unaware of the decay that they had built their nests over. Wrapped in my cloak despite the humid summer air, I began to weave through the trees and grass and stones, looking for a place suitable to hold my father for eternity. Some of the grave markers had flowers and trinkets on them, evidence of friends and family who remembered. Others were so old that they lay alone, the words etched crudely in their faces barely legible after Saints knew how long. I did my best to avoid stepping on any graves, but the clutter of the Backwoods made it nearly impossible.

Thwack. The sound of a shovel hitting loose dirt echoed through the trees. Dirt hit the ground. *Thwack.* I shuffled my way around a twisted tree trunk that had grown almost sideways until I saw a figure about 100 feet away. He was facing away from me, tall, broad shouldered, intent on his work as he covered *someone* in dirt. By the looks of it, he had just begun to return the dirt to the pit he had dug.

"Have you seen any other good spots?" I called, hoping he could help me return to my mother quicker. He jumped, whirling around, hoisting the shovel in front of him as if it were a weapon. I put my hands up as I approached. "Apologies. It wasn't my intention to–"

Calomyr. He lowered his shovel as he surveyed my face, half hidden under the hood of my cloak. "Petra," he said, the smoky voice low and shaky.

"Apologies," I said again, the word short. I glanced behind him at the pit in the earth. "And apologies for..." I lowered my head. He simply stared at me, the pigments of his eyes still as unbelievable as they had been the first time I saw him. They were maddening, the clash of ice and emeralds in his left eye impossible to ignore, even through my grief. He shifted from one foot to another. "Don't stop on my account," I muttered. "I'm just looking for a suitable spot for..."

"For your father?" he cut in, his face immediately flooded with regret.

"How did you know that?" What the fuck?

"I just assumed. I've seen him around town. His...tremors," he said awkwardly, lowering his face. I gave a short nod, looking away, tears threatening to spill. "Apologies," he said to me, and the word reverberated through me so thoroughly that I shuddered. "Are you okay?"

That question again. Aside from my Da a few weeks ago, was he the only person who'd ever asked me that? Was that why my reaction to the words was so disconcerting to me? The tears spilled then as I choked back a sob. I simply shook my head. He dropped his shovel and started to walk toward me. I threw my hands up to

172

him. "Don't come near me," I snarled. "I don't know who the fuck you are or why I keep running into you. But I do know that for somebody who isn't from Inkwell, you sure seem to be there a lot."

"How do you know I'm not from Inkwell?" he breathed, the breathiness of his voice wrapping around my nerves.

"The cloak, you *fucking* idiot. Never mind the fact that you *told me* you lived in Ockhull." I fell into the pattern of speech Larka had used when speaking with strange men who didn't know how to keep their hands to themselves. Sharp. Despite the fire I spat, I felt weak, fragile. "Why are you in Inkwell so often? What business could you possibly have there?"

He sucked on his teeth, his face unreadable. "My sick aunt lives there. *Lived* there."

I had no strength to conjure up any pity for him, not while the last day and a half had changed my entire life...again. "So I'll no longer be running into you in Inkwell then, correct?" I sniped.

Hurt flashed on his face. He opened his mouth to speak, then closed it. "Correct," he finally said quietly.

"Good. Now *please* tell me if there are any more suitable spots where I can lay my father to rest."

◆ ◆ ◆

The exhaustion that pounded through my body was unlike anything I'd ever felt before. I dug a hole with Solise's shovel next to a mangled tree, one of the branches dipping low enough to the ground to serve as a makeshift bench. With blistered hands and an aching back, I stood beside the hole where my father lay wrapped in a sheet. Larka's face flashed in my mind, wondering how it would have felt to look into a hole in the ground and see her covered form.

It almost made me thankful there had been nothing left of her to bury.

Solise had steadily been falling into the role of a friend since the first time she came to our home, our conversations when I stopped in for more tonic growing longer, more personal. I had no idea what my mother and I would have done if she hadn't been there to stitch him up, to make him look more like himself, to dress him in fresh clothes for his ascent to the Saints. So it was a comfort, small as it was, to see her standing at the head of the grave, ready to pray over his body.

Kolvar and Selina stood with Elin, their arms linked and heads bowed. A few acquaintances of his that neither my mother nor I knew stood by as well. My mother had curled herself on the ground, hugging her knees to her chest, deep sobs breaking from her chest as Solise began to read simple prayers from the Book of Benevolent Saints.

"Glorious Saints, divine lights that guide us, please lead Sarek Gaignory into your arms. May he live forevermore under the protection of the Benevolent Saints and kept from the wrath of the Blood Saints." My mother's wail pierced the air as she began to scream his name. Solise's steady voice began to crack as she continued to read, placing a hand on my writhing mother's shoulder. "May Cyen, Saint of Death, grant him mercy as he moves into the next life."

I looked down at the shape of him in the dirt and it hit me.

He had been wearing a cloak when he left on his walk, hadn't he?

"May he be welcomed into the skies by Soren, Saint of Heaven, and kept safe from Liara, Saint of Hell."

And when the fisherman brought his lifeless body to shore, he was without his cloak.

"May he be spared the wrath of Faldyr, Saint of War."

In the pile of clothes he had been wearing that was given to me by Solise, his cloak hadn't been there.

"May Onera, Saint of Miracles, smile upon him now and forever."

It fastened around his neck with two buttons and a tie. It was unlikely that it would have been ripped from him by the fall or the waves.

"May he be freed from the earthly hands of Noros, Saint of Pain, and always have shelter from Idros, Saint of Storms."

Why was he on the Cliffs of Malarrey when his normal route didn't take him anywhere near them?

174

"May Tolar, Saint of Wealth, and Aanh, Saint of the Home, bless the family he leaves behind."

Why would he remove his cloak?

"May Rhedros, Keeper of the Blood Saints, allow him to pass into the hands of the Benevolent Saints."

Why would he remove his cloak?

"And let him live in the light of Katia, Keeper of the Benevolent Saints, Heart of the Eleven, for all eternity."

He wouldn't.

"To our Saints, we pray."

Chapter 19

Now

Alira whispered prayers beside me. "Are you ready to become privy to another secret, ladies?" Higgins breathed, a smile on his lips. I braced myself and felt the movement make its way down the line of Initiates. "Now where do we get the lowly commoners?" My chest heaved because I knew. In my heart of hearts, I knew.

"The bottom of the barrel. The *sludge* left behind," Ludovicus snarled, staring right at me. "Inkwell."

"I do believe, dear brother, that we have an Initiate this year that hails from Inkwell, do we not?" Garit asked mockingly.

"Yes," Ludovicus purred, his eyes not leaving mine. "Sweet Petra here is a native of Inkwell."

"What a shame that the Saints never chose you as our sacrifice," Garit said, narrowing his eyes. I shuddered. "The Saints make their presence known in our actions. Each year, the newest Initiated members have the privilege of selecting a sacrifice. They are allowed to do whatever is necessary to lure them to the castle for the ceremony." I swallowed back vomit, my throat burning. The white hot rage that had become a part of me flared.

"Sometimes it doesn't take much. Some years the Initiates are clever, promising high paying work. Those who are a bit slower..." Raolin trailed off.

"They find their way to the brothels, enticing them in a different way," Arturius added. He let out a low, menacing laugh.

"In the name of the Saints, of course," Anton added. "And in the name of the Saints, my brothers, we must only allow the strongest to advance to this honorable stage. Now that you've learned the secrets, the fun can begin." The members hummed in agreement. "You will be presented with three challenges in which the Saints will identify you as worthy or unworthy."

"Balthazar, would you like to do the honors?" Ludovicus asked, walking behind the row of chairs to retrieve a small leather chest bound with golden buckles.

"Oh, how could I let such an opportunity pass?" Balthazar answered, rising and approaching the chest which had been lowered to the floor at the end of the dais. My heart pounded as he pulled the lid back.

A noise I had never heard before rose from the open chest, and the five remaining girls tensed beside me. I heard Alira's breathing quicken, becoming shallower. The noise sounded like the rattling of beach pebbles in a jar. Ludovicus handed Balthazar a pair of thick elbow-length gloves, his gaze traveling the room as he pulled them on.

"This," he said, reaching into the box, "is a Nesanian serpent." He grabbed the snake behind its head, four feet of muscled body ringed with red and black. We didn't have snakes in Eserene and I had never seen one before, but I heard stories of slithering nightmares that inhabited the deserts on the other side of the world. The end of its tail shook, producing the rattle that had been coming from the box.

All the other Initiates gasped. "The sage here in Eserene keeps a variety of reptiles for study and has been so kind as to lend us a serpent each year since we began conducting Initiations," Garit explained.

"For the next phase of your Initiation, the serpent will be placed around your neck in honor of the Blood Saints. Should Rhedros and the Blood Saints he presides over deem you worthy, you will remain unscathed, but if Rhedros finds you unworthy of the Royal Court..." Ludovicus jeered, a smile rising on his lips. "Let's just say the venom is swift...but it takes longer than Onyxian beasts."

"Augusta, my dear," Balthazar called. Her face has gone gray, eyes wide. He approached her, the serpent writhing in his grip, still secured. "Are you worthy?" he whispered, lacing the snake around her neck until it curled across her decolletage. Her eyes were on the ceiling, her lips moving in a silent prayer. "You ask the Saints for help now?" Balthazar cooed. "Darling, your fate has already been decided. Now we must wait and see." The snake writhed around her neck, its scales glittering in the light of the sconces and chandelier. Slowly, it slithered to her shoulder and down her arm where Balthazar retrieved it once again. "Worthy," Balthazar declared. Augusta's shoulders dropped.

Balthazar stepped down the line to Iridia. She stood tall, her shoulders back, visibly fighting the urge to give in to cowardice. "Are you worthy?" He placed the snake around her neck, across her shoulders. Her eyes stayed on Balthazar. Her pulse thrummed in her neck as the serpent wrapped around the base of her throat, tensing for a moment.

Iridia shook violently. Tears had pooled in her eyes. "Now, now, sweet girl," Balthazar breathed. "It is a great honor to be in the presence of the Saints," he said. "And anyway, should the Blood Saints wish to take you now, they will make it known."

It happened so quickly that had I not heard Iridia's scream, I would have missed it altogether. The snake sank its fangs into her neck, the noise from his tail seemingly sent from Cyen himself. Her scream contracted in her throat as Balthazar pulled the serpent from her neck. Her hands clawed at the fang marks, panic in her eyes. He clicked his tongue. "Unworthy. A pity."

The veins around the bites started to darken, all the blood vessels in her neck suddenly as visible as roads inked on a map. "Truly a shame," Raolin tutted and the Board hummed in agreement. "Such a beauty. I thought she would have served the court well. It seemed Rhedros and the Blood Saints had better plans for her."

"Arturius, do you mind taking care of our dear Iridia? It seems she is not in possession of the strength the Royal Court requires," Balthazar called, eyes never leaving the writhing girl in front of him.

"It would be my pleasure." He descended from the dais and grabbed her by the wrists. The black veins had spread into her face and down her chest, small beads of blood trickling from the tiny puncture wounds. She fought against him as her screams became garbled. Having none of it, he threw her twitching body over a shoulder, crossed the room and dumped her on the ground next to Willow, who was still unconscious.

He chained her to the column, but the screams continued to erupt, her agony palpable. My stomach began to churn harder. He pulled a handkerchief from his pocket, balled it in his fist, and stuffed it to the back of Iridia's throat. I watched as she tried to stay conscious, pulled against the chain, but it was no use. Her eyes began to fall back in her head, her breathing becoming ragged. She eventually collapsed against the column, chest rising and falling quickly and slightly, the blackness in her veins crawling over her body.

Willow and Iridia. Two lives set to end. Just like that.

"Cora, dear," Balthazar crooned, stepping in front of the third girl. Her eyes were wild, her breathing almost as erratic as Iridia's as she lay dying in the corner. "Are you worthy?" The hiss of his voice could have come from the serpent. It slithered around her neck, but her chin stayed high. I saw her lips moving, praying to the Saints, no doubt.

It writhed to her shoulder, back to Balthazar's grip, and I felt the remaining Initiates sigh in relief along with her. "It seems the Blood Saints have deemed you worthy," he said with a wicked grin and a slow nod.

Estelle held her chin high as the snake was draped across her neck. I could see its tongue flicking from its mouth as it glided over her shoulders. "Worthy," Balthazar confirmed.

Alira straightened beside me. "Beautiful Alira, almost identical to your sister." His voice was smooth and rich, filled with years of torturing others and delighting in bloodshed. Alira cringed at the mention of Willow who was still breathing in the corner. "Are you worthy?"

Once again, the snake was placed around her neck, slithering sickeningly past arteries and veins that were beating like war drums. She kept her breathing even as it caressed her neck.

The serpent slithered back to her shoulder as a single tear slipped down her cheek. "Excellent," Balthazar purred.

His gaze caught mine before he began to walk toward me, menacingly slow. "Our little lowborn," he tutted. He came close enough that I could feel his breath on my cheek, smell the years he'd seen, like old books bound with dusty leather. "Let's see if you're worthy." He brought his lips to my ear. "If it were up to me, you'd be in the Onyx Pass already, my dear." I heard Ludovicus laugh so low that I wasn't sure anyone else did.

Up close, I was able to see the snake's eyes as he neared me, piercing black...but not empty. No, the black was deep, the candles around the throne room setting them ablaze. The snake was otherworldly beautiful, the fact that this creature with no sense of right and wrong, of life and death was here to decide my fate. As I gazed into those deep eyes that held so much more life than the matching onyx eyes of Ludovicus, a slight peace washed over me.

Its cool scales touched my shoulder and I began to revel in the feeling that this, *all of this,* may be over for me soon. Maybe revenge wasn't what I wanted. Maybe I just wanted to die. It would be a lot easier.

It slid against my neck, my heartbeat surprisingly even, my breathing calm. I stared at Balthazar as he watched the snake coil around my throat.

His eyes widened slightly as the snake began to coil around my neck again, though not tight enough to choke me, the scales barely grazing my neck. The cold weight was steady. And then...

It stopped. It simply stopped and rested, its body wrapped around my throat. Balthazar's head cocked almost imperceptibly, then his eyes narrowed as he inhaled.

I felt the weight of every pair of conscious eyes in the room against me. I heard the near silent slip of the snake's tongue as its head rested beneath my ear as if relaying the message from Rhedros himself. "You are worthy," Balthazar said quickly, reaching for the serpent.

It hissed, its tail rattling in warning. He snapped his hand back at the sudden noise. I kept my face straight. He reached for the serpent again and it snapped at his gloved arm, menacing fangs bared, narrowly missing his wrist. Maybe snakes weren't so bad after all.

I didn't know what to do and it seemed no one else did either. "How peculiar," Higgins murmured. I slowly reached my arm up, holding my hand in front of the snake. With a flick of my head, the snake uncoiled itself from around my neck and twisted itself around my forearm, placing its head between my thumb and forefinger. It looked at me again, the black eyes seeming to lighten, expand. I gently clamped down my thumb and forefinger, silently thanking the snake — I was thanking a *fucking snake* — and handed it to Balthazar.

I had made it through.

He said nothing before flinging the snake to the ground and stomping his boot on its head, the crunch of its little skull loud in my ears. The snake rattled frantically until it slowly faded into stillness. The familiar rage bubbled inside of me thinking of the soul I had seen in those eyes. Another soul extinguished. Another death I had witnessed.

The dagger once again burned at my thigh.

"Why?" I whispered through gritted teeth, quiet enough that only he could hear. Balthazar met my gaze but said nothing.

The limp body of the snake remained on the ground as Balthazar silently took his seat, his face slightly drawn.

I kept silent, thinking of the pain I'd inflict upon every one of these weak minded pieces of *shit.*

Chapter 20

Then

I didn't tell my mother where I was going when I slipped out the front door four weeks after the funeral. She didn't ask. I had turned over every possibility in my mind, followed every thought to a dead end. I didn't want to admit what I knew was true.

That my father hadn't fallen.

Gormill Road was buzzing with movement. Filthy, patched cloaks billowed behind Inkwell's residents. The harbor opened in front of me, the salty air hitting my face the same time the sun broke over the wall.

The harbor only coated my tongue with bitterness now. After Larka died, I could sit on the waterfront and go numb. Now, it was forever frozen in my mind as a synonym for death. If I stared too long, I'd fall back to those days, Larka's screams, Da's empty eyes—

Snap out of it. I had to stay focused. There was no time to relive those nightmares while I was in the middle of another one. I trudged across the waterfront, the sun beating on the wild hair

I'd braided back. The cliffs loomed in the distance, towering over the harbor like a reaper.

He had been wearing his cloak when he left. And it was gone when he was pulled to shore. I repeated it to myself so many times that the words started to lose meaning. The Cliffs of Malarrey grew closer, my legs already protesting at the incline. The same incline Da had walked a few weeks ago.

The wind rustled the thick grass on the plateau of the cliff, the noise of the city far behind, nothing but the waves and the breeze and the gulls. I stood facing the water, the waves crashing over the breakwall furiously, the waters of the harbor remaining relatively calm. I could see the entire city from here, all of the rich and all of the poor falling beneath a single gaze.

I inched toward the edge of the cliff, my heartbeat quickening. Jagged rocks stared up at me from their bed of seawater, momentarily hidden by the waves before emerging as the water sluiced off. I lowered myself to lay on my stomach, my face hanging over the cliff as I ignored the instincts to jump back.

I let one arm hang over the edge, the feeling turning my stomach but not unwelcome. It could all be over right now...the pain, the longing, the *guilt*. I could slide my body off this edge and be done with it. A fisherman could pull me to shore and I'd be laid to rest next to my Da. No more strife, struggle, or suffering.

I slid the other arm over the cliff. The waves smashed up against the cliff's face, angrily spraying saltwater through the air as my fingers traced the jagged wall. My eyes closed of their own accord and I relished the feeling of being on the precipice of the ether. I inched forward, my chest and shoulders now hanging above the rocks. Just a few more inches.

Hands closed around my ankles and yanked me back. I quickly flipped over and–

"Don't," Calomyr said, his breath ragged, his eyes wide. His body rose and fell with his deep panting, a sheen of sweat on his brow.

"What the *fuck* are you doing?!" I yelled in his face, his body still crouched over mine.

"Please don't," he said, just above a whisper, the silken voice running over my skin.

"Don't *what?*"

"Don't do what you were about to do." He looked behind me as he said it, to the harbor and the sea beyond.

"Why does it matter to you?" I began to rise, his mismatched eyes following me. I had meant to turn back to the view, but I couldn't tear my eyes from his.

"You just can't," he objected, reaching out a hand. I stepped back, already dangerously close to the cliff's edge. The relief that lay just beyond the rocks below called to me, beckoned me to leap. "Petra, the world needs you here."

"It was bad enough when you were in Inkwell. Now I'm on the other side of the city and you're here. What the fuck?"

"I had some...business to attend to." He looked away.

I raised an eyebrow and scoffed. "Business to attend to. Okay," I said sarcastically, cringing at the cliché. Our eyes met again and locked in place until I finally willed myself to turn toward the sea.

"What are you doing here?" he asked quietly. If I were lucky, I could jump and drag him down with me.

"I have my own business to attend to, thank you."

"Are you going to jump?" His voice remained small. I didn't answer. "Are you looking for something?" Something in his tone made me turn to him. I squinted my eyes, scanning his face.

"Why are you asking me that?"

I hadn't realized that he was moving toward me until his face was mere inches from mine. He smelled of wood smoke and cedar, the richness of his scent matching his voice. I was stuck between death and Calomyr. His eyes bored into mine as I searched his face. "I can see it in your eyes. You're looking for something."

I flinched involuntarily, the heat of his body brushing against my cheeks. He was intoxicating, so much so that I had to keep myself from moving to touch him. All I could do was nod weakly as his eyes held me in place.

"You're looking for his cloak."

The fog that he had cast over me dissipated. My rage caught up to me in that moment, a tornado of anger and grief swirling around me as his words sank into my bones. How the

184

fuck did he know I was looking for Da's cloak? I did not take his outstretched hand. Instead I stepped forward and pushed him back. My vision was red as my breathing quickened. His face flashed with surprise. "What did you do to him?" I continued shoving him back down the cliff's plateau. He easily had almost a foot on me and I knew my blows did little, but he still retreated a bit with every push. I was screaming. "What happened to it?!" His jaw clenched.

"I did not hurt your father, okay?" He cut me off, grabbing my wrists, his voice raising and his head stooping to meet my searing gaze. "I saw him that night, you know. I saw him walking. And I was there when that girl brought you to the beach to see him." His eyes almost welled as he blinked furiously. "You have no reason to believe me, but I did not touch him."

I opened my mouth to protest, to scream at him, but I couldn't. A small part of me believed him. Or at least a small part of me *wanted* to believe him. And that small part had begun to govern my actions.

I stood in his grasp staring up at this strange man. The sun from the east shone behind him, illuminating his short dark hair like a halo. The sea breeze lifted the shaggy strands, setting them dancing across his forehead. The concern and sincerity in his eyes made something pool in my gut, though I'm not sure what it was.

"I meant what I said, Petra. *Be careful.*" The words fell from his lips with such intention that I swore I could feel them clang against the inside of my skull. I nodded and he released my wrists. Without another word, he turned away.

I stood in the wind and the grass and the salty air, my head left swimming in the harbor.

"Wait!" I yelled. I'm not sure what possessed me to call out to him as he walked back toward the city, but the word flew from my mouth before I could stop it. Calomyr halted, half-turning back toward me. "I have questions for you." I marched toward him, aware of how small I must have looked considering his towering height.

He looked past me, to the harbor. Worry creased his eyes as he turned his gaze down toward where I stood in front of him. "I'm afraid I cannot answer them." The smoke in his voice was upsettingly tempting, feelings of warmth colliding with feelings of grief in the pit of my stomach.

I leaned closer to him with each question, my finger jamming into his chest. "How do you know that's what I'm looking for? Why is that something you'd notice?" I pressed. He drew in a deep breath, trouble written across his features as the wheels of his mind turned, grinding against each other. He simply shook his head. "*Why?*"

"It's a part of my job," he murmured.

"And what, pray tell, is your job?" I stabbed a pointed finger into his chest.

"I'm... I'm in the Royal Guard." He was visibly uncomfortable, squeezing the back of his neck.

I scoffed. "The Royal Guard?" He nodded, his gaze still distant. Impossible. He was far too young. "How and why the fuck does the Royal Guard know what happened to my father?"

"I was there after Cindregala too, you know," he blurted. My brows furrowed. "The day your sister died. And I did my job then, too. Tried to figure out what went wrong. Tried to figure out if there was any threat to Eserene." My nostrils flared. "Cigar," he confirmed.

"That doesn't explain why you know anything about my father's cloak."

"I need you to trust me." I searched his face, thinking of a thousand reasons I shouldn't trust him. Something in the back of my mind caught my attention when he spoke — a tiny shimmer of *something* that told me to trust him. "Do you trust me?"

"No!" I spat, my gaze falling to the thick grass. "Why the hell would I trust you?" I could see words begin to form on his lips before dissolving into silence. His pupils dilated and constricted as his mind ran a mile a minute. "*What?*" I seethed.

"One day, I will tell you everything," he said quietly.

"What the fuck are you talking about?"

"One day, Petra, I will tell you everything. I swear in the presence of the Saints that I will tell you everything." My veins turned to ice.

186

"I don't know what kind of game you're playing, Calomyr. I don't know who you are. I don't know what to do with these bits and pieces of the truth."

"I'd like to show you something," he breathed. "Come with me."

I planted my feet firmly in place and crossed my arms. "Absolutely fuckin' not."

"Please," he said.

Da's face flashed in my mind, his warm smile, his kind hazel eyes. Calomyr knew a lot more than he let on, all of which I was determined to find out. "Where?"

He flashed a smile that was heartbreakingly beautiful, full of every answer I needed but he wouldn't — or couldn't — give me. "You'll see."

And somewhere in the hurricane of raw grief and confusion that thundered in my brain, I told myself that if I followed him, he'd give me what I needed.

◆ ◆ ◆

"You're out of your damned mind," I snapped, assessing the narrow path that butted up against a tiny inlet in the cliffs I didn't know existed. We were on the western side of the cliffs with only the sound of the wind and each other. I shook my head for emphasis.

"I swear to you I won't let anything happen." He was below me on the steep decline, one foot propped on a small boulder.

"And why should I believe that?"

"You believed me earlier, didn't you?" I still wasn't sure I did, but the grief that was a constant presence in my body muddied my emotions, my decisions. Maybe he'd kill me. Maybe that would be easier for my mother to understand than suicide. All I knew was that I felt reckless enough to entertain the thought. He reached out to me with a calloused palm, evidence of time swinging a sword. Soldier's hands.

Honest hands.

I glared at him as I stepped forward and took his hand. "Are you going to kill me?" I asked, eyes narrowed.

His face drew in shock. "Is that what you think of me?"

"I don't know what I think of you."

"Why don't you find out?" With that, he guided me to stand in front of him and step out onto the path. "You walk in front and I'll make sure you don't fall."

"Sounds like something one might say before pushing another off a cliff."

He chuckled, the sound somehow gruff and soft at the same time. A muscled arm became a barrier between me and the sharp rocks that waited in the harbor below. The inside of his arm brushed my shoulder with every step I took, trying to keep my focus on the path ahead. "It's not too far."

"And how did you find this mystery location?" I asked incredulously, my gaze forward.

He gave a short, deep laugh, his breath tickling the back of my neck. I could have sworn I heard a bit of melancholy in his chuckle. "My brother and I stumbled upon it as children." The smile in his voice was sad. "We'd trek out here and spend the day climbing the cliffs and playing with wooden swords in the caverns."

"The caverns?"

"In due time, Miss Petra."

"And where is your brother now? Is he out harassing Inkwellian women with cryptic answers on their search for the truth?"

"He fell from the cliffs when he was twelve years old."

I stopped in my tracks, his steps pausing behind me. I pivoted to face him, staring up into his eyes. I recognized the pain on his face, had seen it on my own a million times. The world ceased around me, the sea and the cliff and the dangerously narrow strip of rock we stood upon just a wisp in the wind. "How old were you?"

"I was fourteen."

"Is he buried in the Backwoods?"

"He wasn't buried. We never...no one ever found him. Swept out to sea."

"I'm sorry," I said, my words clear and intentional. "No one in this world should have to lose a sibling so young." He gave

188

a curt nod and nudged me forward, but I placed my hands on his broad chest. It was solid beneath my palms, a sure, steady presence that was most welcome. "I mean it, Calomyr." His eyes hit mine once again. "I am so, so sorry."

Something about the way his face softened, the way his shoulders loosened caused my stomach to flip. In that moment, we weren't strangers that had somehow found ourselves standing on the side of a cliff. I wasn't searching for answers and he wasn't withholding them. I wasn't a stupid, stupid girl blindly trusting a man whom I had no reason to trust. We were simply two souls that had broken in a way that not many souls broke, the fault lines jagged and sharp enough to tear up every other part of us.

I turned back to the path and began walking, Calomyr close behind.

◆ ◆ ◆

The cave was no more than a chunk of rock gouged from the cliff face. Enough light reflected from the harbor, barely illuminating the small space, the only sound the lapping waves forty feet below. It was dank, the smell of stale water clinging to my nostrils. Every surface dripped from condensation.

I raised an eyebrow at him. "I'm assuming you *did* bring me here to kill me, then." I was only half kidding.

A rich, sensual laugh broke from his lips, his cheeks dipping into dimples I hadn't noticed before. "I brought you here because I know what you've lost, and that you could use something to remind you of the here and now." He stepped toward me, his gaze intense.

"A damp hole in a cliff was your idea?" My words were sharper than I had intended them to be. "The same cliff my father fell from?"

He recoiled. "That's not what–"

"It's fine," I muttered. "Though I do question your judgment on that one."

Another laugh escaped his lips and I couldn't help but watch as his cheeks rose, crinkling his eyes with a kind of boyish joy. "I brought you here because soon, the sun is going to hit the harbor just right. *Then* you'll see." He lowered himself to sit on a wet rock, reaching into his pocket and pulling out a hunk of crusty bread. "Join me?"

I assessed my options, which included sitting directly on the damp rock, sitting on the equally damp ground, or hurling myself from the mouth of the cave into the sea below. Luckily the rock was wide enough to give us some separation, and I lowered myself to face him, though the third option was tempting. He passed the bread my way, but I put my hand up, shaking my head. "You don't like bread?" he asked, his mouth full.

I had to keep myself from telling him I fucking loved bread. I could eat it for every meal for the rest of my life. But even though I was able to put food on the table, I'd still had a hard time eating for the past few months. "Not hungry," I murmured. The reality of what I was doing, where I was, who I was with sunk into my brain, and I shifted nervously. He could kill me easily if he wanted to. Push me from the cliffs, take the blade from his hip and shove it through my heart, kill me with his bare hands. What the fuck was I doing here?

He swallowed hard, looking at me with his eyebrows raised. "Are you okay?" There was that question again, that question he had asked me on the dirty streets of Inkwell. I hadn't realized how weak the floodgates in my eyes were, buckling under the weight of his question almost immediately. Tears flooded my vision and I turned my head away, but it was too late. He had seen them fall, watched my face contort with pain for a split second.

He sat quietly as I fought the tears, trying to keep my sobs silent. But as I fought my own mind tooth and nail for control, I knew the truth was looming, lumbering closer, no matter how long I avoided it.

I was not okay. I had watched my sister die in front of me just last year. My father had been found dead in the harbor, presumably falling from the cliffs due to his tremors. The absence of his cloak turned that theory on its head and I was spinning along with it. We didn't have enough to eat. My mother was a walking void of despair. She couldn't take care of herself. I slept in the same bed I shared with Larka, waking to Ma's screams every night.

190

I was *not* okay.

I let the sobs overtake me, my heart fracturing into shards that stuck into my ribs. My body shook so hard that I swore the floor of the cave moved. My wails echoed in the dark as I threw my head back in agony. "No!" I screamed, saliva thick on my tongue. "No, no, no!" I beat my fists on the rock beside me, the skin breaking after the first few strikes. Blood began to pour down my wrist. "They're gone!" I screamed, over and over, my throat raw, blood splattering on my face with every strike of my fist, just like it had when I beat my father's chest. I rose, looking for something, *anything* to destroy, anything to represent a tangible piece of this pain, this agony. I wanted to tear my heart out and throw it in the harbor, let the beasts of the sea rip it to shreds. I didn't want to feel anything anymore.

Arms around me. Warmth behind me. A chin resting on the top of my head. And calm. I was calm. The storm inside of me settled, the violence quelled. The screams that had formed in my throat dissolved in the heat that radiated into my back. My breathing evened. I had never felt more...calm. Protected. I knew I should have wanted to wrench myself from his grip, but I just...couldn't.

Calomyr turned me to face him, his face plastered with concern as those liquid oceanic eyes looked into mine. "You won't be okay for a while. But you will be okay again."

"Why do I believe you?" I murmured. A peculiar feeling set in, because for some reason, *I did.* I believed that he hadn't hurt my father. I trusted him with the knowledge he couldn't give me. Why?

"Why shouldn't you?" he said quietly. I inhaled deeply, grounding myself. "Sit," he said, motioning downward as he lowered himself to the rock. "Tell me about them."

Chapter 21

Now

None of the members of the Board of Blood so much as looked in my direction as the snake lay dead on the ground.

Except Ludovicus.

His stare was so intense that I felt like I could reach up and grab it, like it was a tangible thing that I could wring dry and snap in half.

Augusta, Estelle, Cora, Alira, and I remained, the whistling of Iridia's painfully shallow breathing echoing in the large hall. Willow had awoken screaming soon after Iridia had been dumped beside her, but her shouts were quickly extinguished by Garit's handkerchief shoved down her throat.

"My darlings, you have done wonderful thus far," Raolin said, clasping his hands together. His gaze never once rested on me. Murmurs of agreement rang through the line of men on the dais as the nervous energy fluttered. "It is time to see whether the Benevolent Saints deem you worthy of Royal standing." His voice sent a shiver down my back, the goosebumps pulling my skin taut. "Let's begin."

The brothers rose, each approaching a large wooden box that sat on the left edge of the dais. Ludovicus stayed seated, his chin propped on his thumb while his fingers rested on his cheek, his onyx eyes playful. A smile tugged the right corner of his mouth upward. I didn't break his stare no matter how badly every ounce of me yearned to be free from it.

The other brothers approached us holding manacles, each of their faces adorned with menacing smiles. "Stay still," crooned Arturius. They began to shackle our hands behind us, lifting the hems of our monstrous gowns to chain our feet together. Higgins and Arturius tended to my chains, neither of them saying a word nor looking at my face. I didn't fight it. The thick metal cuffs on my ankles were a stark contrast to the delicate silver high heels they rested against. All this time spent practicing walking in these Saints damned things only to be given steel cuffs to wear over them.

"The rules are simple," Anton tittered. The men stood in front of us, their gazes still intentionally avoiding me. Ludovicus stayed perched in his seat, preternaturally still. A cold sweat broke on my brow as my mind ran over the possibilities of what was about to transpire. Was this what Marita was talking about when she said I wouldn't be able to defend myself? "Each brother will commit one...*act* against each of you beautiful ladies. If the Benevolent Saints approve of you, you will be rewarded." A wicked smile painted his face. "Your life remains yours. You will need a favor from Onera, Saint of Miracles, to survive this." Anton strode over to a box, clicking his tongue as his hand hovered over it. "Ahh," he breathed. "Like an old friend." He pulled out a long whip, the braided leather dull in the candlelight. My mouth went dry.

He stepped toward Augusta. She recoiled, which only made Anton's amusement flare. "Turn," he said. Her eyes were wide, her shoulders forward in as much of a defensive position as she could manage with her hands behind her back. Her porcelain skin looked pallid in the light of the throne room. I saw the wheels of her mind turn as she contemplated how she could escape, how she could end this — then saw it melt to defeat as she realized there was no way out. She turned around slowly, the top half of her back exposed above her pure white gown, her hands laced so tightly together that her fingers were red.

Silence fell. Everyone was still. I had expected Anton to predicate his strike with a snide remark, but before I knew it the whip was flying through the air, landing across Augusta's back with a nauseating *snap*. The scream that left her shook the room as she sank to her knees, the manacles clacking together. An angry red welt had appeared with a canyon of broken skin down the middle. Blood dripped, the top of her perfectly white gown turning the color of Raolin's ruby eyes.

Alira turned to me, her eyes wild with fear. I set my jaw and kept my face blank, hoping that my lack of emotion would calm her down. Her head flew from side to side as her twin whimpered through her gag in the back of the room.

Anton gave a slight nod before moving on to Estelle, Augusta's cries of pain still echoing through the chamber. He pointed his finger in the air, wagging it in a small circle. The rest of the board members' faces were set in sickening grins, watching the horror in front of them as if it were a theater show put on just for them. Estelle turned, her head held high but tears streaming down her face. The whip came down across her back and her scream matched Augusta's. An identical wound opened, splitting her slim, pristine back in two. Her gown began to turn red.

Cora's fear was palpable, and her blood curdling scream clanged through my head like a cathedral bell as Anton snapped the whip across her back. I could feel Alira's eyes on me but I didn't look over at her — I couldn't, or else I'd break not only a rule, but I'd break in fear as well.

Anton moved before Alira, gesturing to her to turn. She did so, her body shaking with sobs. Willow screamed through her gag, kicking her legs on the marble floor as she watched her sister concede to the wicked man's order.

Her eyes were squeezed shut, harsh tears pouring from the corners. Her mouth moved in prayer, barely above a whisper. "Onera, Saint of Miracles, please offer your protection and guard my life with—"

Snap.

The whip landed higher than Anton's previous strikes, catching her in the back of the neck as the whip wrapped around her throat. Anton followed through with his motion and pulled the whip back, but it had already encircled Alira's neck. Her body flew backwards, the sound of her neck snapping pierced the air before her head smacked on the marble.

The muffled scream that left Willow could have brought this castle down. It was the sound of a sister watching her other half die in front of her. Willow's screams were my own.

"Oh, dear," Anton said quietly, standing over Alira's body. Her head was angled as if a single movement would sever it from her body, eyes wide and staring into the abyss. "That was certainly not my intention." The other board members chuckled beside him. "Now her pretty dress will stay white forever. A shame to meet the Saints having bled not for them. Higgins?" Higgins nodded and stepped forward, slinging Alira's body across his shoulder, the ruffles of her skirt cascading across his torso. He dumped her next to Willow, whose sobs had gone quiet, so deep and so painful that they could not be heard by others.

Slowly, Anton raised his gaze to me. I sensed something ripple off of him — uncertainty. This tiny vulnerability was all I needed to keep going. He stepped over the body of the dead snake toward me, looking down his nose wearing a mask of disdain. "Turn."

I made sure to stare into his eyes for one extra moment. An extra moment I used to communicate that he would not break me, that not a single fucking member of the Board of Blood would break me. For a split second, his gaze folded in on itself in understanding. It was enough to give me the strength to turn.

Shoulders back, chin high, jaw set, I bared my back to him, but the snap of the whip and the pain that followed proved to me that even though I bore a keeper's crown, not a single Saint was listening.

◆ ◆ ◆

Cora fell to the ground when an arrow sank into her thigh. Her screams were just a few of a constant symphony of pain and terror echoing off the columns of the throne room. She clasped her hands together, staring up at Arturius. "Mercy! Please, Sir, I beg of you. Mercy!"

Arturius looked down his nose at the girl on the floor, a red rose of blood blooming on the skirt of her dress around the arrow that had impaled her. *An arrow. They were shooting us with arrows.* He bent down on one knee, slinging the bow across his back and meeting her gaze. "You, sweet girl, are not worthy." He stood, grabbed her by the shackled wrists, and dragged her across the floor to the columns in the back. The red rose on her gown left its petals in a trail behind her as she begged and pleaded. She was chained and gagged like the rest of them. Her cries of pain made the bile rise in my throat as Arturius wrenched the arrow from her flesh and her head dropped back. Her chest still heaved, but she was unconscious.

The blood didn't flow from my leg as quickly as Cora's had, thankfully, but my dress still showed the evidence. I took Arturius' arrow in my leg just as I took Higgins' mace strikes to my ribs. I could feel my consciousness slipping away as my ribs cracked, but I remained standing. I was almost positive that every one of the bones in my left foot was broken after Garit's hammer came down upon them, crushing them all under its wide iron head. Augusta finally broke and begged mercy through pained screams over her broken foot, promising to dedicate herself to the Saints and the service of the Board of Blood in exchange for her life. Her pleas fell on deaf ears and she was chained to a column and gagged.

I stayed silent as Raolin's fist landed solid in my gut, his knuckles encased in a large ring of metal. Estelle made it as far as Raolin's blow before emptying her stomach onto the floor, the vomit mixing with a pool of blood. She and I looked at each other, strangers understanding that death was imminent.

Balthazar approached Estelle with a wooden club as thick as his leg. Estelle's chin was as high as she could hold it, her white dress now crimson. He raised the club, but Estelle yanked against her chain, trying to cover her face with her hands. He stopped. "Have you forgotten the rules, darling Estelle?" he purred. She said nothing, returning her arm to her side. Without another word, Balthazar swung the club, striking her across the face. The force knocked her to the ground where she landed with a wet slap, the blood and vomit on the marble splashing like harbor waves around her. Teeth flew from her mouth, landing like pebbles in a puddle. I couldn't tell if the blow had killed her or simply knocked her unconscious, but Balthazar chained her to a column nonetheless.

I was the only one left.

Balthazar strode to me, smacking the club in his hand. "Ah, my dear Petra," he hissed. "Such strength you've shown." I said nothing, my stare steady on his. "Let's see if the Benevolent Saints will see you through."

I heard the air whoosh around the club and then I was on the floor, stars swimming in my vision–

"Petra," I heard in a sweet voice. "Petra, come downstairs. I made breakfast." I tried to move my feet toward the familiar voice but they wouldn't budge. "If you don't come down here, Da's going to eat it!" Larka. Da. And another voice calling my name, a female voice I didn't recognize. I was afraid to move because I knew that the moment I began to pad toward the stairs, the words would dissipate. I knew this wasn't real. Tears flooded my eyes as I rolled my head back and forth, spitting blood. I opened my mouth to scream that I was on my way, sure that if I responded it would make it real, but candlelight was flooding in, the room was on fire and–

I was alive. *I was alive.*

Rolling onto my side, I let reality take hold again. I sat up, my bones protesting, my muscles on fire. I pushed myself clumsily off the bloody floor, the shackles clanging against each other as I stood once again. The Board of Blood stared at me, their faces blank except for Higgins whose mouth hung slightly agape. Wiping my face on my bare shoulder the best I could, I straightened as tall as my broken ribs would let me, my blood soaked hair stuck to my back. My right eye was beginning to swell shut, but I made sure to look at each and every one of the men in front of me.

Ludovicus rose, stepping down from the dais. "My turn."

The men parted to make way for their leader as he strolled toward me. My shoulders rose and fell in great heaves, each breath seeming to crack my ribs further. My thigh throbbed where the arrow had been wrenched away. Ludovicus circled me, his hands behind his back.

"The Saints have smiled upon you today, Petra," he said in an amused growl. "Inkwell must raise them scrappy. Strong." Still, I stayed silent, keeping my eyes locked on his, blood dripping from my chin down my dress. I was unsure whose blood I wore, but I was sure not all of it was mine. "Born on the Night of the Holy Stone of Blood Saints. Did you know, Petra, that you were the only child born in Eserene after the sun went down that day? The only child born when the world was darker than Hell itself?" I fought the urge to narrow my eyes. The pain in my ribs grew worse as rage built inside my chest at his pointless babbling. Ludovicus continued to circle. "It comes only once every three hundred years, you know. Some say those born that night are given the gift of Saints' blood." He paused in front of me, leaning his head close to my face. "What do you think of that?"

"Bullshit," I said flatly, spitting blood onto the floor. Eyebrows raised throughout the room.

"Excuse me?" he hissed.

"Bull. Shit." The words were daggers coming out of my bloodied mouth.

Garit lunged toward me but Anton and Higgins held him back as Ludovicus raised his palm in their direction. Ludovicus cocked his head, his eyes narrowing as a nauseating smile graced his lips. He leaned closer to me, his lips just inches from mine, but I did not break my gaze. "The holiest night of the year, and the Saints decided to grant life to a disgusting little *bitch.*"

"The Saints have done nothing for me," I uttered, my voice low, just as solid as his.

He pushed his lip out in a mocking face. "That isn't true, now is it?" His voice had turned whiney, his tone a knife on glass. "You've survived thus far, have you not? You don't believe there is any divinity behind that?" He leaned closer still and I was afraid that if our lips met I would gag. "The time has come to find out," he whispered in my ear, each word clinging to my bones. I swallowed hard, staying silent. Finally, he nodded, pulling his head away, motioning for the brothers to retrieve something from the chest.

The Book of Saints.

"The time has come to take your vows," Ludovicus said. "Then you will be ready for your final challenge. Please step forward, sweet Petra." I obeyed, holding in a groan at the pain. He dipped his chin slightly and Arturius and Anton shuffled to me, producing keys from their pockets and unlocking my shackles. I rolled my wrists and ankles.

The fucking dagger. I still had the dagger strapped to my leg, something I had forgotten while having the life beat from me. My hands were free, if I could just–

"Right hand on the Book," Ludovicus commanded, holding the Holy Book in his hands. I reluctantly placed my hand on it, the leather uncomfortable and unfamiliar, like the Saints knew I was a waste of their time. I just needed the dagger... "Please, recite the following vows. For the crown, you will bleed."

I took a deep breath, flexing my jaw against the pain. "For the crown, I will bleed." My hand grew warm upon the book. It felt every bit of wrong.

"For the Court you will bear."

"For the Court, I will bear." The other brothers snickered quietly.

"For the King you will live."

"For the King I will live." And where was King Belin through all of this?

"And for the realm..." A pause, the leather growing warmer under my fingers. Ludovicus' eyes rolled slightly back in his head. If I could maneuver the right way, I could get to the dagger and send it flying into his throat before he knew it. "You will die."

"For the realm, I will die."

"Very good," Ludovicus whispered.

The men moved behind me. "Your final test, my darling." Balthazar walked to the wooden box and picked up a sheathed dagger, the gemstones laid in gold catching the light as he placed it in Ludovicus' palm. I didn't know if those chained alive to the columns had died or if my brain shut them out, but a silence fell, so thick and eerie that it made me want to weep, made me want to hide. "Katia, Keeper of the Benevolent Saints, deserves something so precious, don't you think? And how lovely that you've worn a diadem matching hers." He unsheathed the dagger. "Walk to me, curtsy, and present your wrist, please."

The brothers looked to me expectantly. Everyone was dead or dying. No one was here to save me. It was on me to make it through.

My feet moved of their own accord, my eyes glued on Ludovicus as his lips turned up in a smile so wicked I felt it in my bones. I reached him, the humiliation of conceding to the cocksucker creeping in. My knees bent and I dipped into a curtsy in front of him, raising my wrist to his waiting hand, just as I'd been instructed. Just as I had practiced. *Do something, dammit.*

As I thought he would, he placed the dagger to my wrist, a bead of blood forming where the blade broke my skin. Without a word, he dragged it across, an angry stream falling to the floor. The pain was nothing compared to what I had already endured, barely a wince passing my face. "In the name of Katia, Keeper of the Benevolent Saints." The brothers repeated the sentiment. The room vibrated. He lifted my chin with a spindly finger, urging me to rise.

Then, without severing his gaze from mine, he pulled my wrist to his mouth and closed his lips around the wound. Horror wrapped its fist around me as I watched him suck the blood from my veins, his pointed fingernails caressing the back of my hand. The brothers were silent behind him. My face heated at the violation, the familiar all-consuming fury pounding against my broken ribs. I was unable to move, unable to pull away.

Ludovicus dropped my wrist, throwing his head back as my blood dripped down his chin, tiny droplets splattering at his feet.

His head dropped forward again, eyes slowly fluttering open. The onyx had somehow grown darker, layers of obsidian and ink and the deepest pits of Hell swirling like a midnight storm. The veins in his eyes swelled until there was no white left — only the colors of death.

"My darling Petra," he whispered, his voice thick with my blood. "It's you." He closed the gap between us but I jumped out of his reach. The brothers were closing in around me as the wound on my wrist oozed. "It's *you*."

My brain swelled with fear as they closed in around me. I scanned all of my escape options, my vision red as I blinked the blood from my eyes that dripped down from my scalp. What had the soothsayer said? *Your blood will spill, girl, from your eyes like they're hoping.*

Shit.

I needed to get the dagger, but my skirts were so thick and heavy with blood that I didn't know if I could raise them quickly enough to grab it. I could attempt to break through the circle of brothers, but I was sure I wouldn't make it far before being killed or captured. I could attack and hope to injure one severely enough to throw off the others. But then where would I go?

"We've been waiting a very, very long time for you, my dear," he hissed, a crooked smile exposing his blood soaked teeth. "We did it, brothers," he purred. "And we've found you while you're still human. Absolutely delightful." *Still human?* How the fuck could I get this dagger into my hand, into his chest—

All seven doors to the throne room flew completely off their hinges with an ear splitting crack, the wood splintering as the doors hit the floor. Dozens of masked men sprinted in with bows and swords drawn and ready.

A bellowing voice cleaved the air. "Get the fuck on the ground!"

Chapter 22

Then

I stared at the ground, silent for a long while. How could I tell a stranger the memories that made up a life? How could I put into words the dynamic of our little family? I didn't know where to start.

So, I started from the beginning. The tiny upstairs bedroom. The cold. The stale porridge. Death. So much death. My mother, and how she and I no longer had the relationship we once had; how frustrated I was with her that I had to bear the burden of our survival. Tears came and went from my eyes as memories passed, smiles and laughter following. Calomyr listened intently the entire time, asking questions when he needed to.

"Why do you think the healer treated him without charge?"

"Do you really think there are people watching you?

"Where would you go if you could leave Inkwell?"

When I had exhausted every possible detail I could think of, I turned to him. "And you? What is your story?" He straightened, averting his gaze. "I laid my entire soul bare before you, a stranger. The least you can do is tell me *something*."

He chewed the inside of his cheek, stifling a smile, looking out of the mouth of the cave at the gulls hovering over the harbor. He was so uniquely beautiful I struggled to tear my gaze away. "Bastard born in Taitha." My eyes widened. Everyone in my life was born and raised in Eserene. I had never met someone from the outside. "We had a small hut on the outskirts of the city, in the rolling farmlands to the south. My mother was a baker. She baked everything in our own kitchen. If I close my eyes I can still smell the biscuits and pans of layered pastries she baked every day." I saw his eyes move behind their lids. "My younger brother was a bastard, too, but we never considered what it meant to be fathered by different men. Tobyas was my brother, plain and simple. We looked very much the same, a bit different in the jaw and cheeks, but the main difference was our eyes. My green is identical to my mother's eyes. She always told me the blue matched my father's, that it was so unique, so unlike anything she'd ever seen that I'd know him the second I met him. And Tobyas' eyes were dark, close to black, like his father's. I had hoped that one day I'd meet a strange man with the same blue eyes and know it was my father. Tobyas wanted the same." The blue in his eyes was indeed unlike anything I'd seen. "We always imagined that our fathers would be best friends." A sad chuckle left his mouth. He shook it away, rolling his neck.

I inhaled sharply as I watched the pain flash across his face. "My mother... she—" My palms started to sweat. His words were quiet, clipped.

"You don't have to tell me—"

"I think I want to tell you."

I narrowed my eyes. "You think?"

"Yes. I'm not sure why. I probably shouldn't. But I think I want to tell you. I haven't told anyone in a long time." I could tell by the look on his face that a part of him died a long time ago. Who had he told before? Had it been harder to talk about it then? He rested his elbows on his knees, letting his hands hang between them. "The only experience I had with death before that day was an old woman who lived on our road. She was covered in veils,

203

carted away to be buried, and that was it. For death to enter my home like that, to see the contents of my mother's head spill on the floor, to watch the light leave her eyes..."

I gasped at his words. "She...she was–?"

"Murdered. Yes." He ran a hand through his dark hair, a stray strand falling across his forehead. "All I could do was jump in front of Tobyas to try to protect him."

"You saw the whole thing?"

His mouth settled into a grim line, a silent confirmation. "A man kicked the door down into our hut. No warning, face covered in a black mask. We barely had time to react before he grabbed my mother and without a word drove her head into the stone floor. Over and over and over again, until..." He swallowed hard. "Until I couldn't even tell it was her anymore. She fought at first, but it didn't take long for..." A silent inhale. "And that was it. The man stared at me and Tobyas for a moment before he ran out the door. Just...stared. I felt him looking past me, at Tobyas, even from behind his mask. And then he was gone." He paused, looking around the cave as if he could see the day among the dips and shadows. "There was an old man who lived next to us, and he heard the screams. When the killer fled, he ran to us. 'Get to Dry Gulch and find the caravan. They'll lead you over the border of Widoras to Eserene.' He pulled us into his hut, filled a canvas bag with bread and honey apples and pushed us down the road. 'Go!' he screamed at us. Dry Gulch was only a day's walk to the south, but the day was filled with Tobyas' constant questioning. 'What's happening?' 'Where is Mother?' 'Where are we going?'"

His brow angled up, the anguish on his face not foreign to me. His eyes were suddenly molten and frozen at the same time, the line between green and blue hardening as I watched the emotions flow through them. Sadness. Anger. Pure *rage*. And bitter, bitter defeat.

"When did this happen?" I whispered.

"Eighteen years ago now. I was nine." Nine years old. He was a *child*. "A kind woman, no older than you are now, found us wandering in the town square at Dry Gulch and pointed us to the caravan. I don't remember being able to speak much, but it was like she knew exactly what had happened the moment she saw us.

She gave us a piece of parchment and told us to wait near the city gates when we arrived in Eserene, that someone would come for us. It turned out her sister had been taking in displaced children that found their way to the city. Lived in Prisma."

"Displaced children?"

"There had been a lot of violence and unrest across all of Cabillia, Taitha especially. It had been going on for years at that point. Still is. There were uprisings and riots and so many things a nine year old boy shouldn't know about. But we joined the caravan. King Umfray wasn't too keen on letting in refugees, so not many groups were let in. We were lucky, and sure enough a woman found us waiting by the Eserenian city gates."

"Was that..."

"My aunt, yes. Berna." He gave the same sorrowful, reminiscent smile I had seen more than once today. "Not my aunt by blood, of course. But she's the one who took us in."

The aunt he had buried. I thought he said she had lived in Inkwell, not Prisma...but now was not the time to pry. "I'm so sorry." I fought the urge to reach out and touch him. That maddening half smile appeared on his face, one dimple on his cheek.

"Such is life, Petra."

"Such is life," I sighed. "And what's your position in the Royal Guard?"

Before he could answer, thousands of glittering specks of light suddenly flooded the cave, tiny rainbows refracting across the walls. It was raining diamonds, a swarm of crystalline honey bees in a hive. The sun had hit the waves in the harbor just the right way to reflect its light on the ceiling of the cave, which I now saw was a solid bed of crystal.

"This," Calomyr murmured, his head slowly bobbing from side to side, watching the lights, "is what I wanted you to see."

I stood slowly, looking down at my hands as the glitter drifted over them, the movement in time with the crashing waves. The crystals that covered the ceiling were set far enough into the rock that unless light shone directly on them, they would be nearly invisible. The jagged points jutted out haphazardly, completely irregular yet somehow arresting in their beauty.

How could something so beautiful, so magical live so close to the dirt pit that was Inkwell? How could this exist in the same world where dirty brothels and empty bellies and decrepit houses are commonplace?

My mouth dropped open in awe. I was aware of how childish I looked but I didn't have the mind to care. "This is the most beautiful thing I've ever seen in my life," I whispered. The specks of light moved across my face, every other one landing in my pupil, the glint captivatingly bright. I felt Calomyr's eyes on me, heard a slight inhale as if he were trying to speak, but couldn't tear my gaze away from the magic that swirled around me. I slowly spun in a circle, following the glimmers across the walls as they moved forward, back, forward, back.

And as suddenly as they came, they were gone. I finally turned to Calomyr to find his intense stare looming, his mismatched eyes burning, the dimples of his cheeks showing. I could feel confusion cross my face as I worked out the logistics of what just happened. "Everyday, the sun hits the harbor *just* right. Magic." The earthiness of his voice filled my senses as quickly as the glittering lights had, consuming me just as completely. I nodded at his explanation, unable to form words. "I told you to trust me."

Chapter 23

Now

I froze, a dozen arrows drawn and pointed directly at me. "Get the fuck on the ground!" someone screamed again.

"I beg your pardon," Ludovicus hissed as my blood still ran down his chin. He stepped forward. "You have interrupted a sacred ceremony. I'm afraid you'll need to see yourselves out." His words dripped with quiet ferocity and self-control. He flipped his hand to shoo the intruders away, as if they were nothing more than a pesky swarm of flies. I could feel the gash across my wrist weeping blood and I held it against my gown that was no longer white. My heart pumped as hard as it could, the sound of it raging in my ears.

A hulking man stepped forward, his bow drawn, silver mask sculpted to look like a roaring bear's face. In one fluid motion he shot at the chain that held the grandiose chandelier above the throne room and it crashed to the ground, exploding in a mess of glass and candle wax across the marble floor. The room was dimmer then, somehow even more sinister.

Ludovicus jumped out of the way stealthily and tutted. "What a shame. Such an elegant chandelier." He crossed his arms and approached the man, glass crunching under his feet. He was only a few inches shorter than the masked man, but he looked miniscule as he stared up. "I am Ludovicus the Wicked. These are my brothers, and we are the Board of Blood. We have been chosen by the Saints. You have intruded upon a sacred Initiation ceremony, and I'm afraid if you don't leave immediately, my brothers will have to act upon the rage of Rhedros at this sign of disrespect." The conviction in his voice made me shiver.

"Ludovicus, you say? I've heard all about you, Ludovicus." I could almost hear a smile come from behind the mask.

"How peculiar, because I have no idea who you are," he muttered.

The man stepped forward, only inches remaining between him and Ludovicus. "You will soon enough. Get. The. *Fuck.* On. The. Ground. Now," he snarled.

Ludovicus simply stepped back, crossed his arms, and raised an eyebrow.

As quickly as a lightning strike, the masked man retrieved an arrow from his quiver, nocked it, and let it fly.

It landed straight in the chest of Arturius.

Anton was the first to scream, hitting the ground beside Arturius who gasped for breath. Blood spurted from Arturius' mouth, dripping down his chin the same way mine adorned Ludovicus'. The humanness of the scene, of witnessing a brother struggle in front of his brothers, the red of his blood, the sound of him gurgling... It almost made me pity him. *Almost.*

I watched Arturius' eyes go dead as the other brothers hit the floor, curling in on themselves in fear. They were able to inflict absolute horror but cowered at the first sign of death. *Fucking* pathetic. I didn't have much time to relish the thought. Ludovicus had remained standing, barely a wince on his face. "Now, now. No need to overreact," he said tauntingly, as if his brother had not just *died.* The masked man raised a fist and struck him across his smug face, knocking him to the ground in a gasping heap.

Ludovicus whipped his head back to the masked man, who was growling under his breath. "I told you to get on the ground."

"If it's violence you crave," Ludovicus said, rubbing his jaw as he stood, "I have five brothers left for you to do with what you please. Take them if you wish, but leave me and the girl." I flinched as much as his brothers did. He would simply hand them over? In exchange for *me*?

A gruff laugh from behind the mask. "You seem very interested in this girl, though I'd say she's more of a woman." The way his voice curled around the words paralyzed me. He leaned into Ludovicus, whispering something to the man who still had my blood on his lips. For a split second, Ludovicus' face blanched, but a fist flew into it. He was unconscious before he even hit the ground.

The sight of Ludovicus falling to the marble would have been satisfying had the masked man not caught me in his gaze. He stepped toward me, his looming figure casting me in the shadows that cloaked the throne room. "Aren't you a pretty little thing," he sneered. "I can think of a few reasons he'd want to keep you." I kept my stare on Ludovicus' unconscious body, letting the sight give me what little strength it could.

The sound of rustling fabric came from the back of the throne room. The masked man turned toward it only to find the eyes of the other girls still chained to the columns watching him. I swore I smelled the fear radiating from their trembling bodies. Estelle was prostrate, dead or close to it. Iridia was still alive, her skin marred with black veins, her eyes swollen, but somehow still choking out ragged breaths. Cora and Willow writhed against their chains as the man in the bear mask walked toward them. Alira's dead body was a heap in the middle of it all.

He looked down upon them, slumped in the corner, chained to the columns. "Already too injured," he called to no one in particular as he gave a slight nod and turned away. "Useless." I watched as two other men, both bearing silver dog masks, stalked toward the other Initiates. One by one, they lifted each girl, dead or alive, and slit their throats. The shock I should have felt never bloomed within me, the previous events of today numbing whatever part of me controlled my flight or fight response. I watched the remaining live girls die and felt nothing.

His boots were heavy on the marble floor as he walked back to me. "On the ground," he spat through gritted teeth. I lifted my gaze to meet the slitted eyes of the mask.

"Who are you?" I said, barely above a whisper but strong. Even.

The bear cocked his head and stepped back. I could hear a smile in his voice when he spoke. "I am Commander Camus Vorkalth. We are the Saints' Regime, and we're here to take you to Kauvras."

Chapter 24
Then

The moonlight cast my room in a soft silver. The sounds of my mother's weeping echoed from downstairs as it had every night since my father's death. Nothing I did quieted her cries, so after a few weeks I began to retreat to my room, leaving her alone.

I lay in bed replaying Calomyr's words from the earlier part of the morning.

And...I believed him. I believed that he was telling the truth, that he was doing his best to help me without compromising his position. It was impressive that he had such a prestigious role at such a young age — he was twenty-seven, from what he'd told me. Even Inkwell trash knows the honor that comes with the role of a Royal Guard.

Then came his story. The heartbreaking image of a little boy trying to protect his younger brother. A lowborn, just like me, trying to make his way in the world, somehow landing a job with the Royal Guard. No father, dead mother, dead brother. The scars he bore to me, the pain he let me see, I wanted to hear more about it.

I wanted to hear more about it.

A feeling of disgust swept through my mind...disgust at myself. Why the fuck did I care about this man's story? I needed to find out more about my father's death, about his missing cloak, about what *really* happened, but here I was enthralled by some gumshoe's tale of woe. The bastard could have been lying about the entire thing. I turned in my bed, pulling the poor excuse for a blanket up to my chin as I pouted. This was *not* a feeling I enjoyed.

Plink. The sound of something hitting the side of the house broke me from my thoughts. *Plink.* What was that? A sick feeling gathered inside me, the creeping suspicion thick in my belly. It was replaced by annoyance when the sound rang again.

Plink.

I sat up in my bed, staring at the dirty, drafty window. Standing and all but stomping to the window, I threw it open to see Calomyr standing on the path that butted up to our house, his palm full of pebbles. Even from here I could see the color of his eyes as the moonlight illuminated his face.

He flashed a smile that made the dimples appear on his cheeks. A shock rang through my body, bouncing off my bones. "Hello," he called quietly, that rich voice smoldering in the moonlight.

"How the fuck do you know where I live?"

"I'm a member of the Royal Guard, remember? Wasn't hard for me to find out."

"Don't members of the Royal Guard have to... I don't know...guard?"

"I have some time off."

"Time off? Didn't think that Royal Guards got time off."

"I can be very persuasive." His eyes almost glowed now.

"Invading my privacy is not a becoming trait," I huffed.

"All this vitriol after the morning we shared together?" A devious grin appeared on his face, his brows raising. I snorted in response. Another smile. "Care to join me for a walk?" *A walk?*

"Why?" Disdain colored my voice. He let out a laugh. It was so genuine, so pure that I almost laughed along with him, reveling in this small moment of joy. I forced my face into neutrality, disgust even, intent to not give him any satisfaction.

"Because today was nice. And I'd like to continue the conversation," he said matter-of-factly.

I pondered his statement. I wasn't afraid of any dangers he could throw my way — I knew Inkwell like the back of my hand, all of its alleys and side streets. I could escape should I need to. Hell, if he killed me, I'd probably welcome it. But did I want to further complicate my life when it was already a mangled mess of grief? Did I want to invite in the struggles of other people while I battled my own? I rested my elbows on the grimy windowpane, never looking clean no matter how much Larka and I had scrubbed it.

Lips pursed, I pulled myself back inside my room and shut the window. What should I do? Larka would have known. She would have told me to toughen up, to march my ass out the front door and take a moonlit walk with a handsome stranger. And she would have waited up until I got home to hear all about it. Saints, she would have loved this. *Don't think, you idiot,* she'd tell me. *Just go.*

I tied my cloak around my neck and padded down the stairs. My mother's weeping had grown quiet but still audible from the kitchen. "I'm going out, Ma," I called toward her bedroom. She didn't respond, and I hadn't expected her to. I stood inside the front door, took a deep breath, and stepped into the summer night, chilly under the stars.

◆ ◆ ◆

The smile that lit his face as I descended the front steps sent heat through my chest. "I didn't think you were going to accept my offer," he said quietly.

"Yet, you waited."

"I did."

"You thought our conversation was so great that you had to track me down at my home and come calling in the night?" I asked incredulously as we fell into step together, walking south toward the harbor.

He looked down at me, the colors of his eyes just visible in the low light. "What if I did?"

"I'd say that's quite disturbing." My tone was firm, because I meant it. It *was* disturbing.

"I didn't mean to disturb you, Petra." His lips formed around my name like honey on a silver spoon. I closed my eyes and shook my head, ridding myself of the fog that had settled over my brain. "Is it okay if we walk to the waterfront?" he asked.

I stopped in my tracks. "Why are you asking me that?" I spat the words with venom, brows furrowed. He turned around to face me, a strand of dark hair falling over his forehead. "Why are you always asking if I'm okay?"

"Because of...what happened," he murmured. "Because it may be a place you'd rather avoid. Because I want to make sure that you're okay."

I couldn't believe what I was hearing. "I'm fine," I said firmly, picking up the pace again. "You asked me if I was okay once. I told you I was fine. You don't need to ask again."

He was quiet. I considered apologizing for my tone, but I kept quiet. We passed the street where the Painted Empress sat, music and screams billowing from the open windows. The torches mounted outside revealed his contemplative expression, the thoughtfulness resounding through me.

"What's your favorite animal?" he asked suddenly.

"What?"

"What's your favorite animal?" He repeated and looked at me expectantly. "It says a lot about a person." I furrowed my brows at him and he offered me a slight smile, innocence on his face.

"A ciakoo," I said without thinking. The answer came out of nowhere, and a small rift began to open in my heart.

"A ciakoo? Really? I haven't seen one of those in ages," he replied.

"Very rare," I added flatly. We walked in silence for a few strides. "What does that say about me?"

His face turned introspective as his gaze stayed fixed on the road ahead. "Well, the ciakoo looks to be solid black at first glance, but the closer you get, you can see that it's not. It's like a painter's palette if they were to try to paint the night sky. Not the canvas, but the palette, where they mix the paint together to try

214

to get the perfect color. It's always a mess but it's always more interesting to me than the actual painting. Blues and purples, even some emeralds if you look at the palette in the right light. I think it means that there's a lot more to you than what you see at first glance."

I rolled my eyes. "Wow, all that from my favorite animal?" I said sarcastically.

He laughed and I swore the night sky lightened a shade, revealing the colors on the painter's palette. "Make of it what you will." He shrugged.

"What's your favorite animal?" I asked.

A half smile revealed a single dimple. "A kelpie."

I scoffed. "Kelpies have been extinct for a hundred years."

"Doesn't mean they can't be my favorite," he quipped.

"Okay, and what is that supposed to say about you?"

"I embody a kelpie. They're soldiers of Katia. I'm a soldier of the Kingdom. Strong. Elusive. Mysterious." I couldn't help but roll my eyes again and laugh.

"You're not doing a very good job at being elusive or mysterious. I thought you said you had no further business in Inkwell?"

"So you think I'm strong?" he retorted.

"Answer my question, you prick."

He chuckled. "I have no further business in Inkwell."

"So why are you here?"

He laughed and shoved his hands in the pockets of his trousers. He inclined his head slightly, then looked down at me. "Why do you think I'm in Inkwell?"

Heat rose in my cheeks and I was grateful to be away from any torches that could reveal my blush. I didn't answer. Larka had always been the one to catch the male gaze, not me.

The harbor yawned in front of us and the familiar chilly breeze wrapped itself around me. We walked in comfortable silence under the cloudless night. Stars dotted the sky as if a needle had been poked through black silk and a candle lit behind it. The air was cool enough to feel crisp in my lungs, the bite a welcome feeling.

We strolled to the railing, both resting our elbows against the wood. A few hundred feet away, a piece of railing had snapped that changed my life forever, the explosion resounding across the harbor, off of the buildings–

He let out a contented breath, snapping me from my spiral. "So the Royal Guard, then?" I asked.

"The Royal Guard," he sighed wistfully, nodding his head.

"How'd that one happen?"

He was silent for a moment. "My aunt had been married to a civilian commander in the Eserenian army before a fever took him years and years ago. Before I was even born. He still had friends serving who owed him a few favors." He let out a soft chuckle. "Getting me in was where their favors ended though. Worked me harder than any other cadet."

"Sounds shitty."

"It *was* shitty." He blew a breath through puffed cheeks and ran his hand through his untamed hair. Without another word he lowered himself to the ground, his feet dangling over the seawall, forehead resting against the handrail. I sat down next to him. My forehead was nowhere near the handrail and my legs were comically shorter than his, but his looming presence was somehow a warm comfort next to me. I was careful not to inch too close to him. "The training panned out, though. His old buddies became my buddies, even if they had twenty years on me. Worked my way up the ranks to the Guard." A half smile, the moonlight bouncing off the harbor to those eyes, shining like two tidepools in the soft glow of the small hours of the night.

"And tonight is just a night off?" I asked, raising an eyebrow.

"More or less."

"Like I said, I didn't think guards got nights off."

"Like I said, more or less." I shot him a sideways glance signaling that I wouldn't question him further, and the comfortable silence surrounded us once again, punctuated only by the sound of the waves lapping on the seawall.

"Tell me about your brother." The words came out before I realized I was speaking them. I clapped a hand over my mouth. "I'm so sorry, I didn't mean to–"

216

"It's okay," he said with a sorrowful smile. "Tobyas."

"Tobyas, right," I repeated back to him.

"We used to climb the cliffs," he started, his gaze remaining over the water. "My aunt would tell us we were going to break our necks, get stuck on some jagged outcrop, drown in the waves below, but she never stopped us from exploring. So we'd each grab a honey apple and set out, walking through the city to the Cliffs of Malarrey, scaling faces that were far too steep, jumping off of rocks that were far too high. We'd come home with skinned knees and bloody noses, the occasional jammed finger." He flexed his hands, bracing them on the handrail. "We were untouchable out there, or so it felt like. We'd spend hours looking for hidden caves, finding Eserenian crystals, discovering new footholds that would get us to new parts of the cliffs. I think the day we found the cave with the lights was one of the best days of my life. We couldn't believe it.

"And then one day it happened." The light in his eyes dimmed as his voice lowered. "He just...lost his footing. Nothing exciting, nothing any more daring than usual, just one bad step." The familiar pain of loss lanced through me, my stomach turning. "I was a bit ahead of him, on a plateau above. Heard a rock slip and a scream, and the rocks below just..." He took a deep breath. "By the time I got to the edge of the cliff, his body had already gone under. But there was...there was blood. In the water." He paused, silent. "I still hear it though, his scream. Still see the red in the water."

I was silent next to him, sorting through my emotions like tangled yarn in a basket, grief knotted with longing knotted with empathy. "I do too," I breathed. "I see it everyday, hear it everyday. It doesn't leave me. *She* doesn't leave me."

His gaze turned to me, pinning me in place. His hands wrung together and I wanted so badly to reach out and hold them. "It's why I still go to the cliffs," he said. "You'd think it would hurt, being there, and it does sometimes. But *he's* there." I nodded in understanding, so many unspoken words on my tongue that I thought I might choke. "And when I watched what happened at Cindregala...when I realized what was happening, what I was witnessing, what *you* were witnessing..." He shuttered. "I've thought about you every day since, Petra. How I could have stopped it."

The words took me by such surprise that I had to repeat them in my mind. The guilt, the rage I felt at myself for standing there as it had happened, for freezing in place like a fucking idiot, it all bubbled up inside of me. Elin's words. It should have been me. I took a breath to steady myself, the air cooling my insides slightly. I looked up at him, my brows angled upward. "I think about it too," I managed to spit through teeth so tightly gritted that it was a wonder none of them cracked. "You would have liked her."

"If she was anything like you, I'm sure I would have."

"Usually men went for Larka, not for me. Everywhere we went, people stared at her."

"I was staring at you."

I was again grateful that it was too dark for him to see me blush. I didn't know how to answer. Shaking his dizzying words from my head, I turned to face him again. "Everyone loved her. She should still be here. Tobyas should still be here."   .

He rubbed his palms on his thighs, the muscles sculpted by intense training evident even through his trousers, even in the moonlight. I had to tear my gaze away, biting my lip. "And such is life, Petra," murmured, head dropped.

"Such is life, Calomyr." A small smile graced his lips, his golden brown cheeks silvery in the moonlight.

I heard the cathedral bells toll signaling midnight had come. I turned my head to the noise, the spires of the ornate building at the base of the castle just visible over the city skyline. He laid back in the grass, and I slowly joined him. And there we lay, admiring the palette the Saints had created while painting the sky, the colors of a ciakoo melting together as if it were just for us.

218

Chapter 25

Now

Kauvras. I fought the bile that stung my throat, the sheer terror threatening to break me. Commander Vorkalth was growling. "Now, pretty thing, get on the ground." I willed my knees to bend knowing this was not a battle I'd win, but they froze just as they had when I watched Larka die. "Or would you prefer to get on your knees for me?" His breath escaped the mask, hot on my face as he took my hand in his, his calloused palm dwarfing mine. A few of the masked men chuckled behind him as he held my hand. My heartbeat was wild. I didn't feel the pain in my wrist or my foot or my ribs or the wound in my thigh. I only felt where his skin met mine and the pure, unadulterated dread that poured into me from his touch.

I hadn't been afraid of death the day I hung over the cliff. I hadn't been afraid of death the day I inhaled so much smoke that my vision turned black. I hadn't been afraid of death the day I was caught stealing in Inkwell. I hadn't been afraid of dying today. I'd been expecting it. I sure as hell wasn't afraid of dying now. But living... The idea of living under the command of Kauvras, the

219

idea of submitting to the commander in front of me stripped me bare. Of *that*, I was afraid. He finally dropped my hand. "Down," he snarled.

I lowered myself to the ground, pausing on my knees to meet the invisible gaze behind his mask. The remaining members of the Board of Blood were silent behind me. Slowly, I crouched to the ground under his glare, making sure to keep as much in my field of vision as I could. How could I get him to kill me rather than kidnap me?

"Prepare the leechthorn," he called behind him.

From the corner of my eye, I watched three masked men move toward Vorkalth while the rest stayed back, bows and swords still drawn. One man produced a cloth bag, while another produced a long glass pipe, and one held matches in his hand. The pipe was dipped into the bag, emerging filled with a fine violet powder. The same hue of violet that had flashed through my mind the past few years, since the day we sat in Ingra's tent.

"Now, since we are on holy ground," Vorkalth started, pacing across the room to the members of the Board, "I will give you each a choice." The remaining brothers were huddled on the floor, Ludovicus still unconscious. "You surrender and take the pipe or you die here and now. I honor the Saints by giving you this choice as in any other situation, it would be made for you. Understood?" His voice dripped with amusement.

He didn't wait for an answer before boots started rushing toward the Board of Blood, masked men yanking huddled figures by pale necks and black hair. Small bolts of satisfaction rushed through me as I watched the soldiers scream in the pasty white faces that had loomed over me mere minutes ago, delighting in my pain. Ludovicus was still in a heap on the ground as the brothers he had turned on so easily were given the choice to live a slave or die now.

I wanted to say I was worried at how much I enjoyed the sight of what came next. I wished I could say that terror was the only thing I felt. But the shock of it all was dotted with bits of pure elation as I watched the so-called sacred group of men be dismantled.

I couldn't hear exactly what was being said through the chaos that echoed through the throne room, but suddenly Higgins was face down on the ground, a man in a stag mask driving a dagger into his back over and over as he cried out, blood pooling around him until he finally stilled.

Raolin was pulled to his feet, his black hair wrapped around the meaty hand of a man in a wolf mask. Raolin's red eyes met mine, pleading and terror emanating from his gaze. I smirked. I *fucking* smirked. It was the tiniest kernel of power, even while I was crouched on the ground. Watching the terror in his eyes melt into outright despair was enough.

A match was lit and held to the bowl of the pipe, small sparks fizzling as the contents began to glow. It was pressed to Raolin's lips as he pulled back, but he was wildly outnumbered and eventually gave in to the visceral instinct to breathe. He writhed against the hands that held him, and Wrena's story flashed through my mind, of the soldiers that ripped each other apart, that ripped themselves apart. In a twist of irony, a masked man produced manacles and shackled his wrists, then his ankles, the entire process taking a team of six to keep him subdued as he raged.

The noises that left his mouth were not human. He writhed against his chains, his limbs thrashing as much as they could while being held by the restraints. An animal. He was passed from soldier to soldier and shuffled to the back of the room.

Garit's throat split open under the dagger of a man in a dragon's head mask as he was propped on his knees. With a nauseating laugh, the man lifted a heavy boot and kicked him over. Anton attempted to fight the man in the lion's head mask holding him, his amber eyes flying about the room. "Hey!" the lion screamed, motioning to a group of men. They came running, methodically pulling Anton to crouch and face the floor, one man pulling his hair toward him while the others secured his body, pulling it away from his head. I realized what was happening as the lion unsheathed a broadsword and held it above his head. A cry erupted from his throat as he swung the blade, severing Anton's head. The men laughed, the one holding Anton by the hair tossing the severed head to the man with the face of a lion.

Balthazar was shuffled to the awaiting men with the pipe, his mouth in a firm line. He looked more dazed than terrified, and like Raolin he glanced in my direction. It took every ounce of me, every single bit of intestinal fortitude to keep myself from shrugging at him. That failed, though, and I raised my shoulders as best I could from the ground. Death may have been reaching for me, but before then, I would revel in their pain.

Balthazar turned his head toward his fallen leader, Ludovicus, the man who had been so willing to give up his brotherhood in exchange for...me.

Balthazar inhaled in a great gasp, having held his breath until he physically couldn't any longer. He sucked in a huge drag of smoke, the coughing fit ebbing momentarily before turning into blind violence. It ripped through him as it had Raolin, and he was chained and paraded to the back, the sound of jeers and shouts from the other soldiers filling the room.

The two chained men had gone feral. "What do you think, Commander Vorkalth?" One of the soldiers holding the chains said. Vorkalth's head nodded once.

The men were held down long enough for their chains to be unlocked before exploding into a tornado of brutality. The masked soldiers stood back and whooped as the men ripped each other apart, blood and hair and chunks of skin flying off of too-sharp nails.

In less than a minute, both men lay dead on the ground, skin ripped to shreds.

Vorkalth raised a fist and all the men went silent. He surveyed Ludovicus' limp body, still crumpled on the floor. He cocked his head, a movement made all the more beastly because of the mask he wore. Suddenly, he turned to me, looking down to where I crouched. "Ludovicus the Wicked, yes?" I gave a slight nod, unsure of the meaning of his question, my face still on the ground. He chuckled as I kept my face straight, peering up from the floor. "Truth be told, with a name like that, I'd always pictured him to be a bit more intimidating. I suppose every time the story is told, the monster gets bigger." He nudged the limp body with a boot. "Seize him," he called to no one in particular, and soldiers descended to chain him. "Kauvras will be happy to see his old

222

friend." *Motherfucker.* The piece of shit knew Kauvras the whole time. Two men lifted him and carried him out, leaving only me.

"Up on your knees," he ordered, and my stomach dropped. I slowly pushed myself up, the bulk of the pain replaced by adrenaline. Keeping my chin down but forcing myself to meet his gaze, I peered up at him from under my lashes. "What a pretty sight. You look as good on your knees as I thought you would," he snarled, eliciting more snickers from the men behind him. "If only we weren't on holy ground..." I swallowed back vomit once again as he grabbed the back of my head, pulling my face to look at him. "So, what will it be for you? Will you take the pipe? Or do you prefer to die by the hands of my men? Either way, I will be having my way with you." His voice was gravelly and his words slithered down my spine like a serpent. Not the regal Nesanian serpent that lay trampled on the bloodied floor. No, the snake that slithered down my spine at his words was wrapped in scales of hatred and unforgiven sin.

"Death." It was an easy answer. Death was an old friend calling to me. Larka and my Da were waiting for me beyond the line that separated life and death. I could almost hear Wrena's sweet laugh, see Marita's gray eyes, feel Cal's hands on my skin. If there was one Saint I knew existed, it was Cyen, Saint of Death, and he was damn good at his job.

My mother's face flashed through my mind. She would be married to Castemont for the rest of her life. But if I survived, what use would I be to her? I'd be carted away, fiending for a drug, ripping myself apart to get it. Ripping others apart to get it. I was dead either way. She was losing her only other child, but even if I had survived today's Initiation, a part of me had died and would never awaken. Death. Easy answer. "I choose death."

Commander Vorkalth lifted his brows. "Do you now?" He paced around me in the same sickening way Ludovicus had. I nodded my head. "Very well then." He jerked his chin and three men were upon me. I didn't fight as they held my hands behind my back, my broken body screaming in pain. I didn't fight as one of them wrapped my hair in a fist and yanked my head back. I didn't fight as one of them pressed a dagger to my exposed throat.

I simply closed my eyes and waited for the blackness to swallow me.

A laugh echoed through the hall, one that was so deeply rooted in depravity that I swore this laugh could have burned down a whole forest. Vorkalth's shoulders jolted as it came from the deepest, most evil pits of his soul. "You thought I'd kill you?" My eyes flew open to find the silver bear's eyes of his mask looking in my direction. "Release her." The soldiers did so with more force than was necessary, and I skidded across the filthy marble floor, rushing to stand. "You're too pretty to kill. You'll be taking the pipe." I opened my mouth to protest but a man had covered my lips with his palm, pulling me back to a kneeling position.

Tears formed in my eyes, blurring my vision. I wanted to reach for the dagger only to plunge it into my own chest. I willed the wound on my thigh to open, to bleed, to drain me of life. I flexed my hand and wrist as much as I could, silently commanding the gash to split further, to bleed quicker. I took deep breaths, fighting through the searing pain of my broken ribs, hoping one was fractured and jagged enough to puncture a lung.

Anything but this.

I fought with everything I had to pull away. It was useless. The burning pipe was brought to my lips. I did all I could to keep from inhaling. "That's it, sweetheart," Vorkalth's abrasive voice hummed in my ear.

No. *No.*

My vision began to darken and I prayed that I could somehow suffocate myself, that I could hold my breath *just* long enough to slip into oblivion...

Vorkalth slammed his fist into my stomach and I gasped in response, the soldiers shoving the pipe into my throat as the smoke poured into my lungs.

Chapter 26

Then

I tried to keep my breath even as we walked, every glance at Calomyr knocking air from my lungs. "So you've met the cowardly Invisible King then?" I prodded. We walked leisurely through the sunlit streets. I wasn't sure if Calomyr noticed we were walking in circles, but I didn't want to point it out. It was an exceptionally clear day, the sun beating down, dust from the poorly kept Inkwell roads hanging like smoke in the air. It was not a pleasant place to be, but I found I didn't mind the tickle in my nose or the grit in my eyes.

"Cowardly?" Calomyr asked.

"What kind of man hides his face from his kingdom?" I didn't understand it.

"You have a point," he answered, contemplative. "I've never met him, but I've seen him. Once."

"Was he ugly?"

"What?"

"Maybe he's hiding his face because he isn't very attractive."

He let out a deep, hearty laugh. "*Not* ugly. Not by my standards, at least. He's young," Calomyr said, shrugging.

Surprise marked my face. King Umfray had been old since before I was even born. I had assumed that the long lost cousin of the King would be close to his age, ancient the day he took the throne and ancient the day he left it to someone else. "Young? How young?"

"Close to my age by the look of it." I gawked at him. "Tall," he continued. "Built like an ox, broad of shoulder, and strong." My mouth bobbed open and closed like a fish out of water. "What?" he laughed.

"Calomyr, are you describing yourself?" I asked sardonically. He laughed, the sound reverberating through my core in a way that caused my cheeks to flush. *Saints dammit.* How the hell was I supposed to hide my blush in the daylight?

"There's the answer. You *do* think I'm strong." His laughter flowed as my face continued to heat. "You can call me Cal, you know. No one ever calls me Calomyr."

I smiled, still trying to hide my face. "Cal," I repeated, my blush rising.

"Are you okay?" Calomyr asked, his voice suddenly dripping in concern. "Your face is red."

Oh my fucking Saints. I felt the shade deepen. "Yes, just the heat, I think. I'm fine." *Stop looking at me.*

He looked around, spotting an alley with a few crates stacked on top of one another haphazardly. Without a word he led me to the shaded alleyway and motioned me to sit on one of the stacks. I did so, reluctantly, trying to hide the embarrassment that was plastered to my face. He reached for his belt where he had a canteen strapped by its neck, unscrewed it and handed it to me.

I wasn't sure if what I was feeling was humiliation for making him think I was overheating when really I was blushing because of his laugh, or disbelief of the fact that the man who knelt in front of me had moved to accommodate me without a second thought. It sat in my chest, and I wasn't entirely sure I disliked the feeling. It was the only thing that concealed the grief, that made it fade away, even if just for a moment. Larka had always told me to trust no one, but she didn't know Cal. She would have trusted him.

"Drink," he urged. I let the sensation of cool water in my throat ground me as he placed the canteen on my lips.

"Why do you do this?" I breathed as his gaze met mine. Kneeling on the filthy ground while I sat on the crates, our eyes were at the same level. I lost all sense of self as I walked the line between the icy blue and emerald green peering back at me.

"Do what?" He cocked his head, furrowing his brows.

"Care."

His face crumpled. "What?"

"You've done nothing but show me kindness." My gaze rested on my hands folded in my lap.

"Petra, I just want to make sure you're okay." The worry in his voice was palpable.

"There's that word again. *Okay.*" I couldn't let him know what those words did to me. Absolutely not.

He let out a breathy laugh. "Would you prefer another word? Alright? Fine?" His hands were on my knees now, dangerously close to my own.

I opened my mouth to assure him that I *was* in fact okay, alright, and fine. The words caught in my throat as I once again met his gaze. Some sort of primal intensity lay just beneath the surface of him, his stare binding me in place. It was somehow ancient, steadfast, lasting, but at the same time it was unfamiliar and strange and new. I had never seen that look in a person's eyes before. A fire that burned blue, a frozen mountain engulfed in flames. Pure want. Pure *need.* A thousand unsaid words that he'd never need to say, because a part of me already knew.

"I'd like to try something," he whispered. I breathed in his smoke and cedar scent, my mouth open slightly, his face mere inches from mine. "Something I've been thinking about since the moment I first saw you." His lips pulled up in a soft smile before he flexed his jaw. His eyes flicked to my mouth. "Something that haunts my mind as I fall asleep every night." His hands rose to each side of my head, his palms flat on the wall behind me. "Something I really, *really* shouldn't do. A *very* bad idea."

I wanted to ask him how anything he ever did could be a bad idea, but my heart pounded so loudly and quickly I could feel it in the base of my skull. I couldn't form words. His lips hovered so close to mine that I could feel the heat from them. He had stopped moving, stopped leaning toward me, his eyes once again locked on mine, something pensive in his gaze.

His gaze flicked from my eyes to my lips, lingering on the latter in a way that set my core on fire. I wanted him, and I wanted him *now*. I took a deep breath and dipped my chin ever so slightly, afraid that if I moved, the moment would dissipate like mist over the harbor.

A smile split his lips, the dimples deep in his cheek as he pulled his hands from the wall, one palm finding my cheek and the other one finding my waist. "The best bad idea I've ever had."

Before he could pull me to him, alarm bells snapped our heads to the street. People began running past the alleyway as shouts began to rise. We looked back at each other the same moment the sunlight that had been spilling into the alleyway turned to swirling shadows. Floating above our heads was a thick cloud of black smoke so dense that it blotted out the sun's rays. "FIRE!" The word was screeched repeatedly by those running down the street.

We rose, silently joining in the crowd, following their movements. Cal's hand rested on the hilt of his sword as we ran. What could cause this much smoke?

My heart lurched into my throat as I saw the crowd pivot left from the butcher's shop, funneling down Copper Street.

My street.

Calomyr reached for my hand as we rounded the bend, a crowd so thick that the street ahead was obscured.

He drew his sword, his other hand still gripping mine. "Royal Guard!" he shouted, ramming his shoulders through bystanders. "Royal Guard! Clear out! Now!" He dragged me behind him, his hand the only thing keeping me standing. I kept my gaze on the dusty ground, sure that if I didn't look, it wouldn't be happening.

We finally broke through the crowd as the sound of my mother's wailing and crackling embers hit my ears, the sound so familiar to me after the last few months that I almost didn't register it. I couldn't tell if her screams came from the house or somewhere in the crowd as our house burned. It was a blazing mass of red and orange and black, flames shooting from shattered windows, black smoke rising to the heavens.

Where the hell was she? Every ounce of my body ached as I considered the possibility of her still being inside, screaming for help, watching death creep in on her. "MA!" I screeched, dropping Calomyr's hand and making a dead sprint for the house. He called out behind me, but his words were garbled by the terror that rattled through me. I heard bits and pieces of her screams, but the noise of the bystanders obscured them. Glass shattered. Planks fell. She was inside.

She was going to die. She was going to die. *She was going to die.*

The front steps had been charred but were still standing, the door wide open to the inferno inside. I leapt up the few feet to the opening, bracing myself against the suffocating heat, the smoke that choked me.

Her figure emerged through the kitchen, silhouetted by flames, her cries blood curdling. "COME ON!" I screamed as loud as my lungs would allow. She had pulled the hem of her shirt up to carry something. Maybe it was the grief, maybe it was the shock, but her movements were slow. *Too slow.* Cracking wood sounded from overhead and the entire house shook. She finally reached me just as Cal appeared in the flaming doorway. "Get her out of here!" I choked out, the smoke coating the back of my throat as my eyes watered.

I watched her figure lower into his arms as I moved back toward the door, toward the clean air. *Almost there. Almost there. Almost th...*

Darkness.

◆ ◆ ◆

My name was being called from some far off place, like the voice that reached me was only an echo that bounced off the mountains and valleys and sky. The darkness was warm, molding to every dip and curve of me. The voice sounded again, a little louder this time. I wanted it to stop.

Let me rest. Please, let me rest now.

My skin was the night sky, the stars freckled across me, a map of everything that was and everything that had ever been and everything that was yearning to be. In this void I was free, I was powerful, I was whole. In this void I felt the Saints calling me home.

"Petra!" It was clear as day, pulling me closer to it. A man's voice. I willed myself to sink back down, deep in the comfort of the darkness, into the arms of Katia. But my vision shook, my brain rattling in my head.

"Go," a new voice whispered, soft and feminine. "You cannot stay here yet. Go."

"She's waking up!" I heard in a voice so rich it ran over my body like smooth velvet. The darkness faded to pewter, to white until an empty street yawned in front of me. The stars on my skin weren't stars at all, but rain — pouring rain.

I gasped, the warmth and darkness pushed out as the suddenly overcast sky materialized in my vision and a deluge of fat raindrops kissed every inch of me.

And then he was there.

Cal stared down at me and I realized the darkness I thought cradled me wasn't darkness at all but his arms under me, his knees propping me up as I lay in the running mud of Copper Street.

Dry. My throat was so, so dry. My eyes burned. My lungs ached. The only respite was the rain that poured down, drenching my skin and hair. "Hello," Calomyr said quietly with a relieved smile, his dimples appearing cheeks streaked with soot and rain.

Before I had the chance to speak, my mother crouched on my other side, throwing her arms over me, her sobs shaking my body. "Petra!" she screamed over and over, her face buried in my neck. I met Cal's eyes over her head, his gaze a steady mix of concern and relief and something darker, deeper. My Ma pulled back, grabbing my face, her hysterical words indecipherable. "Y-you inhaled so much s-smoke and y-you weren't breathing," she said through broken sobs. "I thought... I thought–"

"I'm sorry," I rasped, the words scratching my throat. I nodded my head as much as I could, reassuring her that I was alive, that I was here. "I'm sorry you thought you'd lose me." She threw her head into my neck again and I couldn't tell if it was my tears or the rain pouring down my cheeks.

My mother peeled herself from me, Calomyr still holding me against him. I turned my head at the sound of footsteps to find Solise running up the muddy street, face creased with worry. "*Saints,* Petra!" She kneeled beside me, her fingers going to my wrist to check my pulse. "Are you hurt?"

"I'm okay," I croaked, offering a weak smile. Cal's thumb began tracing circles against my shoulder, the sensation blurring my senses more thoroughly than the smoke had.

She gave me another assessing look before meeting Cal's gaze briefly and turning to my mother. "Irabel?"

"My legs," she whimpered, "I think they're burned."

"Let's get you both somewhere safe. You can stay at my house for now," Solise said.

"I think I'd like to lay here for a while longer," I answered, face heating at the idiocy of asking a healer to leave me lying in the rain. She raised a brow, her keen gaze pinning me in place.

"I'll deliver her to you safely," Cal blurted. "I promise."

Solise pursed her lips before giving a slight nod. "I have a salve for you," she muttered to my mother as the pair turned to leave.

I turned my face back to Calomyr. His gaze was so heavy, so intense that it felt like his very soul was staring directly at mine. I felt his look in every fiber of my being, and I could have sworn I saw him break and come back together all at once. It was a look I'd never seen and didn't think I would again.

"What?" I whispered.

"You're beautiful," he whispered back, raindrops falling from his hair to his slick leathers.

I grimaced at the compliment, turning my head away in embarrassment, but his hand found my cheek and pulled my face toward him again.

"Petra, you are the most beautiful woman I've ever seen," he breathed, voice full of the same pure need I'd seen in his eyes in the alleyway. My chest swelled with emotion as his eyes searched mine. I fumbled for words, but each time I tried to speak they tangled in my charred throat. "I didn't know if you were going to make it out." His features contorted into dismay, his chest rising faster against my cheek as his arms pulled me closer to him.

"Thank you," I started, "for getting my Ma out."

His grip loosened slightly, his face relaxing. "I, uh... I may have dropped her on the ground," he mumbled, his eyes finally tearing from mine. "Yeah. As soon as I was far enough away from the house, I dropped her. Apologies for that."

My face broke into a smile. "I'm sure she'll be fine."

"I didn't drop her hard, I just needed—"

"She'll be fine, Cal," I said again, reaching my hand to cradle his face. His eyes closed momentarily against the touch.

He ran a knuckle over my cheek, his brows upturned as anxiety crossed his features. "I needed to get you out."

His words set my mind spinning as I remembered the last moments before the smoke took me under. I had lost consciousness in the house, which meant... "You...you pulled me from the fire?"

Calomyr's only answer was a slight nod, pulling my hand from his cheek to press his lips to my knuckles. He held them there, eyes closed in a silent prayer.

My breath caught in my throat at the sight, and I knew I needed to look away before I lost consciousness again. I let my gaze wander behind him, to the pile of rubble. The house...it had *collapsed*, wisps of smoke creeping through the air as the last of the embers sizzled out under the rain.

"Are *you* okay?" I asked.

"I'm more than okay," he answered, finally opening those heart-stopping eyes, his lips quirking up in a roguish smile. "Never a dull moment around here, huh?"

Despite the sorrowful truth of that statement, I returned his smile. "Such is life, Cal," I whispered.

His tongue ran across his lips, the smile still lingering. "Such is life, Petra."

And in the muddy street, in the pouring rain, Calomyr lowered his face to mine and kissed me. I surrendered fully to the moment, his movements slow and intentional, as if the world had halted just so we could lose ourselves in each other. He caught my bottom lip between his teeth, smiling against my mouth as he let out a breathy laugh.

This brief moment was my lifeline in a stormy sea of loss.

◆ ◆ ◆

The high of kissing Calomyr quickly disappeared as reality set in once again, my worries beginning to deepen the more I thought about all that had happened.

"Your breathing should improve soon, dear," Solise said as she mixed a small vial into a mug of steaming tea. Every breath came with a slight wheeze. My mother sat in the chair next to me with her hand over mine, silent tears still adorning her face. "Drink this. Good for the throat and lungs." I nodded as I accepted the mug, wrapping my hands around it and savoring the heat. I had been rain-soaked and freezing when Cal walked me to Solise's, and the healer was kind enough to dress me in some of her late son's clothes since hers were far too small. I tried not to think about the fact that we buried my father in the same man's clothes just a month earlier.

I had no choice but to accept them.

We had nothing. And that was still true, even more so now.

Cal had left after ensuring we arrived safely at Solise's home, his weeklong watch at the castle beginning shortly. My mind moved back and forth between quiet contentment and wicked uncertainty. I was questioning *everything.*

After examining my mother, Solise determined that her only injuries were minor burns on her shins and ankles, evidence of where she stumbled too close to the fire in her hysterical state. They would heal.

"I don't know," she mumbled when Solise asked her how the fire started. "I was sweeping the kitchen and suddenly there were flames shooting down the staircase. All I could think of were his things. I had to get Da's things, Petra."

I took a long sip of my tea as she spoke, the warmth on my lips an echo of the past hour.

"You have no idea at all?" Solise asked. The tiny bit of joy I felt quickly soured as I thought of how helpless my mother had been. Once again. But if the fire came down the staircase...

"I can't think of–"

I cut her off. "Did you say the flames came down the staircase?" I sat forward, my hands clenched on the mug.

"Yes," she answered, confused.

"So the fire started upstairs?"

"I... I suppose so." She narrowed her eyes as if looking for the reason I was asking.

"What could have caught fire up there?"

"Petra, what are you–"

"What would have caught fire up there, Ma? There's nothing up there save for the mattress and the dresser! The sky was clear when the fire started, yes?" My breaths quickened, burning in my throat as I tried to catch my breath. "What the hell could have caught fire? *How?*"

"Petra, darling, you need to calm down," Solise said gently from her work station on the kitchen table.

I was beginning to spiral as my vision turned crimson. Cal and I had searched the rubble but hadn't been able to find Da's tiny piece of lapis lazuli. My mother hadn't carried it out. "Did you know that Da's cloak is missing?!" I shouted.

She flinched at the question, clearly taken aback by the sudden change in subject and tone. "What?" my mother asked, the confusion on her face amplifying.

"Da's cloak. He left for his walk that day wearing his cloak. He was found without it. I have no idea where it is."

"What does that have to do with any of this?"

"You don't think it's *odd* that his cloak mysteriously disappeared?" I panted. My head began to spin as my breathing increased.

"I just don't understand–"

"And that a month later our house burns *from the top down?* Not from the kitchen, not from the hearth, but from *my bedroom?*"

"Honey, I think you've inhaled too much smoke," Ma interjected.

"Why was he found without his cloak? How did *my* room catch fire in the middle of a perfectly clear day? None of this makes any sense."

"Thank the Saints for that storm," Solise cut in nervously, attempting to diffuse the tension. The day had been clear when the alarm bells drew us from the alleyway. By the time I woke up I was lying in a deluge like I'd never seen. "I've never seen a storm roll in that quickly. Looks like the Blood Saints may look over you." I didn't know if that was supposed to make me feel better. She took a sip of her tea. "Idros put the fire right out."

My head was swimming. Hysterics would get me nowhere. I took as deep a breath as I could manage, trying to keep my brain from spinning in circles.

Silence settled over the room as the energy shifted away from my heated rant to reflection. "Calomyr," she tested the name on her tongue. "He said he's a friend of yours?" my mother asked, her tone calmer. "Thank Onera. Dropped me on the ground, but if he hadn't been there..."

"What?" I snapped.

"Well I wouldn't have... I don't think I could have made it."

I raised a brow at her. "If *Calomyr* hadn't been there? Calomyr wouldn't have been there if it weren't for me. *You* wouldn't be here if it weren't for me."

Her brows furrowed, face puzzled. "I only meant—"

"I can't listen to you speak any more, Ma." She flinched with hurt. Her Saints damned helplessness filled me with rage.

"Thank you, Petra," she said sheepishly.

I nodded absentmindedly as my brain collapsed in on itself, exhausted from running in circles, unconsciously falling through the unknown and escaping death. I was overwhelmed.

My glance unintentionally landed on Solise, who had shifted uncomfortably where she stood. She took a long sip from her own mug of tea. "What?" I asked her, sensing *something*. She gave a curt shake of her head, dismissing me. "*What?*" I snapped. I hadn't meant for my tone to be so harsh.

"Petra!" my mother scolded.

"He just... Something about Calomyr is..." she blinked rapidly as she searched for the words. "It's *off*."

"How so?" I pressed.

"It just is," she shrugged, her brows furrowed. "Just...be careful." The words struck me, echoing through my mind in his pleasing voice. I thought back to our conversations, to his kindness... What could be off about him?

"He saved our lives, Solise." My mother's tone was firm. I shot her a look.

"He did, as did Petra," she amended. "That I do not deny. But call it instinct or intuition or the soothsayer in my family line... I advise you to be wary of him."

Soothsayer?

"I need to lie down." I quickly stood, feeling faint and placing my tea on the table. "Thank you, Solise," I said curtly, hoping the sincere appreciation that I felt permeated my sharp tone. I did not want to be rude, but my mind was raging hotter than our house had.

She had made up her son's small bed and a palette of quilts on the floor to accommodate my mother and me until...well, until we figured everything out.

The light whistling in my breathing subsided as I laid down, the soft chatter of Solise and my mother drifting around the corner from her small kitchen. I'm sure they were writing off my outburst as the rants of someone who'd inhaled too much smoke.

We lost our house. Da. Larka. I lost the life I knew. I rolled to my side, the smell of burning wood still lingering around me, and fell into a sleep so dreamless I wondered if death had indeed taken me.

Chapter 27

Now

The violet smoke clung to my throat as it filled my lungs. The cough that erupted from my chest was powerful enough to push the men with the pipe off of me as I choked and gagged, doubling over as I clutched my stomach. The pain from my ribs shot spots through my vision. Every gasp pulled the smoke deeper into my lungs and I waited for the loss of self control to hit me, the rage that had roared through Roalin and Balthazar. When my throat cleared enough for my breath to go from gasping to ragged, I righted myself, my eyes closed.

When I opened my eyes, my entire life would be centered around leechthorn. Every fiber of my being would yearn for it, hunger for it, kill for it. This was the end of me.

A calloused hand grasped my chin, my eyes flying open on instinct. A wolf mask stared down at me. I...

I was fully conscious.

I had no more desire to rage and destroy than I had before the masked men stormed in. My throat was dry and felt swollen, like I had crushed dry autumn leaves and swallowed a handful.

The brokenness of my body caught up to me once again as pain shot from my ribs through my chest, my broken foot throbbing. No longing for another hit, no fiending so violently that I erupted into a furious frenzy.

Realization hit me as the man in the wolf's mask turned my face in his grip. "She needs more," he called behind him.

"More?" Vorkalth sputtered.

"Yes, Sir," the wolf confirmed, and the same men who had held me down before descended upon me once again. His voice was firm enough to sound like he was sure of himself at that moment, though I didn't know if he was. I sure as hell didn't know what was going on. Why wasn't I exploding into a storm of fists and nails and teeth? Why didn't I crave another hit? From everything I had learned and now everything I had witnessed, I should have descended into madness by now.

The pipe was brought to my lips again. I willed myself to fight it once more, through the confusion that roiled within me, over the questions that tore through my mind.

The smoke poured down my throat, stinging the raw tissue that remained from the last hit. I coughed so hard that my head filled with pressure, my vision spotty again. Doubled over, I took stock of my mental state as the coughs continued to tear through my body, plumes of violet smoke still erupting from my mouth. The only thing I was fighting for was clean air. The only thing I craved was escape. My mind was clear, my will intact. Which meant...

It didn't affect me?

Wrena said it took one hit, right? I had taken two.

I had to think. *Think think think. Keep coughing while you think, Petra. Draw it out. Give yourself more time.* Every cough threatened my consciousness once more as my ribs screamed in protest. If I stood up and *didn't* fly into a boiling rage, they'd make me take the pipe *again,* and I didn't want to test my luck, lose my control...because what if it *did* affect me?

I recounted the sights of Raolin and Balthazar's tantrums in my head, the primal roars that ripped from their throats, the flying limbs and thrashing movements as they fought against the soldiers who restrained them. The bloody pulp that remained of them. My plan laid itself out in my head but it didn't have time to form completely. I could only see the first step. It was time to pretend.

A final cough burst from me, so intense I swore my throat would be left bleeding. I stood. One last breath as deep as I could manage.

The violence overtook me. For a split second, I wondered if the leechthorn had a delayed effect, the rage coming from so deep inside me that I wasn't sure it belonged to me. The pain of my earlier abuse faded to the background more and more with each movement as adrenaline coursed through me. My mind was clear as I exploded. I punched and clawed at the soldiers closest to me, writhing the way Roalin and Balthazar had. The soldier's grips were like the manacles I had worn around my wrists just minutes ago, in another lifetime, in another reality. I did everything I could to make it look believable, make it look like I was succumbing to the madness. Screaming began to feel like it was ripping my throat from the inside out. I felt the pain creep back into my broken foot with every kick I landed. Saliva flew from my mouth, angry tears streaming down my cheeks. And behind every kick and punch and swipe was something more that threatened to burst forward.

I let them subdue me, securing me in shackles once again while putting up enough fight to keep them from suspecting. Not so much that I lost my wits, which I was coming dangerously close to, but enough to keep their eyes from lingering too long.

I didn't have the stomach to consider what was going to come next. I was now one of thousands, maybe hundreds of thousands. I'd be marched out of the throne room, out of the castle, out of Eserene. Probably out of Widoras. Were there other people like me? What about—

My mother. Had she told me where she'd be waiting during Initiation? How secure was the castle? I hoped to every fucking Saint that the bastard Castemont would protect her. I knew she wouldn't be able to protect herself.

My arms flailed in my pretend hysterics. As long as I kept fighting, kept exploding, I'd have time to think. I hadn't the freedom to wander during my time here so I had no idea of the routes the soldiers would have taken through the castle, the guards they would have come across to get to the throne room. How many had been slain? How did the intruders even get in?

When my screams finally went hoarse, sweat dripping down my blood-caked cheek, I slowed my fists. They dropped to the crimson ruffles of my skirts. It felt like every inch of my skin was bloodied, either beginning to dry and crust over or still dripping from the various wounds that marred my body. My chest moved slightly, rising and falling within the corset that bound me so tightly it may have been the only reason my ribs hadn't burst from my chest.

Vorkalth walked toward me, every drop of his foot wet with the sound of blood on marble. He was a mountain towering over me in the honeyed light of the sconces, foreboding and terrifying and *massive*. A low growl rumbled in his throat but without being able to see his expression behind the mask, I didn't know what it meant. How was I supposed to stand? I stared straight ahead at his chest, the top of my head barely reaching his shoulders.

He bent down, hooking a finger under my chin and pulling my face to his mask. "In all my days," he murmured, his voice barely above a whisper. "I've never seen the likes of you." I willed my eyes to reflect the fire that burned inside me praying that it looked close enough to the real thing. "The leechthorn always works the first time. Kauvras is going to have fun breaking you." He trailed a calloused finger from my temple down my cheek, as light as mist. He continued down my chin, my neck. Goosebumps rose from my skin as his finger caressed the hollow of my throat. "Oh?" he mused. "It seems your skin is prickling under my touch." His voice dripped venomous amusement. "You welcome this."

My goosebumps rose from fear, not arousal. Vorkalth didn't seem to know the difference. I fought back the nausea once again, willing my features to stay straight, my eyes wild. My mind was screaming for him to back away from me, to leave me alone. Something about staring into a mask was so much harder than staring into a man's eyes. "Maybe you *will* get on your knees for me after all." He finally turned away, stalking back to the center of the room.

"Take the prisoners. Keep the girl under close watch. Do what you want but leave her face. Burn the dead." A flurry of movement and I was being pulled by the chains toward one of the doors at the back of the room. Ludovicus was in chains, his still unconscious body thrown over the shoulder of a large man and carried out the door down an obscure hallway. The bodies of the slaughtered brothers were dragged to the pile that lay in the back. I was able to turn my head just far enough to see one masked man pour something across the bodies while another lit a match.

I only saw the light of the fire reflect off the back walls of the throne room. I couldn't turn to look at it. If I did, I didn't think I could stop from hurling myself into the flames where everyone I loved waited for me.

Trudging forward, still in my high heels and gown, I couldn't keep the whimpers of pain from escaping. Every step on my broken foot shot icy pain through my entire body, the ice meeting the fire of my broken ribs and colliding in a thunderous crash. Any hope of getting to the dagger was gone. The men didn't look back at me.

◆ ◆ ◆

There wasn't a guard in sight as I was yanked through the castle by my chains. I peered through my blood crusted lashes, trying to get an idea of where I was, but with my head down it was impossible to mentally map these foreign halls. I did my best to control my screams, but every step I took threatened to be the one to break me, to make me beg the men for a death I knew they wouldn't grant me.

Vorkalth led the group of soldiers, walking with conviction through the corridors like he knew them well. We came to a stop at a wooden door I didn't recognize. I could see light shining around the edges of the door — sunlight. We were facing an exterior wall. A possible way out, if I could find a way to get from the castle down the winding road to the city below. There was noise coming from the other side, so muffled by the thick wooden doors that I couldn't decipher exactly what it was.

The doors swung open from the outside, two men standing at attention as their Commander walked through. The sunlight was blinding compared to the dimness of the torches that lined the halls, and at first all I saw was white. The men yanked on the chains, pulling me forward. I grunted at the movement, willing my eyes to adjust to the light.

And then I wished they hadn't. I wished I wasn't seeing what I was seeing.

A small stone courtyard was lined with an intricate wrought iron fence, the east and south sides of the fence acting as railings for the hundred foot drop from the castle to the city below. Statues of Rhedros and Katia stared at each other from their respective pedestals, a look of angry longing carved into each of their faces. Katia's crown was gilded in gold and rose high above the courtyard. The diadem still sat on my head, and I wondered how long it'd be before one of the men took it.

On every surface, people were chained, arms at their sides or behind their backs, feet shackled. There had to be at least sixty people in the courtyard, maybe more, most writhing against their chains in various states of moaning and screaming and sobbing. Some sat despondent, heads hanging. Bloody boot prints zigzagged across the stone, tracked by a dozen rebel soldiers prowling the chaos with a variety of weapons. In the furthest corner of the courtyard where the railings met in a point was a *pile* of bodies, some still oozing blood from their necks and heads and innards.

The noises that rose from those chained in place were not cries of sorrow for a lost loved one. They weren't screams of pain. They were the same noises that Roalin and Balthazar had been making before they tore each other to shreds. The same ones I would need to try to imitate.

Every single person here was forced to take the pipe.

Every single person here was now under the control of Kauvras, currently at the mercy of his lackeys. My eyes frantically scanned the faces for any sign of my mother. No sign of her or Castemont. I didn't see a face I recognized, but the clothing told me they were all members of nobility, Lords and ladies and barons and baronesses. Were any of them the parents of one of the other Initiates? I couldn't remember, couldn't discern their screaming faces from the other screaming faces around them. Even — oh, *Saints* — even children hadn't been spared.

I wondered if the Invisible King was among the broken.

"Secure them," Vorkalth barked to a group of soldiers holding the chains of two noblemen. They held one man in place against a bare area of wrought iron fence, the other to a stone bench. A long piece of chain was wrapped tightly around their bodies once, twice, three times. They unhooked their manacles at the last second, holding their hands at their sides as a guard gave a final tug of the chain, cementing them in place and rendering them incapacitated.

"And you..." Vorkalth purred, once again standing over me, so close I could feel the heat from his body, distinct even in the sweltering summer. He *reeked* of sweat and dirt and blood. I made my eyelids appear heavy, once again hoping it was the right thing to do. "Allow me to show you to your accommodations." He took my chains in one massive hand and placed the other on my lower back. I bristled at his touch, covering it with a quick thrashing movement. We were walking toward Katia's monument. "You remember this part, don't you sweetheart? On the ground," he snarled in my ear, an unsavory smile marking his tone from behind his mask. I thrashed again, which turned out to be a mistake, as he grabbed my shoulders and slammed me back against the pedestal of the statue and down to the ground. Another soldier came with the chain.

When it was pulled tight, the pain from my broken ribs threatening to take my consciousness once again, Vorkalth crouched to the ground next to me. "I'm very much looking forward to our time together, but unfortunately it will have to wait until I can join you in Taitha," he hissed before standing and striding into the mass of writhing bodies.

I laid my head back against the pedestal and closed my eyes. I didn't have to pretend as the tears began to fall.

◆ ◆ ◆

I didn't know exactly how long it had been, but hours had passed. My neck ached from leaning back against Katia's marbled feet. Screams had turned to moans, and eventually, a restless silence, the sound of limbs knocking together as they twitched and the odd jangle of shifting chains. Behind the silence was a low roar. It was quiet enough, obscure enough that I couldn't tell whether it was coming from beyond the castle or within my own head.

As the sun inched closer to the western side of the castle, the masked men began to pick up their pace. Their postures straightened, their grips on the hilts of their swords tightening. I kept as alert as I could though staying lucid was a battle, a tug of war between my mind and my broken body. That low roar, barely a rumble continued in my ears. Was it death coming for me?

I hadn't been able to check on the arrow wound in my right thigh or the cut on my wrist. Trying to wiggle the toes on my left foot stole the breath from my chest, causing my fractured ribs to scream in pain. The marble pedestal of Katia was smooth against the wound on my back caused by the whip. I wondered what kind of stain my blood would leave when I stood.

Vorkalth burst suddenly into the courtyard from the castle, hand on the hilt of his sword, nodding to the guards. His pacing slowed as he settled in the center of the courtyard, his chin lifting under the bear mask. "You have been chosen," he announced to the prisoners, his voice booming and somber. "Just as the Benevolent Saints have chosen King Kauvras as their prophet, you have been chosen as his missionaries." I flinched at the mention of the evil incarnate, Wrena's words from only three nights ago feeling like distant, unfamiliar memories. I scanned through the conversation in my mind trying to remember any key detail, anything that could help me escape.

"Who the hell is Kauvras?" a rugged voice yelled from behind me. It took me by surprise. I hadn't heard anyone aside from Vorkalth and the soldiers speak since they'd invaded. I didn't dare turn around to see who had spoken.

"What did you do to us?" a frantic female voice shouted.

244

"Silence!" Vorkalth yelled. He pulled his sword from its sheath so quickly that the sound of the metal echoed off the castle walls.

All at once, shouts erupted as people suddenly found their voices, as if they were coming to the realization that the head-lolling and initial pain of the come down were gone.

"What do you want?"

"Why are you here?"

"Where are the Royal Guards?"

He walked up to an older gentleman chained to the wrought iron railing who hadn't uttered a word and swiftly struck him in the face with a closed fist. The crowd of prisoners gasped. I could tell by his surcoat that he was a lord. The expensive gold material of the garment began to turn red under the blood that gushed from his nose. Nausea hit my stomach at the thought of the once-white dress I still wore, how different things had been just twenty-four hours ago. "You will stay *quiet*. Understood?" Vorkalth screamed at the prisoners. The man gave a slight moan as he righted his head. "Anyone speaks again and I will take a life." He leaned in to one of his soldiers. "Though I don't think they'll be able to speak much longer," he said with a chuckle.

The restless quiet settled again, the low rumble reverberating through my bones as I saw Vorkalth straighten. "You've been given leechthorn," he began again, a few soft gasps sounding from the crowd, quickly dissipating. "As you've experienced, the high is nothing short of euphoric. It's a high that has caused women to kill their babes with their bare hands, men to shred their neighbors limb from limb." He began pacing through the crowd slowly. "The come down is..." he chuckled. "You've all had the pleasure now, haven't you? The chains around you are a mercy. You would have ripped each other, *yourselves* apart, skin from muscle, muscle from bone, bone from socket. I've watched men gouge their own eyes out and bite their own fingers off. After a few hours, it subsides." He paused in his walking, staring down at a woman who looked only a few years older than I. He crouched down, running a finger over the dark purple smudges beneath her cloudy eyes. "It subsides, but then the real thirst starts to build.

You will no longer have the urge nor ability to speak, and your only thoughts will be about receiving your next hit."

It does not affect me. It does not affect me. It does not affect me. I chanted it in my head over and over and over, my palms beginning to sweat beneath my chains. What if it had? What if my adrenaline had been pumping so hard that I didn't feel the effects now? What if I were addicted?

It. Does. Not. Affect. Me.

He rose again, resuming his pacing. "You see, you will get stronger as your need does. You will have the urge to kill. If you do not get your fix, if you go too long, you will die by your own hand." A woman to my left began to whimper weakly, her face gray. Vorkalth stomped to her side and swung his sword so quickly that she didn't have time to scream. Her head rolled to the ground, the stump of her neck spraying blood on the prisoners next to her.

He *laughed.* A cacophony of muted screams sounded, and it didn't take long before a snarl rose from his mask. "Shut the fuck up!" he screamed, his voice rough and ragged. The soldiers paced in time with him, staring at prisoners from behind their masks. What kind of cowards would hide their faces this way? "Shortly you will begin your journey to Taitha where you will join the army of King Kauvras in his holy mission." I fought the terror that threatened to contort my face.

"Mission for what? What the hell is going on?" another man shouted, this time only a few feet in front of me.

Stomp. Stomp. Stomp. Swing. Thwack.

His head fell to the side, rolling once and landing just inches from my feet, blood pooling on the stone. His eyes stared up at me blankly.

"Sainthood."

Chapter 28

Then

I knew we couldn't live off of Solise's kindness for long. She may continue to offer, insist on helping, but she wasn't much better off than we were to begin with. I could tell we were a strain on the kind woman, though she'd never admit it.

My mother drifted off to sleep in the nest of blankets on the floor while I laid awake letting my mind run rampant. The thoughts overlapped each other, another thought starting before the last one had a chance to finish. I tried to sort through each thread, pull it to the end to see what it was tied to, but I just ended up creating more of a tangled mess. The cause of the fire. Solise's warning. Her mention of a soothsayer in her family. Da's missing cloak. And of course the dire need for shelter and food. My focus was split between all of them. One thought continued to rise above the others, demanding my attention in a low, decadent voice. Eyes that I needed to stare into. Arms that I needed to be in.

I hadn't seen Calomyr in almost a week, since his watch began at the castle. I didn't like that I spent so much time thinking of him. I didn't like that the grief wasn't so strong when he was around. I didn't like that the thought of his lips claiming mine in the middle of the street made my stomach flip, made my breathing ragged. I replayed that mud-soaked moment over and over, adding it to the mess of thoughts ravaging my mind. Before he kissed me in the alley, he'd told me it was a bad idea. Why? How?

Stop.

I had no time to escape into the fantasies that had intensified over the last few days. I knew he was on duty at the castle, but his absence was making me anxious. He had been so insistent on making sure I was okay before. Would he be here now if he weren't on duty? What if he regretted kissing me? What if I'd made a huge mistake allowing him to get closer to me? I was second guessing every word, every touch, that *kiss*–

I banished the questions from my mind. I needed to focus on what lay ahead of me, not a kiss from a man who was essentially a stranger.

◆ ◆ ◆

The bitter coffee burned my tongue the next morning. Solise had laundered the clothing I had been wearing the day of the fire, soiled with soot, ash, dirt, and rain. The rest of my pitiful closet had gone up in flames, leaving only what I had been wearing: a pair of simple black trousers, a matching black tunic, my too-small boots, and my cloak. I brushed and braided my brown hair so it fell down my back. I splashed water across my tired face, imagining clarity spreading through my mind as I patted my face dry, hoping the cool water would lessen the look of the purple smudges beneath my brown eyes.

My mother had returned to her state of dejection over the last few days. As the shock of the fire wore off, so did any sign of lucidity. She had quit fussing — a small mercy, but a signal that she was mentally, emotionally, and physically retreating once again. I couldn't blame her. I often had to fight off the feeling of spiraling into my own soul where Larka and Da lived happy and healthy and whole. If I hadn't had my mother to worry about, to take care of, I too would spend my days in a state of detached sorrow. I resented her for that.

I fastened my cloak around my neck, careful not to rouse any thoughts of my father's cloak for fear of becoming distracted. Today, I *had* to make enough money to feed us and secure another place to live. I would fret over everything else once we were fed and sheltered. My halfhearted attempt to find work at the washbasin yesterday was met with no luck. I would prowl the streets *one more time* before I gave up and turned to something far more unsavory.

The front door clicked behind me as I stepped into the dirty street. Though it was well into morning, the sun had not yet crested over the wall. Inkwell was cast in a blanket of dawn, illuminated only by a few torches and the lightening blue sky laced with a disconcerting violet. This hour had always filled me with a heady mix of possibility and eeriness — the promise of a new day lay ahead, yet the darkness that remained from yesterday still loomed.

The promise that lay ahead of me was survival. Food. A roof. The bare minimum of what we needed. The darkness however...

I had the sinking feeling of eyes on me once again as I strode down the street, headed for Gormill Road. I fought the urge to throw my hood back and whirl around to see if there was anyone lurking. But there was no one staring at me. There never was. No one gave a rat's ass about another piece of Inkwell trash blowing through the street. It had to be the anticipatory guilt and thrill of what I was about to do settling into my bones.

Even though I knew it was a mistake, I didn't have much of a plan. The landscape of my mind was not conducive to any sort of strategizing at present. Come to think of it, the less I thought of it, the better. The streets would be packed for the next hour or so as people rushed to their menial jobs, gathered food for the day, and tried to sell what little they could. There was buzz on the street about a group of Low Royal Lords visiting Inkwell today. The streets would continue to fill in as people tried to get as close to the Lords as they could. The noblemen would pass out bread and fruit from their horses, just like they did a few times every year, and pretend their presence and their *generosity* made a difference in the lives of the derelict and otherwise neglected.

I rolled my eyes behind the edge of my hood. Unless one of them could give me enough to put a roof over our heads, I had no interest in taking anything from them.

Rounding the corner to Gormill Road, the day was already well underway. *Good.* People rarely paid enough attention to notice me, consumed by their own thoughts and conversations and survival. The more people that were on the streets, the more cover they offered. *And* the more items I had to choose from. Caroline, the seamstress, waved from her shop window, but I pretended I hadn't seen her.

The idea was to swipe as many things as I could, whatever I could get my hands on. The pockets on my cloak were deep enough to conceal a small bounty of stolen goods. Damn the guilt. Damn the feeling of being watched. Damn the suspicions of the man in the shop. We needed a home.

The uneasiness. The immorality. The shame. I pushed another wave of guilt down, reminding myself of my mission, feeding the monster inside of me that found the hunt thrilling.

Shadows in nooks and alleys offered me cover as I surveyed the residents walking up and down the street. I saw a man pulling a cart overflowing with burlap. I cursed silently, knowing I was unable to steal something so large and conspicuous. I was sure a few yards of it would bring in a couple coins. I ducked between buildings, the smell of piss overwhelming my nose. Dozens of people strolled by, unaware of my presence. No good prospects passed; few people had pockets, most women clutched their bags so tightly that there was no way to stage a collision and spill the contents. My lungs were still not back to normal after the fire, so I had to be careful with my movements so as not to breathe too loudly and attract attention.

When the smell of the alley became too oppressive and the sun had finally broken over the wall, I slipped out and began walking back down Gormill Road. A thought I had been pushing off for awhile now prodded at the back of my brain. As much as I wanted to shove it away, to stuff it down into the deepest part of my mind so it couldn't be seen again, I couldn't. The brothel. The Painted

Empress. I opened the door and let it in as I plopped down on a dusty curb to catch my breath. *You can do this because you must do this. This is the only way you can provide for your mother. You need a house. You need to eat.* I let the reassurances roll through my head, trying to keep the disgust from my face at what I knew I had to do. Though I considered it in the past, I hadn't *really* ever meant to. I stood, righted my cloak, and turned to walk toward the intersection of seedy side streets.

Commotion sounded from the south, pulling me from my concentration. I saw a mass of people gathering. On the small hill that blocked the view from Gormill Road to the harbor, mounted horses began to appear. Four finely dressed men sat straight on the horses' backs. The lords. Two dozen armored guards surrounded them. My heart leapt. Could he be here? He never told me specifically who he guarded, so the chances of him being on Gormill Road today were slim...right?

The parade continued my way, the lords waving every so often, but I didn't focus on them. I was scanning the faces of the guards that circled the Low Royals, their helmets only revealing their eyes. That was all I needed. They passed in front of me, and I stood as straight as I could, hoping, *praying* that those eyes would meet mine. But not a single guard so much as glanced in my direction. I told myself that he wasn't there at all. I told myself that maybe he was here, he just hadn't seen me. I couldn't bear the thought that he *had* seen me and then chose to ignore me.

Why did I feel like this about him? We've had a handful of conversations. We'd kissed...once. That's *it*. I needed to sever this thread and focus.

I fixed my gaze ahead, moving forward, four blocks south and one block west, to the Painted Empress.

◆ ◆ ◆

I heard it before I saw it. I clenched my jaw as I turned the corner from Gormill Road to Iron Avenue, the street packed with the lowest of the low, the scummiest of the scum. The pressure that built in my head kept my thoughts at bay. I needed to keep from talking myself out of this.

It stood a story taller than the buildings around it, though it was just as dilapidated. The paneling on the outside had once been red, but it had faded and cracked to a sickening muddy brown in the spots where paint remained. The door was open, held that way by a large, sleeping man who was sitting on the top step, head thrown back in a way that suggested he'd been very, *very* drunk. I stared up, trying to tune out the various noises that were floating through the open windows, trying not to look too hard at the men shuffling in and out. The bar on one side expelled its patrons, even this early in the day, drunkards headed straight for the brothel. On the other side was a shop just as seedy. They displayed an assortment of goods so random that it was obvious they were stolen.

"Ye headed in there?" a ragged voice called from behind me. I whirled around to find a wisp of a man leaning against the brick building that faced the Painted Empress. His clothes were grubby, visibly soiled, but the boots he wore were noticeably nice. My attention lingered on his boots, so out of place among the rest of his rags. Something about him was...not right. Even though I had a few inches on him, the sight of him made me want to recoil in disgust.

I didn't give him an answer before I turned back to the building. *I can do this. I can do this. I can do this.* My stomach was a bag of knotted ropes. *No,* a bag of snakes twisting and writhing and tangling together.

"Ye deaf, girl?" he called. "I asked ye if yer headed in there." His accent was thick, evidence of no education but the one Inkwell streets could provide. "Dumb bitch."

I shot him a sharp glare and returned to the pep talk I was giving myself. *It's a surefire way to make money. It is not forever. It's just until we get back on our feet. A few months at most.*

Walking. I was walking, fists clenched. I took a deep breath and lifted my foot to the first step when something caught my attention. At the shop next door, among the rickety shelves that held items of questionable origin was a beacon of bright blue.

Lapis lazuli.

I didn't feel myself turn before I was moving toward the chunk of stone. The color was so vivid it burned my eyes. There was no way this *wasn't* stolen. This didn't come from Eserene.

I had never stolen from a shop before, only from people on the street. Stealing from a shop felt too...official. Like if I ventured into this side of thievery, then I was truly a thief, not just someone trying to survive. I felt like petty pickpocketing left room for my soul to be saved yet.

But this stone would bring in enough to rent a shitty little flat for at least a month, and probably enough to feed both of us for just as long. It was only the two of us now, anyway.

The sound of the parade rounded the corner, the streets opening up as the four Lords leaned off of their horses to hand out bread and honey apples, surrounded by guards. It was the perfect distraction. I strolled through the store leisurely, the shopkeeper paying me no mind as he hooked his head out of the storefront to see the oncoming spectacle.

They drew nearer, the sounds of cheers and hooves on dirt mingling with the screams erupting from the brothel next door. I stared at the stone on the shelf, silently praying to Onera for a *fucking* miracle. I knew that once I did this, my soul was damned. But this was about survival. Something about it made me even more nervous than I had been walking toward the Painted Empress.

A quick glance over each shoulder and the stone was in my pocket. I had to leave *now*. The rush began to set in, my heart pounding, blood whooshing–

"THIEF!" the wispy man with the nice boots screamed, running into the street and causing the procession to jolt to a stop. He stood in the middle of the road, directly in the path of the Royal Guards and Lords, a bony finger pointed at me. "This dumb bitch is a *thief.*"

My body went hot and cold at the same time, the skin on the back of my neck tightening as my guts loosened. *Every single person* that stood on the street was looking at me. The shopkeeper stalked toward me.

"Call the constable! Call the watchmen!" the wispy man cried, hysterical. The Royal Guard at the front of the parade turned his head back toward the Lord who rode in front. I couldn't make out his face but I *prayed* it wasn't Calomyr. Good fucking Saints, *please* don't be Calomyr. I didn't want him to see this. I was going to be thrown in prison. My mother was going to die hungry and unsheltered and alone. The crowd that lined the streets murmured quietly.

The wispy man continued screeching as the Lord at the head of the parade gave a slight nod to the guard. Both dismounted and the crowd went silent. I was sure I was about to vomit or shit myself or both as they walked toward me, my gaze pointed to the ground. I could see the thick leather boots of the guard. *Please don't be Calomyr.*

"Hello," a low voice said. I slowly looked up to see the Lord staring down at me. His jaw was squared, his face pleasantly rugged. He looked to be in his early fifties, the silver throughout his dark hair framing his face. His brown eyes were warm as they peered down at me. He gave another slight nod to his guard who then turned to the rest of the procession, giving a hand signal that caused them to start moving again. The guards began to call out to the crowd to scatter.

I saw the wispy man give a sneer before disappearing into the crowd. *Bastard.*

"*Hello,*" the lord repeated. I inhaled sharply.

"H-hello." Saints dammit. Not only was I a thief but I was a stuttering little shit too.

"What do you have there?" My face was on fire. I slowly reached into the deep pocket of my cloak and closed my fist around the stone. I kept my eyes down as I pulled it out and opened my palm. "Beautiful," the lord remarked. "Lapis lazuli, yes?"

I realized he was asking me a question. Of course he knew this was lapis lazuli, but I gave a hesitant nod.

"A hand, my Lord?" the guard asked from behind the helmet that covered his entire face. "Or should we take the whole arm?"

My heart stopped. I moved to shake my head but it seemed like the muscles in my neck were frozen stiff. "Always the hasty one," the Lord said, clicking his tongue at the guard. He stared down at me, cocking his head as he searched my face. I was simply waiting for the command, waiting for my arm to be held away from my body then severed. If the bleeding didn't kill me, an infection would. I couldn't go to Solise for help again. "Why, pray tell, did you make the decision to steal this?"

His question caught me so off guard that for a few seconds my mouth just bobbed open and closed like a fish out of water. I still held the stone in my hand, which was now thoroughly slick with sweat. "I... I, uh..." What joke was he making at my already obvious expense? "I need to feed my family, and we need shelter," I blurted. I had no control as my gaze moved back and forth between the stone in my hand and the Painted Empress looming beside us.

The Lord's eyes widened, following my eyes. "No husband to provide for you?" His tone was thoughtful, without edge. Was that kindness? Condescension? I shook my head. "No father to provide for you?"

I shook my head again. "Not anymore," I breathed, barely above a whisper.

His brows raised. "And your mother?"

"Grieving."

"Ah, I see." The Lord's face had softened, though his guard stayed unnaturally straight, hand on the hilt of his sword. "How long ago?"

"Four weeks." I blinked back tears from my eyes and swallowed the bile in my throat.

"My deepest apologies, Miss..."

"Petra."

"Miss Petra. A beautiful name." He offered a small smile.

"Thank you, my Lord." I wanted to run away.

"You're very welcome. I, too, lost someone very dear to me only a short time ago. Close to the time of your father's death." He gazed down at his hands, his fingers briefly wringing together. No betrothal ring. "A terrible fever. Took her within two days."

"Apologies, my Lord."

He stared at me silently. I didn't know where to look, so I settled on my boots that were painfully tight on my feet. His voice was deep and warm, bewilderingly so. He turned to his guard and nodded, and I watched the armored man place an obscene amount of coin on the shopkeeper's counter. "Take me to your home, Miss Petra."

"What?" I snapped, shaking my head vigorously at the informality I had let slip in front of a fucking *lord*. Good Saints. I quickly corrected myself, staring between the Lord and his guard at the counter. "Pardon?"

"I'd like to see where you live." The look he gave me had some level of comfort in it. His eyes were sincere, thoughtful. He patiently awaited my response. Patrons walked past us from both directions, slowing down enough to scan the scene in front of them. My cheeks were on fire.

"It...it burned down, my Lord. My home is gone." Gone.

He lifted his brows once again. "Well then, Miss Petra. Lead me to the rubble."

My face contorted with confusion. Why would he want to see my house to begin with? Let alone a pile of rubble? I nodded. "This way." The Lord and his guard trailed behind me. The uneasiness in my gut swelled.

"This is Tyrak," he started, gesturing to his guard. "And I am Lord Evarius Castemont."

Chapter 29
Now

My eyes moved warily over the forms of Kauvras' soldiers. Somehow, the diadem was still on my head. Maybe Onera *had* granted me a miracle, but I knew it wouldn't be long before one of these fuckers took it from me. Looking over both shoulders, I feigned a spasm, throwing my head forward, the diadem falling into my lap. I had little use of my hands beneath the chains, but I brought my knees to my chest and managed to shove the diadem under my skirts, tearing it through the layers of ruffles, hoping it would stay put through whatever was to come.

"In line!" The words were howled over and over as soldiers spun keys around their fingers. A soldier had begun to unlock chains and push the prisoners to line up by the castle door. Two other soldiers began locking a new set of manacles around each pair of hands, hitching them to a long chain. We were to be chained together. Like cattle. I knew that it would be pointless to reach for the dagger at my thigh.

The soldier who unchained me said nothing. His hands lingered too long on my skin, the grime under his fingernails like black crescent moons against my wrists. I felt his eyes on me from behind a mask sculpted into a ram's head. I wanted him to *get the fuck away.*

I made sure to follow the cues of the other prisoners, most of which were cycling through dejection and spells of weeping. My gown was stiff with blood, the ruffles crusted and rigid, but the knowledge that the diadem was nestled among them gave me the tiniest sliver of comfort. I kicked my high heels off when the swelling of my foot made them impossible to keep on. I still hadn't been able to look, but it felt like the arrow wound on my thigh and the whip mark on my back had at least clotted — maybe another miracle to thank Onera for.

We were pulled from the courtyard back through the halls of the castle, the soldiers taking advantage of their authority by hurling fists into the stomachs, spines, or faces of anyone who so much as stumbled. I was on the receiving end of more than one punch to the gut as I limped, trying to keep weight off of my broken foot. *Good fucking Saints.* Weren't we supposed to be missionaries? Did other missionaries receive beatings like this from their leaders?

The buzzing roar that was background noise in my head had subsided, replaced by the echoes of cries bouncing off the stone walls of the corridors. I kept my eyes low, trying once again to get a lay of the castle that was so foreign to me. Had I been here before? Was this familiar?

Stairs. Crimson velvet drapes. A large set of doors. I knew where we were. We were in the entry hall where the Board of Blood had made their introductions. It seemed like a lifetime ago, but just three days had passed since Ludovicus paced the marble floors before me. There was no sign of guards and I realized they probably had taken the pipe too.

The chain was yanked, pulling all of the prisoners forward in a lurching mess of limbs and lavish clothing. Sunlight dissolved the dusty darkness of the hall as the massive doors swung open. The low roar in my head resumed immediately.

The doors opened to a drive high above the city.

The city that now burned before me.

Columns of smoke rose from every direction, ashes drifting like snow. I could see people running through alleys and lanes to escape masked men. People were being pinned to the sidewalk, to buildings, pipes being shoved in their mouths. Bodies both whole and in pieces littered the streets. Horses ran amok, rearing at the sight of swords and smoke.

The roar hadn't been coming from inside my head.

It had been screams. A symphony of yells, screams, and sobs from the residents of a city that lay in ruin, ricocheting off the city walls to echo in my bones.

The rage in the air was palpable as lives were lost one way or another to the violet smoke. From high above the city, it looked like nothing but a swarm of ants on crumbs, the movements so erratic and sudden that it was impossible for my eyes to rest on one person at a time. Every scream was fingernails dragging down my back. I watched the residents of Eserene rip at their hair and clothing and skin as Kauvras' soldiers tried to subdue them. There weren't nearly enough soldiers to hold everyone who had taken the drug.

So they raged.

A man slammed his head against a brick wall until it was bloody, until the movements grew slower and he collapsed in a heap on the ground, blood pooling from his crushed skull. I saw a small child scream as she ripped at her hair. Two women close to my age tore at each other's skin, the blood on the ground collecting the falling ashes like leaves on a pond.

The chain snapped forward as we were pulled toward the road that wrapped around the castle, connecting it to the city below. As we rounded each bend, new screams pierced my ears, many falling silent shortly after. Everywhere I looked, there was someone taking the pipe or fighting it or erupting with need or lying dead.

The other prisoners chained alongside me did not have any sort of reaction to the melee below. They all remained silent, their faces betraying no sense of terror. I harnessed every ounce of strength I had to keep my face blank. Neutral. No cause for suspicion that the drug may not be eliciting the same response from me as the other poor souls. But every new scream made the bile rise higher and higher in my throat. Smoke from the leechthorn and burning buildings and charred skin stuck in my nose, the smell suffocating, my eyes watering.

Pellucid Harbor had been breached, the breakwall missing large chunks. Massive, ink-black sails rose above the water, the Cabillian crest's gold dragon flying menacingly through the smoke. The docks were on fire, planks slowly slipping under the surface of the water. The waterfront was crawling with soldiers.

My gaze stayed on the ground as we reached the east side of the castle road, where I knew the very edges of Inkwell could be seen pushed up against the city wall. I needed to look, needed to know, even though a part of me already did.

Slowly, I forced myself to lift my gaze. Not only black smoke, but angry flames rose into the air, the entire view of Inkwell obscured by fire. Everything I had ever known prior to the last four months was burning in that little corner of Eserene. I clenched my jaw so hard my teeth ground out in protest, threatening to crack.

If I weren't chained, I would have thrown myself over the edge of the road and let the cobblestones deliver me to Cyen's doorstep.

The soldiers leading us said nothing as we reached the bottom of the castle's road. They simply pulled us toward the city streets slick with blood, to the carnage and the slaughter..

From a street that had been obscured by a crumbling brick building, figures began to emerge. Even though they were still hazy behind the smoke, I could make out the whirling silhouettes of Eserenian citizens as they violently bucked against the two soldiers that held each of them.

"Hold!" the soldier at the front commanded. The chain stopped as soldiers who had been in the front rushed to the back of the line. The sound of clanging metal pierced the air as the chain rattled to a stop. One by one, person after person, men, women, children, elderly, disabled, all of them were chained behind me. Anyone they could get their hands on, anyone they were able to force the pipe on then subdue. "Proceed!"

260

Through the city we walked, a chain of prisoners in varying states of agony and anger. Every few blocks we stopped and more links were added to the chain, more Eserenians whose lives were over.

I'm not sure if it was shock or numbness or maybe both, but as we neared the city wall, I stopped seeing the fires, smelling the smoke, hearing the screams. I no longer felt my broken foot or the gaping wound in my thigh. I didn't feel my head singing with pain, my burning back, my broken ribs, my jaw that was undoubtedly swollen. My brain melted like wax. My vision glazed over. I fell into the rhythm of being yanked and pushed.

Our shadows grew longer as the sun sank toward the wall.

◆ ◆ ◆

The sight of the city gates brought me back to my own head. I had never seen them before. A massive portcullis was pried halfway open to a wide tunnel, another portcullis on the other end, leading beyond the wall. The metal spikes at the ends of the beams were mangled, the wood cracked and jagged. Dozens of Eserenian guards lay slain on the ground, their throats slit, heads severed, viscera spilled. One body was surrounded by so much gore that he had to have fallen from the watch post on the wall two hundred feet above.

"Prisoners!" boomed Vorkalth from somewhere behind me. "Tonight, you begin your journey to righteousness. You begin your journey to holiness. *You* have been chosen by the Saints!" If we'd been chosen, why the hell were we being beaten and killed? "Follow orders and you will receive your next dose of leechthorn." The crowd reared, cries erupting all the way down the chain. I joined in, throwing my head back like I saw the others do. "Silence!" I heard the sound of fists making contact with bodies. "Tonight you camp in the Onyx Pass."

My stomach turned leaden as I fought to keep my eyes from widening. There was little reaction from the other prisoners. Had they no idea of what lay beyond the wall? Or were their brains already so gnarled by leechthorn that they weren't scared?

"Some of you will die tonight," Vorkalth yelled, his voice flat as he neared me. "That is the Saints extinguishing the weak." My eyes almost rolled. "But, if you make it through the night, you will be granted your next dose in the morning." A subdued murmur washed through the prisoners. I felt him behind me, his hand finding my lower back. "I'll see you in Taitha," he whispered. Then he retreated, his voice bellowing once again. "Onward!"

And we walked out of the gates of Eserene.

◆ ◆ ◆

I'd imagined what life was like outside of the Eserenian walls thousands of times; a desolate, rocky landscape teeming with nightmarish beasts, human remains in various states of decay littering the craggy mountain trails.

I had never pictured the calm openness that lay before me now. I hadn't noticed how impure the air within the city walls was until I breathed in the air of this unknown beyond. Without the wall to hide it, the sun still had a considerable way to go before it set. Everything the light touched had been dipped in the halcyon of the final hour of sunlight. The Onyxian Mountains loomed in the distance behind a sweeping plain, the Onyx Pass somewhere among the peaks that wore gilded crowns of sunlight.

Had the rattling of the chain, the moans of the other prisoners, and the shouts of the soldiers not destroyed the silence, it may have been peaceful.

We began to cross the plain, the short, dried grass crunching underfoot. Someone in front of me soiled themselves and I did my best to avoid the mess as we continued to walk. But every step was like needles on the sole of my broken foot, the pain becoming more and more unbearable as it finally caught up to me. My limp was so severe that I wasn't sure how I was keeping up. I had gone numb so long ago that it seemed the throbbing came back with a vengeance, insistent on making up for lost time.

The edges of my vision darkened. I should have lost consciousness by now. What would happen if I did? I'm sure I'd just be unhitched and tossed to the side, left to die on the plain. When I thought about it, it wouldn't be the worst way to die.

Peacefully slipping into oblivion, dying under the biggest sky I'd ever seen. It would beat death by the hands of the wicked men who pulled our chain or by the hand of the Board.

The Board. *Ludovicus.*

He'd been taken alive. Unconscious, but alive. I let my mind wander through the possibilities of his fate. The more I thought of it the less I thought of my broken body and how it was beginning to shut down. The plain stretched on for about two miles, the flat terrain allowing my mind to leave my body completely as I trudged forward, imagining Ludovicus shackled and gagged.

◆ ◆ ◆

"Halt!" a soldier screamed from the front of the chain. I lifted my eyes to see that the golden crown the mountains wore had been exchanged for one woven of darkness. The peaks rose against the sky like a tear in the universe, so black that they had no discernible features aside from the outlines of their craggy peaks.

Pure onyx. My heartbeat picked up as the back of my throat turned sour. Ingra's words floated through my head.

The beasts of the Onyx Pass prowl the mountains with your blood on their jowls.

The sounds of ragged breathing filled the air. The prisoners in front of me had begun rolling their heads again. My shoulders ached, every matching roll of my head sending pain throughout my body.

"Over this next ridge, we will find ourselves in the Onyx Pass," shouted a soldier, his voice stern. "You will be unchained for the night. Stay with the group and you should survive. Venture off and face the consequences of the Pass. We will not stop you, nor will we rescue you when you find yourselves in the jaws of an oxbear or the talons of a Rivodian crow." Goosebumps pricked my skin at the mention of the beasts. "Next dose will be in the morning, if you make it."

The beasts of Onyx Pass prowl the mountains with your blood on their jowls.

263

Stay with the group and you should survive.

The chain was pulled forward as we began to climb a slope, the rough plain grass thinning as softer, more forgiving dirt spread before us. A small mercy. The soldiers lit torches, the light casting formidable shadows over the trees and boulders that had begun to line the path. I was thankful for the jangle of chains and the moans of the other prisoners. While silence on the plains would have been peaceful, silence in the Pass would be unbearably eerie.

It was impossible to gauge the distance left to walk as the darkness smothered everything that was not directly touched by the soldiers' torch light. Some of the prisoners around me began to thrash periodically, quick spasms that jerked the chain this way and that with a force that seemed impossible. Were they beginning to get stronger already? I had no idea how long it would take.

Creatures called through the night, the air filled with howls and caws and cries straight from a nightmare. Screeches so high pitched I thought my ears would explode were followed by bellowing snarls that sounded like they were pushed through sharp, dripping fangs. Wings flapped in the trees. Twigs snapped. I fought the urge to whip my head toward every noise, every ounce of my body telling me to get the hell out of here. No one said a word about the noises as we continued deeper into the darkness.

My Da had told us legends of the beasts outside the wall only when we had enough money for him to overindulge on wine and build a fire in the hearth. Larka and I would beg him to tell us of the world beyond our little corner of it, of what was lurking just on the other side of the wall. Never mind the fact he'd never left Eserene.

Everybody knew of the common beasts like oxbears and wolfhounds and Veridian raptors. But the truly fearsome monsters were the ones Da only spoke of in hushed tones, when Larka and I wore him down with constant begging. Sharpstingers with wings as wide as I was tall and a sting so venomous it would paralyze a human in minutes before ripping limbs away and feasting. Rivodian crows, picking at the bones and flesh other beasts left behind, ruthlessly territorial. Bonehogs with massive tusks and eyes the color of blood. Venomous hell serpents and deadly vulgites and arachnas with eight legs and fangs the size of daggers. There were mountain folk, too — the Onytes, he'd called them, who were hardy enough to survive the monsters that hunted them.

I hoped Da had been very, *very* wrong.

An hour passed in the pitch black night lit only by the flickering light of the soldiers' torches as we moved through the mountains. The towering, menacing shadows of the trees seemed to repeat, little variation in their shapes and sizes, all the while animals screamed until it was nothing but threatening background noise.

The soldier in the front stopped abruptly, signaling to the other soldiers that we'd reached our resting point for the night. One by one, prisoners were unlocked from the chain, the freed moving awkwardly into the dark. Most of the prisoners had fallen into a fragile silence. Some let out an occasional cry. The chain rattled and clanked, echoing through the forest.

A few of the other soldiers began assembling fires throughout the camp. I couldn't tell how many captives there were now that we had picked up so many on our way out of Eserene, but easily more than five hundred people were slumped on the ground, curling into the fetal position or throwing their heads back in despair. The fires cast an eerie, dancing glow across the gaunt faces that surrounded me. I cringed at the thought of Eserene's thousands and thousands of citizens being reduced to a fraction of the zombies that sat around me now. Did anyone from Inkwell even make it out? The flames I'd seen just hours earlier coming from the streets of the slums made me think that Inkwell – and everyone in it – were nothing but ash.

I had settled against a tree when I heard footsteps. Whirling around, I saw a man with a Prismanian surcoat bounding into the pitch black, away from the camp. He was silent, but his face was frantic with fear, his movements jerky and uncoordinated. The prisoners stayed silent, but the guards began to chuckle.

"An hour," one of them yelled from the back of the line.

"That's generous, Artem. I say thirty minutes," another guard yelled back. "They don't usually last that long."

The man called Artem and the other guards heckled each other back and forth when a growl ripped the air, my lungs turning leaden and my skin prickling. A garbled scream, the squelch of flesh separating from bone, and...

Silence.

I fought back the rising panic, every instinct telling me to *run*. But I stood less of a chance out there. I didn't want to meet the same fate that man had, didn't want Ingra's words to come true.

"Oh *fuck* you lot," a guard in a dog mask shouted down the camp. "Didn't even get to place my bet."

"Not our fault you're slow as shit, Len," Artem yelled back, cackling with laughter. *Bastards.* I couldn't tell how lucid the other prisoners were around me. No one moved much as the soldiers patrolled through camp, staring down at sullen faces.

I bent, curling my body on the ground at the base of the large tree, draping my arm over my eyes. I wanted to go home. To Inkwell, to Copper Street, to our little shack, to the cave with the dancing lights. All that remained of that life was ghosts.

◆ ◆ ◆

Acrid smoke filled my nose, coated my throat, stung my eyes. My sight was red, my skin was burning, the forest—

I shot upright, my pain catching up to me as I shook the vision from my head. I hadn't fallen asleep but was caught in the void between consciousness and unconsciousness, the first images of a nightmare worming their way into my brain. Sweat creeped down my brow and back. The darkness was heavy, the fires burning low as they sent embers floating through the air – nothing like the raging inferno that seemed to haunt me. The other prisoners were slumped in heaps, limbs turned at unnatural angles. Were they sleeping as fitfully as I had?

Food. I needed food. My hands shook slightly, emphasizing my empty stomach. Did they plan on feeding us? A group of three soldiers chatted in hushed tones toward the southern end of the camp. I watched them pass a canteen around, wriggling it beneath their masks and taking quick gulps, their jaws hardening against the burn of whatever was inside. I hoisted myself up on aching legs, my broken foot nauseatingly swollen.

Their gazes roamed to me as I approached them. Vorkalth had stayed in Eserene, but I felt just as violated by their stares. I kept my eyelids heavy and my mouth slightly open, looking as distressed as I felt. I hated that I didn't know if any of these men had been in the throne room, if they recognized me. "Will there be food?"

"I see something I'd like to eat," one of the guards blurted, looking me up and down before turning back to his fellow soldiers and chuckling. *Ugh.* His stag mask was tarnished and glowed dully in the fire light.

"I'm hungry." My voice was firm and flat.

The soldier turned back to me. "What?" he snarled. I fought the instinct to cower beneath his gaze. I did not repeat myself. The smell of rum smacked me across the cheek as he leaned in closer to me. "Don't know why the *fuck* you can still talk. You get your next dose tomorrow, but I could give you a little something tonight." He hooked his arm around my back, pulling me close to him. The smell of rum was immediately overpowered with the stench of unwashed skin and weeks of sleeping in the forest. The other soldiers whooped and cheered as he ran a grimy, calloused hand down the bloody skin of my bare back. I was utterly frozen, unable to move, unable to think. My ribs were searing. "Such a pretty dress you're wearing," he breathed into my ear, his hand roving the corset, moving closer to the bow tied at the bottom.

No. No. *No.*

"Ythan." A low, raspy voice boomed from behind me, the roughness sounding like he had something caught in his throat. The soldier's arms stiffened around me, his hands stopping their wandering. "Let her go."

The soldier let go only to immediately turn me so his body was pressed to my back, his arms across my chest. I felt something hard against my backside. *Fucking Saints–*

"Let her go," the man repeated. The same man with the ram's head from the castle faced us, his hand on the hilt of his sword. I noticed then that his leathers were different from the soldier's who held me. *Ythan,* he had said. Ythan and the other soldiers' leathers were dirtier, more rugged. This man's leathers had clean lines, sharp cuts.

"Oy, Miles. Always ruining my fun." Ythan ran the back of his hand down my cheek, still crusted with blood.

"You will address me as Lieutenant Landgrave."

Ythan smirked. "Don't you want to join in, *Lieutenant Landgrave?*" He moved his free hand to my hip, yanking back and pressing himself into me. I was going to be *sick.*

Steel rang as Miles pulled his sword from his sheath. His voice was jagged granite. "Unhand her."

"Blood of the Saints, mate," he cawed, his grip loosening slightly. My breathing was shallow, my lungs burning.

Miles took a step forward. The soldiers behind Ythan rose, each unsheathing their swords. Ythan threw me to the ground where I landed with a yelp, the pain causing my vision to flicker black.

The men faced each other, and though I couldn't see their eyes, I could feel the heat radiating from behind their masks. Miles growled. "You will do as I instruct or you will be handed over to Vorkalth."

Ythan and his men did not falter. "Well, *Lieutenant Landgrave,"* he said again with a sneer. He lifted the very bottom of his mask and spat on the lieutenant's boots.

It happened so quickly that I didn't see Miles' hand around Ythan's throat until I heard a gag. It seemed that Ythan's men noticed too late as well, because Miles had Ythan pinned against a tree with one hand, his other hand raised to the men in warning.

Ythan continued to gasp against Miles' hand, which was impressively large. Both men were of similar size — taller than the average Eserenian man, broad shouldered and solid, but Miles was clearly superior when it came to brute strength.

"You do as I command or I will skin you alive in front of your cronies. You'll be wishing I'd handed you over to

Commander Vorkalth instead." His voice was measured, even, the roughness of it edged with lethal calm that broke through the sound of Ythan's choking. "When I release you, you are to return to your post, unless you'd like to see what lies beneath your own skin. Do you understand?" He cocked his head, the movement so primal, so animalistic that I could feel Ythan's fear from where I lay on the ground.

"Yes, Lieutenant Landgrave," he barely heaved out.

In one swift movement, Miles released him, the sound of his gasps echoing through the forest as he greedily gulped down air. "To your post. *Now.*" Ythan righted himself, still grasping at his throat as he shuffled away, trailed by his men.

Do I thank this man for saving me? Do I berate him for stepping in when I could have handled it? No, I couldn't have handled it. If he hadn't interrupted...

"Are you okay?" The gruff words traveled down a fault line in my soul, jagged chunks of rocks flying as every part of me broke in half, each piece shattering into a million more. I had dreamt of hearing those words again instead of simply repeating them to myself, dreamt of the pleasing taste they would leave in my mouth, the molten eyes that would accompany them.

I sat up, averting my gaze from the gilded mask. He squatted beside me, coming as disconcertingly close as he had when he removed my chains earlier today. I gave a slight nod, wrapping my arms around myself and recoiling at the pain in my ribs.

"You're hurt." The words were sharp, his voice so raspy it almost made my own throat ache. He reached for my arm but I swatted his hand away, the pain lancing through my body once more. He reached for me again, and again I lifted my arm to push him away, but the pain from my rib shot straight to my head, to my vision, dark speckles intruding, going dark...

I hit the forest floor.

Chapter 30

Then

We walked silently down Gormill Road, the energy surrounding Lord Castemont easy going and mild. I felt the eyes of fellow lowborns on me. The stolen stone was still in my fist. "Just this way," I murmured as we turned left onto Copper Street. The Lord fell into step next to me then, Tyrak behind us.

"How did your house catch fire, Miss Petra?" His tone was relaxed, as if he were taking a leisurely stroll along the waterfront, chatting with an old friend about something much more inconsequential than my impending homelessness.

"I'm not sure, my Lord."

"Not sure?"

"No, my Lord. We only know the blaze began upstairs." The words were hard to say. They made little sense to me.

"And was there anything upstairs that could have caught fire? Maybe a candle?" So he thought it was odd, too.

"No, my Lord."

He sighed. "Sounds like a stroke of bad luck. Have you prayed to Aanh?" Saint of the Home. I had absolutely not prayed to Aanh. He sensed my hesitation and nodded, his voice soothing as he said, "I will say a prayer for you, Miss Petra."

My brows furrowed as I processed his words. Who the hell was this man?

We walked until we stood in front of the rubble that had been our home. It was a pile of blackened planks and soot, nothing recognizable in the ashes. It still smelled faintly of that day, of my mother's screams, of Cal's eyes looking down at me. My heart broke all over again thinking of the lost piece of lapis lazuli.

"You weren't lying," he remarked, surveying the rubble. "Your house has well and truly burned down." What the fuck was he expecting? I kept my mouth shut. "And you have no place to live now?"

"No, my Lord. We don't. We've been staying with a friend who has been kind enough to shelter us, however I'm afraid we've overstayed our welcome"

"Any siblings?"

A dagger to the chest. I pulled it out. "I had a sister. She passed. At Cindregala last year."

His eyes widened as he shook his head. "Was she...?"

I nodded somberly.

"Such horror you've been through. And so young."

"Am I to be punished?" I felt my control fly away as I blurted it out. Tyrak stirred slightly behind us.

Lord Castemont stared down at me, assessing. His warm brown eyes narrowed. "Do you believe you should be punished?"

I chewed the inside of my cheek. "What I did was wrong," I said quietly, looking away.

"And do you believe it warrants punishment?"

The control I had lost moments ago scurried even further away as my lip began to quiver. I didn't know why, but suddenly my cheeks were wet and my eyes crinkled. I fought off the sobs that threatened to take over my body. I'd been bending for so long, I was ready to break. I was ready to succumb to the pain, the madness, the numbness. I was *exhausted.*

"I will not punish you." The words suddenly punctured the air. I furrowed my brows in question, my eyes still swimming.

"I will not punish you simply because you were trying to provide for your mother."

"I-I don't understand, my Lord–"

"But I will make a deal with you." I cocked my head, my lip still trembling. I could feel the confusion on my face as I fought it back. "If you can promise me that you will refrain from theft, I am willing to offer you an allowance for food and shelter."

My mouth went dry as I straightened. "What?"

Castemont stared at the rubble, his face thoughtful. "During my prayers this morning, I had an overwhelming feeling. I can only assume it was the Benevolent Saints speaking to me. I couldn't explain why, but as soon as I saw you in the shop, the feeling returned. I believe the Saints want me to help you."

Excuse me? I took a deep breath. My cheeks burned with shame. Did he think I was asking for... "The Saints want you to help me?" It was half whisper, half snarl. Why would I trust him?

"I believe they do."

My first instinct was to berate him for assuming that I couldn't provide for myself or my mother. Then, when I realized his assumption was probably accurate, my instinct was to berate him for believing the Saints had spoken to him. But all I did was stare at him in disbelief. It was all I *could* do. This absolutely wasn't real. "I don't understand."

"Nor do I. But you strike me as someone who will do anything to ensure the survival of her family. I'd like to make things a bit easier for you." I shook my head, backing up. No. *No.* Something about this wasn't right. Is the only reason he came to Inkwell today to find a charity case? "Please, I'd be happy to find you housing in any part of the city you prefer." I continued backing up, anger, disbelief, embarrassment, and shame flooding my veins.

"No," I growled. Tyrak's helmeted form stepped forward at the sound of my voice.

His face was puzzled. "I beg your pardon?"

"*No.*"

"I only wanted to–"

"I don't know what you're trying to do here, Castemont. What do you want from me?"

He flinched at the informality, but quickly recovered. "Like I said. I only want you to promise me that you'll refrain from theft." His voice was as calm as ever, even as I spewed poison from my lips.

My head shook as I continued to back up. I had the stolen stone. I could turn right here, duck through a few alleyways and be in front of the shop in no time. I'd surely get some looks from the shopkeeper, but I knew he'd buy it off me. It was better than accepting a fucking handout.

"Please, just consider the offer. I'll return to Inkwell tomorrow at midday. I'll wait right here. And if you decide to decline the offer, then I'll leave you be. But I urge you to seriously consider it."

His words ricocheted off of me as I turned and ran for Solise's.

◆ ◆ ◆

My fingers were red as I wrung them together beneath Solise's small table. I decided I'd give her the lapis lazuli that Castemont had paid for. It was the least I could do to thank her. The old healer sat across from me, various jars and piles of dried herbs littering the tabletop. Her brow furrowed over her dark eyes, intent on her work. My mother sat in the sagging armchair by the fire, staring into the flames as if she could see her family among them.

Should I tell them?

Our entire lives could change if I returned to the burnt remains of our home tomorrow. If Lord Castemont was to be believed, we'd be sheltered and fed and clothed.

Should I go?

But this man had absolutely no incentive to help us. And he was fucking crazy if he believed the Saints spoke to him.

Should I believe him?

We could move out of Inkwell, start new lives, learn to live within the loss. Find a new normal.

Should I accept his offer?

My mind rolled like marbles in a jar, the clattering blunt and irritating. I rubbed my temples. Solise, too observant for her own good, paused her mixing. "Aching head?"

"I'm fine," I murmured.

"I can make you a tonic," she offered.

"I'm fine, really."

"What's troubling you?"

Fuck. "Nothing is troubling me."

"It's that Saints damned man, isn't it?" I had spent an embarrassing amount of time wondering about Calomyr, what he was doing, what he *wasn't* doing. It did not bother me at this moment, but I would be lying to myself if I said he hadn't been at the forefront of my mind since the day of the fire. Was he thinking of me as he patrolled the castle halls? Did he hear my heartbeat in every footstep like I heard his? No, he wasn't thinking of me. He couldn't be. I let my head fall back, willing the thought of him to tumble out of my head. "I'm telling you Petra, stay away from him."

I fought back the irritation that rose within me, the irritation that was a constant companion now. My jaw clenched, the marbles in my head plinking around. A flood of words pooled in my mouth but turned to ash on my tongue as I considered the conversation that would follow. I stood from my seat. "I'm going to lie down."

"I see you, Petra." I froze. "I see you. You're doing everything you can. It's a role you never thought you'd have." She continued mixing her concoctions, her voice even. "But you do, now. And I see you working, and I see you pushing. I want you to know how absolutely incredible that is. How absolutely incredible *you* are. I see that *you're* the one carrying your family, this burden." She looked up from her work, her eyes on my face. "You don't need him complicating things."

The words were like droplets of sap on my heart, thick and uncomfortable but somehow warm and sweet. My eyes flooded, and I didn't exactly know why, but the tears quickly crested and began falling down my cheeks. "You will never move on," she started, petite, wrinkled hands pouring powder into liquid and stirring it with a long stick. "You will never forget. It will never stop hurting. It will be a part of the load you carry for the rest of your life. And that load will never get lighter, rather you will grow stronger. That's how it's been for me, with Novis." My lip quivered as I dropped my face into my hands, the utter exhaustion threatening to break me once again. "You have held yourself together as your world fell apart. You have been the solid earth under your mother's feet. You were never a victim." She laid her tools down, and raised her head to face me. "You're a warrior. You've *always* been a warrior, fire burned and ocean tumbled."

"Fire burned and ocean tumbled?"

"A stone can be put to the fire and end up burned, but it will not crumble. It can be thrown around by the sea, jagged edges smoothed by the waves, but it will not crumble." Her deep brown eyes beheld me with reverence. "You will not crumble, Petra."

The sobs took over then, violent and loud and all consuming.

But she was right.

I was a fucking warrior, fire burned and ocean tumbled.

◆ ◆ ◆

Tiny raindrops showered the city in the dull mid-morning light. Walking through the misty rain, I felt the moisture seeping into my boots. I let the feeling remind me of what was real, what was happening now. What I was about to do.

It was far earlier than midday, but I stood in front of the sooty rubble that had been our house. Our house may have been bare and in disarray, but it was still *home*. Numbness threatened me, but I pushed it back as I stepped into the ash, the burned remains damp from the rain.

I stood where my parents' room had been, the little cove at the bottom of the stairs. I tried to find my Da's lingering scent in the air but all I smelled was stale, charred wood. Their straw mattress had disintegrated. What remained of their headboard crumbled into ashes as dark as night.

I turned to where the staircase would have risen. How many times had Larka yelled that breakfast was ready up the creaky steps? How many times had we run up those stairs giggling or bickering or scheming? A pile of blackened planks jutted out from the ground, remnants of the time Larka and I spent in our little room.

The kitchen, or what was left of it, was just like the other parts of the house. Destroyed beyond recognition. I crouched down, running my hand through the soot, hoping with every ounce of my soul that I'd pull Da's tiny lapis lazuli stone out.

"Saying goodbye?" a warm male voice called from behind me. I whirled around to find Lord Castemont standing with his hands behind his back, Tyrak's at his side in leathers, black hair shining in the sun free of his helmet. I wasn't sure how to respond. I rubbed the back of my neck as I realized I *was* saying goodbye. Castemont smiled. "You're early."

"*You're* early," I countered, not at all concerned with my sharp tone toward a Low Royal.

I should have been concerned, though, considering what he had offered. He chuckled, a deep, jovial noise that warmed my bones. "Have you made your decision?"

I straightened my tunic, stepping over soot and ash as I approached him. I inhaled deeply, letting the mild chill in the air deep into my lungs. This was it. "I accept."

His face lit up immediately as he clapped his hands together. "Good decision," he laughed. I couldn't help but feel embarrassed, my cheeks reddening slightly. "So, Prisma? Ockhull? We can find you two a nice place near the patisserie."

I couldn't even imagine what life would be like in other districts. The thought made me...uncomfortable. Itchy. Awkward. How the hell would we fit in in Prisma? Ockhull may not have been as rich as Prisma, but what it lacked in funds it made up for in pretentiousness. None of the other districts appealed to me.

"Inkwell."

"*Inkwell?*" he repeated back to me.

"Yes. I'd like to stay in Inkwell."

"Why, pray tell, would you want that?"

"It's home." The words flowed so naturally that my tongue felt like a rock that had been smoothed by a stormy sea.

He inhaled deeply and flashed a look to Tyrak. "Very well, then. I will arrange the finest living quarters that this...corner of

Eserene has to offer." I couldn't ignore the slight crinkle of his nose as he said it. I breathed back my anger. I felt so unstable, so close to erupting at any moment.

"Thank you, Lord Castemont," I bit out.

"This is the start of something very special, Miss Petra."

◆ ◆ ◆

"And it's paid for?" my mother murmured, apprehension in her words but not her tone.

"Yes, Ma. You don't have to worry about anything."

Solise peered over her workspace at me, her face grim.

"Are you ready? It's just a short walk." My mother didn't answer and instead lifted herself from the armchair and walked toward the front door without a goodbye to Solise.

"I'll be back in a bit," I said to Solise. She stayed silent as we walked out the door.

The small cottage was on Jasper Lane, a relatively quiet side street off the southern end of Gormill Road. We were close to the harbor and far enough away from the bustle that accumulated on the northern end of Gormill.

Men — guards — were heaving furniture up the front steps and through the door, empty handed guards returning for another load. My mother stared blankly as I wrapped my arm around her shoulder. "I don't understand," she murmured.

I wanted to tell her that I didn't understand either, that none of this made any sense to me. But Lord Castemont strolled out the front door, immediately spotting our approach, a dazzling smile across his handsome face. "There's someone you should meet, Ma."

◆ ◆ ◆

My mother and Lord Castemont sat on an overstuffed leather sofa, *our* overstuffed leather sofa, a fire blazing in the hearth...*our* hearth. Though her face remained vacant and hollow, she was holding a conversation. It was an improvement.

I retreated to the small kitchen, placing mugs and plates and pots in various cabinets. We had never had so much space, so many belongings. Guards shuffled around the cottage, in and out of the two bedrooms upstairs, the small breakfast nook off the kitchen, out the back door that led to a quaint garden and an outhouse that wasn't terrible.

I was reaching for the top shelf in what I had designated as the cup cabinet when I heard him. "What do you think?" I paused as his voice rolled across my body. I turned to him, the mug almost crashing to the counter as I all but threw it in its place.

Calomyr stared down at me, his sapphire and emerald eyes glowing with excitement. "Hello." The half smile, the dimple. The stray strand of hair that hung over his forehead. I forgot all about the frustration, the wondering that had plagued me all week. He wore his uniform, clean cut leathers sculpted to his body and a shining breastplate bearing the large ship of the royal crest. His sword was at his side. The sight of him, of his eyes, of his broad chest plated in steel...

"On Low Royal duty now, hmm?" I asked, fighting the rising blush in my cheeks.

"I caught wind of his little plan." He nodded toward Castemont. "Asked if I could help." He ran a hand through his hair as the smile on his cheeks grew. "The catch being no more stealing." I blanched at his words. *He knew.* Embarrassment coursed through my veins.

"I only did it because–"

"I understand, Petra." My name on his lips set my stomach flipping. "I do." The tension melted away and I couldn't help but smile at him, the guards all around us fading into the background, my mother's hushed words to Lord Castemont a whisper in the distance. "Let them handle this," he said, gesturing to the guards still buzzing about the house. "Take a walk with me?"

◆ ◆ ◆

"How are you feeling?" Calomyr asked. We strode side by side through the low hanging mist as the sun fought its way through, making our way toward the harbor.

"Better. Much better. No more coughing."

"Good. I was worried about you," he murmured, turning his head.

My face cracked into an involuntary smile. *Keep it fucking cool.* "Oh, were you now?" I said as coolly as I could, but the words were rough.

His answering laugh was warm honey. "Of course I worried about you. I watched you *barely* survive."

I scoffed. "I was nowhere close to death." The remaining scratch in my throat reminded me that wasn't true.

He stopped in his tracks, turning to me. "I thought of you every waking moment this week, Petra. I need you to know that." The words were so sudden, so severe, so serious that I straightened. I swallowed hard under his fervent gaze. "If I hadn't been on duty, I would have been at your side. And I really, really shouldn't be feeling this way."

My heart raged against my ribs. "Why not?"

"Please, just trust me when I say that." I blinked in shock, but the bite of the words dissipated as he placed a hand on my side, his touch immediately warming my core, his fingers flexing against me. "Please." His other hand reached for the other side of my waist. I was completely paralyzed in his grasp, his eyes baring down on me with an intensity I didn't understand, couldn't comprehend. I couldn't speak to tell him that I did trust him, that I'd believe anything he told me. Damn being cool and composed. My entire body went loose and rigid at the same time, warmth pouring from where his hands rested on my waist.

"Do you remember the day we met?" he breathed, his face hovering dangerously close to mine, the ghost of a smile on his lips. His scent of smoke and cedar enveloped me, pushed against every inch of me.

"Of course." My voice was barely above a whisper as the tips of his fingers dug into my waist once again.

"I may have been the one to bump you. And it *may* have been on purpose." The corner of his mouth quirked up in a smile so maddeningly beautiful I could have lived in the light of it. The tip of his tongue ran over his teeth. I couldn't speak, couldn't think. "And I'm so fucking glad I did it, because the moment I saw you, I knew I needed you."

My voice shook. "You knew?"

"Like it was all I'd ever known."

He finally closed the distance between us, pulling me against him as his lips claimed mine, the taste of him even more intoxicating than when we kissed in the street the day of the fire. A low groan sounded from his throat as I clung to him. It felt like the first time and the millionth time, our lips in perfect sync. His hands roved my back, gripping me so tightly against him that I didn't know where I ended and he began or whether we were two people or one person or simply a burst of light. I looped my arms around his neck, tangled my fingers in his hair that was damp from the rain. His tongue slid against my lips, into my mouth, somehow gentle but urgent, soft but demanding.

I buckled beneath his touch, needing him closer, closer, *closer*. At that moment I didn't care that we stood in the middle of a public street, that people walked by. I cared about being as close to him as I possibly could.

He tore his lips from mine, the cold absence immediately threatening to swallow me. "Come on," he laughed, grabbing my hand.

◆ ◆ ◆

Carnal heat exploded from him as we tumbled into the cave in the side of the cliff. His hands were immediately on my hips as he backed me against the cave wall, the stone smoothed by wind and sea doing nothing to put out the fire that was raging beneath my skin.

There was nothing in the world other than the places where our bodies touched, where he pressed me to the wall. In one swift movement I was in his arms, my legs hooking around his waist, pulling him as close as I could. His hips ground into me, the evidence of his want pressing hard between my legs.

He moved his hands to my face and wrenched his lips from mine. His eyes, the colors molten, stared into mine with a look I'd never seen, and I swore I could see the ocean in his eyes

280

widening and deepening and churning. It was savagely fervid and somehow tragic, so agonizingly consuming that my core turned to liquid with pure *need.*

Without breaking his stare, he carried me to the middle of the cave and laid me on the ground. Standing over me, his towering figure aroused a primal want deep within me. He was *beautiful.* His fingers worked to remove his breastplate, the buckles on his shoulders falling, the long sleeves of his tunic leaving defined, muscular arms in their wake. I gasped at the sight of his broad, bare chest as he removed the tunic, tossing it aside.

He lowered himself to the ground, moving close to my face. "Are you okay?" he breathed. "With this?"

I wanted to scream that yes, yes I was absolutely okay with this. But the words caught in my throat. I pulled him to me, hoping the urgency showed him that I wanted it more than anything in the world.

I clawed at my own tunic, needing to feel his skin on mine, his hands following my own as my skin met the cool cave air. He pulled away, staring down at my naked breasts with burning hunger. I didn't want to hide. I didn't want to turn away. I wanted to feel his eyes on me, feel the heat of his stare where I so desperately wanted his hands, his mouth. "Absolutely perfect," he whispered, shaking his head slightly before lowering his face to my chest, pulling a nipple between his teeth with a force that made me gasp. I felt him laugh against me as I gulped down air. His tongue flicked after his bite and I threw my head back as he moved to my other breast, his hands roving my body while his mouth worked.

"This," he murmured against my skin. "I thought of this." I was headed toward delirium, and he hadn't even made it to—

His hands fumbled at the laces of my pants. I grabbed them from him, needing them gone that second. He sat back and pulled my left foot into his lap, yanking my boot off before moving to the other. My chest heaved at the sight of him kneeling before me. He pulled at the waist of my pants, his eyes boring into mine as he took his time, every graze of his skin on mine agonizing as he threw my pants on the cave floor.

"And this," he said, lowering his face between my legs. "I thought of this." He planted kisses on my inner thighs, his breath hot enough that I could feel it through the thin fabric, the last barrier keeping us apart. I panted as his eyes met mine, words dissolving on my tongue every time I tried to speak. His fingers trailed over the fabric until it was slick beneath his touch. "And I thought of *this* every night." His voice was enough to make me cry out. Just as the thrill of his words sunk in, his arms looped around my thighs, his fingers gripping hems, and the sound of fabric ripping echoed through the cave as he tore the last bit of modesty I had in half, exposing me to him. Every inch of my body was on fire.

"Absolutely *fucking* perfect." His mouth settled over me as his tongue followed suit, feasting on every nerve. Euphoria reverberated throughout my body as he worshiped me with his tongue. I was the palette and he was the artist mixing the perfect color, leaving no empty space as he painted.

He pulled away, licking his lips before descending again. A finger joined his tongue as he used the other hand to hold my legs open, baring me to him completely. Up and down his fingertip moved until it hovered over the place I needed him most. He sucked the very core of me into his mouth as his finger finally entered me, immediately hooking against a spot that made me scream. I was close to coming undone, his name on my lips with every movement of his finger, his tongue. I was inching toward the edge of oblivion, grinding against his hand, his mouth, my moans echoing through the cave.

He pulled away and stood, staring at me with a want so deep that it destroyed the last remaining bit of my sanity. He clawed at his pants, the bulge straining against the fabric as he peeled them away. His pulsing length sprang free, my core throbbing at the sight of it. "When you come, I want to *feel* it," he growled, lowering himself to me. "I'll have time to taste it later." I could have combusted right there, leaving nothing but smoldering embers on the cave floor.

My fingers dug into his muscled back as he pushed against my entrance, teasing me with movements that were infuriatingly slow. "I want to *feel* you come. Do you understand?" My mouth hung agape as he breathed the words into my mouth. I managed to move my head in some semblance of a nod.

Little by little he sheathed himself in me, each thrust deeper and deeper until we melted into one. The fullness was almost overwhelming, the friction pulling the breath from my lungs. Only when my eyes rolled back did our gazes stray. I relinquished all control at that moment, surrendering wholly to his movements, his taste, his stare.

Glimmers of light began to dance across the cave as the sun broke through the mist, a blizzard of diamonds swirling around us. I swore I could feel them move across my skin as Calomyr buried himself deeper in me. His eyes glittered as he let out a laugh so carefree, so airy that the simple joy of it sent me over the edge. Climax ripped through me like a summer storm sent from Idros, thundering against every part of me the way the waves crashed on the breakwall.

"My fucking Saints," I breathed as he smiled against my lips.

"Just as I'd imagined it." I was dizzy with pleasure as his words moved through me. He suddenly pulled back and stood, offering me a hand but only letting me stand halfway before scooping me up again. "Let me tell you how much I thought of *this*," he growled as he pinned me to the wall once again, entering me with such ferocity I wondered how the entire cave didn't collapse in on us. "Every. Fucking. *Day*," He nipped at my neck between words. "I thought of fucking you like this every day." *Oh my Saints.* Diamonds danced around us. We breathed in unison, his lips leaving my body only to stare at me with eyes of shattered gemstones. He watched as I slowly unraveled again, the same look reflected in his eyes. "Are you going to come for me?"

I gasped at his words.

"Yes," I hissed, my eyes locked on him.

"Come for me, Petra," he whispered.

Stars swam in my vision as I once again came undone, my legs wrapping tighter around him, my nails tearing at the muscles of his back. Nothing in this world came close to this feeling. I was quaking as he unsheathed himself and spilled across my belly, my hips, his moans telling me just how deep his pleasure ran. The glimmers in the cave dissipated as he lowered me, both of us panting. We sank to the ground, chest to chest as I clung desperately to him. "Most of all," he whispered. "I thought about this. You."

His smile was brighter than the diamonds that had just danced for us.

Chapter 31

Now

Diamonds covered the night sky, the sight carving another slice from my soul. Darkness still cloaked the earth as my eyes focused on the treetops pinned against the sky. I had lost consciousness from the pain, and as my lungs found their breath, I braced myself for that pain to resume.

I remained on my back, willing all the air out of me before slowly breathing in, my chest rising beneath my bloodied gown.

There was no pain.

I was dead. Or dreaming. Or delusional.

My hand found my cheek, still crusted with blood, but no longer swollen. I wiggled my toes wildly as I realized the agony of my broken foot was gone. I clutched at my thigh, poking and prodding beneath the ruffles, relieved that the diadem was still there and finding only a puckered indent where an arrow had been just hours ago.

I shot up, wrapping my arms around myself, jabbing my fingers into the ribs that had been cracked like twigs. I let the air flood into me, filling me so that there was no room for disbelief, no room for doubt.

Dead, dreaming, or delusional. Those were my only options. Afraid my senses would awaken and cripple me again, I stood, testing my balance. I was *whole*. I could move, I could breathe, I could think.

I could think.

Shit. What the hell had I done? Had I been so deluded by pain that I decided this was a good idea? Pretending to be a slave to leechthorn...for what? What was my plan when I was brought before King Umfray's mad brother, Kauvras?

I took a deep breath, savoring the feeling of my body restored. As far as I knew, the guards were still none the wiser to my mental state. No one had questioned me, no one had looked in my direction a second too long. And Vorkalth said he'd never seen the leechthorn fail on the first inhale...so there's no way he would even consider the possibility that the second didn't work.

The atmosphere lightened and I could tell dawn was close to breaking. I stood, stepping over sleeping prisoners, past barely-conscious soldiers, shuffling to the edge of the woods to relieve myself.

I rose to turn back to camp when a twig snapped in the forest. My heart jolted, panic immediately rising in my gut as I spotted a figure between the trees. He was tall, each step careful, and...he was wearing a ram's head mask. Miles. What the hell was he doing so far into the forest? Surely he wouldn't need to wander so far off simply to relieve himself. What could be worth the risk of being mauled?

I turned away. It was neither my business nor my problem. My back burned with the feeling of eyes watching me, the hair on my neck standing up. Turning back around, Miles had disappeared into the forest. *Something* told me not to go back to camp. *Something* was urging me to follow Miles. Maybe it was the shock of waking up free of pain. Maybe the leechthorn *was* getting to me.

If Larka was here, she'd surely go after him, not a lick of fear in her mind as she entered the land of beasts. "You worry too much," she'd tell me. I remembered Ingra's words about the Onyx

Pass, my heart thudding against my chest as Miles moved further and further away. But what did I have to lose if I were going to die anyway?

I stepped as lightly as I could, yanking up the crusted ruffles of my gown, each footfall calculated to avoid dried leaves and loose rocks. I couldn't believe I was walking without pain, without a limp. His figure materialized in the distance again as I gained ground. He walked deeper into the woods, further up the mountain. The sun broke over the peaks, watery light warming the earth.

Suddenly he vanished from sight. I quickened my pace to find myself on the lip of a large valley, the clearest stream I'd ever seen weaving a lazy path through the grassy landscape.

And there was Miles, walking down the slope, mask glinting in the early morning light. A tunic and trousers had replaced his leathers. I crouched behind a small boulder, waiting until he cleared the other side of the valley so I could cross, but when he reached the stream, he stopped. He sat on a stone and bent to untie his boots, tossing them to the side. He then stood and began to unbutton his shirt and–

Oh, *Saints.* He was going to bathe in the stream. He pulled the tunic over his head, a massive divot of a scar on his right shoulder. Tattoos covered his entire left shoulder, though I couldn't see what they were from this far away.

My cheeks flooded red as he reached for the waistband of his pants. What the hell was I thinking? I needed to leave. I had no choice but to make the trek through the woods back to camp all alone. I turned myself away slowly to lean against the boulder.

A pair of hollow, deep red eyes stared directly into my soul.

Nostrils flared just inches from me, the slits expanding and contracting silently. Two massive tusks jutted from its jaw. Teeth protruded from its mouth, each as long as my hand. The scars... Good *Saints*, the scars zig zagged up its jagged back, cutting valleys through the coarse, wiry hair that covered a bony spine. It had to be at least my height on four legs, each ending in hooves the size of a dinner plate. It was a nightmare incarnate.

It stared down its snout at me, eyes the color of freshly spilled blood assessing its prey. I had no way out with my back against the boulder.

Something clattered from behind me, a sound like metal on stone, and the beast's gaze strayed, narrowing on something in the distance. It leapt clear over me, over the boulder, and bounded toward the riverbank.

Toward Miles.

Still masked — and thankfully still wearing trousers — he whirled toward the hoofbeats and lunged for the dagger he had dropped on the stone. An ear piercing roar split the air and I wasn't sure who it came from as man and beast collided. The animal was *massive,* charging and snapping its jaw, but Miles was quick on his feet, evading every rush. He swung his dagger, catching the monster across the side with a shallow gash. Black blood began flying, and the beast seemed to swell with anger, growing stronger, more formidable. It backed Miles closer to the river, the soldier handling the dagger like it was simply an extension of his arm.

A stone. He tripped on a fucking stone as the beast pushed him back toward the stream. His head slammed into the water then the stony streambed below, and I swore I felt the impact inside of me. His dagger flew from his hand, landing in the water behind him. The beast approached Miles slowly, hooved foot pawing the ground in agitation. Miles shook the impact from his head, trying to keep it above water.

But it was too late. A massive hoof came down on Miles' chest. The beast paused, almost seeming to revel in Miles' spastic movements as its hoove pressed harder. Miles was punching and tearing and ripping at its flesh, fighting to keep his head above the shallow water.

The dagger. I still had the dagger strapped to my leg. I had the fucking dagger on my leg!

Before I knew it, my dress was hiked to my thigh and the blade was in my hand as I sprinted for the riverbed, praying the diadem stayed put in the ruffles.

The sound of Miles' frantic gasps from under his mask and the gentle rush of the stream masked my footsteps as I approached, leaping through the air and desperately clawing onto the creature's bony back. I stabbed the beast in the side of the ribs, dragging the knife back with a feral scream that matched its furious screeching roar.

It bucked, releasing Miles, who rolled and sprung to his feet as I clung to the animal.

I wrenched my dagger from its side, reaching around to jam it into the thick skin of its neck. It was running in circles now, frantically trying to buck me off as black blood sprayed across the bank of the stream.

Anywhere I could make contact, I drove the blade in. I lost track of Miles as dizziness began muddying my vision, and still the beast lived. I needed *one* solid slice across its neck, *one* deep enough to sever something vital...

A primal scream bellowed from its mouth as Miles threw his own dagger, the blade piercing one of its eyes, the blood spurting like the geyser. I clung to it as it sank to its front knees, then its back, moaning as the blood flowed and flowed.

I managed to hop off as it toppled over, chest heaving, legs kicking weakly. Sorrow sent a bolt through my chest for the beast that was just acting in its nature, for the beast that didn't know any better.

A final groan and its chest stilled.

"What are you doing here?" a thick, gravelly voice growled from behind me, panting.

I spun to face Miles, his mask *still* in place despite the fact that he was half naked and dripping water, sweat, and blood. I was able to make out the tattoo now — ocean waves with two ships between them, wrapping from his shoulder to his chest. "What *was* that thing?"

He was breathless, an odd warmth moving through me at the sight of his chest heaving, at the fact that he was still alive. His tone quickly cut that warmth into pieces. "What are *you* doing here?"

Snapping me from my stare, I raised a brow at him. "You said we were allowed to 'wander.'"

"Why would you do something so *stupid?*" he snarled.

I began to straighten my gown, my chin inclined slightly. *Nothing to lose.* "Came out looking for food."

"Food?"

"Yes. Food."

His shoulders loosened. "The leechthorn sustains. Some people don't break the habit of eating at first. You don't need food anymore."

Fuck. Fucking Saints damned cocksucking shit.

I would certainly need food. Which meant I would not only need to find food but a way to eat it without being seen. I schooled my features into neutrality and gave a slight nod. "What happened to me last night?"

"Seems you already know." He reached for his tunic, splattered with black blood, and began to pull it over his head.

I shook my head, his words sticking in my brain but making no sense. "But...what did you do to me?" I swallowed hard, the gravity of the situation beginning to unfold in front of me. My body was no longer broken.

"I did nothing." His words were short and dismissive, and he didn't look up at me as he adjusted the hem of his tunic. He tied the cord at his neckline, sighing at the putrid blood stains that had soaked in.

"How am I healed?" I pushed.

Bending down to the stream and splashing water over his forearms, he was silent for a few moments. "You're very talkative, you know that?" I stepped back, his words biting. "Too talkative. I don't know why you're healed. It's not something you nor I should know," he grumbled, "and things will be a lot easier for you if you don't know. Keep your head down. Not a word of it to anyone else. Understand?"

I was blinking rapidly, looking like an utter idiot as he turned to face me. Not something I should know? "What are you talking—"

"Keep your fucking mouth shut. Or I will inflict every wound upon you once again and savor every Saints damned moment of it. *Understand?* And keep that thing hidden," he spat, pointing at the dagger. He stood over me now and I swore I could feel his stare through the metal mask. I wanted to rip it off, to see

290

the expression underneath. My throat bobbed as I nodded at him. "Next dose is—"

A horn sounded, echoing through the forest, birds flying from the trees. "Now," he muttered, storming past me and heading back up the slope to the edge of the valley.

"You're welcome for saving your life," I yelled. The words had left my lips before I realized I was speaking. He stopped in his tracks, turning slowly to face me. He stalked toward me and I recoiled under his stare.

"*You're* welcome," he snarled through a clenched jaw, "for saving *your* life." I inhaled sharply, praying he would back off, that he would turn back to camp.

The beast lay in a stinking heap as I strapped the dagger back to my thigh, tore the diadem through another layer of fabric, and followed Miles back to camp.

◆ ◆ ◆

"Single file!" a soldier screamed to the crowd of prisoners. "Anyone who steps out of line will be executed on sight." Prisoners scrambled to form some semblance of a line, spastic limbs twitching and groans permeating the morning's small sliver of silence. None of them were talking, and I cringed at the thought of how much I had just spoken to Miles. I had lost track of him as soon as we entered camp. What a pompous dick. I saved *his* life.

A group of masked soldiers produced a number of pipes and cloth bags. Four other soldiers began to lay yesterday's chain and shackles out as a pipe was lit, the first captive greedily gulping the smoke down. His head lolled back in sweet, fleeting ecstasy before his hands flexed, knuckles going white. His chest erupted in a scream. The rage set in, two soldiers subduing the slight man rather easily and shuffling his thrashing form to the chain where they shackled him, this time shackling his feet as well.

Indistinct shouting rose from behind me. Soldiers rushed to the noise, the sound of steel unsheathing over a cacophony of footsteps. No one in front of me turned, so I stayed facing forward, but I didn't need to see it to know that what I heard was fists on flesh then the swing of a sword and a wet thud. "Anybody who steps out of line will be executed on sight," a soldier yelled again. My stomach turned leaden.

One by one, the former residents of Eserene descended into screaming, flailing animals. The scene I had witnessed yesterday began to unfold in front of me once again as I inched closer and closer to the front of the line.

The man in front of me split the air with a shriek as he exhaled the violet smoke, the lion-masked soldier with the pipe stepping back as the man was subdued. I shuffled forward, but when I raised my head, a lion didn't stare back at me.

Horns curled around a ram's face.

Miles scooped a pipe into the bag while a small torch was held to the powder inside. It was killing me that I couldn't see his face, couldn't tell if he was smirking or snarling or staring at me with pity or disgust or remorse. He held the torch to my lips.

I inhaled a heavy, intentional breath, staring at the vacant ram's face above me, the slits for his vision too small for me to see his eyes. *Please.* I didn't want to play this game anymore. I willed the leechthorn to *finally* soak into my blood so I could descend into a mindless madness. Closing my eyes, I pushed the smoke out of my lungs, erupting in a cough before dropping my head back as I had seen so many of the victims do before me.

Please. Please. Please.

My eyelids opened to a world no more or less vivid than the one I had closed them to. This was the way it was going to be.

I pushed myself into a rage, whipping my limbs around haphazardly, the only pain in my body now my aching heart.

◆ ◆ ◆

We were dragged out of camp by the chain, moving further up the Pass. I threw my head around as the others did, letting real tears fall in time with theirs. My feet grew raw as we traversed stone and gravel. The initial rage had passed for the chained prisoners, and at midday we were unshackled on a stretch of trail that looked identical to the miles and miles we had already traversed. The soldiers apparently needed time to rest and eat.

I leaned up against a boulder as I felt the first true pang of hunger roil my gut. I had been hungry before, but this emptiness was now undeniable. How the fuck was I supposed to find my way out of this? I knew *nothing* about the forest, just that there were some things you could eat and some things that would kill you. A great start.

Prisoners scuttled off here and there to relieve themselves along the edges of the trail, most opting simply to succumb to their mental states and soil themselves. Letting out a groan, I rose and headed toward a reasonably secluded tree stump a few yards into the thicket. I stared at what was around me. Towering trees with green leaves of varying shapes, dried twigs on the ground, bark, pebbles, ferns... Nothing looked any kind of appetizing, even as my hunger began to deepen.

A small sprig of thick green leaves jutted up from the base of a tree. *Onera, if you're real, please save me.* I plucked a leaf from its stem and folded it into my mouth. It was bitter, my face contorting against the sour juices that leaked onto my tongue. *Chew, chew, chew. Swallow.* I fought a gag as I reminded myself I *needed* to eat.

I choked down three leaves before turning back to the convoy. The path was blocked by Miles' imposing figure.

He said nothing as he stared at me from behind his mask and turned back to camp.

◆ ◆ ◆

The soldiers told us this would be our last night camping in the Onyx Pass, that tomorrow we'd move closer toward the border of Widoras and Cabillia. We camped at a fork in the road, the western trail marked with a wooden sign, "Blindbarrow" painted crudely. The northern trail, the one we were taking, had no sign. The prisoners grew quiet again, only an occasional cry breaking the noise of the forest around us. I found myself curled between two other prisoners. They did not respond when I tried to start a quiet conversation.

As tiny bits of ash floated through the dark night air from the fires that burned around me, my mind wandered. How had

Miles healed me? Why was there no evidence aside from a small scar on my thigh? Even if he were a healer, which I doubted considering his gender and general abrasiveness, there was no way he would have been able to heal my shattered foot, arrow-torn leg, whip-carved back, and cracked ribs...overnight.

Did the Onyxian Mountains grow some kind of powerful herb? I had never heard of such a thing in Eserene. Was he touched by the Benevolent Saints? No.

Footsteps sounded through the forest, probably a catatonic prisoner or a drunk soldier looking to take a piss. Another set of footsteps, then another, then...

"Onytes!" a deep voice bellowed.

"Up!" a soldier screamed, the other soldiers springing to attention. "Get the fuck up, you lousy shits!" he screamed. The footsteps in the forest became louder, quicker. "Every man for themselves!"

The forest shuttered as a shadow descended. The shadow turned into lumbering figures, a line one hundred men wide careening toward camp. All at once, the Onytes screamed, beating clubs against wide wooden shields.

Some prisoners scrambled around me, their half-lucid grumbling sounding like a mix of panic and disbelief. Some simply sat on the ground, their eyes glazed and empty. I pulled my skirts up, felt for the diadem, and grabbed my dagger, the only chance I had.

The Onytes rushed the camp, seeming to ignore the prisoners and go straight for the soldiers. Chaos. Masked soldiers heaved their swords through the bellies of the wild men, entrails flying as they swung their clubs in an attempt to maim, screaming in their mountain-born language. The Cabillian soldiers were much more skilled, but they were severely outnumbered, and it didn't take long for clubs to strike the unprotected backs of heads.

Arrows began to fly from both sides, several captives getting caught in the crossfire and dropping into screaming heaps.

I clung to the dagger, the blade still crusted with the blood of the beast from the stream. Without warning, an arm wrapped around me from behind, pinning my arms to my sides, my hand

294

still gripping my dagger. A blade pressed to my throat and suddenly I was being shoved toward the woods.

The steel at my neck sent such a chill through my body that I couldn't think enough to fight it. The havoc continued behind me as my captor pushed me, pinning me up against a wide tree trunk. "The perfect distraction," a voice growled in my ear. "No one will think anything of your screams." My blood turned to ice as my mind worked on placing that voice. "Miles isn't here to ruin my fun tonight."

Ythan.

If I could get an arm free I could try to drive the dagger into his flesh.

He spun me toward him and I took the chance to raise the dagger in front of me. The bastard had the same idea as I did, because his own blade was clutched in his hand pointed straight at my chest. The smell of rum radiated from him, his scuffed stag mask icy in the low forest light. I inhaled, willing my face to remain neutral, knowing that any show of emotion would trigger him further and I'd lose any chance I had. His voice was eerily measured as he spoke. "You're not supposed to have that."

"Don't you fucking dare," I whispered.

He huffed a laugh from under his mask and in one swift moment my blade was on the ground, Ythan's face just inches from mine. "Let me ruin you like Landgrave ruined last night."

He shoved me to the ground, my head striking the soil hard enough for stars to swim in my vision. With his blade still in one hand, he used the other to reach for the ties at his waist as I willed my sight to clear and my ears to stop ringing from the impact. My arms flew out to my sides, wildly searching for the dagger I knew I wouldn't find. I squeezed my eyes shut, steeling my resolve.

His blade dropped to the ground as his hands spasmed, suddenly covered in a ruby river as his neck erupted in a spray of blood, an arrow protruding from the side of his throat. His mouth hung open, the arrow quaking with the movement as his jaw opened and closed. He dropped to his knees before me, the blood pouring from his neck in spurts, giving me a look of pathetic desperation before falling forward. I had just enough time to scramble out of the way before Ythan landed face first in the dirt. His last breath choked out as a gurgle.

The initial shock faded and I sprang to my feet, fumbling for my dagger and whirling around toward the source of the arrow. I saw no one, only the spastic movements of combat throughout camp. Leaving Ythan's body crumpled, I inched toward the noise, ducking behind thick tree trunks.

Carnage. In the firelight, the Onytes had lost significant numbers to the hands of the soldiers, but now a number of prisoners lay slain, their bodies being trampled by those still engaged in battle. The prisoners that attempted to fight made feeble, uncoordinated attempts at best, the others sitting leisurely as if hell wasn't raining down around them. The reek of blood and gore hung in the air.

When the last of the Onytes fell to the ground, neck sliced from ear to ear, Kauvras' soldiers panted with exhaustion. I stumbled from the tree line back to the group as it was announced that a dozen soldiers had fallen, not including the one unaccounted for. Ythan. I kept my mouth shut as his comrades shouted for him, knowing they'd find his body soon enough, the soldiers having no knowledge of what he had been attempting when he was struck. I saw no sign of Miles. I wasn't sure I hated the idea of him being among the fallen.

I wrapped my arms around myself as soldiers shuffled to and fro, separating fallen soldiers and prisoners and Onytes. The Onytes' bodies were heaved into the forest, discarded like trash. Soldiers began digging holes — a mass grave for prisoners and individual resting places for the fallen soldiers.

The dark of night hadn't yet lifted as bodies were lowered into the pits, the other surviving prisoners showing little interest, limbs twitching. How long would it take for the leechthorn withdrawal to make them stronger?

I surveyed the forlorn faces of the prisoners glowing by firelight, but I was met with nothing but cold, vacant stares. It had been two weeks since I'd first heard of leechthorn. Two weeks since Castemont told us it had come over the border of Widoras, that it had been here for a while. And here I was, rubbing elbows with its slaves. Face after face, shadow after shadow, until...

Slumped against a small boulder a hundred feet and twenty prisoners away, hair tangled and gown filthy, was my mother.

The only thing I could hear was the beating of my own heart as it exploded in my ears. I fought my initial instinct to rush to her, to throw my arms around her, shake her. If the leechthorn did nothing to me, maybe it was the case for her. I stood slowly and trudged to the edge of the forest, ducking behind a tree to feign relieving myself. Careful not to seem too eager, too obvious, I stumbled back to camp, this time in her direction, and sank to the ground directly in front of her, placing myself directly in her eye line. Her mouth hung open like a door off its hinges.

"Ma," I whispered, tears welling in my eyes. She stared at me, eyes narrowing so slightly I almost didn't notice. "Ma, it's me. It's Petra." *Please.* Her expression didn't change. The same vacant, far-off glaze clouded her eyes. "Please, Ma." She looked at me for one more second before turning her head, staring off in the direction of the plains. I threw my head about, looking for any sign of her bastard husband. Castemont's face was not among the prisoners.

It took everything in me to keep myself from crumbling, from breaking into hundreds of broken shards of despair that would ignite and burn this camp to the ground. My jaw clenched as I stared at the husk of my mother.

As dawn broke, two soldiers dragged a body out of the forest with an arrow in his throat, dug him a grave, and laid him to rest. While the soldiers called us back to the chain to march out of camp, I spat on the dirt that covered him, before taking my place on the chain behind my mother.

◆ ◆ ◆

Dusk came and I could see the plains yawn open at the base of the mountains through the branches of trees, the grasses dusted with the pink of the setting sun. My mother stumbled ahead of me as her knees and ankles seized every so often. I was thankful to be headed out of this Saints forsaken mountain pass.

Ingra hadn't been completely right, after all. No beasts prowled the Onyx Pass with my blood on their jowls.

My mouth felt like I'd swallowed sand and my stomach grumbled so loudly I was afraid the soldiers would hear it. If we camped on the plains tonight, there would be nowhere to hide as I found and ate what I could. I had gone longer without food before, but I hadn't done so while exerting so much energy.

We started our descent down what seemed to be the last slope of the mountain pass, the trail opening wide, when a soldier near the front threw a fist in the air, signaling everyone to stop. Prisoners collided as they missed his signal, and the sound of clanking chains reverberated through the forest.

Then, silence. Eerie, too-still silence. My bones went cold.

Like an explosion, the trees erupted with every nature of beast I could have possibly imagined and some I couldn't. Dozens of winged rats the size of dogs swooped from the trees. Rivodian crows. Hounds with shoulders as tall as a horse rushed from the overgrowth, lips pulled over their maws to reveal a row of razor sharp teeth. Wolfhounds. The same kind of beast that had attacked Miles yesterday, now bellowed toward us in droves, letting out the same blood curdling screech — a bonehog. Beasts of every size and shape spilled from the forest.

And we were chained in place.

I saw soldiers scream but couldn't hear what they were saying over the roars, caws, and screeches. Soldiers ran for the chain, unshackling as many prisoners as possible as the stampede descended upon us. Some prisoners stirred, having the sense to run even though the beasts were closing in from all directions. Most prisoners simply stood in place, oblivious to the onslaught of certain death.

My mother and I were released as the first of the animals reached the group, soldiers swinging their swords furiously. The crows swooped down, chunks of flesh ripped from vacant faces and thrown about.

"What the hell?!" I heard a soldier scream, sword drawn. "I've never seen this before!" The panic in his voice was unmistakable.

"Get the prisoners out!" another soldier yelled as he slashed a Rivodian crow clean in half.

I grabbed my mother by the wrist, dodging sprinting soldiers and the beasts that chased them, careening around hounds that ripped the innards from bellies. I swallowed back vomit as I made my way to the front of the chain where there was a small break in the commotion.

One soldier was trying to corral the prisoners together as some kind of animal the size of a bull with horns and spines on its back charged toward him. I heard bones snap as the creature made contact.

"I'm getting us out of here, Ma," I shouted more to myself than her.

I slipped between the chaos to the edge of the forest where it seemed to be clear and I ran, my mother in tow. Weaving through the trees, trying to keep her on her feet, I hiked my dress up as high as I could.

A noise straight from the deepest pits of my nightmares sounded — a low, menacing snarl that sounded like death.

It stood at least two feet taller than me, its large, blocky head cut in half by a massive jaw. It looked like it had no skin, only gleaming, rippling muscle, and its legs bent the wrong way. Thick fingernails — no, talons — jutted from hands that were far more human than animal.

It stepped toward us and I backed up, one step, two steps, until my back was against my mother and my mother was against a tree. The dagger at my thigh was useless against this monster.

Ingra had been right after all.

It lurched, tackling me away from the tree and ripping my mother's hand from mine. Pinned to the ground, a talon grazed along my cheek as the animal cocked its head at me.

Oh Saints. Oh Saints. Oh Saints.

The past day had been one near death experience after another. But at this moment, with glistening teeth inches from my neck, talons the size of my forearm resting against my face and chest, *I knew this was it.*

Its neck was so broad, so inviting that I wished more than anything to slit its damn throat. If only I had unsheathed my dagger, held a sword, *anything.*

Blood showered me as the muscular creature's neck opened in an explosion. It gagged, choking on blood as it poured from its mouth, splattering on my face. It began to waver and I pushed its massive body away, letting it fall to the ground in a lump that continued to choke and sputter.

I whirled around, looking for someone who could have thrown a dagger, shot an arrow... I saw no one but my vacant mother. And when I whipped back around to the dead monster, I met the glowing green eyes of a massive wolfhound, stalking toward me.

It jumped, easily catching my arm in its mouth. I was too stunned to fight, so in shock that the hound shook me like a doll, its teeth sinking into my skin. But then I heard a crack and a yelp and the hound released my bloody arm and fell to the ground, its mouth pried so wide that the bones of its jaw tore through the skin. Again I saw no one and no weapons around.

What the fuck?

Winged monsters dove only to explode into a flurry of feathers and gore that rained over me. One after another, beasts pounced on me only to have their skin ripped from their faces, their paws and legs and spines snapped, their throats slit. Some of them managed to catch one of my arms in their mouths, their teeth ripping at my flesh for only a split second before they fell, the wounds small but burning. I was finally able to get the dagger into my hand, attempting to strike, carving out any measly wounds I could as some *force* made animals implode around me.

The final animal came at me, paws as wide as my hands and claws almost as long swiping for my face. The beast let out a demonic roar as it lunged at me, but it was cut short as its spine was wrenched through its back, falling to one side as the rest of its body fell to the other.

At least three dozen animals lay dead around me, not including the ones so thoroughly dismembered that I couldn't tell paws from snouts.

My arms and shoulders were covered in blood, only some of it my own. Puncture wounds and gouges covered my body, my hands and arms mangled by teeth, fangs, tusks, and talons.

I leaned over and vomited, my body heaving so hard that my vision went scarlet. What the fuck just happened? No one was around me. There were no weapons around, nothing to suggest someone had been throwing daggers. No spears or arrows or blades. *Nothing.*

I sank to the ground, resting my elbows on my knees, telling myself to *breathe.* My mother was still leaning against the tree, her gaze as empty as before, completely unaffected by the sight of monsters exploding into nothing but blood and bones. My body felt like I'd been thrown off the Cliffs of Malarrey, smacked around by the sea, and left to bake in the sun. Every part of me stung and burned, my energy so depleted that the world began to go dark, a looming figure appearing in my vision as the color seeped out.

Ingra's words echoed in my head. *The beasts of the Onyx Pass...your blood on their jowls.*

As the fingers of darkness began to close around me, I was lifted from the earth, and I remembered something else that Ingra had told me.

My Saints are showing me fearsome beasts laying slain in your wake.

Chapter 32

Then

My mother and I fell into a comfortable routine. There was always enough to eat, always firewood in the hearth, and plenty of clean clothes free of tears and patches. Lord Castemont had stopped by every week or so for the first few weeks, ensuring we were doing well and taking time to speak with my mother. His visits soon grew more frequent, though, and he sat with my mother almost daily now. She slowly began to speak more and more, little bits of her former self peeking through the calloused crust of grief. Solise stopped by frequently, too, offering to fix supper or clean dishes. She was sure to voice her skepticism of the arrangement.

It didn't take long for Cal to begin accompanying Castemont on his visits, standing beside Tyrak as one of Castemont's personal guards. "He doesn't need more than one guard," Cal whispered to me one afternoon while I lay tangled in his arms, legs wrapped around him. "You know that, right?" We had taken to making our way up to my new bedroom during their visits, first trying to play it off as just a simple, private conversation. Both my mother and Lord Castemont saw through that quickly, and since nothing was ever mentioned about it, we stopped being so discreet. He would make love to me, a hand held over my mouth when it became impossible to stay quiet, our bodies melting together again and again.

"And may I guess why he has two guards now?" I teased, my fingers drawing lazy circles over his bare chest. He nodded. "You're just so persuasive that you convinced him he needed you."

"How did you know?" His sensual laugh wrapped around me. I giggled as he began to plant kisses down my cheek to my neck, my skin prickling into goosebumps.

"You're not guarding him *now*, are you?"

"I'm not sure how much protection he needs from your mother. Besides, he seems to be smitten."

I pulled away, propping myself up on one elbow. "What?"

"You can't tell me you don't see it."

A sour feeling pooled in my stomach. "She's grieving." My tone was short.

"Petra, I…" He planted a kiss on my forehead. "I know she's grieving. But she seems…better. Lighter." I couldn't deny that. "And as long as he's smitten with her, it means he'll be visiting. Which means I get to see you even when I'm on duty." A smile pricked at my lips. "And, I get to do *this.*" He ran his thumb across my lip, the touch moving down my chin to the hollow of my throat as he pushed himself on top of me. He looked down on me with a smile as I relished the warmth of his weight, the smoke and cedar scent of him creating a heady mix in the midafternoon light. The light danced off his eyes, the blue and green meeting like salt and freshwater.

"So is this the plan from now on?" I asked.

"Is what the plan?"

I leaned up to kiss his nose, reveling in the feeling of his eyes on me. "What we've been doing. You visiting with Castemont."

His eyes crinkled with a smile. "For the foreseeable future, I hope."

"What about after that?" I blurted. I didn't know why I asked, but the words were out before I could reel them in. His smile melted into a thin line, his eyes fortifying. I wanted to take the words back as my face reddened. "I only mean...because–"

"Do you remember the cave?" My brows raised as I nodded. "And how I told you I thought about being inside you *every single day*?" My face grew hot. His lips grazed my ear, my neck, before he pulled back and looked at me again. My face began to scorch under his gaze. I swallowed and nodded again. "The only thing I think about even more than that, even more than fucking you on every surface in this Saints forsaken city..." I inhaled sharply. "Is a future with you. I'd marry you in a heartbeat. We'd have a house and children and you'd be the most amazing mother. I want *that* future." The air left my lungs at his words, at his molten eyes, and I wondered how I ever could have doubted his feelings for me. "But I don't know if that's even possible..." The heat inside of me went frigid and I tried to conceal the hurt that I knew was visible in my eyes.

He sat up, pulling me with him, cradling me to his chest. "My future... It's in the castle, Petra. Guards may only marry if they receive the Saints' blessing."

"So how do we get the Saints' blessing?" I whispered.

He breathed in, a thick, heavy sigh. "It's only happened twice, Petra. The last time was before the War of Kings."

I bit my lip. "So our future is...nothing."

"No," he said, a palm cupping my face. "No, it's not nothing. But I don't think it looks the way you'd like it to. The way I'd like it to."

I inhaled. "I never wanted to marry," I said quietly, looking at him. His eyes widened. "At least, I didn't think it would ever happen. Larka and I, we...we assumed we'd need to provide for our parents for the rest of their lives. Marriage was never really an option." The left side of his mouth quirked up in a sympathetic half smile. "I don't care what the future looks like as long as you're there." A smile erupted across his face, dimples appearing in his cheeks as he leaned his forehead against mine.

"I have to go away for a few days," he said. "I'm on duty for a tour to Blindbarrow. A few barons are headed there, and I have to accompany them." He shifted to lay beside me, again placing a hand on my cheek. "But when I get back in three days, there's something I'd like to show you. It'll have to be late at night, and you can't tell anyone."

He gave a mischievous grin and I matched it, raising a brow. "A secret, then?"

"A very big secret. So I hope you can keep your mouth shut, or I'll have to do it for you." I laughed as his lips collided with mine. He laid me back, his hands moving so urgently across my skin that I felt I'd ignite. I clung to him, breathed him in, savored the feel of his body on mine as he set about holding a hand over my mouth.

◆ ◆ ◆

The late summer haze had swallowed the city, the days sweltering but the nights whispering promises of autumn. I found work at the washbasin when it was available, but Lord Castemont was happy to provide us with everything we needed, no matter how persistently we declined. The money found its way to our home one way or another, be it deliveries of fresh fruits and breads, new clothing hung sneakily in our closets, or small gifts left on the doorstep. Never anything excessive, always respectful of the life we lived in Inkwell.

I had a book spread across my lap, the story of a peasant turned king painting itself in my mind. My mother had taken to weaving scraps of our old clothes into blankets and hot mitts and rags, most of them ending up in a pile as she started another. She sat idly on the couch, lazily twining fabric together. I was just happy to see her doing something other than staring into nothingness and weeping. The late morning sun had been baking the city for an hour now, the heat slamming into our roof and creeping its way inside the house.

"Would you like to take a walk?" my mother asked suddenly. The question took me so much by surprise that I flinched, her wide, hollow eyes staring at me.

"Together?"

"Yes. Maybe to the harbor." Her words were small, mousy.

My heart picked up its pace. "I'd love that."

We strolled silently together through the few blocks that separated us from the waterfront. My mother was slower than she had been before, but seeing her take in deep breaths of the salty air loosened something inside of me I hadn't realized was tense. Her pale skin had turned paler in the past few months, her fine blonde hair lacking the sheen that had matched Larka's, but seeing her in the sun struck a tiny cord of hope within me.

We began our descent down the small hill to the waterfront. "I'm glad he stuck around," my mother murmured. We stopped, lowering ourselves to the grass on the eastern side of the waterfront, far from the scorched grasses that had caused our worlds to spin out of control. "He does you good."

I scoffed, my cheeks reddening. "He's very kind."

"And he's very handsome," she chided. I laughed at her, at the little flicker of her past self. He really was breathtaking, his honey-brown skin and dark, unruly hair setting his eyes on alight in a way that made my heart race.

"Yes," I said with a smile, "he is." We sat in silence for a few moments, the lapping waves against the seawall like a drumbeat for the city. "You and Castemont seem to be getting along."

She turned away and nervously cleared her throat. "Evarius is also...very kind."

"Evarius?" I raised a brow.

"He's asked me to call him by his first name."

I inhaled as I processed the statement. "He *is* very kind." I thought back to what Calomyr had said. "Do you believe he has feelings for you?" The words coated my tongue with a bitter film, the thought of my father still fresh in my mind.

She turned to me, disbelief on her face. "Petra!"

"I'm just asking, Ma."

"I... I love your father." Her words were sharp.

"I'm not saying you don't."

"It's been less than three months, Petra." She twirled strands of grass between her fingers as she looked out over the water. "I can't begin to think of what another man might feel for me."

It was more than understandable, and quite honestly I preferred it that way. But the color had begun to return to her cheeks, the sight of her smile, no matter how subtle... It was a welcome sight. Lord Castemont's kindness still made me a bit uneasy, but I could overlook it if that kindness brought some of my mother back.

"We're going to be okay, Ma." I laid a hand in the grass. She laid hers on top of mine, then her head on my shoulder.

And for the first time in so, so long, I believed it.

◆ ◆ ◆

Three days crawled by as I waited for Cal to return, my mind running rampant at the possibility of what he was planning. Night fell and deepened, his knock sounding quietly through the house close to midnight.

"Are you ready?" he whispered in the dusty moonlight. No armor, just leathers, his sword at his side, and boyish anticipation on his face.

"I don't know, am I?" I asked, biting my lip.

"Do you know what it does to me when you bite that lip?" His voice was low burning fire. He moved closer to me, leaning his forehead against mine and resting his hands on my waist before grabbing my hand. "Come on."

We walked hand in hand through the districts, out of Inkwell, out of Sidus, closer to Prisma, the castle growing larger and larger as we neared it.

Realization hit me as we turned down an unfamiliar street lined with well-kept homes and flowering trees with petals that fell to blanket the cobblestones. "Don't tell me we're going to..."

"Surprise," he whispered, squeezing my hand.

I paled, dread clenching at my chest as I stopped walking. "What?"

"We're going on a little tour," he said in a voice laced with mischief.

"I can't go into the castle." No fucking way.

"Why not?" He didn't slow his pace, pulling my hand.

I could think of a million reasons. I wasn't royal. I wasn't *welcome*. There had to be some rule against it. A guard couldn't just bring in a commoner, could they? "I'm not dressed for it," was all I could say.

He scoffed, continuing to pull me along. "You look perfect," he said with a quiet smile.

My heartbeat quickened. "You're going to sneak me into the castle?'

"No sneaking required. I can bring in whomever I choose."

"That's a lot of freedom for a Royal Guard."

"I've already told you, I'm very persuasive."

Ascending the winding road from the city to the castle was not for the weak, and my legs protested the higher we got. But the excitement that radiated off of Cal was contagious as he chattered on and on about his trip to Blindbarrow, about his friends on the Guard, about the history of the castle.

Two guards stood at a pair of doors and merely nodded at us, swinging the doors open as we breezed through. No questions asked, no second glances. I assumed it wasn't the main entrance to the castle as we were greeted by a torch-lit hallway, though I barely had time to look around before being pulled deeper into the castle. What came next could only be described as a labyrinth as Cal led me through corridor after corridor, up staircases and through doors and around corners. "Almost there," he said more than once, a smile plastered to his face. I was in a daze trying to take notice of everything around me, though I saw nothing that I'd call recognizable.

Up one final dark stairwell and through a set of doors, we arrived in a massive antechamber, our footsteps echoing as we approached another set of doors. Two guards pulled them open as we approached. "Evening Cohen, Marcus," he said to the guards, nodding. They nodded back to Cal as we entered. My jaw dropped.

A chandelier dripping in crystals hung from the ceiling, which was painted with scenes of Katia and Rhedros in battle. The white marble floors were pristine, the walls covered in large pieces of art framed in gold. A winding staircase rose above us, the carved banister a work of art in itself. Cavernous halls stretched out in every direction. It was breathtaking.

"Lady Petra," Calomyr chimed, sketching a bow. "Welcome to the King's Keep."

My stomach lurched. "*What?*"

"He's traveling," he offered as an explanation.

"I thought you were on Low Royal Guard duty?" I whispered.

"Some days," he said and shrugged. "Other days, I'm here. I haven't seen King Belin save for once, but he seems to appreciate the same level of opulence King Umfray did." My eyes shot so wide I thought they'd fall from my head. He'd never once told me that. "You said you trusted me, right?" I spun in place, taking in every shade of opulence and wealth, the sight of it overwhelming every one of my senses as I moved my head in a weak nod.

He led me through dining rooms, sitting rooms, and dozens of bedrooms, each just as luxurious as the last. I was speechless as he told me what purpose each room served. I had no idea someone could need a family dining room and a formal dining room, a dining room just for tea and another for informal suppers. There were bedrooms for visiting dignitaries and some simply for show, each one with their own palatial bathing room.

"But this," he said, pulling me toward a set of doors carved with intricate roses, no guards to be seen, "is why I brought you here." He swung the doors open to reveal a bedroom the size of my house five times over. Every inch of the marble walls and high ceiling were carved with artwork, scenes of the Saints and their lore. Plush sofas and chairs surrounded a massive hearth, a fire blazing within, casting the room in varying shades of red and gold. The white marble floors boasted massive woven rugs, and I knew each cost more than all the money I'd make in my entire life. Crimson velvet was draped from the posts of a massive four-poster bed.

Then I realized where we were standing.

I whirled to Calomyr. "Is this the King's *bedroom*?" He simply smiled in response, the dimples creasing his cheeks as he ran his tongue across his teeth. "Calomyr, we *cannot* be here!" I whispered.

"But we can," he said, his voice low as he approached me. "But what if–"

His lips met mine, cutting me off mid sentence, my knees buckling. "What if we just enjoy it?" I pulled my lip into my mouth, biting down as I felt my nerves fray. The groan that came from his throat was animal. "You bite that lip," he breathed, "and it makes me want to–"

He pulled me to him, his mouth searching mine so urgently that I had no control over the way my body melted in his arms. "I was tired of being quiet," he panted, his hands roving my body. "I won't have to cover your mouth here." I almost crumbled at the words as he lifted me up, my legs wrapping around his waist. "The Keep is ours for the night."

"Cal, this is too much, this is–"

"Petra," he said against my neck, the sound of his lips around my name sending me reeling before he pulled back to stare at me, "if you don't mind, I'm going to fuck you in the King's bed now."

There weren't words for the sinful feeling that washed over me. I fought to choke out a response. "As you wish," I managed to whisper. His mouth moved back to my neck as he laid me on the bed, pulling my skin into his mouth, the feeling sending shockwaves to my core. My chest heaved as my eyes continued to nervously dart around the room, convinced we were going to be caught.

A wicked grin split his face as he stood, pulling his tunic over his head. *Saints*, the sight of his chest undid me every time, but in the brilliant light of the King's bedroom, it set every one of my nerves on fire. He tossed his tunic to the side and started on his belt, placing his sword on the rug before staring at me, his trousers hanging off his hips, indecently low. He leaned over me, a hand on each side of my head, his thumbs grazing the sides of my neck. "You are my Queen, and I'd like to treat you as such."

I turned my head to where his hand pressed into the mattress beside my neck, catching his thumb between my teeth and sucking it into my mouth as I looked back to him. His eyes all but rolled back in his head as he groaned, pressing his thumb deeper into my mouth. He leaned further toward me, prying my knees apart with his own and nestling between them, already straining against his pants.

We were in the King's bed. Holy shit. The idea that we could be caught at any moment was not far from my mind, even as one of his hands moved lower, lower, even as the other began to find its way beneath my tunic. I couldn't wait any longer.

I pushed him off of me, a flash of confusion on his face quickly turning to hunger as I spun and nudged him toward the bed. He collapsed, propping himself up on his elbows, watching me as I frantically pulled my tunic over my head and unfastened the laces on my pants. "Off," I breathed, gesturing to his own pants. His mouth hung agape at my sudden audacity, one side quirked up in disbelief, eyes positively molten. I stopped, raising a brow at him. "Your Queen commands it."

He leapt up without hesitation, his face painted with lust, and made swift work of his pants. He stared at my naked form, dropping to his knees in front of me and cupping my waist in his hands, leaning in to lay kisses on my stomach, on my hips, getting dangerously close to the heat I radiated.

But my impatience caught up to me again as I felt him looking at my face. "I could worship you forever," he breathed into my skin.

"Worship me later," I whispered, my bluntness taking even me by surprise. "Your Queen would like to be fucked now."

He was an animal and I was his prey. He lifted me with ease and threw me to the bed, his every movement purposeful as he flipped me on my stomach and pulled my hips in the air. *Oh, Saints.* Leaning over me, pressing his chest to my back, his palm found my throat. "As you wish, my Queen," he whispered. And then we were one, my name on his lips as he braced his hands on my shoulders. "Scream for me," he grunted. "I want to hear you scream my name, Petra." I couldn't have stopped it if I wanted to, my voice echoing off the gilded surfaces of the bedroom that belonged to the King of Eserene.

He pulled me to him so I was kneeling, my back pressed against his chest, one arm hooked around my waist as he buried his face in my neck. He reached in front of me, his fingers landing between my legs and exploring the flesh, my want obvious by the slickness that awaited him. Every nerve in my body was on fire. Sweet heat built inside of me at his touch, the sensation dizzying. "Oh, Saints," he groaned, the vibrations of his mouth against my throat my undoing, and I threw my head back against him while my soul came undone, his name like a prayer on my lips while his fingers continued to dance. I was drunk on him, every one of my bones liquid beneath his touch. I reared against the wall of muscle behind me, needing him as close to me as possible, wanting no part of the world between us.

He slowed, unsheathing himself, leaving me uncomfortably empty, but quickly flipped me on my back. "I want to look at you," he said, his voice suddenly laced with longing, his eyes pained. Cal leaned over, pulling me to him as he buried himself again. I gasped at the sudden fullness, his eyes glowing with vivid want. "For as long as I live," he whispered, leaning in so his lips hovered above mine, "I will remember this night." The urgency of his lips, of his movements inside of me told me that I'd remember it, too.

He was setting me on fire, and for him, I'd gladly burn. Release rippled through me again, my shaking legs locked around him as he pulled back and spilled across me. "Petra," he hissed in that smoldering voice, his head thrown back as he gripped himself in one hand, my waist in the other. "*Fuck*, Petra."

He was so beautiful, the firelight making his eyes glint like gemstones, his voice reverberating through the room. His arms trembled as he held himself over me, his lips barely an inch from mine. "Every day," he whispered, the energy radiating from him so intense that every part of me felt like crackling lightning, "I thank the Saints every day that they sent you to me."

◆ ◆ ◆

I handed the vendor three silver pieces, my basket heavy with a sack of flour and the best butter in Inkwell. Turning back to our house, I smiled beneath the hood of my cloak at the twinge of soreness I felt coursing through my muscles from last night.

My mother had an idea to make meat pies for dinner and have Lord Castemont and Calomyr join us. The betrayal I'd felt at her suggestion to serve Da's favorite meal to another man dissipated as soon as I saw the excitement on her face. Actual *excitement*. She'd been buzzing around the kitchen all afternoon, making plans and preparations. When she asked me if I'd go out to fetch the remaining ingredients she needed, I was happy to do so.

I rounded the corner of our street, mouth watering at the thought of the savory meal ahead. I wondered if Cal had already arrived. I climbed the steps, nodding at the ever-dutiful Tyrak who stood guard as I pushed the front door open.

My mother sat deflated on the couch, eyes on the smoldering hearth. I knew that look. That was the look of–

"Petra," Castemont said, his voice grave. The air was thick as I inhaled. I began to shake my head, knowing the tone of his voice all too well.

"Where is Calomyr?" I felt the skin of my neck tighten, my collarbone jut out as my chest collapsed in. Castemont said nothing as he looked to my mother. "Where is Calomyr?" I demanded again.

"Petra, he..." I saw his mouth form around the words but no sound came out. My ears rung. "There was an accident. In the training yard. Calomyr... Calomyr is dead."

Chapter 33

Now

A head and two shoulders silhouetted above me. I wondered why he wasn't cradling me against him like he had when we fell asleep in the King's bed. I opened my mouth to tell Cal about the dream I had, of the nightmarish life I had seemingly lived overnight. My breath caught. His head was misshapen, its outline rounded and twisting. From this angle, I could see an angry puckered divot beneath his chin. The scar was thick, jagged, not a singular slice or puncture wound but a furious mix of both. How did Cal get that?

Features began to take shape as I realized a ram's head was staring down at me. I pushed him away and shot up, shuffling backwards, shaking reality back into my brain. I fisted through my ruffles, the diadem still there, but no sign of the dagger. *Fuck.*

"Where is my mother?" I shouted.

"Quiet," Miles commanded, the gravel in his voice making sense now that I had seen the marred underside of his chin. He was squatting, a blade in his hand.

My volume did not change. "Where. Is. My. Mother?" I began to rise, every muscle in my body protesting.

"She's with the others."

"Where are the others?"

"Halfway to Taitha by now."

I cocked a brow at him. "Excuse me?"

"She was gone. There's no saving her." His tone was flat.

"Where is my dagger?" I hissed.

"Safe and sound right here," he said, patting another sheath on his already-crowded belt.

"Give it back."

"Do you know how to use it?" he asked incredulously.

"Give me my *fucking* dagger."

"Of course you don't. Why would an overindulged royal bitch know how to use a weapon?"

White hot rage bloomed in my chest, steam building in my head. "You *bastard*." I stalked toward him, my skin blistering. "You absolute *fucking bast–*"

"You're a bit lucid for three days off the thorn," he quipped. I stopped in my tracks. Three days? Had I slept for *three days*? He stared from behind his mask, not stirring from his crouched position. He began cleaning his fingernails with his blade. "I've seen thousands take the pipe. They all react in some way. None like you though." He pointed his dagger to me for emphasis.

I blinked. "I don't know what you're talking about." My tone was not convincing.

He scoffed, which quickly turned into...a laugh. A deep, hearty laugh with a cadence so warm that it momentarily threw off my guard. Rising from the ground, he stepped toward me. "We've already lost three days. Get up, we're going to Taitha. And I will be delivering you directly to Kauvras."

I planted my feet firmly on the ground, knowing that my physical strength was comical compared to his. "You will not."

"Oh, but I will."

"*Why?*"

"Kauvras is looking for you, and I'm looking for answers. Answers I know he has. You're my bargaining chip."

I scowled at him. "And why are *you* the one bringing me to Kauvras? Not one of the other soldiers? Why aren't we with the rest of the group?" With my *mother*.

He let out a low, gruff laugh. "They think you and I were ripped to shreds when the beasts attacked. Didn't take much for them to move on. Imagine how surprised they'll be when I show up with you."

"So that's why you 'saved' me from Ythan that night? So you could use me as a bargaining chip to get what you want?" I demanded, my arms flying wildly with my words.

He didn't flinch. "Ythan was a piece of shit. I'd been looking for a reason to off him." My eyes flicked to his belt, to the quiver of feather tipped arrows that hung there, a bow peeking out from over his shoulder. *Holy shit.* I bit my tongue. "I didn't know who you were then. But damn if I'm not glad I do now. You will wed Kauvras and I will get my answers."

I charged at him without a thought, a ball of fists and red hot fury. I wasn't sure what I was aiming for, but he caught my swing in one hand, easily pushing me to the side. "Fuck you, fuck Kauvras, and fuck your stupid fucking cause!" Punch after punch he deflected me. I grew angrier each time. "Take me to my mother! *Now!*"

I wound up a punch that I intended to land under his jaw, where the mask wouldn't protect him, but the bastard blocked my swing. When I turned around to face him again, his dagger was pointed at me. I froze. "You're coming with me to Kauvras. Your mother is a lost cause."

I seethed, knowing one wrong move would end my life. I debated running, taking away his prize, or at the very least, making his mission that much more difficult as he would inevitably pursue me. He inclined his head, silently telling me to turn and walk.

◆ ◆ ◆

We walked in silence down the Pass, all the while my eyes on my sheathed dagger at his hip. Within two hours we had leveled onto flat land. The grass looked dry and crunchy but was surprisingly soft on my bare feet. A balmy breeze blew toward the mountain. If only my fucking jailer wasn't here to ruin it.

I tried to will myself into feeling fear, knowing that fear would keep me cautious, and caution would keep me safe. But I wasn't afraid for myself at all, only my mother. I resented her for being so Saints damned helpless throughout the years, even more so now. I resented her for depending so heavily on me when it should have been the other way around. I resented her now more than ever for marrying Castemont. But I feared for her, simply because I knew she was no longer able to fear for herself.

Miles marched behind me. I didn't turn to look at him when I spoke. "What will happen to her?" The words flew from my mouth with palpable vitriol. The pale blue sky stretched all around us, the sun somehow milder, gentler than in Eserene.

"Same thing that happens to the rest of them," he answered curtly.

I waited. "And that is...?"

"She'll have a bed in the barracks and a dose of leechthorn as needed."

"And then what?"

"You ask a lot of questions for a liar," he snarled. I was so taken aback that I almost missed a step.

"*Excuse me?*" Damn. Larka would have been proud of the venom in my voice.

"You heard what I said." The rasp in his voice was maddening, grinding against every nerve in my body.

"I'm no liar."

The tip of his dagger pressed into my back hard enough to make me jerk. He threw a hand out and grabbed me, whirling me to face him as I felt the now familiar feeling of blood dripping down my spine. His eyes were undetectable behind the mask, but I could feel his stare boring into my soul through the tiny slits. "You're immune to leechthorn," he growled.

I felt my face go white. The energy that radiated from him was calm, steady, but I knew what brewed beneath it. "No." I said matter-of-factly.

"*Yes.*"

I bit my tongue, calculating my next words. "How?" And I wasn't sure whether I was asking how he knew I was immune, or how one could tell if they were immune, or how the actual fuck I was, apparently, immune.

He laughed, the noise husky and harsh. He seemed to laugh a lot for a hateful soldier. "You're not nearly as strong as the others. Your eyes are clear. You can *speak* far longer than the others can after a dose. You had the sense to throw a fucking dagger at a bonehog that day in the valley. And you're hungry enough to eat a bitterfern, which I'm sure you found has a very accurate name." He finally lowered his blade to his side, resheathing it. My shoulders slackened. "How long have you known you're the Daughter of Katia?"

I recoiled. "What?"

"How long have you known?" Though his weapon was sheathed, his words were sharper than any blade.

"The Daughter of Katia? I don't understand."

"I watched you kill dozens of bloodthirsty monsters without so much as a blade. I watched their throats explode and their bones snap. I've never seen *anyone* kill a Veridian raptor, and you killed *three* of them." I didn't even know what a Veridian raptor looked like. In the mess of fur and claws and feathers that had hurled themselves toward me, I didn't have time to distinguish one monster from another.

Speaking to a mask rather than a person was maddening. My stomach roiled. "I didn't kill anything."

"Then who did?"

"Someone must have been shooting arrows, or throwing daggers, or–"

"Did you see any arrows laying around? Any blades? I'm not sure how an arrow could snap an oxbear's spine in three places, or pull it clean from its body, for that matter."

"It wasn't me."

My Saints are showing me fearsome beasts laying slain in your wake.

"And you healed yourself overnight. I'm not sure why you didn't do it earlier, but to each their own, I guess." He pushed past me to resume walking.

He was the last person I saw before I collapsed from the pain the night before last. "*You* healed me," I insisted.

Pausing, he reached into a small satchel on his hip, pulled out a honey apple, and scoffed. Pulling the mask away from his face just enough to wedge the fruit in his mouth, he took a massive bite, the sound of the crunch fraying my nerves. Stupid *fucking* mask. I fought the urge to learn forward and rip the Saints damned thing off myself, to see the identity of the man who had somehow healed me of my gruesome injuries. "No, actually. That was you."

"*Me?*" No. I was dizzy with confusion, with questions. "How–"

"Shit if I know. You're the one who's — how do they say?— touched by divinity." I shook my head. He kept walking but turned back to see me standing in place, mouth ajar, eyes wide. "Born on the Night of the Holy Stone of Blood Saints, yes?" I looked at him blankly. What the fuck was happening? Is this what Wrena had been talking about? "Thought so. Though I was expecting someone...different."

I didn't have the mental capacity at the moment to process the presumed insult. *Me?* The Daughter of Katia? Ludovicus' declaration passed through my mind, that they had been waiting for me, that he would gladly hand over his brothers in exchange for me, that they'd found me while I was *still human*. "I'm not the Daughter of Katia. I was born in the poorest part of Eserene, to my parents. My very *human* parents."

"You said the woman in the forest with you was your mother?" I nodded, looking anywhere but at him. "I'd be surprised if you were even distant relatives. You look nothing alike."

"I–"

"Listen, all I know is we've been told to look for you, and that we'd know when we found you. And I think I know."

"You're not looking for me. This is some kind of misunderstanding. Now please, take me to my mother." My brain was doing somersaults, chills running up and down my spine.

He looked me up and down from behind the mask, took in the ridiculously gaudy gown hardened with blood and torn in places. "You really didn't know?"

I clenched my jaw. I felt inferior under his gaze, a feeling I most certainly didn't like. "There is nothing to know. My step-father is Lord Castemont. Reunite me with my mother *now* or I will call upon him." His name on my lips was like a razor blade, but I'd use it to cut this bastard down.

Miles raised an eyebrow and let out a breathy laugh. "Castemont, huh? An Eserenian Lord holds no power in Taitha, sweetheart." My stomach dropped. "I will be delivering you to Kauvras, and I will get my answers when you wed."

I almost vomited right then and there. "I will do *no such thing.*"

"You won't have a choice, *sweetheart*," he sneered.

I charged him again, but before I could make any headway, he flicked his wrist and threw his dagger straight for me. Without a thought I moved to dodge it, but it stopped and fell to the grass as if it had hit an invisible wall. What the actual *fuck*?

"Just as I thought. You *are* her daughter."

◆ ◆ ◆

There was no firewood on the plains. We laid a few feet apart on the grass, the moon making its way across the early evening sky. My chest was aching, my mouth inflamed with questions I hadn't been able to ask. Every time I tried to speak, the tears would well.

Not that Miles seemed to mind the silence.

He had passed me a small hunk of cheese, telling me to eat. I was somehow starving yet my appetite was nonexistent. Miles all but pushed it down my throat. "How the hell am I supposed to get my reward if you die of hunger? No bitterferns out here, sweetheart." The cheese was tasteless and tough, but I made myself swallow it.

I needed my dagger. I had no idea where we were, and I knew if I killed Miles I'd also die out here. But I wanted *my* dagger back. Even if I didn't know how to use it, I could figure out which end to stab the bastard with. "What's with the masks?" I finally pushed out. Maybe if I could throw off his defense enough, I could steal back my blade while he slept tonight.

"Separates us from you lot." He said the words with such disgust that I had to fight back the urge to scream at him. "And keeps the smoke out."

"What do they mean?"

"The animals? Nothing, really. They're supposed to intimidate the Vacants."

I raised a brow in question. "Those addicted," he clarified. "We call them Vacants."

"Well, the *Vacants* don't seem to be aware of what's going on around them. Why would they be scared of a mask?"

"Wasn't my idea."

"I'm guessing Kauvras wears some sort of elaborate mask," I mused.

"I've been told Kauvras doesn't wear a mask."

"You've been told? You've never seen him?" The air chilled slightly while the last wisps of warmth seemed to leave the earth all at once.

"Very few people get to see him."

"He wants to be a *Saint* but won't let the people see his face?"

I heard the sneer in his words. "I don't make the rules, sweetheart. Besides, I've heard King Belin of Eserene is a rather elusive man."

"At least he isn't murdering people for a pointless cause. And you may not make the rules, but you enforce them. That's just as bad."

"I do what I need to do to survive." The statement shot through me. Shame bubbled within me at the thought of what I once did to survive.

"So you don't believe in his cause?" I pried.

"So many questions."

I needed to push the conversation toward what I *really* wanted to know. "And I have to marry him, *why?*"

Miles sighed. "Because you are the missing piece to his claim to Sainthood. He marries the Daughter of Katia, he ascends to Sainthood."

I wasn't worried because that wasn't going to happen. I wasn't worried because I wasn't the daughter of anyone but my parents, Irabel and Sarek Gaignory.

Homesickness began to swell in my chest, for Inkwell, for my old life, for the first time marriage had seemed like a real possibility. I would have done *anything* to bring Cal back, to marry him.

"Sleep," he ordered. "We've got days of walking ahead until we get to Taitha."

I rolled over in the grass, staring at the Onyxian Mountains in the distance, and wished on every star that this wasn't real life. I couldn't wallow for long, though, because tonight, after Miles fell asleep, I was getting my dagger and leaving.

◆ ◆ ◆

I fought the urge to sleep until I heard Miles' breathing slow and deepen, fighting to keep my eyes open. I hadn't realized how exhausted I was, how my body was begging me for rest. I waited a bit longer, until I knew his sleep was deep enough not to be easily disturbed.

Hopefully.

I righted myself, sitting up and feeling for the reassuring presence of the diadem among the ruffles of my dress. I couldn't wait to get this thing off of me.

Miles had kept his belt on while he slept, his bow still slung over his shoulder. It looked uncomfortable, but I suppose it was a smart decision on his part. Not smart enough though — because he had fallen asleep on his right side, my dagger there for the taking on his left.

Gathering my ruffles as best I could, I padded over the grass, every tiny *crunch* sending my heart racing faster and faster. I stood over his sleeping form, the diamond on the hilt of *my* dagger peeking out of the sheath, reflecting the starry sky above. What a *stupid* man, falling asleep and leaving my blade so exposed. He deserved to have it stolen.

With a deep breath I leaned over, my hand closing over the hilt as I pulled it free. Slowly, slowly, slow—

Miles' arm shot back, deftly swiping the dagger from my grasp without looking and pointing it straight at my throat, all without so much as turning over. *Fucking* Saints.

"Sleep," he commanded flatly, neither raising his head nor opening his eyes. He fluidly sheathed the dagger at his hip once again, completely unphased by the almost-attempt to escape.

I evened my breathing as best I could, dropping my ruffles as my face heated with embarrassment. I let the lack of control stoke the heated fury within me, and I added him to my growing list of people to burn.

Chapter 34

Then

No no no no no.

Calomyr couldn't be dead. Because that would mean that every single person who meant something to me, aside from my mother, had been ripped from my life. Because even a world devoid of Saints, devoid of a higher power, devoid of a universal truth, couldn't support a world with so much pain, so much devastation. My grief was heavy enough to fracture the world beneath it.

"Petra, I'm so sorry," my mother whispered.

Before I could ask how, my legs began to move. I bolted out the door, past Tyrak, the air closing in around me as I sprinted through the streets. Shabby buildings flew past me as my feet carried me to the water, then west to the only place I could think to go.

My lungs burned as I reached the cliffs, shuffling along the small ledge, willing my eyes to stay clear until I turned the last corner.

My feet hit the cave floor and I crumbled to the ground, wishing the walls would collapse over me, crush me into the oblivion that held Larka, and Da, and now, Calomyr.

Fists and feet and knees and elbows connected with stone, blood beginning to run down my limbs. My knuckles split and I welcomed the pain, anything, *anything* to distract me from the gaping wound in my chest.

Calomyr was dead. The man I loved was dead. My future was dead.

I laid back, staring at the dark crystals on the ceiling of the cave, and willed death to find me, too.

◆ ◆ ◆

Inkwell was empty, its residents having flooded the other districts to try to steal a look at the King as he and the rest of the High Royal Court left the city for some foreign business. The King's bedroom would be empty, then, just as I was. I relished the silence that so rarely found its way into Inkwell, the empty streets leaving room for my grief.

I laid in front of the fireplace that raged despite the warm summer day. The suffocating heat against my skin was the only reminder that I was alive. I shouldn't be this close to the flames — I knew that had I not been consumed by grief, the heat would burn. But I didn't think I could be in any more pain than I was right now.

Castemont told me they buried Cal in the Royal Cemetery, in a section designated for fallen guards. He told me I wasn't allowed in the castle, and I wanted to scream at him and tell him I'd already been to the castle, but I'd promised Cal I'd keep it a secret. And I was afraid. Afraid that if I saw Cal's lifeless form nestled in the dirt, I'd throw myself in with him. Afraid of what the sight would rip open within me. So while his funeral was attended by the guards and royals he knew and the rest of the city tried to catch a glimpse of its Invisible King, I inched closer and closer to the fire.

A training exercise had gone wrong. That's all it was. A demonstration for new recruits had somehow ended with a sword in his abdomen. That was all Castemont knew.

It was all I could think about.

Every time I closed my eyes, I saw his, the blue and green burning my insides just as the fire should have burned my outsides, the light leaving them as he fell to the ground, blood pouring from his wound. I could picture his hands flying to his stomach, the same hands that had held me.

My mother set plates of food down on the wooden floor near where I lay. I didn't touch any of it. How could I? She eventually coaxed me to chew and swallow a few bits of bread, but they quickly came back up in a fit of vomit and tears. She stopped trying after that.

Day turned to night and night to day as every bit of the future that I'd briefly dreamed of turned to cinders in my hands.

◆ ◆ ◆

Four months had passed by the time I looked in the mirror again. I couldn't stand the thought of staring at my reflection, at the face that he had stared into. When I finally mustered up the courage to look, my cheekbones were protruding from my face in a way that made me look thoroughly Inkwellian. My hips were sharp. My wrists were like twigs.

Solise funneled tinctures and tonics down my throat, assuring me that they'd keep me healthy while I wasted away. I didn't have the energy to fight her. "You are strong, child. You are loved. You were never a victim, always a warrior," she'd whisper to me as I wept, running her hands over my back. "Fire burned and ocean tumbled."

With Larka and Da, I hadn't had the luxury of grieving, because without me, we'd have starved. At first I thought that was why Cal's death hurt me so much, because I had the time to hurt, the time to grieve. But somewhere between the flames and smoke, I realized that he was the only person who made me feel alive, who made me feel like life was for more than simply surviving, that I could *live*. And now, he was gone.

Now, in our little house, with our stack of firewood and cupboard of food, I could grieve the loss of the other half of my soul.

◆ ◆ ◆

Lord Castemont proposed to my mother the same day I was able to feed myself for the first time, to lift a spoon to my mouth. The ring was exquisite, and even in my vegetative state, even though the color hurt me to even think about, I could tell that the emerald that sat atop the gold band was beautiful.

But no. It had been four months since Calomyr left me. Only a year since Larka. And seven months since my father. *Seven months.*

My mother could not marry Lord Castemont. Somewhere in the haze of my grief, my mother had bloomed again, the sweet, delicate bits of her personality opening their petals to the world, petals I'd never seen before. But each time her laugh floated through the cottage, each time Lord Castemont placed a hand over hers, I swelled with such rage that I felt I may explode.

How could she disrespect Da like that? Why did she get to be happy while I was shattered once again?

It sickened me knowing my Da was rotting in the ground. Knowing that *my* Cal was rotting in the ground.

◆ ◆ ◆

"No," I said absently, lying on my side, facing the raging fire in the hearth.

"No?" my mother asked quietly. She and Lord Castemont sat together on the leather couch behind me, the sound of their breathing quickening.

"No. You do not have my blessing. What a stupid fucking question."

"Petra!" my mother gasped.

"Irabel, darling, of course this is a shock to her," Castemont's voice chided. "I should have asked you how you felt about it first, Petra, and for that I'm sorry."

I heard my mother take a deep breath. "He's done so much for us, Petra, and I didn't realize it, but...but we were falling in love."

Give me a *fucking* break. I rolled my eyes so hard I was surprised my head didn't roll with them. "Da died seven months ago, Ma. *Seven months.* You were in love with Da seven months ago.*"

"And don't you think Da would want me to be happy?"

I sat up so quickly that stars swam in my vision. Slowly, I rose to my feet, turning to face them on knobby knees. The look on her face was filled with heartbreaking longing. I schooled my features into neutrality, not wanting any of my empathy to escape.

"Your mother will *always* love your father," Lord Castemont said, his hand squeezing my mother's. "Just as I will always love my Berna. But your mother and I have found great comfort in each other, and an even greater love."

Unbelievable. Un-*fucking*-believable. I debated what I should say, whether I should fly off the handle or deliver a cool, calculated blow. But I simply walked through the room, up the stairs, and to my bedroom, where my tears slid silently down my face for the rest of the night.

My days became a blur as I began to spend them sitting on the cliff's edge. I hadn't been able to return to the cave since the day Cal died. I wasn't sure I'd be able to stomach it. I knew I'd either feel him there or feel nothing, and I didn't know which one scared me more.

My feet dangled off the cliff, my back pressed against the frosted grass of the cliff's plateau. It was shaping up to be an icy winter rather than a snowy one. I was thankful for the sting in the air. It made everything else hurt less.

Life had been hard. But it was simple. And now...

Now life and death were in a duel, and death wielded a sword while life swung a stick. If the Saints were real, Rhedros had the upper hand, Cyen leading the charge from atop his black stallion. Everything I'd known had been touched by the fingers of death, corroded and rotting in a smoking heap of pain and guilt and ash.

◆ ◆ ◆

I sat in the sagging armchair and stared at the woman as she read the tiny print on each bottle, separating them by whether they could be purchased anywhere or if they were only available in Eserene. She muttered to herself, scribbling notes on parchment as she sorted, filling a crate with those she chose to take. "When will you be back?" I tried to keep my tone from sounding too nervous, too eager, but she saw right through it.

Solise gave a close lipped smile as she tallied off another vial. "You know the answer, Petra."

I did know the answer, and I didn't like it. I knew that more likely than not, Solise would never return to Eserene. "And the letter said *what*, exactly?"

She silently pushed a folded piece of parchment to the edge of the table.

Dearest Solise,

I'm afraid I must ask you to come to me. I've fallen ill and am in need of care. I have no one else to ask.

Sincerely,
Your sister

"A bit nondescript, no?" I asked suspiciously, placing the letter back on the table. The script was hurried, smudged in places.

Solise sighed. "I know this is hard, Petra. Believe me, I don't want to leave Eserene. But my sister needs me."

I nodded in understanding, because I knew I'd have dropped everything if I got the same letter from Larka. Solise was headed to some tiny town on the border of Widoras and Xomma, the third country on the continent of Astran, where her sister had found herself living after she'd fallen in love with a traveling bard. A bard who, I assumed, was dead now, if she was asking her sister to make the journey across the country.

Castemont had arranged a private escort for her to ensure safe passage through the wild lands outside the walls of Eserene. The smallest of comforts. Solise didn't want to accept the gesture, but I told her she had to. Her herbs, tinctures, and elixirs were the last things she needed to pack, and I watched as she got closer and closer to the end of her stash.

"What do you think?" I asked.

"Of?"

"Castemont."

She didn't look up from her work. "I think he loves your mother very much."

"But what do you think of *him?*" I pressed.

She stopped and folded her hands on the table. "I think he is a very kind man with a very kind heart." I could tell she had more she wanted to say, but she pursed her lips.

I stayed silent, simply cocking a brow at her.

She sighed through her nose as her eyes looked everywhere but at me. "I told you how I felt about...about Calomyr." I tensed at the mention of his name, steeling myself against the rush of pain that accompanied it. "And I'm sorry. I'm so, so sorry, Petra. I feel the same way about Castemont. Something is off." I didn't have the energy to push her on it. I knew, deep down, what she was saying, because I felt it too. "But love..." she continued. "Love overshadows all else. All reasoning, all sense, all logic. I wish it weren't the case, but you know better than anyone that it's true."

I knew that regardless of what Solise had told me about Calomyr, no matter how true, that reason, sense, and logic would not be present. Because even though our time together was short — too short — I think I would have loved him to the ends of the earth. I still did.

I sat back down with the realization that Castemont and my mother shared that same kind of love.

A knock sounded at the door. "Come in!" Solise yelled up from her last few bottles. Lord Castemont pushed the door open,

Tyrak in full armor close behind. I hadn't seen Tyrak in full armor since the day I met Castemont — gloves, a full-face helmet, multiple swords on each hip. He was usually a solid, steady presence in his normal leathers, but his armored form was noticeably imposing in Solise's small cottage.

"Almost ready?" Castemont asked, his voice light.

"Just about," she answered. "Everything that's coming with me is there by the door."

Tyrak immediately set to work picking up a large crate of even more jars and vials and heading to the front door. Castemont pulled the door open for him and I caught a glimpse of the horse-drawn cart in the street.

Castemont lowered himself into the worn chair opposite mine. I know I looked miserable; my eyes had been swollen and puffy for months, my face gaunt, my shoulders sagging. I managed a slight nod. "I'll be sure she gets there safely," he offered, a sympathetic smile on his face.

"Last one," Solise called to Tyrak as she placed the final crate on the dwindling pile then moved to stand in the doorway to watch him. Each box, bag, and crate that Tyrak took was like a ticking clock, counting down the minutes I had left with Solise.

"Tyrak will formally brief her escorts at the gates, hence the full armor. She'll be well-guarded throughout the entire journey. I've arranged a carriage so she'll be protected from the elements and any wildlife." I bristled at the word, thinking once again of the soothsayer's words. Solise's journey to the border of Xomma wouldn't take her through the Onyx Pass, but the rest of the Onyxian Mountains were dangerous nonetheless.

To be honest, I wasn't thinking about Solise's journey, selfish as it may be. I was thinking about the loss of yet another person of significant meaning to me, not to death but to circumstances of life. Solise's sister needed her, so she had to go. But I needed her too.

"Looks like that's the last of it," Solise murmured quietly, walking to the small living area.

"I'll give you two a moment," Castemont said, bowing his head before ducking out the door.

My lip wobbled and I fought to stop it, but it was no use. Looking into Solise's deep brown eyes, I saw they too were glistening. We wrapped our arms around each other, both of us losing control of the emotions we'd tried to hold back.

I pulled away, her hands grabbing mine and squeezing. "What am I going to do without you?" I whispered, my cheeks thoroughly wet.

She pushed a strand of hair behind my ears. "You're going to be just fine, Petra. You are stronger than you think you are."

Salty disbelief stung my eyes, and I let them flutter closed at the words. "How can I ever thank you for everything you've done?"

Her wrinkled face softened into a smile. "You can thank me by continuing to fight," she offered. "You can thank me by continuing not to break when the world has stretched you to your limit and beat you against the ground. You can thank me by *living*, Petra, not just surviving." My eyes welled again, her words resounding through me and settling in my bones. "You will find happiness again, the happiness that you so rightfully deserve. It's out there. And when you find it, you can thank me by grabbing hold of it and claiming it as your own. You can thank me by being happy."

She folded me into her arms again. "Thank you," I whispered.

"Thank *you*," she whispered back. "I didn't know if I'd find happiness after Novis died." The mention of her son's name caused my breath to catch. "Thank you for letting me be a mother again."

The words settled between us, the realization that we'd both been exactly what the other needed at exactly the right time. Solise righted herself and cleared her throat, straightening her robes. I tried to pull myself together, but I knew any attempt would be futile. She looked at me and nodded, then headed for the door. I followed her onto the street, watching her tiny figure crawl on the back of the cart, legs dangling off the edge. Castemont and Tyrak sat in the seats at the front, Tyrak taking the reins of the two brown horses and snapping them, the horses beginning to move.

Tyrak turned back to look at me, giving a slight nod from behind his helmet as they departed. Solise simply raised a hand, a sorrowful smile on her face as they turned the corner to take her away from me.

Chapter 35

Now

It had been days and days of clipped conversations and shitty bread as we moved over the middle of the continent. I didn't know when we passed into Cabillia, but the grassy plains became drier and drier until the horizon was interrupted by small bumps and shapes.

Taitha.

As we neared the city, I began to identify the outlines of buildings — there was no wall like the monstrous one that surrounded Eserene. Just the slight rolling hills of the farmlands that lead to the city. "What is *that*?" I asked, pointing at a structure that rose high above the houses, cathedrals, and shops. It was blocky, a harsh mark against the blue sky.

"The castle."

I raised an eyebrow. "That doesn't look anything like the Eserenian castle." I had no other castle to compare it to.

"Oh, I'm sorry. Does it not live up to your royal standards? What were you doing when we sacked the city, having a tea party with other royal bitches in fancy gowns?"

"I was getting the absolute shit beat out of me."

"I said *before* we sacked the city."

"And I said I was getting the absolute *shit* beat out of me."

His footsteps stopped behind me. "What?" I kept walking.

"Initiation. I'd ask if you've heard of it but apparently it's only done in Eserene." The anger stewed hot within me.

"Oh, I've heard of Initiation. I thought it was a story that Cabillian parents told their daughters to make them behave. That they needed to be good or they'd ship them off to Eserene for Initiation. I didn't think it was real, even when..." He trailed off. I stopped and turned to where he stood about twenty feet behind me. I stared at him, pursing my lips. "So your *own* people did all that to you?" I clenched my jaw in response. "I thought my men had done that to you for being disobedient."

I cocked a brow at him. "So it was okay for your men to beat me?"

"I only meant that I wouldn't expect *your own people* to do that to you."

"They're *not* my people." Every scream I'd held back since moving into the Low Royal Castle tangled in my throat, my chest swelling with an anger so turbulent that it felt like Rhedros was inside my rib cage.

"What's your name?" he blurted.

He hadn't asked before this. And I hadn't told him.

"It doesn't matter."

◆ ◆ ◆

My stomach twisted as I beheld the small huts sprinkled like specks of dust across the fields, rickety fences containing even more rickety cows. I didn't want to look too long at any of the small structures, knowing one of them could be the walls that had stood around Calomyr and his brother.

"Your palace awaits, my Lady," Miles muttered gruffly as we followed a beaten path to the city.

I snarled at him.

I'm not sure what I had been expecting. Maybe streets filled with zombies, vacant eyes staring into the ether while bloody attacks happened on every corner. Wrena said Kauvras had forced the pipe on anyone he could get his hands on. But this city was...normal.

Vendors yelled from carts about breads and cheeses, fabric and ceramics. Children ran around their mothers, pulling on skirts to ask for sweets and trinkets. There were beautifully kept horses, clean people with clear eyes.

I stayed close to Miles as he wove through the crowds, past lively conversations and the smell of baking pastries. People jumped out of the way at the sight of Miles. I felt the stares of the townspeople on me, my Initiation gown beckoning for attention. Perhaps I'd have some leeway to demand clean clothing when we got to the castle. And a bath.

"I thought everyone would be addicted to leechthorn here," I said just above a whisper. We moved deeper and deeper into the city, into the shadow of the castle.

"If everyone is on leechthorn, who the hell is going to tell the story when it's over?" When it's over? His tone was unbothered as we turned a corner, wide steps rising to massive wooden doors at the castle. Masked guards stood every few steps, hands on the hilts of swords, metallic masks gleaming in the sun. "Any city resident who swore fealty to Kauvras and his cause were allowed to stay in the city, *uncorrupted,* as some may say."

"And I'm guessing anyone who didn't...?"

He gave a low laugh. "The city reeked of leechthorn for weeks, and the sidewalks were stained red just as long." I bristled at his words.

Figures began to take shape on the walls of the castle, figures that looked a lot like–

My stomach jolted as I realized I was looking at a dozen bodies in all states of mutilation and decay hanging from the walls. I couldn't keep my eyes from scanning them even as I tried to tear them away. The one closest to the massive wooden doors was a hulking man, blistered burns across his arms and dried blood crusting his leathers, having poured from the gaping wound on his neck. The flies swarmed, crawling across the metal bear mask that sat on his lolling head. I froze midstep, barely noticing Miles stop on the step above me.

"Is that... Is that Vorkalth?" I whispered.

"Huh. Looks like it is," Miles said nonchalantly, cocking his head.

"Why is he *dead*?" My voice caught in my throat. Nausea churning in my gut. But it was nausea laced with something pleasant, something slightly sweet at the sight of him.

"I'm guessing when Vorkalth arrived back in Taitha he told Kauvras of the woman who needed two doses of leechthorn. I'm sure Kauvras asked him where you were, but he lost you. So...it's the wall for him." Miles continued his ascent and I finally managed to tear my eyes away.

Not a single guard protested as Miles and I approached the doors which swung open in time for us to stride in without losing speed. It reminded me of the night Calomyr took me to the King's Keep.

The entry hall opened in front of us, soaring ceilings higher than I'd ever seen. Everything was stone — cold, gray, merciless stone. Nothing beautiful, nothing ornate, nothing worth a second glance.

A band of young women snapped to attention, their heads lowering as we neared. "Lieutenant Landgrave," one of them said, stepping forward. "Welcome back to Taitha." She was small, dark haired with petite features, her beauty at war with the harshness of her surroundings. "May I show your guest to her rooms?"

"That won't be necessary, Anna, thank you," Miles answered. My heartbeat quickened. I swallowed as he turned to me. "I will show you to your rooms and give you some time to...freshen up." I could hear the sneer with his last words. "I'll send someone to check you over and bring you a gown, and I will collect you in an hour's time to meet your groom." I tried not to tense up.

Winding, empty corridors blurred together as I followed Miles, finally stopping outside a door that looked identical to the dozens of others we had passed. "One hour," he said, before turning and leaving.

I pushed the door open. Cold, gray, lifeless. Just like the rest of the castle.

I didn't take the time to check the room for possible escape routes. Where would I even go if I managed to run? A door to the left of the room was propped open, leading to a bathing room with — oh, thank the fucking *Saints* — a bathtub. It was already full of water, tendrils of steam dancing over its surface. I was terrified to look in the mirror, to see what the journey had done to me, so I carefully avoided it as I untied the corset and peeled the dress from my body. I let it crumple to the floor, a sinister bouquet of red and white roses. I sifted through the fabric to find the diadem, closely inspecting it to make sure it wasn't damaged. It looked just as perfect, just as comforting as ever.

Other than the small dent of a scar in my thigh from the arrow, my body showed no evidence that *anything* had happened. My feet were sore, but beyond that, nothing hurt.

I stepped into the steaming bath, the water immediately sullied as the caked blood and dirt dissolved. I dunked my head, wondering if I could hold myself under water just long enough to end this nightmare.

The need for oxygen took hold as I broke the surface, and questions began to flash through my mind as I took a deep breath.

Daughter of Katia?

And I healed myself?

And I *killed* dozens of wild animals without any weapons?

What the fuck was I going to do when I was presented to Kauvras?

I dunked my head again, hoping that the answers to every question would magically appear in my head when I came up for air. That was not the case.

A small knock sounded at the door to my room. "Come in," I shouted, not moving from the tub. I heard the door click open softly, then the sound of fabric rustling as the person, who I assumed to be someone Miles sent to my room, moved toward the bed. More rustling fabric, then the sound of glasses on a tabletop. "I just need a minute," I called to the person, my voice raspy and weak. They didn't answer.

I took a bar of soap from a small basket on the side of the bathtub and scrubbed my skin until it was raw, the dirty water swirling around me. Four years ago I would have dreamed of a bathtub, and I wouldn't have cared when the water became filthy with my dirt and grime. Now here I was, with what should be an indulgence, wishing I was anywhere else.

I finally stood and let the water fall from my bare skin. I wasn't ready to step out, knowing that when I did, I was one minute closer to facing Kauvras with no idea what was going to happen. I reminded myself of the time limit Miles had given me and the fact that someone had brought me a gown. I figured I should let her check for any wounds I may have overlooked, considering...well, everything.

I toweled off and finally looked in the mirror. And I looked...surprisingly strong. Tall. The time without any real nourishment hadn't transformed me into the gaunt wisp I had been in Inkwell, and sure enough no major evidence remained from the Board's assault.

Wrapping myself in an ivory silk robe I plucked from a hook on the wall, I hurried out the bathing room door. The person Miles had sent turned to greet me and dropped the vial of herbs she held, the glass shattering on the floor.

Looking back at me from across the room was Solise.

Chapter 36

Two Years Ago

"One? Or two?" I called through the kitchen to the living room.

"One is fine, thank you," my mother responded.

"I'll have two, darling," Castemont answered.

I took a deep breath, ignoring the nicety and subsequent chatter drifting in from where they sat in the living room. I poured three small dollops of batter across the sizzling pan, the smell immediately filling the cottage.

For two years, I missed Solise, and for two years, Solise's words swirled through my mind. *Something is off.* But what? She'd been wrong about Calomyr and there really was no reason for me to hate Castemont. He'd been nothing but kind to us, providing us with a life we could live rather than survive, just like Solise had wanted. He appeared to love my mother fiercely, irrevocably.

The biggest issue I had was *why. Why the hell* would a man — and not just a man, but a Lord of Eserene, a Low Royal — personally fund the lives of two strangers? The Benevolent Saints told him to. That's what he'd told me. But *why* stick around a weepy, mopey widow until she was no longer weepy and mopey?

Why insist on taking in her child — her defiant, unagreeable, *adult* child — as his own? He was handsome, he was excessively wealthy, and he was *royal*. He could have had his pick of eligible women. Women who were raised for the position, knew the role they were expected to play. Women who were younger and richer and more beautiful than my mother.

Maybe love was all it was. Simple as that. *Without reason, without sense, without logic.*

I took a deep breath, knowing that Castemont would ask me soon enough–

"Have you given any more thought to my proposal, Petra?" There it was. I was grateful to be facing away from them, because my face contorted into a puckered mix of annoyance and anger at the sound of his voice. He brought it up at least once a day.

"I do not wish to live in the castle." My answer was the same as it always was, my tone even, flat. Unemotional. They may be without their mental faculties, but I didn't have to be.

"Think of the opportunities that await, Petra!" my mother chimed.

"Like what, marriage?" I shot back. "To some snotty-ass nobleman's son? I've said it before, and I'll say it again. No, thank you."

"If you agree, you still have a year to prepare," Castemont added. It would take at least that long to make preparations for the wedding, to get approval from the court for the marriage. Apparently royals couldn't just marry whomever they pleased.

My mother had come across *some* sense and had agreed not to move into the castle, not to follow through with the wedding until I gave my full approval. Castemont understood without question, willing to play the game I laid in front of him.

And shit, if he didn't play it well. His wealth seemed to know no bounds, and neither did his motivation to win me over, even after two years of my constant rejection. He showered me with gifts and compliments, tried to help with housework and hired a maid when I refused his help, invited us to fancy dinners, ceremonies, and events, all of which I declined.

I was not a nobleman's daughter, and I had no desire to pretend I was.

Castemont got to know the neighbors, offered them help with patching roofs and sealing gaps. He and my mother would stroll through the streets, Castemont offering smiles to the poor and the wretched. Though he never gave up his courtly appearance, he had thoroughly embraced life in Inkwell. He'd told me over and over that he wouldn't stop until I knew his intentions were pure.

"Breakfast is ready," I called, placing the plates on the small table in the breakfast nook.

"Thank you, darling, so very much." His tone was sincere as he and my mother approached the table. I had come a long way and had only recently begun to offer him food when I cooked. It had felt too intimate, too real before. I gave a tight lipped smile as the three of us sat around the table. "Your birthday is fast approaching," he said.

"Twenty-three," my mother answered with a smile, placing a small forkful of pancake in her mouth.

I nodded. "Twenty-three."

"What would you like for your birthday?"

I chewed hard, knowing that this was going to turn into another attempt to buy my approval. "I have everything I need."

"But what is something you *want?*" he pushed.

For you to leave. For you to stop smothering me. For you to go back to your castle without us. "I don't want anything."

He looked down at his plate a bit awkwardly, a pang of hurt on his face. I fought back guilt at the fact that this man was doing everything he could to help us and I was all but spitting in his face.

But my brain kept circling back to the same question. *Why?*

◆ ◆ ◆

I could hear the wind whistling through the cave as I stood on the ledge. One more step and I'd be back for the first time since that day.

342

My back was pressed against the cliff side, my fingers running over the rocks behind me. The first full moon of autumn had brought uncharacteristically cold air that nipped at my cheeks and nose. The harbor was choppy today, and the sea beyond it even worse; glimpses of the wrath of Idros visible in the spray that flew over the breakwall. But the sun shone, and I knew that it was a matter of time before the lights came alive inside the cave.

Just do it. Just walk in.

It wasn't the first time I had stood in this exact position in this exact spot, listening for an answer in the waves. "Go," they seemed to call to me. I stepped around the corner.

A silence that was louder than the crash of the waves pushed in on me as I beheld this little slice of my past. *You are okay. You are okay. You are okay.* I closed my eyes, wishing to hear his voice, wishing to smell the smoke and cedar, but nothing came. Nothing but stale air and cold and heartache.

"You're not here," I whispered, the weight of reality sinking into my chest. It was going to crush me. "I need you, and you're not here." I moved to the middle of the cave and stared up at the crystals still cloaked in shadow. "You're not here! Why did you have to go?!" I let myself hit the floor, the same spot where he had laid me down. Where I realized I was going to fall in love with him. Where I thought to myself that maybe I already had.

The lights started then, the harbor's furious movements causing the glimmers to sprint back and forth across the cave erratically. I closed my eyes and let them wash over me, let the tears flood my eyes, let myself remember him. I had never let myself wonder if he had thought of me in his last moments, never breathed life into the possibility that he had or hadn't. I suspected both would be just as painful, just as heart wrenching, just as devastating.

I opened my eyes again when I knew the lights had ceased, gone back to live in their crystals until tomorrow came. My head fell to the side, facing the rock we sat on the first day he brought me here. I tried to make his figure materialize, tried to find his outline in the cave wall, but it was no use. I rolled onto my side, content to lay in my misery, but something caught my eye.

There was something dark behind the boulder, something that didn't seem to belong.

I rose and shuffled over to see whatever it was neatly folded and tucked between the rock and the wall of the cave. Did anyone else know about this cave? Did someone leave something here? I grabbed it, the fabric falling open, and as I unfolded it, I saw... Two buttons and a tie.

It couldn't be.

I didn't want to turn it over in my hands, to look for the little flaw that would tell me what it was, but my hands were moving to the hem.

A small tear with frayed edges.

It was my Da's cloak.

Chapter 37

Now

I stood in the silk robe, my mouth gaping at the woman before me. Solise's eyes were the size of the moon as she stared at me, pure disbelief on her face, the same familiar face I hadn't seen in almost three years.

And then we were rushing toward each other, tears streaming, the sobs saying what we couldn't. She pulled back to hold me at arms' length. "What are you doing here?" I cried.

"We don't have much time. Your mother?" she choked.

My head shook in some semblance of a nod. "She's here. She's here somewhere," I said through tears. "She's...gone." Solise nodded in grave understanding. She wasn't surprised. "How are you here? What happened? Where is your sister?"

"I will explain everything soon. I heard rumors a few days ago that Eserene had fallen." I nodded frantically. "I've been praying to my Saints every single day, Petra. Praying that you and your mother weren't hurt or killed, that you hadn't taken the pipe, that Castemont had gotten you two out safely." She searched my face, and I saw the confusion across hers. "Why didn't they make you take it?"

"They did." Her eyes widened.

"What?"

"I've taken it three times. And I feel nothing, no different than before. It...it doesn't affect me." The confusion didn't leave her face, but I could see her working over my words in her head.

"What are you doing here? In the castle?"

How the hell was I supposed to explain all that had happened? The fact I had decided to move into Castemont's residence? The Board of Blood, the trip through the Onyx Pass, the healing and the...powers? Miles and his insistence regarding my true identity? The fact that she was *right about Castemont*, that what was off about him was the fact that he was a self-serving bastard? "Solise," I started, grabbing her hands. "I will tell you everything as soon as I figure it out for myself. I don't know what's happening, I don't know why I'm here, but I'm to be brought before Kauvras in less than an hour."

Her face went ghostly white. "Why?" Her whisper was shaky.

"I... I don't exactly know."

"I've heard whispers, Petra," she started. "Whispers growing louder between the guards that the Daughter of Katia is coming. You don't think... They couldn't think–"

"No, that's ridiculous," I blurted, pushing Miles' words from my head.

A solid pounding on the door broke through the room. "Twenty minutes," Miles' raspy voice called.

I inhaled sharply, looking at the woman who had been like a mother to me. Marita had reminded me so much of Solise, and I pushed down the last image I had of my tutor.

For so long I assumed the role of provider when the responsibility should have fallen on my mother. I was tired of being the one to take care of everything, tired of being depended on, tired of being lost. "What do I do Solise?"

Her eyes didn't leave my face as she raised her hand to her mouth, chewing on a fingernail. "We need to get you ready. Are you hurt?"

"No," I said quickly. She nodded and pushed me toward the bed where a gown of crimson satin lay. It was beautiful — thin gold filigree stitching from the delicate straps through the deep vee of the bodice to the waist made it appear to be dipped in gold, the skirts blood red beneath. As I dressed, I thought of the expressions she'd make when I told her about my apparent power to heal. She'd be wonderstruck. I let that thought keep my mind from spiraling.

She herded me toward a chair that sat before a small vanity and began frantically brushing through my tangled hair, still wet from the bath. She braided and twisted and pinned, and all the while, she spoke.

"Listen to me Petra, and listen closely. Kauvras will not kill you, at least until he knows you are not the Daughter of Katia. If he believes you are this prophesized Daughter of Katia, he will want to wed immediately." I swallowed hard. "You need to make him think you are."

"What?" It was almost a shriek.

"If he believes you're not descended from Katia herself, he will kill you without a second thought. *Play along.* Make him think there's a chance. It will keep you alive long enough for me to get you out of here." My head spun at her words. I realized I was biting my lip so hard that the skin almost broke. "Petra! Are you listening to me?" I nodded, wide eyed. "I am going to get you out of here."

"My mother–"

"Petra," she cut me off. "If she's addicted–"

"No. I know she's not coming back." I steeled my heart against the words, staring at Solise in the mirror. "I just want to know she's alive."

She pursed her lips, the veins in her neck bulging, but she gave a small nod. "I'll see if I can find out where she is."

She pinned the last piece of my hair up, the wetness of it much less obvious. "My diadem," I whispered.

"What?"

"I have a diadem that Castemont gave me." I rose, rushing to the bathing room to grab it, nestling the replica of Katia's very own on my head.

I emerged to see Solise's dropped jaw again. "Is that..."

I nodded. "Yes. A little too perfect, considering the circumstances." Her face was grave as she straightened the straps on my gown and smoothed the skirts.

My mind was still circling around the fact that Solise was *here*. "Tell me, is your sister here?"

"No," she said, narrowing her eyes at my question. "I'm not even sure if she's alive. I was halfway to Skystead when I was captured."

"Skystead?" I whispered, my own eyes narrowing as I wracked my brain for why the city sounded so familiar. Skystead. *Skystead.* "Solise, what is your sister's name?"

"Ingra," she murmured, questioning in her eyes.

"Ingra of Skystead," I whispered. Bile shot up my throat and I fought to keep it down, my mind spinning, swirling, spiraling around the threads of my life that somehow had knit themselves together. Her sister wasn't married to a traveling bard...her sister was a traveling soothsayer.

A knock sounded at the door.

We looked at each other, a river of unspoken words between us. I wanted to crumble right there, to tell her everything that had happened, to tell her about how I had met her sister, how I had found my father's cloak and still had no answers. But I knew now was not the time.

"Remember, Petra," Solise said, voice low. "You've always been a warrior," I choked on my tears. "Fire burned and ocean tumbled."

◆ ◆ ◆

"You tell him who you are," Miles growled in my ear from behind his mask. "Tell him you're the Daughter of Katia."

"I am *not* the Daughter of Katia," I snarled back, words thick with unsorted emotions. We stood outside the throne room, the stone antechamber heavy with masked guards.

He leaned in, the cold metal of his ram's head mask grazing my cheek. "You will tell him you're the Daughter of Katia and you will do what he asks of you, or your burned body will be hung from the city gates. Understood?"

I didn't have time to answer before the doors swung open. Miles straightened next to me, his hand moving to the hilt of his sword. "Enter." The word echoed as we stepped across the threshold.

Taitha's throne room was nothing like Eserene's. Everything had been constructed from the same gray stone; the floors, the walls, even the vaulted ceiling seemed to be made of stone. It was dull and cold and void of any sign of opulence, anything I had ever known a castle to be. Sconces sat on pillars at the edge of the hall, and a chandelier much too small for the space loomed overhead. Masked guards were stationed around the room, a cluster of guards in front of the throne.

The throne.

It was a massive chunk of the gray stone, the throne itself carved into it. The seat and back had been smoothed and polished, but everything else about it was jagged and raw. I had never seen anything like it, the sight so jarring that I didn't immediately see the figure nestled in the stone.

A rugged, handsome honey-brown face atop broad shoulders peered down at me as we approached him. He sat lazily in the throne, ankle over knee, slouched against the left side of it. As I got closer, his features began to take shape, a straight jaw, high cheeks, and then I saw them.

His eyes were the color of molten sapphire.

My gut pooled with ice. I knew those eyes. They were unmistakable. I'd memorized their shape, the way the light set the blue ablaze. I'd gazed into them so many times and it had still not been enough. It never would have been enough.

In the dusty, unfamiliar light of a foreign castle, I met Calomyr's father.

Chapter 38

Then

The world was silent around me as I sprinted back to Inkwell. I didn't hear the waves or the clopping of horse hooves or the shouts of vendors. I only heard the whoosh of my breath in and out of my lungs and the steady beat of my feet on the ground. Da's cloak was bundled under my arm.

Tyrak, waiting outside as always, saw me round the corner and opened the door for me as I burst into the house. Castemont was in the kitchen, his eyes scanning the heaving, disheveled woman in front of him.

"Petra, are you hurt?" I shook my head, unable to form my mouth around the words. "What–" I fanned the cloak open and he stopped, his eyes going wide. "Is that..."

I nodded, nausea bubbling in my gut. "His cloak." My voice cracked.

His face was unreadable, his jaw clenched, lips a thin line. "Where did you find it?"

But the answer didn't come. I choked on the realization, the confirmation that he hadn't fallen, that it hadn't been an accident, he hadn't jumped either. I had known the truth, it was buried deep in my bones, but I so desperately wanted to pretend it wasn't so, to give myself closure, even if that closure was built on a lie. All I could do was shake my head, my mouth opening and closing as the tears began to roll. The cloak fell to a heap on the ground. Before I knew it, I was folded in Castemont's arms, his chin resting atop my head as I shattered.

My mother came down the stairs then, her eyes flicking from our embrace to the crumpled fabric on the floor, her head shaking slightly. "It can't be," she whispered. She gathered the fabric, holding it in front of her before finding the hem, coming to the same conclusion I had.

She crumbled along with me, Castemont's arms wrapping easily around both of us as the pain of my father's death grew new roots in my soul.

◆ ◆ ◆

The three of us sat on the overstuffed leather sofa, the fire Castemont built in the hearth casting the cottage in a warm glow. I had opened my mouth to speak but couldn't find the words.

I wanted to tell Ma that I told her so, that I knew his death hadn't been an accident or premeditated on his part. I wanted to scream at her for denying it, for moving on with her life so quickly. "So...suicide?" she whispered into the room that had been silent save for the crackle of burning logs.

"I'm so sorry, my love," Castemont murmured, a hand on her knee.

"It wasn't suicide," I blurted. They both turned to me, puzzled. I shook my head, sorting through the night of his death and the days after and what was happening now. "How did his cloak end up in the cave?"

"Maybe that was where he..." She couldn't finish the sentence.

I continued shaking my head. "No, because I've been to that cave since he died. More than once. I would have seen it."

"You must have missed it," Castemont said, his voice coated with unnerving calm.

351

"No. I didn't. I would have seen it," I repeated. *I would have seen it.*

I hadn't been prepared for the haphazard stitches across this wound to be ripped open again. I hadn't come to terms with his manner of death, but when the cloak was still missing, it was easier to pretend that maybe it *had been* a fall. Finding his cloak, and finding it in a place where it had been placed purposely...the wound was not only ripped open but widened and doused in whiskey.

"He jumped, Petra," Castemont whispered.

My breath began to quicken, my lungs not able to hold enough air. "No, he didn't."

"I'm so sorry," Castemont continued. My mother's cries began again, and he moved to hold her against him. How could she accept this? My father would *not* have ended his own life. Not a fucking chance. But even if he had, how did the cloak turn up in the cave *all this time later?* Who had put it there? It made absolutely no sense.

Silently I rose, collected my own cloak and walked out the door.

"My Lady, may I be of any assistance?" Tyrak called as I descended the porch steps.

I pivoted to face him, staring up at him from the bottom step. He was handsome, like Castemont, but more rugged, his edges rougher. His cropped black hair was thick, pushed back from his olive face. "Tyrak..." I started, unsure of what I was going to say. "Is he a good man?"

Tyrak gave a small smile. "You're asking me if I think the Lord I've sworn fealty to is a good man?" I nodded. "Don't you think I'd be a bit biased?"

This was the longest conversation I'd ever had with Tyrak. I narrowed my eyes at his words. "I know your answer will be biased. But I have no one else to ask, no one else who would know." I walked up the steps to stand before him, my voice low. "I have a rather large decision to make. One that will change my life, and my mother's life, forever. I'm sure he's told you." He looked down at me, his dark, hooded eyes neutral. "I'm lowborn. You know this. I know nothing about royal life, nothing about what's expected of me. I am terrified to my core, Tyrak, to make the wrong decision. Your answer will stay between us, but your answer will decide my fate. I need to know. Is Castemont a good man?"

He stayed stone-faced, but I saw a muscle in his jaw feather as he thought. He turned to the front door, behind which my mother and Castemont sat. My mother and my potential step-father, the man she loved. He faced me again, his dark eyes alight and his brows furrowed.

"Lord Castemont is one of the most well-respected Lords in Eserene. He didn't earn that status without reason." I nodded, my eyes still on his, fully aware that he didn't directly answer the question.

"Let me rephrase," I said quietly. "Should my mother marry Lord Castemont? Knowing we'd move into the castle, that I'd be expected to take on the role of a nobleman's daughter?"

His face softened with contemplation, but the muscle in his jaw still twitched. He took a deep breath. "Yes."

I nodded, backing up. "Thank you, Tyrak," I said as I turned to the stairs again.

"I'm sorry, Petra." I stopped, whirling back to him, "for everything." He stared at me, brows furrowed slightly. I gave him another nod and walked into the street.

◆ ◆ ◆

The painter's palette of the night sky spread above me as I laid in the frosted grass on the waterfront. The din of the city behind me had grown quieter as the night deepened until nothing but a low chatter hung in the air.

"Mind if I join you?" I heard a rich voice say as Castemont walked up behind me.

I sat up, surveying him. He held a glass decanter as he looked down at me. I waved my hand to the side and he lowered himself to the ground.

"Your mother isn't much of a drinker," he said, pulling the cork out of the decanter, the smell of some kind of dark liquor hitting me almost instantly. "I realized tonight I've never asked if you like to drink." He offered me the decanter, and though I wasn't much of a drinker and didn't particularly like the taste of alcohol, I took it from him, taking as big of a swig as I could manage. My eyes watered and I fought back a gag, but the warmth that ran down my throat was satisfying. "Ah, your father raised a whiskey girl, huh?" he chuckled.

I didn't have the heart to tell him that we'd never once been able to afford whiskey. Wine, on occasion, and only the cheap stuff that left you achy and nauseous. "Guess he did."

"I'm truly sorry. From the bottom of my heart," he said, his voice sincere. I knew he was. "I'm sorry he did that."

"He didn't do anything. He didn't commit suicide," I snapped back.

"I'll never be him, Petra," he said suddenly, tipping the bottle to take a drink for himself. "I will never replace him. I know that. Your mother knows that. And you know that." He popped the cork back in and rested the decanter on the ground. "But I have fallen in love with your mother. And that means that I will love you, too, as long as you'll let me."

I turned my head away, my lips beginning to tremble. My question of why he would do this was being answered. It was love. Stupid, nonsensical, love.

Fuck.

My forearms rested on my knees, my head hanging from my shoulder. I took a deep breath and motioned for the whiskey. He popped it open and handed it to me, and I took another sip, the delicious burn returning, reddening my cheeks. I wiped my mouth on the back of my hand before turning back to him. I had no idea what the future held, but that was true whether I lived in Inkwell or in the castle. Why wouldn't I say yes to Castemont?

As soon as the burn dissipated in my throat, I spoke. "I accept."

His eyes flew open. "What?" he whispered.

"I accept. You can marry my mother, and we will move into the castle."

His eyes welled with tears as a smile the size of a crescent moon cracked across his face. And, despite everything, despite my

354

unanswered questions and unresolved pain, I couldn't help but smile back at him, at the man who was ecstatic to give us a new life.

Chapter 39

Now

"Petra," Kauvras crooned. He knew my name. I hadn't even told Miles my name. I clenched my jaw. "Petra Castemont, formerly Petra Gaignory. Born in the poorest part of Eserene. Your sister and father are with the Saints now — Benevolent, I hope." I took a deep breath, fighting the nausea that rose higher and higher in my throat. "When Commander Vorkalth told me of a woman unaffected by leechthorn on the first drag, I just knew it was you. I was a bit disappointed when he told me the second one had taken. Then he said you'd been killed en route. I was so terribly disappointed. I'm so glad Lieutenant Landgrave was able to ensure your safe passage, and to think the leechthorn hasn't affected you *at all*." The image of Vorkalth's limp body flashed in my head as Kauvras' eyes went wild.

"I would introduce her, but it seems you've already met," Miles said, a touch of questioning in his voice.

"Oh, we haven't," Kauvras answered, the blue resembling Calomyr's eyes boring down on me. "I haven't had the pleasure of

356

meeting the Daughter of Katia until now." He rose, his hulking figure taller than I'd expected. His shoulders were Calomyr's, the resemblance causing the familiar boiling storm within me to flare. "Though I feel after all these years I already know her." All these years? I kept my face blank as I stared into his eyes. *I am okay. I am okay. I am okay.* He grabbed my left hand and raised it to his lips, planting a kiss across my knuckles. Had Calomyr known Kauvras was his father? "I'm just surprised you haven't figured it out already."

My breathing instantly quickened despite my efforts. "What?"

A low laugh escaped Kauvras' lips, the echoes bouncing off the stones and multiplying. "While I'd love to be the one to tell you, someone else had the honor of orchestrating this little charade." He looked over my head and nodded, and the large wooden doors opened. I whirled at the sound of footsteps.

Lord Evarius Castemont stalked toward me.

The smile on his face was nothing short of wicked as his eyes roved over me. "A lovely, lovely dress, my darling daughter Petra," he sang. I stared at him in disbelief, the confusion coursing through every vein in my body. "I trust the journey wasn't too difficult," he said to Miles.

"No, my Lord," Miles answered. "Thank you for granting me an audience today. I'm glad I could deliver."

"Thank *you*, Lieutenant Landgrave," Castemont answered.

"What the *fuck* is going on?" I seethed, every inch of me burning.

"Oh! You did tell me she had a mouth on her," Kauvras laughed.

Castemont laughed along with him. "She does. It's made the years slightly more interesting." He faced me. "Petra, do you know who the Bloodsingers are?" I didn't respond to the sudden question, instead only staring into his face. "They worship only the Blood Saints. You see, they practice blood magic. They sacrifice to the Blood Saints for glimpses into the future."

I looked to Castemont, to my *step-father*, to the man who had sworn to the Saints that he would protect me, protect my mother at all costs. "Remind me, when is your birthday?" I didn't answer him. He knew. "I trust you haven't heard the legends of the Daughter of Katia? I know your education was...lacking. I tried to glean as much information about your upbringing as I could, but you weren't always the most talkative, and the Saints know your mother wasn't very useful." I stayed silent. "The Bloodsingers have long predicted that the Daughter of Katia would be born to human parents on the first Holy Stone of Blood Saints after the War of Kings. They were able to foretell that she'd have a daughter, born in Eserene to poor human parents, but they saw nothing after that."

"We had to get creative," Kauvras added.

"Inkwell was the obvious choice. I sent scouts to seek out any pregnant women a few months before you were born. And on the Night of the Holy Stone of Blood Saints, all we had to do was listen for the screams. They were easy enough to find. Your house *barely* had walls. Irabel screamed like she was dying. Then came the hardest part of all — the wait."

"I hope my spies weren't too obvious," Kauvras said.

So I was right — I had been watched my entire life. The footsteps in the dead of night were not a coincidence. The men who would stand outside my house were not simply waiting. Every time my back burned with an invisible gaze and I convinced myself I was crazy... "I almost thought you'd figure it out the morning I met you," Castemont started. "You stared at that street rat's boots for so long, I thought there was no way you didn't know. He had actually been on his way to the healer's home to check you were still staying there. Found you outside the Painted Empress and saw an opportunity. Tricky little bitch you are."

"How *could* you?" I breathed, my jaw clenched so tight my head began to pound. The heat continued to grow behind my ribs, becoming unbearable.

"When Ludovicus and his minions arrived in Eserene on the Night of the Holy Stone of Blood Saints, on the night of your *birth*, I knew he had the same plan. I knew he wanted *you*." Miles snickered beside me, but Kauvras let out a low growl. "We couldn't just kidnap you without arousing suspicion. And we needed your blood to confirm you were in fact Katia's divine gift. So I requested an audience with Ludovicus. He had been thinking ahead — smart bastard. Thought of how he could capture you without causing alarm. With my royal standing, I knew I could get you into the castle somehow. So we laid out a plan. A twenty-four year plan. And so Initiation was born." I was going to lose consciousness. "The Board of Blood," he said, annunciating each word and waving his arms in time. "A group led by a Bloodsinger with a band of lackeys. Creative, don't you think?"

"You have the bastard, yes?" Kauvras asked Miles.

"If Ludovicus is the bastard you're speaking of, then yes, Sir. He was captured alive and brought to Taitha."

"Kauvras and Ludovicus have some...history," Castemont said to me and winked. "With King Umfray's desire to strengthen the Royal Court against his brother here, he instantly supported Initiation, and was so thankful that one of Eserene's lords stepped up to help coordinate its inaugural year. And when Umfray died, his replacement was more than happy to play along...for a while. Our righteous Invisible King. Isn't this fun, my friend?" he said to Kauvras, who grumbled in response.

"Everything was a lie," I snarled.

"Don't be so angry, darling. I pulled you from a shithole and put you in a castle. You should be grateful."

I spat in his face. "I should never have trusted you," I growled as he recoiled, wiping his cheek on his shoulder.

He turned to the guards at the doors. "Bring them in."

The doors clanked open, and my worst fears came true. My mother and Solise were dragged through the doors, each escorted by two soldiers. My mother's moping figure hung limp, her steps barely catching as they dragged her. Solise was alert, face set with cold composure. "No!" I screamed and ran for them, but Castemont easily subdued me, grabbing me and pinning my arms to my side. "You fucking bastard! Fuck you!"

"Kauvras' men captured a healer en route. Had I known that Solise would end up their captive, I wouldn't have paid so much for her escort to Skystead," Castemont said to me. "I just wanted her out of Eserene. She was too skeptical. We could have saved four good men that day had the others just identified themselves, realized they were on the same fucking side. Fucking imbeciles," he growled. "But what a pleasant twist it was."

"Solise has *nothing* to do with this, and you know it, Castemont!" I screamed, bucking against him.

"She didn't...until I arrived in Taitha and called a healer for one of my men. What a reunion that was, right Solise?" Still, she kept her face calm. "Unfortunately, it wasn't the happiest of reunions. It didn't take long for my men to break her just now — only took a few minutes before she admitted she was going to help you escape."

He walked to stand before Solise, the woman a picture of silent strength. "To the dungeon," Castemont commanded.

"No!" I screamed, my voice breaking. I thrashed against Castemont, kicking and punching and scratching, but it was no use. He was far stronger than I was, even as my insides boiled, even as steam rose in my throat. "No, no, no! You can't! She has nothing to do with this! Let her go!"

She lifted her head, meeting my eyes. "Petra," she said calmly. I could barely hear her over my sobs. "Petra! Look at me, Petra." Her voice was even, the feeling at war with the firestorm that was raging inside me. "Find King Belin," she whispered.

"Enough!" Kauvras shouted and nodded.

The soldiers that held her began dragging her out of the room, pulling on the small woman with unnecessary force. "Find King Belin!" she yelled again before one of the soldiers took the hilt of his sword and pounded it into her skull. Her head lolled to the side as she lost consciousness.

"*No!*" I screamed, but the doors had already closed.

Silence descended upon the room before Kauvras let out a dramatic sigh. "You should recognize that anyone working against the will of the Benevolent Saints is working against *you*," Kauvras tutted. He stepped toward me, the eyes I almost knew searching my face. "You should be happy that the wretch will rot in the dungeon. Don't you know who you are?" he whispered. "Don't you know the power of your birth?" His breath was hot against my ear. "She told you she'd help you escape, no?" He clicked his tongue. "Don't you see what we've done for you? Don't you see the strings we've pulled to get you here? Why would you want to escape your betrothed? Your *destiny*?" The world slithered over my skin.

I inhaled. "I don't know if I have a destiny," I snarled through gritted teeth, channeling the vitriol I had learned from Larka, "but if I do, it sure as hell isn't *you*."

"But destiny is inescapable, is it not?" Kauvras asked, his words thick with sarcasm. "And your last chance of escape will now be locked away." I let the fire continue to scorch my insides, to grow hotter and hotter. "Darling Petra, you are exactly where you're supposed to be."

I took another deep breath and turned my head to Castemont. "And what is in this for you?"

"When Kauvras ascends to Sainthood, I will become the King of both Cabillia and Widoras."

"All this for a fucking *crown*?"

"You'd be amazed at what people will do for a crown," he whispered, then nodded to the guards at the door again. "Speaking of a crown, I have a surprise for the two of you." He looked to me, then to Kauvras, who raised one brow. "Consider it a wedding gift. Bring in King Belin!" he bellowed.

Find King Belin. I didn't have to look far as the man was shoved in by two guards.

And all at once, my boiling blood turned to ice in my veins. My heart stopped, then began to beat so hard I thought it would explode. But my ribs could have cracked and I wouldn't have felt it. The entire castle could have crumbled to dust and I wouldn't have noticed.

Because the man being dragged toward me was Calomyr.

Chapter 40

Now

No words came out of my mouth as sapphire and emerald eyes met mine. The canyon that had opened inside of me exploded. He was all I could see. The world ceased to turn, the tides refused to rise, rivers dried up and forests burned and the stars fell to the ground. I opened my mouth to speak but all that came out was air.

"Petra, I'm sorry," he choked out before a soldier punched him in the gut. "I'm sorry."

"*How?*" I whispered, my voice shaky. "How is this possible?"

"It had been a bit harder for my men to find him, being the *Invisible King*. And not only the Invisible King, but a king who preferred to live his life disguised as a Royal Guard. I was the only one who knew, isn't that right Belin?" Calomyr was silent, staring hard at him. "Our plan was working perfectly until the bastard fell in love." I could feel the hurt on my face as his gaze moved from Castemont to me, his head shaking slightly. "I needed him under control. A training yard accident was the perfect lie.

"And you never even thought to ask his full name. Stupid, *stupid* girl. We had an alias picked out for the occasion — Calomyr Bellsin. Perfectly believable. The play on words was my idea, thank you." He chuckled to himself. "But apparently just Calomyr worked for you." He clicked his tongue. "Belin Cal Myrin. A bastard born in Taitha. Somehow found himself living in Eserene, eager to please. When I arranged for him to join the Royal Guard, he was more than happy to rise to the challenge. And how convenient for me — the son of Umfray's brother." Realization crashed into me. King Belin wasn't a distant cousin of King Umfray. He was his *nephew*.

Kauvras tensed, as did Miles beside him. "Watch your tongue, Castemont."

"Why? Is it because—" He stopped, looking back and forth between Kauvras and Calomyr. His mouth fell open then erupted into a wicked smile. "You didn't know?" The tone of his voice was liquid evil as he cocked a brow, lowering his chin. "You didn't know you had a son. You believed the lie that our Invisible King was a distant cousin of yours." He let out a breathy chuckle, the noise ricocheting chills through me. My mother still hung between two guards as her husband dismantled multiple lives right in front of her.

Kauvras was silent, staring at Calomyr with the nearly-same eyes that stared back at him. The muscles in Calomyr's his jaw twitched with muscles as he clenched it harder and harder. Kauvras took a deep breath and inclined his head to look down at Calomyr. They hadn't known. *They hadn't known.* "It appears he is my son."

Calomyr spat at his feet, immediately receiving a blow to the face by a guard. Kauvras' face was still filled with pure confusion. He truly hadn't known. "I was told I was a distant relative of Umfray's through my mother's side, that I was somehow next in line for the throne. Whether that is true or not, I never have been and never will be your son," Calomyr hissed. He once told me that he dreamed of the day he'd see a man with the same blue in his eyes as his own, the perfect match that the green in his mother's were to his, and he'd know it was him. His father. His eyes moved from Kauvras to me and back again. "*What* do you want?"

Kauvras only continued to stare down at him, stone faced. "To begin with, we want Eserene," Castemont declared. Calomyr scoffed, a soldier quickly connecting his fist with Calomyr's jaw once again. "Let me rephrase," Castemont continued. "Eserene is ours."

"Over my dead body," he snarled back, mouth bloodied.

"Very well then," Castemont answered. Kauvras hadn't moved from where he stood, his stare still fixated on his son. A nod of Castemont's head and Calomyr was on the ground. My muscles froze but fire burned within me.

He snapped his head up to me. "I wanted to tell you," he whispered. "I loved you from the first day I saw you, Petra." And in the face that I had memorized, in the face that had become less and less clear in the years since, in the face that I mourned so fiercely, I saw it. The truth, whatever it was, lay with Calomyr, and I was going to find it. He had told me to trust him, and I did.

Steel rang as the soldier pulled his broadsword from its sheath. "Belin Cal Myrin, former King of Eserene, you have been sentenced to die."

Castemont leaned in, whispering in my ear. "I finally recognized Marita when I saw the scars, the ones I left on her body when we were young. Just like old friends." My blood ran cold for a split second. Marita's story...it had been Castemont. Tyrak was the one who saved her. Where was Tyrak? "She always looked so pretty in red."

Something was happening inside of me, his words stoking a fire. It was growing too hot, the steam burning my throat, begging for release. "And I *enjoyed* killing her, Petra, just like I enjoyed killing Wrena, just like I enjoyed sending my men to start the fire in your shit hole of a house. I would have enjoyed killing your sister, but the Saints took care of that for me. But nothing," his lips brushed against my ear, "*nothing* brought me more joy than pushing your father from that cliff."

My vision went white as I exploded, white flame shooting from my hands as I screamed from the depths of my soul. Whatever had been building inside of me was now shooting from my skin as tangible fury. Chaos erupted from every one of my bones as they broke and reformed and broke again, as I released every ounce of my hatred for Castemont, for Kauvras, in the form of pure, undiluted power. Every window in the throne room shattered as the stone castle shook. I was no longer in my body but in the flame itself as it scorched and charred everything around me.

It was *agonizing*, the searing pain running through every fiber of my being, every piece of my soul. I felt the source of the power pounding in my chest, beating furiously like a drum in sync with my racing heart, begging for me to keep going, to keep burning. My head was so full of fury that I felt like it would explode. But through the pain, through the torment that was the culmination of every loss I'd suffered, every obstacle I'd overcome, every single thing that had broken my mind, my body, and my spirit, it felt *euphoric*. I was made for this moment. I was made to burn.

This was the firestorm Ingra had spoken of.

Holy *fuck*.

I was her. She was me.

I...I *was* the Daughter of Katia. The thought poured into my head like it was thick black smoke billowing from my fire. I was a conduit for the power of the Benevolent Saints. I was fire, I was light, I was the rage of the sea and the fury of thunder. The earth bowed for me, the stars bowed for me, the wind and the rain and the night bowed for me and only me. I *was* fire burned and ocean tumbled.

"Petra!" I heard a distant echo through the mayhem of power and anger. "Petra!" It was him. Calomyr's voice. But I couldn't stop. Flames swirled around me, winds whipping my hair and the skirts of my gown at my command. My skin felt like it was melting, and I reveled in it, reveled in the fact that this was finally it. I was going to burn myself into nothing more than a pile of ash and I was *ready*.

And then I saw it. A lighthouse in the storm. A tiny speck of yellow light in a sea of red and white fury. A voice sounded through the hurricane, one I'd heard before. "Lay your flames down," she said, her voice as soothing as it had been the day our house burned down. It was the voice I'd heard in the Eserenian throne room, when I'd been struck down so many times that death was reaching for me.

"Hello?" I screamed into the mess of fire and wind.

"I am here," she answered. I raged against her, not wanting to hear that voice, not wanting to face the fact that I now knew who it belonged to. I had to ask.

"Katia?"

"Yes."

Fuck.

The inferno continued to swirl around me. I couldn't tell whether the castle even stood anymore. "I'm ready to die!" I roared.

"Not yet," she echoed through my head.

"Please!" I begged. I wanted it to be over. I swore I began to burn hotter.

"This is not your time, daughter," she called. "Lay your flames down, for there is much to do." What could I possibly have to do? Had I not suffered enough? "Rest now, daughter," she whispered. "The world needs you whole."

"*No!*" I screamed into the fire, the flames licking up my throat, a lifetime of hurt pouring out of me in a blistering heat.

"The world needs you whole," she repeated, her voice fading.

All at once the flames died out as my arms dropped to my sides. Fire still crackled around me before turning to embers and ash. The air calmed, the smoke dissipated as I heaved in a deep breath. My vision cleared as the incessant pounding of fury in my chest dimmed. *Relief.* I looked down at my hands, angry blisters bubbling over every inch.

What had I done?

Castemont and Kauvras were huddled in heaps, the sounds of pained whimpering becoming audible as the roaring in my ears quieted. Miles lay on his side, facing away from me, still masked. I couldn't tell how badly they'd been burned, but the three of them still breathed. How had they survived? My mother sat with her head between her knees, covered in soot but otherwise unscathed, showing no reaction to what had just happened. The soldiers who'd held her had been reduced to ash. Turning to survey the rest of the throne room, I realized that I'd incinerated a number of guards.

Why couldn't I have destroyed the fuckers I wanted to?

Every guard who still stood, who hadn't been caught in my flames, had fallen to one knee, left arm across their bodies, hands on the hilt of their swords, heads lowered. "Daughter of Katia," one of them murmured. The rest repeated. Over and over they chanted, my heartbeat raging to the time of their words.

And Calomyr.

His guards had fallen, and Calomyr stood straight up, soot-streaked but untouched by whatever the hell had just exploded from me. The same broad shoulders, the same calloused hands. The same Calomyr. But he wasn't Calomyr. He never had been.

He dropped to one knee, dipping his head. "Daughter of Katia," he breathed before standing again, taking a tentative step toward me.

"Don't," I whispered, stepping back and putting a blistered hand up. I was dizzy, the feeling of overexertion rolling through my body. He stopped in his tracks, his brows knit together. "Please don't come near me."

He nodded weakly. "It wasn't my choice," he whispered back. Tears welled in my eyes as I looked at him, his own lining with silver. "I prayed to every Saint there is that you would uncover the truth. I went back to the cave." His words were spilling out, coming so quickly that I almost couldn't understand him. "I left his cloak for you."

The words crushed me. "Take him," I called, unable to stand his presence, the command rolling off of my tongue. Three kneeling guards quickly rushed to his side. "Take them all."

"You don't give orders in my court." Behind me, Kauvras stood straight, his clothing singed but his skin untouched by flame or wind or flying glass. The guards who had shuffled at my command paused, their gazes flickering between us. My heart lurched.

Taking a steadying breath, I planted my feet. I wouldn't cower from this man, this man who had worked to orchestrate my entire life to get me to this point. "This doesn't appear to be your court anymore," I said evenly.

"At attention," he barked, and the soldiers straightened. My stomach dropped as I felt my sliver of control slip away. Kauvras simply raised an eyebrow at me, his eyes burning far colder than his son's.

"I will admit," Castemont started, rising from his curled position, surcoat charred, "I was not expecting *that*." Neither was I.

Miles stepped to Castemont's side. They did their best to straighten their blackened clothing and armor, soot covering every inch of exposed skin. I clenched my jaw, looking back and forth between the two men now staring at me, approaching me.

"Take the Invisible King and lock him up. Take her mother back to the barracks," Kauvras ordered without breaking his stare with me, the guards once again moving. I fought the urge to turn to Calomyr as Kauvras stepped toward me slowly, his eyes suddenly wild. "Do you hear them?" he whispered, a finger in the air. One side of his mouth quirked up in a sickening smile, a dimple appeared, so thoroughly Calomyr. "They're telling me it's *you*." His hands cupped my face and I winced as his grin deepened, the silence closing in on me as every one of my muscles tensed.

I... I had exploded. The white hot rage that had been brewing within me for so long hadn't been rage at all...it had been whatever the hell *that* was. It had been flame and air and blinding light. And... I had heard her. I heard Katia, her voice soft and warm, making no sense at all yet somehow melding perfectly with my mind. I *spoke* to her.

And then the words left Kauvras' mouth, like tendrils of poisonous smoke that twisted around every inch of me. "My bride."

The rage bubbled again as flames crackled against my fingertips, but they popped and fizzled into smoke as I cried out. Every spark sent blinding pain up my arms, the skin melting beneath the ghosts of flames. I stared at my gnarled skin as the last of the flames died out, trembling in pain as even more blisters formed.

"Castemont," Kauvras murmured, "Please see my betrothed to her rooms. We wed tomorrow."

I whipped my head to Castemont, to the man who was still my step-father by law. But all I saw in his face was cold, calculated indifference. In his eyes, I was nothing but a means to an end, a shot of whiskey as he grew drunk on power. He took my arm, leading me to the doors of the throne room. Words formed in my throat only to dissolve in my mouth.

The doors swung open to reveal a handful of masked and hundreds of unmasked soldiers, on bended knee, packed into the antechamber, shoulder to shoulder. "Daughter of Katia," they chanted. The corridors off of the antechamber were packed with soldiers as well, their voices echoing off the stone walls. Either I shook all of Taitha, or word had traveled fast. "Daughter of Katia." I stood at the head of a foreign army bowing for me. *Holy fucking shit.*

"Rise! At attention!" Kauvras shouted from inside of the destroyed throne room. And they did — they hopped to their feet, straight as arrows, eyes conflicted yet jaws set with resolve.

As Castemont paraded me through, I swore I felt every pair of eyes follow me. *We see you,* they seemed to say. *Daughter of Katia, we see you.*

Chapter 41

Now

Castemont was silent as he led me through the halls, his face etched in a smirk that made the fire crackle beneath my skin. I was also silent, my mind racing through what the next few hours of my life would look like, what they would amount to. I needed answers that I was not going to get, not now at least.

As we arrived at the door to the rooms I'd been given, two masked soldiers already standing guard, I stopped. "I'm the Daughter of Katia." My voice was emotionless, and though it wasn't a question, Castemont answered.

"You are." That maddening smirk remained.

I pinned him with my stare. "Tell me then, loving step-father." The only thing keeping me from lunging for his throat was my blistered hands. "If I'm the Daughter of Katia, who is my father?"

He let out a low, gruff laugh and nodded. "Smart girl. That's a secret only I know."

"Who. Is. My. Father?"

He licked his lips, inclining his head only to stare down his nose at me, sick amusement lacing his features. "Your father, your *real* father, is Rhedros, Keeper of the Blood Saints." I stilled. "You, darling girl, are the Sin of Saints."

Thank you for reading! Please add a review on Amazon to let me know what you think!

Amazon reviews are extremely helpful for authors. Thank you for taking the time to support me and my work.

BOOK 2 Of THE BENEVOLENCE & BLOOD SERIES COMING SOON

ACKNOWLEDGEMENTS

To the beta readers who started out as strangers and quickly became a sounding board, a source of inspiration, and one hell of a hype team, thank you from the depths of my soul. You guys were the first strangers to read my story and fall in love with it. They say you're not supposed to rely on outside validation, but you guys are the reason I had the confidence in this story to bring it all the way to publication. To Matrasa Connolly, Vesta Nicol, Brigitte McGuirk, Patricia Williamson-Brown, Amber Peterson, Joyce Fernandez, Samantha Guidry, Taylor Moon, Stacie Young, Kristi Cole, Renée Godinez, and Dolene M Hurst, I will never be able to thank you enough for all you did to me. Now how about this second book?

I'd like to scream a massive thank you from the rooftops to Joyce Fernandez for taking on the role of editor, friend, and confidant. I won't ever be able to express how thankful I am that this journey brought us together. Our book talks turned to life talks, and I truly feel like I've made a lifelong friend. You've been such a massive support and did so much for me when you absolutely didn't have to. Words simply don't exist to tell you how much I appreciate everything you've done for me. Now girls trip to Napa!

To Ivy at Beautiful Book Covers, you are an absolute legend. Not only did you take what was in my head and make it real, but you put up with a zillion messages, questions, and requests without a single complaint. Thank you a zillion times. I'm so lucky I found you, and I cannot wait until you start cooking up the cover for the sequel.

To the friend group that became family and gave me the space to be completely myself, I love you. To the infamous Bitches group chat — Ashley Garner, Jenn Rogers, Jessica Pettry, Chelsea Fredrickson, and Maddie Neumann: the TikToks, the memes, and every word of encouragement live forever in my soul (and in our chat thread). And to Alex Garner, James Cook, and Cody "More

Chapters Please" Rogers, thank you for being the ultimate childhood friends I never had. Seriously. Okay, now I'm crying.

A special thank you goes to Ashley Garner for being my bookish bitch, RenFaire pal, and spicy book sloot. That may be inappropriate but this is my acknowledgment section and I can say whatever I want. No one else I'd rather obsess over fictional men with.

Thank you to Lauren Peel for being one of the best friends I've ever had and a cheerleader throughout this journey. You never once doubted me. I've always been able to count on you for whatever I need — encouragement, tea spilling, and, most importantly, our typical bullshit.

To Bianca Bongiorno, my first Florida friend, thank you for keeping me laughing. You're one of the most talented people I know and have been such a massive support to me throughout this process. Love you forever my dude. And to Jess Gallo — thank you for taking care of my B.

A big thank you goes out to every one of my friends who listened to even the tiniest of my ramblings about this story. I have truly made some amazing friends throughout my adventures, and whether you knew it or not, your friendship bolstered my confidence in my story. If I'm lucky enough to call you a friend, then this thank you is for you.

To Dr. Christy Moore, my partner-in-crime, thank you, thank you, thank you. You are my go-to person for a cheer up, the ultimate queen of snacks, and the bargain hunter to end all bargain hunters. I'm beyond grateful that we met and that we've been able to create a space for people to heal, learn, and laugh. You have hyped me up for every single endeavor I've taken, never once preventing me from chasing every opportunity that presented itself. You are one of the most badass women I know and deserve the entire world. I love you.